AUTOGRAPHS!

I0535437

TIME TO FEEL-RELOADED-Time Will Reveal part 5

"Reloaded Version 2013"

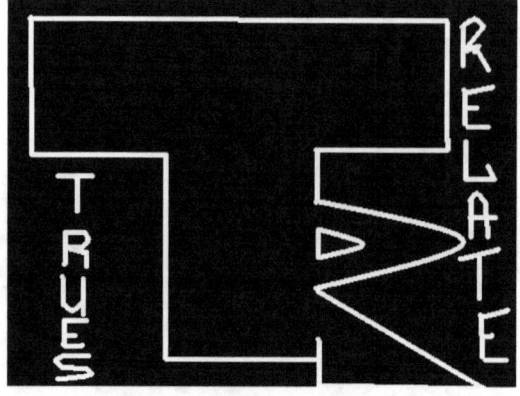

TIME TO FEEL-RELOADED
TIME WILL REVEAL PART 5
BY
BLACK COFFEE

TIME TO FEEL-RELOADED-Time Will Reveal part 5

Published by True's Relate Publishing
Time to Feel-RELOADED (Time will reveal: Part 5)
Library of Congress Control Number: Txu 1-788-504
ISBN: 978-0-9844701-7-4 & 978-0-9892092-5-0
Copyright ©2011, 2013 True's Relate publishing/LTBROWN
All rights reserved

REGISTERED TRADEMARK-MARCA REGISTRADA

ISBN:978-0-9844701-7-4 &
Printed in the United States of America
Set by: True's Relate publishing
Cover design: Gregory Spencer of Misvision Graphics info@misvisiongraphics.com
Logo design by: JayRocOne [@ age 9]
Requests for information on ordering, scheduling the author for signings and
appearances should be addressed to:
Black Coffee's websites
www.truesrelatepublishing.com
www.blackdollone.com
Twitter.com/AuthorBlkCoffee
http://www.linkedin.com/in/lovelybrown
www.facebook.com/BlackCoffee

Manuscript Preparation: Black Coffee
True's Relate publishing company
P.O. Box 2911
Gulfport, Ms. 39505
Email: blackdollone@att.net

PUBLISHER'S NOTES

TIME TO FEEL-RELOADED-TIME WILL REVEAL 5   Black Coffee

TIME TO FEEL-RELOADED-Time Will Reveal part 5

FOR THE BOYS,
Darion, Brandyn and Jalen
Here's the strength to carry on.
I'm already proud. I hope you are too!

THE TIME WILL REVEAL SHORT STORIES

#1 MORE THAN 4 ADMIRERS-RELOADED
"The Threat to a Legacy."
#2 MR. WRONG AND THE RATS-RELOADED
"Sweet Ray, Sonya, Shuntay & Tina"
#3 CREW'S 1ST PRIORITY>FEMALE CREW-RELOADED [TBA]
"Goodbye deviled Angel"

ORDER THE FULL SERIES AT:
www.blackdollone.com/buylinks.html

The Time Will Reveal-the series

TIME TO FEEL-RELOADED-Time Will Reveal part 5

CHAPTER   48

TIL DEATH DO US PART

It's still Thursday and Lynn is trying to get her girls together before club night. She wants this Katrina shit handled and she wants it handled *today*. Nina is almost a month out of labor and delivery. In 2 days, Lynn's godson Lil Tank will be a month old. Lynn knows her sister won't be able to exert anything physically. But mentally, Nina is very important to this fold as far as Ebony and Ajay goes. She needs her to be there. She heads straight to Nina's house from the facility to get her onboard. To Lynn, this feels like the days of old, as she plots on how the crew will rally around Ajay and Ebony and rid them of whatever evil force which has tried to threaten their love and happiness. The crew always comes to the rescue for crew. Lynn is just doing what comes natural to her. Which is taking care of her younger siblings and crew. She wants Nina to help her arrange a dinner for the foursome, Bre, Jan, herself and most definitely, *Katrina*. Gwen, Venitia and the crew ladies will be invited. Whether the husbands come or not, is optional. Except for Ajay. He has to be there.

"Oh and I want Officer Miles to come too," Lynn says to Nina, "Schedule it early so Renee and Tonya can come before time to go to the club. *Fuck it*. Our whole crew needs to be there, on second thought. It's going down at Ajay's house tonight. So make it happen."

"Sis what's gotten into you?" Nina asks with a smile, "Are you still in war mode? You've always been ready to go at a moments notice. But *damn*! Something has really set you off."

She knows when her oldest sister is bothered and today, she's very bothered by something. Nina already knows it has to be something about Ajay, John III, Jb, family or the crew. Nothing makes Lynn emotional unless it's about a loved one. A trait which her and Ajay share.

"You'll be ready to *set it off* too," Lynn says, "Once I tell you what a bitch did to our *only* brother. And how she's trying to play *Ebony*."

"You'd better talk to me *quick*!" Nina says, "What the fuck is going on? What happened? Tell me right now. No more hints."

Lynn tells her the revelation, just as she'd gotten it from Ajay. After hearing it, Nina is seething. Having this revelation has also brought back

every pinned up feeling Nina has about past flings their guys had. Alana is on her mind and in her employment too. Whether she *really* likes it or not. "All I wanna know is why can't we unfold things like this when I can fight?" Nina asks, "So we can invite Alana and her crew along too."
Lynn laughs and says, "Like they'd *really* come. They'd know it was a set up. Katrina doesn't know because Ajay's been quiet for almost a decade."

"I hate phony people with a *passion*," Nina admits, "I just wanna get mine in too, sis. For real."

"One thing at a time, sis," Lynn says, "Renee and Tonya sent me letters about that posse. Then I saw that Farah girl in my husbands face last night. Their time is coming. *Trust!*"

"You know John Brown junior is not about to entertain a white woman, Lynn," Nina says with a smile.

"Oh I know that," she says quickly, "John junior takes pride in the fact that he's named after an abolitionist, a warrior for freedom from the clutches of white rule and slavery. Farah hitting on him is an insult to his intelligence. He said as much. But that's not the point. It's about the disrespect thing for me. You *heard* me?"

"I knew you was upset," Nina says, "I can still see that."
Lynn says, "And for him too. He felt like he always feels when a white woman comes on to a black man. Like she don't care about him or whether he lives or dies. Because many black men died because of transgressions with or about white women. Even when that wasn't the case. That's how he feels. He started talking about *Emmett Till,* for God sake."

"Let me get baby girl on the phone and set this up," Nina says as she dials Ebony. "We can let Crew's House cook for it. Since everybody's working today. We're gonna get this thing *jumpin,* sis. Wow! I feel sorry for Ajay because I *know* he wasn't about messing over my girl during our senior year of high school. Or *since* then. He had pushed all of that off."
She gets busy on the phone, calling their female crew.

By noon they have the dinner scheduled and all of the crew on board, including the husbands, who are ready to rally. Even big mama is coming. After hanging up with big mama, Nina and Lynn feel sure they're doing the right thing for Ajay.

"Big mama is a guardian and a half for Ebony and Ajay," Nina says, "Did you hear how angry she got?"

"Yes. I haven't heard her that emotional since granny died. She sounded like she was ready to whoop Katrina's ass herself," Lynn says.
Before it's done, several parents say they're coming as well. This intrusion
6

TIME TO FEEL-RELOADED-Time Will Reveal part 5

by Katrina didn't set well with big mama. Just as it hasn't with Lynn and Nina. Big mama insisted Pearl, Jo, John, Al, Percy and Jackson Brown be at this dinner too.

Meanwhile Al is hearing the story for the 1st time. Firsthand from Ajay, his only son.

"Ah son you need to out this now," Al says, "Let your wife know about it. And if you find out that Officer Miles knew it. Have Jacobson fire her ass on the spot and let him know *why* too."

"I get the feeling she does know. Just by how she looks when she says something to me about Katrina," Ajay says, "Or maybe Katrina just told her, she likes me. But hasn't told her the real deal. I really can't read her because I'm not able to even look at her."

"Now I know why Katrina wants to play in Cleveland," Al says.

"She came to Miami and tried out for the *Sol*. She made the team," Ajay says, "Then when she found out I was opting out of my contract to come to Cleveland. She told them she was gonna leave. Jarvis told me she made the team but didn't stay there and she made more money *there*."

"She's following you?" Al asks.

"That's how I feel. But then again. That team was folding after the season so she may say that was her reason for leaving. I feel like she's a rapist or something. Stalking me. It feels weird to have a woman coming after me, knowing that *that* woman took advantage of me. It's unnerving, pops. A *powerless* feeling. I can better understand my wife's situation with Neal and with Raymond. It's haunting, man. It's just weird."

"It haunts you because you're trying to keep it a secret. Like Ebony tried to do with Neal," Al says, "It won't work. Just like you had to hear Raymond tell you he wasn't successful in raping her. Even though Ebony had already told you. Her doctor and everybody else had told you. You had to hear it from him. Give Ebony the same opportunity. Put Katrina on that same plank like you did Raymond. Get it out there and get it out *now*. Because it's been nearly ten years. Ebony is gonna have her doubts. Katrina damn well *better* tell the truth. That's all I'm saying."

"We need to have neutral people there," Ajay suggests, "I don't want my wife to catch a charge behind my insecurity."

"We'll have Jacobson come and bring some friends. How's that?"

"Cool."

Big mama calls the facility and talks to Ajay about the dinner Lynn and Nina planned at their Estate. He knows what it's for and why big

7

mama is all for it. He hadn't shared the experience with her completely either. He'd given her the same prefixed version he'd given to Lynn. But he can hear it in her voice. She understands why he hadn't been completely forthcoming. She's on he and Ebony's side. For the 1st time Ajay feels that the time is now or never to put Katrina's actions on blast. So he can move past it and not feel hostage to her whenever she's around or mentioned. Just as Ebony's not coming clean about Neal had done to her. It had burdened her and caused problems in their sex life. He can't allow nor afford for that to happen. It's time to come completely clean with her about Katrina *Gettin Some Head* and taking advantage of him and his trust.

After work everyone shows up at Ajay and Ebony's house. Even some of the junior crew like Kim, Bruce, Steven and Ally come. Ebony and Ajay's parents are here. Big mama, poppa and papa Brown are here. Jacobson, who has been briefed on the occasion, escorts Miles and Katrina. He brings several of his former rescue team buddies to be of assistance should the need arise. Chill's entire crew attend. The Atlanta crew is in the house early and they are already rowdy. They have their kids with them too. Big mama has brought along servers from their restaurant, so no one will have to leave the room once the discussion starts.

They enjoy dinner. Then everyone retires to the basement for the evening. No one knows what's going on yet. Except those who knew prior to arriving. Bre and Jan have learned since they arrived.

Ebony is being the gracious hostess and running behind her twins. They're getting a kick out of having so much company. Lil Ajay is running around the basement and having a blast. Katrina sees him and is about to pick him up.

"Oh hell no!" Lynn says, "I got him. Don't touch my nephew. I don't play that shit."

Katrina looks at her awkwardly but says nothing. Nina watches Katrina with evil eyes. Tank notices Nina and asks her what's going on.

Her answer, "You'll know soon enough."

Rich is the only 1 from Chill's crew who's absent. Wes has taken his place. Lynn takes the stage in Ajay's basement and brings the room to order.

"I don't know if this is the proper way to do this. But it has to be done," she says, "There is a rat in this house. That rat needs to cleanse and purge herself immediately. Or there's gonna be problems."

"What's the problem, Lynora?" Jo asks.

"Mama I had a talk..," she pauses, "I talked to my..," she pauses again and Jb can see she's upset about something.

He asks, "Lynn what's going on?" thinking someone has offended his wife. He joins her on stage. She whispers enough to him for him to get an understanding of the situation. His expression and mood changes instantly. Katrina is his *only* sister's teammate and pretending to be her friend. Just like the rats from Houston had done, she's taking advantage of Ebony's gracious nature. Just by being present in her household and her life. She has never admitted to her wrong doings. Jb isn't going to have it. But he can see that Ajay isn't comfortable with this revelation coming out this way.

"Pops, tell Lynn I don't wanna do it like this," Ajay says to Al.
Al goes up to Lynn. He brings her and Jb off of the stage. As Lynn is exciting the stage, T-baby asks her what has her so angry. Katrina is standing right next to T-baby. Lynn can't contain herself any longer. She stops in front of Katrina while Ebony is asking Ajay to go check on her.

"Something's got Lynn pee owed," Ebony says to Ajay, "She's in fight mode."
Ajay's response is, "I know."
Then Nina suggest they move the party out back onto the large yard. They turn on the track lighting and move the large group outside. Ebony, Ally and Nina volunteer to stay inside with the small children. Everyone else goes outside. Lynn takes this as her opportunity to confront Katrina.

"*You.* Come here," she says, "I wanna know when are you gonna stop *bullshittin*?" Lynn snarls as she glares at Katrina.

"*Excuse* me?" Katrina asks.

"No ma'am. I will not," Lynn says, "When are you gonna let it be known what you did to my brother. And the whore game you're still trying to play right now?" she asks. She continues, "And don't lie bitch. I saw you last night and today too! What the *fuck* do you think this is!? That's a fucked up game you're playing. That's my *only* brother, girl! He's taken and has been. *For life.* I don't play that low down shit you did to him!"
Katrina doesn't answer fast enough. Before anyone can grab her. Lynn begins punching her repeatedly. Katrina fights back. That only unleashes a female crew assault. Officer Deloris Miles tries to pull Lynn away. That's when Jan and Bre step to her and advise her to stay out it.

"Or get *all* the way in!" Bre yells.
Jb and Tank break up the fight by pulling Lynn away. Katrina lunges at Lynn. T-baby gives her a look and a few words.
She says, "Look! You're my teammate but that's my crew! Whatever beef *y'all* have! I suggest you get it worked out. Here and now!"
It becomes clear that Miles doesn't know the extent of what happened when

9

she asks, "So y'all invited my niece to dinner so she can be jumped on? *Why*? Because she has a crush?"

That's when Lynn lets the cat out of the bag. She can't hold her tongue any longer. She isn't about to let this go. Not without a purging of Katrina's soul and a believable apology to her brother, if he wants it. It's so much unrest out on her lawn that Ebony will surely know the story. *Real soon*.

"Ho please!" Lynn yells, "Your niece assaulted my brother while he was past out and laid up, down there in college! And she got the fuckin nerve to be visiting him and his wife's *home*. While she's *still* making passes at him. *In his home*! Grabbing his dick! *In his home!* And at his place of business! She's even sending him mail with the address that my sister-in-law asked her to keep private at their gift shop! And all this time she's smiling in Ebony's face! That's shit that'll get you killed! Do you hear what the fuck I said?! That's my only brother! I don't like no parts of that shit! He didn't want her, Miles! She took advantage of him! So tell me, Katrina. How many times did you fuck him and suck his dick before he came too?!"

The rest of the guest are stunned to hear what Lynn is saying. They're so focused on Lynn. They didn't even notice the woman of the house joined them.

"*What*?!" Ebony yells.

She'd heard all the noise and came out back to see what all the commotion was about. She heard it all. She looks at her husband. He has tears streaming down his face. This makes her *instantly* angry. She wants to get her man away from everyone and hear his side of this assault. She can see that he has a lot of anger. But there's more in his expression. What Katrina did to him has really affected him traumatically.

"Anthony what's she talking about? When? What happened and where was I?" Ebony fires questions at him quickly.

Not in anger but out of concern. She can see her man is troubled right now. Lannie is standing next to Ebony. Lil Ajay has run to his daddy. Ajay picks him up. It's Ajay's turn to speak now.

He says, "Everything my sister just said is true. I want everybody to stay exactly where you are. I need to talk to my wife in private. Then we'll be back out here to address y'all."

With that, him and Ebony go inside to their bedroom. They leave the twins with big mama, Pearl and Jo so they can talk open and candid.

Outside everyone is digesting the information which was just revealed. T-baby and Rebbie want the fight to continue and so does Lynn, Bre and Jan. June and Tank are shocked at the revelation. Ajay had never

TIME TO FEEL-RELOADED-Time Will Reveal part 5

told them anything about this encroachment. But then they were off doing some encroaching of their own. That's something that will have to come out before long. Especially with Jarvis and Gwen vying for crew membership. Immediately Tank and June know this had to have been something Ajay felt was out of his control. Further, they know now why he had a problem with being in the presence of the women's team. From here on, Ajay's crew takes the lead and no one is allowed to leave until Ajay and Ebony finish their discussion and return.

In their bedroom, Ajay tells his wife every detail. Right up to the 1 that happened tonight. He's shedding tears trying to get through it.

"And you didn't tell me because you had just gone through that whole *messing around on me* phase? And after that, Angel ran me off the road and all of that. Right?"

"Yes."

"Anthony this might sound crazy to you. But I understand. I know why you couldn't tell me. I know the feelings you had and have now. What I mean is. I know how you felt then and how you feel now. I knew it was something more to that whole, *me giving you oral sex* thing," she says, "I know you, just like you know me. Because the times before this happened when I visited you in Natty. We was almost about to do oral sex. But we didn't get around to it. You told me we would get to it on the next trip. You was open to it. But by the next time I came to see you. You didn't even want me to talk about doing that to you. That carried over. All the way over and up until our wedding night. And I still get those vibes from you when I wake you up with it. I understand now. It's because you woke up to her doing that to you. I use to think it was because you didn't like how I was doing it. I know better now. This assault with her, it happened right before the men's season of your sophomore year started. Didn't it?"

"Yes baby girl. It did," he says solemnly, "Two weeks after we got the house. It was at our first party. That's why I didn't wanna have anymore parties that your team came too. Just my team and the football team," he says, "And when I talked to you, the day after..-"

"-You cried and you said-"

"I was worried about somebody ending up making a baby at the U and Bruce was sleeping in my bed. Our *old* bed," he says, "But you knew it was more than that."

"Yes that's what you said but I *did* feel like it was more than that," she says as she wipes tears from his face, "Of course I did."

"It was. But I knew you was excited about coming to meet your

11

new team," he says, "When you came down during our conference, I held onto you so tight, we made a baby. I just wanted you in that bed next to me, from then on. So nothing like that could happen again. And I didn't wanna be around her. I didn't wanna be around the rest of your teammates either. Not those who knew about it and thought it was cool. Because baby, a lot of them did think it was cool or funny."

"Because my team was a bunch of whores. Except for me, Claudia, Tee and Shantel," she says as she smiles, "I remember you saying that, so clear. And there I was sticking up for all of them."

"I understood why you was though," he says, "Because you're a team player and I hadn't told you about it."

"You really did understand what I went through with Neal," she says, " Kind of, ha?"

"I understood why you tried to block it out," he says, "I thought about taking her life,…, so many times. That's why I kept up with where she was. I was plotting it before I became a father. Even though I loved you more than life itself. I felt like she took something from me. From us. The same shit you was saying about Raymond and what you felt like he would've done if he had raped you. She did rape me. That is some hard shit for me to say. Let alone live with. My twins came into my life and that's what saved hers."

"I wanna beat her ass, Anthony," she says suddenly, "I haven't wanted to fight in a long time. But I wanna beat her *muthafuckin* ass!"
He doesn't even care that she's using foul language. He's there also.

"Only if you let me help," he says.

"I'm not gonna let you fight a woman and you know it," she says.

"Then you need to cripple her and make sure she remembers what she took from me," he says as he looks into her eyes.

"She didn't take anything from you, baby," she says, "Remember how you talked to me after Raymond? And after finding out about Neal? I even understand why you didn't tell me that night at the Fillmore when we cleansed our souls and told all of our secrets."

"Because you had to go back to school and she would be there," he adds.

"I love you," she says, "This won't change that at all. But if Deloris Miles knew something about this, then she can't work the gate."

"She can't work it anyway," he says, "Jake already said she can't. He'll put her at the mall if we say keep her. But she can't be in charge of who comes and goes, out here. Not even with a partner in the booth. Like its

12

TIME TO FEEL-RELOADED-Time Will Reveal part 5

been so far. He don't want her out here. *Period*. Neither do I. It appears she didn't know about the assault. Not judging from her reactions outside, just now. She thought she just had a crush on me."

"I heard her say that when Lynn was punching Katrina," Ebony says.

"But still. Even with that I don't want her anywhere near our home, the gate or our kids," he says, "And damn sho *not* Katrina. She use to take pictures of me and send them to my email with explicit messages and shit. She took those pictures and made posters and cards. All because she knew I was trying to keep this from coming out. She knew it was because I felt like I was assaulted. But she still did it. I was disgusted."

"I could really hurt her right now," she says, "She's been coming around here like she's a friend. How do I always miss this kind of stuff?"

"Because you're a wholesome woman," he says, "You don't know how to recognize shady ass people. I just want her and her cousin, aunt or *whatever* Deloris is to her, to never have access out here again."

"Then it's done," Ebony says, "Let's go address our guest. Then we can entertain the real guest like we normally do."

"And dismiss some," he says.

"Exactly," she says and they smile at each other while she takes him to their bathroom to wash his face and they return to the backyard.

The crew are happy to see them come back so soon. They know all is alright with them because they're holding onto each other. Just like always. They get everyone's attention so Ajay can speak again.

"I wanna thank all of my crew and family for being here," he says, "I'm sure by now, everybody knows what Katrina did to me. The part that bothers me the most, other than someone taking advantage of me. Is her being dishonest with my wife. Trying to play with my children like she's not a snake. I don't wanna ever lay eyes on you again," he says directly to Katrina, "I don't want you. I never wanted you and you knew that. Didn't you?"

She doesn't say anything but her aunt insists that she admit her faults and apologize. She finally steps forward.

"I admit I came in on you while you was knocked out. I did things you never showed interest in doing with me when you was conscience," Katrina says, "I admit I took the address Ebony gave me at Valentine's. And used it for my own personal gain. I admit that every time I had a chance to get next to you out of anybody's sight. I did. I have always been feeling you. I took things way too far. I'm sorry for everything. I mean

13

that. I'm sorry for what I did to *you*, Ebony and your whole family. It won't happen again."

"Did you drug my brother?" Lynn asks.

"Yes," Katrina admits.

"What did you give my son?" Jo ask, sporting a furious expression.

"*Roofies*," she admits, "I gave him rufilin."

"The date rape drug?!" Jo asks, making her way toward Katrina. Big Al grabs her by the elbow and keeps her from getting any closer.

"I did and that was wrong," Katrina says quickly, "I will never do anything disrespectful to him again. It was wrong and I'm sorry."

"I know you'd better not, Katrina," Ebony says, "Because if you do. I am gonna tear you a new asshole. And that still might come later. So watch your back."

"That's staying power, right there," Chill breaks in and says, "I had no idea either, baby girl. They use to tell me everything. But I didn't get this one because I would've made him tell you."

"Nobody did, Chill," Tank adds. Then he turns to Katrina. He says, "I don't like you being around my family. I don't like it when ho's try to play my lil sister out."

"Neither do I," Jb steps up, "Just because she's a good person. Don't mean she won't beat the hell out of you. I'd even give her a pass on shit like this right here."

"Because it's wrong," Al adds, "I've never seen my son in this position. He hates you and that scares me. Because I know what I'm feeling at this moment. I have no doubts, he's thinking *much* worse."

"You're only okay because of Ebony's reaction to this news," Pearl says to her, "If my daughter hadn't been able to accept this. You would not be so,.... *healthy*."

John can't even speak. The angst he feels can be witnessed in his eyes and on his face as he grimaces at Katrina. When asked for his comment, he waves it off. He's too emotional to speak, so big mama takes a turn.

"When I think about the decades ago when this young man first started talking to me about how he felt about my granddaughter. I smile," big mama says as Ajay pulls Ebony closer to him.

Big mama speaks on them, their past and their foundation. She continues, "My first memory goes back to about nineteen eighty. Ajay was barely six years old. He told me. He said, *'Big mama I want Ebony to be my girlfriend but she don't like me. I like her, big mama. Will you tell her that for me?'* she smiles, "And I did. Everyday since then I've told her that. I made sure she

14

knew that." Ebony smiles and big mama continues, "Myself and my best friend Pearline, you all called her granny. Well we told her and made sure she knew what to look for and what to demand. While the men in this family showed him what to give and how to show what he felt about her. He got it right. I am so proud of these two and all of my babies, for that matter. But these two especially. Because I guided them over the years. Their parents will tell you how me and Percy took up for them. Your love is untouchable, babies. Keep on keeping on and make this the *last* time you allow evil to disrupt your peace and quiet. Men and women can see that you're both fulfilled. They'll try to get that for themselves. Y'all have to be strong and keep evil at a distance. Starting right now."

Big mama waves her hand and with that, Katrina and officer Miles are excused. Then escorted away with Jacobson and his colleagues.

The crew wind down their dinner party. Most of them leave to go open up the club. Ebony and Ajay will join them later. After they spend some private time at home.

****

The following weekend is Father's day. Donovan Darnell Wilson celebrates his 1st birthday at Granny's house. Jr is already trying to convince Tonya that they should try for a 3rd child.

"Since he's already walking," Jr laughs, "We need a girl now."
Tonya acts as if she can't even hear him speaking. They laugh.

Rich has only gotten worse. He's still refusing to leave the house or sign the divorce papers T-baby served him. To make matters worse. At the end the month, he moves Regina and Richanda into the house. That ticks *everyone* off. T-baby tries to get a court order to have all 3 of them removed. Only her and Rich are still *legally* married. She has no real recourse. She's in the middle of her season but she's determined to get some relief on this matter by season's end. She tries to reason with Rich but he won't budge. T-baby stopped paying the mortgage when she moved out. Rich hasn't paid anything. Now the mortgage is 2 months behind. T-baby decides to wait until the mortgage company threatens foreclosure. Then she'll save the house from being taken and have the crew throw him out. They only have a mortgage because he claimed he needed money to pay off the car's he'd gotten. Because he was going to be investigated for NCAA violations. When the truth was, he was getting the equity out of their home

15

to pay for Regina's expenses for his other life and his drug addiction. Now with no team to play for, he isn't receiving income. The crew are taking his share of the profits from their businesses and putting them in an account for his children.

"I know I'm not paying a house note for him and his mistress and bastard child," T-baby says to Wesley, "That's for *damn* sure."
Wesley has even offered to help her with the mortgage. But she stands firm on her decision.
"I am financially able to pay it, Wes. But I'd rather loose it before I pay for it and he's still in it," she states.
Her and Rich III are still living with Ajay and Ebony. Katrina Dobbs is still on her Rockers team too. But she'll never visit her at any Ebony's again.

****

Terrell and Chrissy get married in Detroit, the 1st Saturday in July. Ajay is his best man. Ebony is the Matron of Honor. The twins are flower girl and ring bearer. Their wedding is small but beautiful, none the less. The happy couple will continue to live and work in Atlanta after they return from their Jamaican honeymoon.

Monday night after Ajay and Ebony return home with their kids, he plans a quiet evening for him and his family. He puts on the *Floetry* album, *Floetic*. Ebony loves it instantly. With tunes like, *It's Getting Late* and *Sunshine,* it's enough to keep them grooving all night. Once the twins are asleep, they play *Say Yes* and turn in for bed. His birthday is only 3 days away and he doesn't even care to celebrate it. He doesn't want to deal with any unwanted guest at his party.

Ajay turns 28 years old quietly. But the twins have a huge birthday party at *Big Mama's House* to celebrate their 3rd birthday. Lannie has been tested for accelerated classes. At age 3 she can read on a 2nd grade level. Ebony and Ajay don't want to separate the twins in school. So Lannie will stay in the 3 year old class for the upcoming school year.

For T-baby's 26th birthday, Wes plans an official 1st date for the 2 of them. After her game against the *Shock,* Wes is taking her to a black owned restaurant called *Favor's* which is owned by 3 sisters. It's also rumored that this may be the last season for the *Rockers* team. T-baby has expressed interest in the *Detroit Shock.* They're interested in having her on their team next season. She'll have a tryout with them when the 2002 season wraps up.

TIME TO FEEL-RELOADED-Time Will Reveal part 5

Rich falls further behind on the mortgage. By the end of August, 4 payments are due and have to be paid by September 10th. He hasn't lifted a finger to pay anything. Furthermore, he still refuses to sign the divorce papers. Regina and Richaunda are still living with him but he has the nerve to constantly call T-baby, at Ebony's house. He has even tried to visit her there. Ajay nor Ebony will allow that. Though Rich knows he's on breaking ice, he still hasn't tried to get clean. He keeps spiraling further into his black hole of drugs and deception. He barely shows up for work at the Detail shop or Stoney's. He'd been reemployed at both since his last dismissal from the NFL. He won't go to work because he doesn't want to hear the truth from his father and others. He curses any and every one who tries to advise him. Anna cried so hard 1 evening when she'd come to the house to try and reason with him. He called her out of her name, over and over.

"I learned this shit from watching you and daddy," he'd said to his mother. "That's all he did was whoop your ass and you're still with him! She can stay too!"
Anna was heartbroken. Rich had even hit his sister Roo when she'd come by to visit him. She was home from Louisiana and wanted to see him. She wanted to try and show him some love and talk some sense into him. He slapped and punched her because she told him, he was a bum. Rich Sr, Jesse and Greg Jr had beat him up for that incident. Still, with all of that, he hasn't tried to make any changes. Since the day he hit Roo, not 1 member of the crew has supported him. Him disrespecting his mother and sister is something they will not accept. His parents and family refuse to help him until he helps himself. He mopes around each and every day, feeling sorry for himself. He beats Regina, on the regular. Right in front of their 2½ year old daughter. Regina stays there and takes the beatings, day in and day out.

On September 11, the mortgage company is prepared to call the loan. They've ordered Rich to leave the premises. That's when the crew step in with T-baby and saves the house. Regina had finally had enough of Rich's beatings. She took their daughter and moved into a shelter for abused women on *Lorain Avenue*. Rich had threaten to kill her the day she moved out. He even blamed her for ruining his marriage. He's in the highest state of denial.

The next day, the crew men physically remove Rich and his things or lack there of, from the house. He barely has a car left. Let alone any real property. No one even knows what happened to his other cars. After being

17

removed from the house. He moves to Mentor and into the crack mansion where he'd spent most of this year.

When T-baby does walk back into the house, she's disgusted. Rich had messed it up royally. Everything he could pawn for his habit. He did. She isn't even sure if she can find all of her antiques. But she's going to search every pawn shop within a 100 mile radius to recover her things. Some of the walls have holes in them. Some doors are nearly off the hinges from his fits of rage. The carpets are nearly ruined. The odor in the house is unbearable.

"I can't believe how he ruined my dream house," she says in disgust, "He would do anything to try to get to me and make me upset. But you know. I'm not gonna let it bother me. I'm gonna get this house back in shape, now that he's gone."

The crew men in Jackson Heights had taken Rich's gate key, his other keys and they'd changed the passwords to the security systems when they removed him. They also pitched in to have the house cleaned up and remodeled before T-baby and Rich III moved back into it. Rich had gone to Mentor without the divorce papers. He left them on the kitchen counter. Exactly where T-baby had put them when she served him. She isn't down about it. She has confirmed her tryout with the *Shock*, for next March. She's prepared to move on. She has Lil Rich's 7th birthday party at Granny's House, regardless. Rich doesn't show up for the party nor does he call to wish his son a happy birthday. The party is held on the 28th of September. But by the 30th, Rich calls T-baby at her office. Not to wish their son a happy birthday. But to beg her for visitation.

"You're in no shape to be in his presence, Richard," she tells him, "I don't even want him to see you like that."
She hangs up on him. He calls, over and over. T-baby finally lets him say his peace. He tells her, he's going back to rehab. She tells him, she thinks that's a good thing. He asks her if she'll consider giving him visitation if he gets clean.
She says, "Of *course*."
He asks her if she'll reconcile with him if he gets clean and stays clean.
She says, "Absolutely not."
Rich says he understands and accepts her decision.

"If you'll agree to let me come by the house tomorrow to see my son," he says, "I'll sign the divorce papers and give you your freedom. You can do whatever and whoever you wanna do. But I wanna be able to see my son."

TIME TO FEEL-RELOADED-Time Will Reveal part 5

T-baby thinks about it for a minute or two. She realizes it is their son's birthday and Rich III has been asking to see his daddy. Tomorrow will be Rich's 27th birthday, so she figures she'll let him visit if he cleans up *first*. She lays out the terms of tomorrow's visit. He accepts them. She agrees to let him come to the house to sign the papers and visit with his son. Satisfied that he has made some lead way, Rich hangs up and doesn't call back. T-baby tells Wes about tomorrow's visit. He offers to come over for moral support. She tells him that won't be necessary.

"I can handle him," she says, "But I appreciate your offer."

Wes has to honor her wishes, though he doesn't want too.

"I'll be waiting by the phone if you need me," he adds.

"I know you will and I promise. I'll call you if things get out of hand," she says.

Before the close of the business day, T-baby gets a call from the Detroit Shock's business office. She has already been added to their roster without a tryout. She just needs to report to camp on March 3, 2003. She's elated. The Shock had gone to the playoffs this season. She's confident with her on the team *next season*, they can win it all.

"I'll put my money on that," Wes laughs, "You're just what they need to get a ring."

Her WNBA season has ended and T-baby's back in her office, each and every day. Rich III is in 1st grade. He seems to be adjusting well. Despite his troublesome home life. He's a very bright child and very well mannered. T-baby has done a great job with him, primarily on her own. He still has not met his sister. He doesn't know about her yet and T-baby feels it's Rich's responsibility to introduce his daughter into their son's life. Not hers. If it's going to happen, Rich Jr will have to do it.

}*October 1, 2002*{

This is a normal day and work day for the crew. Archie Jr is looking forward to turning 17 in 3 days. There's a party planned for him and for Rich Jr. T-baby is at work. Her and Wes close out for the evening and prepare to leave.

"Trish I want to ask you a question," Wes starts.

"Yes," she says, "What is it?"

"Well I wanted to know..........., if," he hesitates.

"What is it, Wes?" she ask, "Just ask me."

"Can I cook dinner for you. After you finish your meeting with Rich, tonight?" he asks.

19

He really wanted to ask her to be his woman but he got cold feet.

"That sounds great," she answers, hoping he was going to ask her to go steady. "Dinner sounds great," she adds.

"Say around eight?" he asks for clarity.

"Eight o'clock it is."

"Bring Rich the third too. I'm cooking for four."

They lock up the office. Ebony is leaving at 5pm too. They all meet out front and walk to their cars together. T-baby tells Ebony about Wes cooking dinner for her and Rich III after her meeting with Rich.

"Good," Ebony says, "You'll need a pick me up, I'm sure."

They all share a laugh before driving to Jackson Heights. Ebony has an eerie feeling about T-baby's meeting with Rich. She mentions it to Ajay as soon as she arrives home.

"I just don't trust him anymore," she says.

"I don't either," Ajay says, "But T-baby agreed to meet with him. We can't control that part, baby."

"She's back at home though, Anthony. I'd feel more comfortable if she were still here."

"He's not coming in here anymore," Ajay says instantly.

"My intuition tells me that he's dangerous," she tries.

"Tell your intuition that he'll be in more danger if he comes on my property," he says with a smile.

She smiles and says, "Okay baby. I just have a terrible feeling about the meeting."

"She whooped his ass, the last time," he adds with a chuckle.

"This is a new day."

"And a new ass whooping too," he says still laughing.

Ebony lets it go with that. Ajay doesn't seem worried about Rich Jr being alone in that house with a major drug problem, a wife who wants to leave him and opportunity. Plus the knowledge that he has a crew who is at it's wits end with him. She can only think the worst, though she tries to remain positive. Still she calls Nina and Rebbie for a talking down. She doesn't get one because they're feeling the same way. Rich is suppose to arrive at the house at 6. The girls feel as though they should be there to intercept him. They go to T-baby's house but she tells them she doesn't want them to stay.

"He'll just climb up, feel pressured and he won't sign the papers," T-baby says, "I want him to sign these divorce papers, so I can get on with my life. Thank you girls. I know y'all got me. But I can handle his cracked out ass."

TIME TO FEEL-RELOADED-Time Will Reveal part 5

With that, they leave. It's 6:15 when they head back home. He hasn't shown up. They're thinking maybe he won't come at all. That wouldn't surprise any of them.

Rich does show up but not until 6:45. T-baby and Rich III are still waiting. Rich shows up with gifts for his son's birthday. T-baby gives him the gifts that she'd bought for his birthday, from his son.

"Thank you," Rich says solemnly, "I thought you forgot."

"After more than twelve years of remembering your birthday?" she says, "Nah I didn't forget to get you something."

Rich talks to his son. He plays with him and with his toys, for the first 15 minutes of the visit. T-baby notices how thin he's become. She can't help but notice that he seems preoccupied with something else. She wants to get on with it before he starts a pity party. She has no plans on feeling sorry for him today or any other day.

"Are you ready to talk?" he asks suddenly.

"I guess now is as good of a time, as any," she answers, "Let me get the papers."

She goes into the kitchen to get the divorce papers and returns to the living room. She lays the papers on the coffee table in front of the couch and in front of Rich. He looks at the papers. He looks at his son. Then he looks at T-Baby. She sees a change happen in him, right then and there. It's unfamiliar and desperate. She feels an eerie calm that tells her, a storm is brewing. He starts to speak softly.

"Trisha I really don't wanna lose you," he tries as the tears come.

"Rich, we've already been through this," she says, "You said you wanted a divorce and for me to get the fuck on. It's done now. Let's just sign these papers and let each other get on with our lives."

"I don't wanna go on without you and him, in my life," Rich states, "That was the drugs talking when I said I wanted to leave. That wasn't me, Trisha."

"I will never keep your son from you," she tries, "He's always gonna be your son. No matter what happens with us."

Rich becomes agitated and loses his cool.

"I don't want a divorce, Trisha!" he screams all of a sudden, "I came here to get back with you!"

Verifying his mood change, T-baby sends their son to his room and tries to calm Rich down.

"Richard, you don't have to scream at me," she says calmly, "We can talk to each other, like civil human beings."

21

"I know. I know," he says as he calms his voice.
She can see that he isn't accepting their relationship being over. He has gone from hot to cold, in a matter of seconds. Then back to hot again, then again cold. She keeps her eyes on him, feeling like she's in the company of a stranger and not the only man she's had ever loved and known sexually, in her lifetime.

Meanwhile, Arthur calls Chill on his cellular. Chill is on his way home from the club on this chilly Tuesday October evening.

"Hello," Chill says.

"I wanted to tell you, Rich was out here a little while ago," Arthur says, "He was at the U. He bought some more drugs."

"I know," Chill says disgusted, "That brother won't even try to hide the shit anymore. He just wants to kill himself. I'm tired of talking to him because he's not listening. He's suppose to be at a meeting with T-baby. Signing them damn divorce papers tonight. He probably had to be *zooted* out of his damn mind, to go through with it. I know I would have to be."

"Chill, I think you should know that he had a gun with him too."

"What?!"

"Yea. He had toys for his son and a pistol," Arthur states again, "Find him soon, man. I think he's gonna do something crazy."
Chill hangs up with Arthur and speeds up to get to Jackson Heights. He calls Renee to alert her of the situation. She's already preparing to go the T-baby's house to intervene. She moves double time, after Chill's call.

At Rich and T-baby's house things are about to take a turn for the worse. T-baby has already started to feel uneasy with his mood swings. But he calmed down, just as suddenly as he'd gotten irritated. He wants to talk now, so she lets him.

"I wanna tell you the truth about things," he starts, "Regina......, never really meant anything to me..., she was a mistake."
T-baby listens intensely.

"I was so messed up on this shit," he says as he suddenly takes a rock of crack cocaine from his shirt pocket.

"Rich, how dare you bring that into this house," she says, "You have to leave here with that, right now. Rich, now!"
He reaches into his jacket pocket and takes out a pistol. A .357 magnum and she can see that it's loaded. His demeanor grows even calmer. She tries to speak to him.

"Richard please put that away," she tries, "What are you doing? The baby's in the house."

22

TIME TO FEEL-RELOADED-Time Will Reveal part 5

She reminds him of their son's presence, trying to appeal to his good sense. But on crack, he has none. He's silent as he takes a lighter and pipe from the same pocket the crack rock was in. He lights the crack, right in front of her.

"Rich don't do this," she reasons as she tries not to inhale.

She stands up and makes an attempt to leave the room.

"Sit your ass down!" he yells, "I'm gonna talk! You're gonna listen to me, for once God dammit!"

He's pointing the gun directly at her. She sits down nervously.

"Okay Richard," she says, "Just stay calm. Okay?"

"I wanna tell you when things really got out of hand with Regina," he starts again and this time he's calmer.

He takes a hit from the pipe and she cringes in disgust.

"Don't do this to yourself," she tries, as her eyes well up with tears.

He continues smoking, as he says, "When Ajay had the bachelor party, after that she started traveling to New York with me. The day June and me was leaving on the shuttle, she was going too. That's why I was in a hurry to leave. Because we was picking her up first."

T-baby wants to get angry. But she takes it in stride and remains calm. He's still in denial about his own faults and still wants to blame others for the mistakes he made.

He continues, "Y'all always wanted Ajay to be better than me," he says out of the blue, "Y'all gave him props on everything he did. Chill even gave him run of the crew when he got shot. You probably wanted to fuck Ajay."

"That's not true. Half of our life, me and Ajay didn't even speak to each other and you know that."

"You left me and went to stay with him and took my son."

"Because they, *him and Ebony* invited us to stay with them after you jumped on me. And let's not forget, that wasn't the first time that you jumped on me or hit on me, Richard. And that was the last time I was gonna stay and get beat on."

"He tried to fuck you before...-"

"Richard, please. That's all lies and you know it," she says, "Stop trying to give yourself something to be sad about."

"He knew Ebony liked me, when we was little. So he had to make me look bad to make himself look good." he says.

She doesn't even offer a comment to that. They both know that's ridiculous. She lets him ramble on, making up excuses and slinging accusations until she has to give him some kind of response.

23

"Okay," she says, "I knew something was going on. But Richard, that's all in the past. We can move on."
She knew Ebony didn't like him, *ever*. She hadn't even liked her with him, after the violence started. Ebony didn't even like Ajay when they were young. She didn't like anybody but her baby dolls, her grandparents namely big mama, her parents and her brothers. She was always stand offish and distant. Rich is fishing for anything to set her off. But she isn't going to bite. She just wants him to finish his say, then get out of her life.

"I'm not gonna let you leave me, Trisha," he threatens suddenly, "I love you with all my heart. I've never loved Regina, Tameka, Selina…, none of them, like I love you."

"Okay."
She watches the pistol. He has it on his lap. He lights the pipe again and again until the rock disappears. Trisha feels fear now, more than ever. Because now he's smiling and groggy from his drug. She has seen him like this, many times. But she had never witnessed the transformation until today. The phone rings and breaks the monotony for her. He doesn't seem to hear the phone. Not until she moves toward it. She looks at the caller ID. It's Renee. She doesn't know Renee is calling from the driveway or she would make a run for the door to let her in. Rich doesn't allow her to answer the phone. He's in control of what their fate is, for once, he feels. He's going to see this thing through to the end. One way or the other.

"Tear the papers up," he orders suddenly, "And we can still live happily ever after."
She says nothing. She knows by now that this meeting isn't going to end positive for her.
"When you married me, Trisha. You said till death do us part, right?" he asks looking directly at her.
She looks at him nervously. The gun still lays on his lap.

"You're right," she says, "Okay Rich. We can work it out."

"You're lying!" he screams picking up the pistol from his lap, then laying it back down.
He's very jittery and antsy. She knows him and how he gets, when he's feeling sorry for himself. He's very desperate.

"No No Rich!" she tries, "I'm not lying. We can try again, okay? But you have to get clean, baby and stay clean, this time," she pleads.

"Tear the papers up," he demands calmly.

"Or you gonna sign a note saying that you'll get clean and stay clean?" she asks.

24

"Alright."

"And if you go back on the drugs, then you'll give me a divorce to keep from ruining my life and the babies too? Remember what you told me about your parents and how it affected you?"

He doesn't want to think about that. He shakes his head as if the thoughts of his childhood are shaking out of it.

"Ajay had a better home life than me. His parents didn't fight."

"All of our parents fought, Richard. All of them. Some worse then others but they did. I remember my mama screaming and my daddy too. Throwing things. We all had some of that."

"Did your dad go to jail?"

"He didn't get caught, is all the reason he didn't go. Are you ready to do the note?" she's trying to keep him on the subject of a reunion.

"Okay."

"You'll have to sign the papers and give them to someone for safe keeping, in case you refuse to sign them if this were to happen again. Cool?"

He doesn't answer that part. T-baby looks at the papers laying on the table. She isn't going to tear them up. She knows that. Renee calls again. Once again, they let the phone ring.

Figuring that the ringer might be off, Renee comes to the door. She dials again. She can hear it ringing, so she yells their names. But Rich's voice turns calculating as he stands up and starts toward T-baby.

"Don't you say a word," he says to T-baby, as he moves close to her and puts the gun to her temple.

"Why don't I just put the papers away," T-baby whispers, "So she'll know that we're working things out. We'll just send her back home and try to salvage this married. If we can both agree that it won't work at a later time. Then we'll have the papers already. Rather then paying the money again," she tries.

"I'm not signing them muthafuckers!" he yells, loud enough for Renee to hear him, "Not today! Dammit and no other fuckin day!"

Neither T-baby nor Rich notice their son standing just outside of the living room. He's watching the whole ordeal go down. He has seen his father smoking crack and pointing the gun at his mother. He's quiet as he watches.

"Okay okay, Rich," T-baby tries, "Just stay calm, okay? Don't do something that's gonna make it worse."

"There's nothing worse than the woman you love, not loving you back," he says in a haze, "You wanna try to trick me into signing these papers. Then once they're signed you're gonna go through with the divorce.

So you can be with your new boyfriend Wes, right? Is that why your future sister in law is out there?"

"No Richard, it's not like that."

"Chill, Renee, my whole crew are against me now," he says, "Because of you, Trisha. You could've made them all love me again."

"Richard everybody *does* love you," she tries, "You don't love us. If you did, you wouldn't hurt yourself. We just want you to love yourself, get clean and stay clean."

Renee is still knocking on the door. She has called Nina from her cell phone and ask her to come over and help. Nina is on her way. Chill had called to say he was stuck in traffic but he's on his way.

Inside the house, Rich makes a demand, "Prove it! Tear em up."
She can't do it. She looks at him and tries to reason with him.

"Rich, how about we wait until your head is clear. Then you do the note," she says calmly, "And then we can talk about our next-"

"You think I'm stupid, don't you?" he ask still speaking calm and calculating.

The phone is ringing again. This time from Nina's cell phone, as she runs across the lawn trying to get to their house. T-baby hopes Renee has called the gate and has Jacobson outside, as she continues to try and reason with Rich.

"No I don't. But you ask *me* for a divorce. You don't remember?"
She feels strength because he has sat back down on the couch, across from her. He'd flipped the coffee table over earlier, when he demanded she tear up the divorce papers. But now, he points the pistol directly at her again.

"I'm not stupid, Trisha," he says, smiling at her, "You'll leave me, over your dead body. Do you hear me?"

"Richard, please put the gun away."
That's when she notices their son standing in the doorway of the living room. She can see him, just over Rich's shoulder. She knows she has to end this peacefully, for his sake.

"I'll take you back," she says as she tears the divorce papers in half, "Just don't hurt us."

"I don't believe you," he says, still with that evil grin, "You're scrambling now to save yourself."
She tells him, she's sincere as she rips the papers again so that they're in 4 pieces.

Meanwhile Nina and Renee are beating on the door. Jacobson calls out their names and McDaniel rings the phone.

"Till death do us part, Trisha," he says again, "That's all I can think about right now, baby. So let it be like that."
His eyes are so glossy. He's smiling. A harmless smile.
"Richard! Please put the gun away!" she pleads.
He fires 2 rounds directly at her. He shoots her twice in her chest at point blank range. She falls on the floor *lifeless*. Rich III screams out. That's when Rich notices him. He doesn't want his son to see what he's doing. Renee, Nina and security hear the shots. But Rich has the deadbolts locked on their steel doors. They can't get inside and he's not coming out, just yet.
Rich yells to his son, "Go back in your room, son!"
The phone rings continuously while the 3 outside the house are constantly yelling their names. They're beating *very* hard and desperate on all of the entry doors. Inside, Rich III wants to get to his mother.
"My mommy! My mommy!" Rich III yells as he runs into the living room.
He's trying to get to where his mother's body is lying on the floor, in a pool of her own blood.
"Mama wake up!" he cries as he hovers over her. "Please wake up, mommy!"
"Go in your room! *Now!*" Rich yells at him.
Rich III exits the living room with his mother's blood on his clothes. He doesn't go into his room though. He hides in the hall closet and peeks out. He can still see his father. Rich gets up from the couch. He slowly walks over and kneels over T-baby's body.
"They said it wouldn't last," he says as he starts to cry and blubber, "They wanted you to leave me when we was little. But you loved me then. You don't love me right now. But you will again. God will make it so."
He's sweating profusely. His sweat is dripping onto T-baby's body. He attempts to wipe his sweat from her face and wipe the blood from her chest. Then with his bloody hands, he wipes the sweat from his own forehead and face. He looks like the mad man that he is. He's zoned out and no longer conscious of what his actions are. Or what this will do to his son. He's done. He cries out to the top of his lungs, "Till death do us part!!!!"
From the closet, Rich III can still see his father. Crying, yelling and blubbering over his mother. Rich leans down to kiss T-baby's lifeless lips.
"I love you, Trisha. And I'm sorry," he whispers, "I'll love you. *Forever.*"
He points the pistol to his own temple. "Till death do us part!" he says 1 final time and fires 1 more shot into his right temple.
His 7 year old son sees his father's lifeless body fall on top of his mother's.

27

TIME TO FEEL-RELOADED-Time Will Reveal part 5

Renee and company keep yelling and calling and beating. They're waiting for Sandy to bring the spare key from T-baby's office. Nina and Renee react to the shots from outside. They're calling all 3 of their names while they beat on the front and side doors. No one comes to the door. No one answers the phone. No one answers them from inside. Renee and company are pounding. Trying to gain access after hearing shots fired within the house. They imagine the worse.

Inside of the house, Rich III comes out of the closet slowly. He's numb. He cries as he walks up to the pile of bloody bodies. Moments ago, this was his parents having an argument. But not anymore.

"Mama? Daddy?" he speaks softly.

He shakes them. He wants to get his mother up but his father is on top of her. He shakes them. Then he yells their names, trying to wake them up. Neither of them respond. He sits there, transfixed and deaf to all sound. He sits numb with their bodies on the floor, for another 5 minutes. He's just crying now. Nina and Renee still beats on the door. He can't hear them. Not at the moment. He has to save his mommy. He goes into survival mood and stands up. He goes to the phone and dials 911. The dispatcher answers.

Rich III says, "My daddy shot my mommy. And he shot his self. They're on the floor."

The dispatcher talks to him. At the same time, she dispatches police and emergency units to Jackson Heights. She's telling Rich III to stay on the line but he hangs up and goes back to the pile of bodies. He sits back down, next to the bodies while he waits for help to arrive. When all the while, help is just outside the door. Renee and Nina plus security are knocking and pleading for someone to open the door.

Ebony and Ajay are preparing to leave for a movie night out with the twins, Jarvis Jr and their goddaughter Ashanti. Steven and Ally arrive with Ashanti when they hear the police sirens coming into their community.

"Oh my God! *T-baby!*" Ebony screams.

Without hesitation, Ajay runs out and jumps into his Benz.

"Baby stay here," he says, "All of you. Stay here. Please!"

He tears down the driveway and races around the curve to Rich and T-baby's house. Him, the police and EMS arrive simultaneously. He sees Nina and Renee outside of the front door with Jacobson and McDaniel coming out of the driveway. Chill is arriving at the same time. The house is sealed tight.

"What's going on?" Ajay asks as he jumps out of his car and runs up to the house.

TIME TO FEEL-RELOADED-Time Will Reveal part 5

Nina is already crying as she says, "We heard shots from the house. Three of them. No one is answering us."
Police officers are rushing the property.
"We got a call that there was a shooting here," the 1st officer says. Jacobson is present. He briefs them. He gives them the logistics of the house. Chill tells Ajay about the call from Arthur.
"Damn," Ajay says.
He rushes to the door with the police after Jacobson tells them, Ajay might be able to convince those inside to open the door. The officers asks Nina and Renee to step back to the driveway. They do so reluctantly. The officer knocks on the door but there's no sound from inside. They knock again. Then Ajay knocks and calls out, "Hey! Anybody in here!"
"Who is it?" Rich III asks, recognizing Ajay's voice as the man who likes to play with him and the man whom him and his mommy lived with until school started back.
His little innocent voice gives Ajay a false sense of security. But Rich III isn't going to answer the door to strangers. He knows Ajay's voice. *Well.* He'd come and saved his mommy the last time his mother and father had an argument. So Rich III knows he's going to save her again.
"Lil Cuz. It's me. *Ajay*," he says, "Open the door so I can come in."
Rich III hesitates. Ajay continues to coax him. Finally he unlatches the locks. Ajay turns the knob and gently pushes the door open. Ajay can see Rich III. He's covered in wet blood. From the doorway, Ajay can also see Rich and T-baby's bodies lying on the floor covered in blood and looking lifeless. Ajay grabs Rich III.
"Are you hurt, Lil Cuz?" he asks.
"No but my mama and daddy is," he says, sounding *so* innocent.
Ajay picks him up and runs from the door with him. He takes him straight out to the ambulance. He yells over to his sister Nina and Renee.
"Nina. Renee. Don't go up there."
Sandy is just arriving with the spare key. Ebony, Steven and Ally have arrived with Ashanti, Jarvis Jr and the twins. Ajay sees them and protest immediately.
"Take them back home. Right now baby girl. *Now*," Ajay says sternly. "Take Lil Rich with y'all. This is nothing y'all need to see."
Ebony becomes hysterical when she sees Lil Rich covered in blood.
"Oh God! Anthony! What happened?! Are they okay?!"
"Go home baby," Ajay says, "Go home. *Right now*."
He kisses her. Then he has Steven to drive her Escalade back to their house,

29

TIME TO FEEL-RELOADED-Time Will Reveal part 5

with her and Ally screaming in terror. All 4 of the kids are crying. Ebony and Ally are crying because they know they've just lost 2 more of their crew. The kids are frightened just hearing their mother's upset. Rich III rides back with them. He isn't crying. He's in shock. He doesn't say 1 word. He doesn't make 1 sound.

By 8pm, word of the tragedy has spread and the crew are showing up, 2 by 2 including Wes. They arrive by the time the EMS are allowed to move T-baby and Rich's bodies from the house. The family is hysterical now. They're all asking for information.

How did this happen? Why was he allowed back into Jackson Heights?
The police clear everyone away from the ambulances. There are 3 EMS units on the scene and over a dozen police cars. They've managed to get the family to move back beyond the perimeters they set up while paramedics continue to assess their victims.

T-baby has an *extremely* light pulse. She's barely alive and has lost a lot of blood. The paramedics work hard to bring her back but it isn't looking good. They tell the police to make an opening so they can rush her to the hospital.

"She needs to go right now," the lead paramedic says, "She's fading fast."
The family hears this and a brush of cries fan throughout. The ambulance moves down the driveway. Sirens blaring, as they head to the hospital with T-baby.

At the 2nd ambulance, things aren't buzzing at all. Rich's body is lifeless. No pulse and no reaction to any stimulants. He's pronounced dead on the scene. The coroner signs for his body. The ambulance leaves with T-baby, speeding to the hospital. They haven't given her much of a chance to survive either. The coroner takes Rich's body to the morgue. The crew are stunned and shocked beyond belief. Everyone is visibly shaken and distraught.

"I'm going to the hospital," Ajay says, "I've gotta get baby girl."
He gets into his car and heads home to collect Ebony. Their parents follow him to his house to check on Lil Rich before going to the hospital. They know he's traumatized. Sandy is so overcome with grief when she hugs him, that she can't even stand up. Greg Sr holds her up. Then he loads her, Steven and Lil Rich into his car. They rush to the hospital behind Ajay and Ebony. Most of the crew follow them. Wes rides with Chill and Renee. They leave Destiny and Jada with Ally, Ashanti, Jerica and Tank Jr.
Orian, Kim and Pam are all at Ebony's house where the twins are, as well.

30

TIME TO FEEL-RELOADED-Time Will Reveal part 5

Nina, Tank and Rebbie go to the hospital. Jr and Tonya join the others at Ebony and Ajay's house. They bring 1 year old Donovan and 11 year old Brad III with them. They'll help watch the kids while waiting on news on T-baby's condition.

"I can't go to the hospital, Bradley," Tonya says, "I just can't. Since Stoney died, it's been hard to go back there when family is injured. I can't believe Rich is gone. My God!"

Everyone is heavily devastated. Rich is dead. T-baby doesn't have much life left. Ally and the others sit around Ebony and Ajay's house in disbelief. 1 by 1, the phone calls from Atlanta, Baton Rouge, Oklahoma City and Houston start to come in. Everyone gets the news firsthand. Rich shot T-baby. She's critical and barely clinging to life. He shot himself to death while their 7 year old son Rich III, witnessed the entire tragedy.

}*The Home Going*{

In less than a week, all of the family have arrived from out of town. Anna and Rich Sr made the funeral arrangements for their son. Rich's funeral will be on October 9th.

T-baby is on life support. She's in very critical condition and not expected to recover. She hasn't regained consciousness. The guys from Atlanta and Baton Rouge, fly in today. Kenny comes home from Columbus. The surviving men of Chill and Bruce's crew gather at Chills house, this evening. They talk about the tragedy amongst themselves.

"How did we let this happen?" Chill asks Ajay, "We should've talked T-baby out of having that meeting with him."

"We had no idea he would do this shit, Chill," Ajay says, "He wanted to die. I hate it so much. But look at all the shit we did, trying to get through to him."

"He didn't want our help," Jb says, "I talk to Rich all the time. He knew he was messing up. He didn't wanna do better."

"Look here y'all. We all knew Rich," Tank says, "When he made up his mind about some shit. That's the shit he was gonna do or say."

"He threatened everybody who tried to speak to him about it," June says, "He was like, '*Stay the fuck out of my business. I'm a grown ass man, muthafucka.*' So what could we do?"

"He went off on me on the practice field. Just for encouraging him to do his best," Eric adds, "I was saying it because the offensive coach was pissed off at him. I was trying to help him keep his spot on the team."

"Me too," Bruce says sadly.

31

"He was ready to fight me when I tried to stop him from buying crack in Shaker Heights, one day," Jr says.

"He did the same shit to me," Arthur adds, "He pushed me in the chest when I told him, he was better than that. He pointed that same gun at me. I called Chill, right after. I knew he was going off the deep end."

"He threatened me so many times, man," Jesse says, "He would hurt Ruthie's feeling. I would put him in check. Then he would snap."

"For real, that's why we got at him, not to long ago," Greg Jr says.

"Yep," Steven adds.

"Wasn't anything *no one* could do," Rob says, "From the moment he called T-baby's office yesterday. He knew what he wanted to do."

"I was thinking that too," Sam Jr says.

"That's what I believe," Cedric says, "That's what it sounds like. Like he premeditated the whole thing. It still hurts though."

"This shit is unbelievable," Bruce adds.

"*Fuckin* unbelievable," Reaper concurs.

The CrewLand mall is the destination for all well wishers and those who want to send their regards. The gates outside Jackson Heights becomes a memorial for both T-baby and Rich.

Rich's funeral date and T-baby still has not regained consciousness. The doctors still give little hope that she'll *ever* recover. The crew attend the funeral. And though they're torn by the way his death had come to pass. They're sad nonetheless, that he'd chosen to take such desperate measures to find a solution. They all feel guilty for what they feel was them turning their backs on him. They tried showing him tough love but his solution to being banished, this time. Was killing T-baby and himself. They can't make any sense of it. And no matter how much they try to accept it. They just can't shake this lose from their hearts and minds.

It's been 8 days since the tragedy. Rich is buried. T-baby is still *barely* clinging to her life. Rich III has still not uttered 1 word.

RICHARD TREVON "RICH" WILLIAMS JR.
OCTOBER 1, 1975-OCTOBER 1, 2002
AGE 27 YEARS OLD
YOUR CREW WILL KEEP YOUR SWEETEST MEMORIES ALIVE!
RICHIE RICH, REST IN ETERNAL PEACE!
OCTOBER 9, 2002.
[*committed suicide on his birthday*]
32

TIME TO FEEL-RELOADED-Time Will Reveal part 5

CHAPTER 49

LIFE GOES ON

Three weeks after Richie Rich's Funeral, another tragic death is recorded in Hip-Hop. The night of October 30, 2002. Legendary hip-hop DJ *Jason "Jam Master Jay" Mizell* of RUN-DMC was fatally shot and killed inside a studio on Merrick Boulevard, in Queens New York. The crew are still grieving the loss of Rich. So *JMJ's* death hits them *very* hard. There are still no words to describe the pain, emptiness and grief the crew feel over Rich's suicide. Ruthie hasn't returned to school since coming home for her older and only sibling's funeral. Corey had attended the service. He visits the crew a lot more since the lose of his brother. Ruthie spends every day with her nephew Rich III. She tries to get him to talk about what he witnessed but he still isn't talking. T-baby has been in a coma for 18 days. Her girls have been with her each day. Sandy has barely left her side. They all talk to her and pray. T-baby hasn't shown any *signs* of recovering.

Today a stranger shows up at T-baby's accounting office with a letter Rich had written, months ago. The stranger is an Asian woman. She says she lives in the Mansion in Mentor, at Madison-by-the-Lake.
"I see his *why,* one day," she says in her broken English.
"You saw his wife one day?" Claudia clarifies, as she translates.
"Yea, yea, *Treesha is her, rye?*"
"Yes. Trisha is her name," Claudia repeats, "Okay. Wait right here. I'll go get misses Jackson. Her cousin. Okay?"
"Kay."
Claudia rushes to Ebony's side of the duplex and tells her about this new visitor. Ebony is out front in seconds, to meet this woman who introduces herself as Keno. Keno is Japanese. She's the wife of the Clydesdale owner who owns the mansion where Rich and T-baby use to hang out. The same mansion that became Rich's haven to smoke his crack. Keno is the woman who'd run out to the Benz that day, nearly 4 years ago, when T-baby went investigating and looking for clues as to where Rich had gone during Ebony and Ajay's wedding reception. T-baby thought this was a woman Rich was messing around with. She later learned that wasn't true. She wasn't Rich's mistress. She was his customer. Crack was his *real* mistress. And whoever tolerated him while he used it. He had supplied Keno with powder cocaine for years. T-baby knew they had allowed him to cook and process his crack

at their house. She later learned, they'd also allowed him to smoke crack there too. Today Keno has shown up with what Ebony describes as a depression note, more so than a suicide note. In the letter, Rich bashes Ajay terribly. He also talks about his inferiority to Ajay and how the crew put faith in Ajay and never him. The same things he was saying to T-baby before he shot her. He had written it down and told Keno to bring the note to his wife's office if anything were to happen to them. He had given her this letter in the early summer. Which indicates to Ebony, Claudia and Wes that he had been planning this for awhile. Ebony is disgusted to see the negative things he had to say about Ajay. She's just as disgusted to read that he had a crush on her.

"Oh that's just *awful*. Why would he do this?" she asks aloud but not really expecting Wes or Claudia to have an answer.

She feels terrible and doesn't want to read anymore. So Wes reads the letter in full. He's upset at how Rich describes T-baby as less than Ebony. Second rate compared to Ebony and that Ebony beats her in everything.

"He had some real issues, didn't he?" Wes says aloud.

But not really asking anyone in particular.

Ebony is already crying. She knows she has to tell Ajay. But she never wants T-baby to know about this letter. She feels it'll hurt her deeply to read these words written by the only man she ever loved. She knows if Ajay had said or wrote these types of things about her. She would be devastated.

"I can understand you don't wanna hurt her anymore than he has," Wes says, "And it's not something you would have to do right away."

"I'll show it to Anthony. See what his thinks we should do with it," Ebony says, "I know we have to show it to his parents. They should see it. It's written by their son, who's no longer living."

She still finds that hard to believe. No matter how rude he had been to her. And though he had hurt her and her children and even her dog, when they were kids. She never wanted him dead. At the same time, she has never wanted him in a personal way either. For that part of the letter, it only makes her loathe him more. That part made her feel like those words would leave her cousin with an inferiority complex, if she ever read it.

"We'll figure out what to do when it comes to her," Wes says, "But right now. We don't have to talk about it. We'll just pray for her recovery."

"Good," Ebony says, "Thanks Wes. I'm gonna call Anthony and ask him to come in and see the letter. Then we can decide what to do next."

He agrees with her. Then they take Keno's information, thank her for coming in and send her on her way.

TIME TO FEEL-RELOADED-Time Will Reveal part 5

Ajay comes by and reads the letter. Then he takes it into his possession. He and Chill will take it to Rich Sr and Anna when they see fit. They don't want Ebony or Wes to worry about it. The case is closed.

]East General hospital{

Wes has been in to see T-baby everyday. He hasn't had much of an appetite. Renee is worried about him not eating because he's diabetic. Renee sits in the waiting room with him this evening and talks.

"Wes I need for you to eat, baby brother," she says.

"I haven't had an appetite, sis," he says, "I can't believe I let her talk me out of coming over there for that meeting. I could've saved-"

"I'm not gonna let you blame yourself for this," Renee says, "We all feel like we should've done more. We all feel guilty as *hell* about what happened. But none of us ever thought Rich would do something like this. I damn near grew up with him. I would never have guessed it would've ended like this. My husband is sick over it."

"I wonder do Trisha even know that he's dead?" Wes asks.

Renee is silent. She hadn't even thought about how T-baby is going to react when and if, she recovers.

Nina, Ebony and Rebbie come out of ICU and sit next to Renee and Wes. They're quiet too. This ordeal has shaken the crew like none of the others had. Not since Stoney was suddenly killed and Granny died suddenly have they been this stunned by a death. But Rich's death is even more heavy on them because they all feel guilty for turning their backs on him. Or at least, that's how they think *he* saw it.

"I can't believe Rich is gone," Rebbie says as she cries, "I was so mad at him. But if he was here right now. I would hug him and tell him I love him. Then tell him to get his shit together or I'll beat his behind."

"I was still mad at him for hitting me and hurting the twins," Ebony says, "That seems so small of me when I think about it now."

She's reflecting on the letter from Keno by Rich. She can tell Wes is too. The contents of it makes it hard for either of them to feel sorry for Rich. He had written such hateful things about the very people who are confessing their love for him right now. *Renee and Rebbie*. The letter has mean spirited comments about everyone in Chill's crew. He had even gotten low down on some members of Bruce's crew. Namely Jesse because he dates Ruthie. He said foul things about Bruce, Eric and June too. Ebony feels this was because they were able to enjoy their professional football careers and he had ruined his royally. Renee, Rebbie and Nina are going on about their

35

their love for him. Ebony wonders how reading his letter would affect their present views. Wes feels like it would make them angry to know what he'd said about them. At the office, he'd said not to let anyone read it because he didn't want them to be angry with Rich, now that he's gone. Ebony feels it will make them feel guiltier and blame themselves, even more. Still her and Wes keep silent while the others speak.

"We all feel bad because we didn't want to have him around. Not as long as he was on the drugs," Nina says, "My cousin is dead. My best friend girl is barely alive."

"We've got to find a way to hold it together," Renee says, "We have too. And be prepared for the worst if T-baby doesn't make it out of there."

They don't even want to think about that scenario.

Next Chill, Ajay, Jr and Tank come through to visit again. They sit with Ebony and company in the waiting room. Neither of them will be able to shake their guilt for a long time. Most likely never. After reading the letter, Chill still feels guilty, just as Ebony had predicted. The letter made him feel even more guilt. She can see it in Ajay's eyes. He's angry. She already knows he didn't like reading the admissions that Rich gave up about her. No matter what, he will never live that down. Knowing that his own cousin had thoughts about sexually assaulting his wife, long before she *was* his wife. His letter revealed that he had thoughts of attacking Ebony. Even before and after Raymond had tried. That admission prevents Ajay from feeling anything but anger towards his 1st cousin.

Weeks later and still no one is in the mood to celebrate anything. However Nina and Tank do have a party for Jerica's 8th birthday. All of their children are there including Rich III. He's still not talking and he doesn't play with anyone.

Roo returns to her classes at Southern with Greg Jr and Jesse. The families manage to get through Halloween and even Thanksgiving but nothing has been the same for any of them. They spend Thanksgiving at Bruce and Kim's house this year. By the end of November, Charlotte turns 18 and receives her trust fund from Stoney. It's bittersweet. Ebony handles her transfer, just as she had done for Chaundra.

During the last 2 months Ebony, Nina and Rebbie managed to recover most of T-baby's valuables. These are the things Rich pawned while living in the house. They're still hopeful she'll recover and be normal again. None of them have been back to the house since the tragedy except Chill,

36

TIME TO FEEL-RELOADED-Time Will Reveal part 5

Ajay, Tank and June. The police had long suspended the crime scene. But no one else even wanted to go in. No one wants to disturb anything until they know what T-baby's outcome is going to be.

Lil Rich has gone back to school but for the most part, he's a shell. He's still not talking. Roo comes back home for her 21st birthday. She picks him up from school on her 1st day back home.

"Hey nephew," she says, "You wanna go with me to the hospital to see your mommy?"

He shakes his head yes. She drives him to see T-baby. Before today, he hadn't been allowed to go in by request of his grandmothers, Sandy and Anna. Today though, Sandy and Anna are both there and they decide to let him visit her.

"It can't affect him any worse, ma," Roo says, "He hasn't talked since it happened. It might help him to see that she's not gone too."

She takes Lil Rich into T-baby's room. She's still hooked up to machines and monitors. Lil Rich walks up to her bed side. Then he climbs up on her bed and lays his head down on her stomach. Roo starts to cry. T-baby doesn't respond. Lil Rich lays on her until he falls asleep.

Nina is at the salon. Suddenly Alana and Darlene come in seeking appointments. Nina tells Charlotte, who works as the receptionist, "No way. Absolutely not."

Then Tonya steps in and tells Alana and Darlene to go out and wait in the reception area while she brings Nina to the back office for a talk.

"Nina we're a business establishment. We have to serve people, whether we like them or not," Tonya says, "As long as they follow the salon rules. We take their money. Remember?"

"I don't want that bitch parading up through here, *Tonya*," Nina says, "It's enough that she works in the club."

"Tank don't give a fuck about that bitch Nina and you know it."

"That ain't the point, Tonya," she says, "That bitch is trying to be slick. She's trying to *slowly* ease her way back into our lives. I don't want shit to do with her."

Tonya says, "You don't have to do her hair. Matt already agreed to take clients like her. His daughter Kelly works with him too. *Look*. They'll be on the other side. So you won't have to view them. Just like Farah. Okay?"

"*Tonya?*"

"Okay Nina? I need you to be okay with it," Tonya insists.

"Okay but one of these days I am gonna snatch her ass up and

37

beat the ever loving fuck out of her," she oozes, "That part I promise you. So be prepared."

"Just make sure she starts it," Tonya says, "Cause she'll probably sue us. And as her employer. That changes shit a whole lot for you and our business interest. Alright?"

"Then I'll hire someone to do it," Nina says as she tries to stop herself from smiling.

"Are you gonna handle this?" Tonya asks, smiling now.

"Okay. Only for crew though."

"That's how we do it," Tonya says, "And besides. Think of all the laughs you, me and Justine will have at her expense."

"Right over her dumb ass head."

"We can do that," Tonya smiles.

Her and Nina give each other a pound. Then they go back out front. Alana and Darlene are still sitting in reception. Tonya goes to Charlotte and tells her, they can be added to Matt and Kelly's list *only*. She sets them up with appointments. Then sends them on their way.

"It's not over," Nina says, "Mark my word. That bitch is gonna go there with me. And I'm gonna end her career."

Justine and Tonya look at each other. They don't say a word. But secretly, they hope Alana gets out of hand so all 3 of them can whoop her, Darlene and Farah's asses, right here in the shop. Tonya had all 3 of their appointments set for the same day and the same time block. So they'll all be here every time, at the same time. She's going to inform Renee of the days they'll be here as well.

"The possibilities are endless," Tonya says and they all laugh about it as they go back to work.

Roo had left Rich III in the room alone with his mother. She'd gone down to the vending machines to get some snacks for him. Then she joins her mother and Sandy in the waiting room.

"How is he?" Sandy asks.

"He was laying on her stomach," Roo says sadly, "He fell asleep. So I went to get him some snacks and juice."

"That baby is *devastated* by this," Anna says, "It may not be showing right now. But he is."

"He's in shock," Sandy says, "He needs to see that his mommy is still breathing. It's gonna take all we have to help him recover from this."

"If he *ever* does," Roo says, "I miss my brother and my sister."

38

TIME TO FEEL-RELOADED-Time Will Reveal part 5

She starts to cry. Quickly Sandy and Anna comfort her before they head back toward T-baby's room to take Lil Rich his snacks.

All of a sudden they hear him laughing. They run into T-baby's room where they find Lil Rich laughing hysterically. He's laughing because his mother is tickling him. T-baby is *awake*!

"Oh my God! Thank you Lord!" Sandy and Anna both yell as the happy tears come and they rush to T-baby's side.

Ruthie runs to the nurses station. She tells them T-baby is awake.

T-baby hasn't spoken yet but she's awake. She's very weak. She's smiling at her son. *She's awake*. She keeps hugging her son. She hugs him, looks at him, then hugs him again. She's thinking about the nightmare she has relived for the past 2 months, during her coma. She had relived October 1, over and over. She thought Rich had shot their son too. She was sure of it. But now she knows different. Feeling his presence and hearing him talk to her is what motivated her to wake up and *live*. She didn't want to live without her baby. The nurses take her vitals and determine that she's breathing on her own. She's out of the woods.

"We can take these machines off of her," 1 nurse says, "We just have to get her doctor in here to approve it. But she'll need to keep the I.V. until she consumes some fluids and food."

Anna, Sandy and Roo are thrilled. Anna grabs the phone to call Greg Sr and the crew. She calls the salon first. T-baby even tries to talk but she's still too weak.

"Baby don't try to talk," Sandy suggests, "Just be happy you're awake. Lord knows *I am*. Thank you *Jesus*!"

"My mommy's not dead," Lil Rich says all of a sudden.

"No she's not and you helped her to wake up," Sandy says, hugging and kissing her grandson.

He giggles playfully. That's medicine for T-baby and for them. Just to hear him laugh and talk like a normal 7 year old kid. It's a beautiful sound.

After her doctor gives the okay, the nurses remove the ventilators, oxygen tank and respirators. Dr. Stansfield comes in and gives her the once over and says, "She's on a good road. I expect she can make a full recovery. But it'll be day to day."

By the time her crew arrive, T-baby is smiling and speaking slowly. She remembers the entire incident. She remembers Rich shooting her. She remembers him kissing her and saying he loved her. And he would love her, *forever*. She remembers him saying, *'Until death do us part.'*

39

She also remembers hearing a 3rd shot. She thought he had shot their son. But she can't remember anything after that 3rd shot.

"Did they catch him?" she whispers.

"Yes T-baby. They did," Anna says, "Don't you worry about him right now. He's in the best place for God to fix him. We need you to get better so you can get up and get back to your life."

"Did he miss when he shot at the baby?" T-baby mutters.

"He missed the baby," her father says.

No one wants to tell her that Rich had killed himself. She's just waking up after 68 days in a coma. They don't want to shock her with the news of Rich being dead and buried. Not at this time. They will cross that bridge later. Much later. When she has her strength.

Wesley sits with her tonight. Sandy has taken Lil Rich home with her. Roo went too. She isn't ready to leave her nephew's side. Not just yet.

Tonight he opens up and talks to Roo about the traumatic incident on his daddy's birthday. Roo stays strong for him. He's now on the road to his recovery, just like his mother. Roo holds her nephew and cries, somewhat happier tears. Just to hear him speak about what he had witnessed, gives her chills. But he seems okay.

Now that T-baby is in recovery, the crew decide someone has to go back to her house. They have to access the damages done during the shooting and get it ready for her homecoming. They hope she'll be coming home soon. They want to fix it up for her and Lil Rich.

When they unlock the door and go in, the first thing they see is Rich's gift and Lil Rich's toys. They're still lying on the floor where they had been playing. on that horrible day when Rich had ended his life and nearly ended T-baby's too. The blood is still dried into the living room carpets T-baby had *just* replaced after the guys put Rich out.

"We have to get this place in shape for Tee and Lil Rich," Nina says, "I don't want her to see this vision. *Ever* again."

"We're gonna change this *whole* living room," Sandy says, "I don't want her nor my grandson to ever see this *same* room again either. I'd rather them come home to a totally remodeled front end. With hopes that they can put this tragedy behind them, one day."

They have renovators to come in and redo the entire living room and front hallway. They change the hall closet which Lil Rich told Ruthie, he'd hid in while he watched his father shoot his mother and himself.

TIME TO FEEL-RELOADED-Time Will Reveal part 5

"New furniture, curtains, paint, plants. The *whole* nine," Jo says.
"This will be a totally new room and front end when they come back home," Ebony says with a smile.
They leave the workers to finish up while they go back to visit T-baby.

In the days leading up to the Christmas holidays, Wes runs the finance office. Then he visits T-baby every evening and brings her up on the business. Sandy and Anna get to go home every evening when he shows up. T-baby is in her own room and still recovering. She's able to walk around and she has started to ask a lot of questions. She wonders where Rich is and why she hasn't heard from him.
How come no one is willing to talk about him? Why hasn't he come to visit me?

She wonders if he's in prison. When she mentions him, no one is willing to discuss him. They just say he's not around right now. Or they don't want her to think about him until she's completely well. She isn't willing to accept these answers anymore.
"Is he in jail? Missing again? Has he been to see me?" she has asked but no one will answer her directly.

T-baby is released to go home, 10 days before Christmas. The crew have a surprise for her when she gets home.
"Oh my God!" she says and smiles as she reenters her home, this time in a wheelchair. "Y'all remodeled and redecorated the house and y'all fixed up everything," she says while still smiling.
She notices many of her antiques are back.
She asks, "Did Richard tell y'all where to find this stuff? I know he had too. Since he's the one who sold them. At least he did help me get my stuff back. But why won't y'all tell me where he is?"
"We will Trisha," Anna says, "But we want you to be strong."
"Why?" she asks, "Why do I need to be strong first?"
"Baby," Greg Sr finally says, "He's gone."
"Gone where?" she asks as she looks at her family and crew.
"Where is he? Prison? Another crack house? Rehab again? *Where?*"
"No Trisha," Sandy says, "He shot himself after he shot you."
"He did? Is he okay?"
Anna shakes her head negatively.
"He's dead," Rich Sr says.

41

TIME TO FEEL-RELOADED-Time Will Reveal part 5

T-baby frowns. She has a look on her face like that last statement has entered her head but it's slow to process. She finally speaks.

"He's *dead* mama Anna?" she asks in disbelief.

"Yes," Anna whispers softly.

T-baby sits in silence. She looks bewildered and confused.

"He shot me then he shot himself?" she asks for clarity.

"Yes Trisha," Rich Sr says.

She's numb. She doesn't know which emotion to feel *first*.

"I need to go to my bedroom," she says suddenly as she tries to push herself around her living room in her wheelchair.

She's struggling and not making much head way. So Nina starts to help her. T-baby refuses her help, saying, "No Nina. I really need to be alone."

"Sure Tee," Nina says with doubt in her voice as she watches T-baby try to push herself.

She can't do it. She quickly becomes frustrated. She throws her arms up in angst and screams, "Oh my God! He's dead!! For *real*?! Oh God!"

She screams over and over. She can't believe it. The man she has loved for all of her life is dead. No more arguments with makeup and explanation sessions later on. No more late night crack binges and no more domestic violence. There won't be anymore rehab or new NFL teams either. No matter how horrible he had been to her at times. She never imagined he would be gone *for good*. Her girls are crying like they can feel her pain. Neither of them can imagine Ajay, Tank or June never being here. Most of the crew are crying and reliving the 1st moment they found out about Rich's death. They try to comfort T-baby. She isn't handling it well at all.

"I loved him, mama Anna. With all my heart," she says as she cries, "I never wanted him to die. *Why*?! Why did you do this honey?! Oh my God!"

"I know baby," Anna says and hugs her, "I know you loved him."

"He shot me and then he shot *himself*," she whispers, "I should've known he was desperate. I should've known better. I *tore* up the papers."

She's consumed with guilt instantly, which is another feeling they all understand and relate too as well.

"Yes he was desperate," Sandy says, "And we all tried to be there for him. It's not you alone. We all tried but he didn't accept us."

"Lil Rich was here during all of it," T-baby recalls.

"He witnessed it all," her father tells her.

"Is he okay?" she asks.

They tell her, he's down at Ebony's with Ruthie and that he didn't talk from that day until the day she woke up.

42

TIME TO FEEL-RELOADED-Time Will Reveal part 5

"This is gonna scar him," she thinks out loud, "Oh no. Please go get my baby. *Please*."

Her father goes to get him and brings him home immediately.

Wes is here and he can't help but to feel out of place right now. He asks T-baby if she needs anything. She tells him, she wants to be left alone with her son. They all understand. The crew file out 1 by 1, leaving T-baby, her parents and Lil Rich in the house. T-baby tells Wes to call her later. He feels good about that part.

For the rest of the evening, as Sandy and Greg Sr take care of the house duties. T-baby spends time in her bedroom talking to her son. She knows he'll have repercussions from this tragedy. She wants him to be open about his feelings and not suppress them. He's 7 years old. The same age his father was when he witnessed his own parents fights and troubles. She's determined to break the *Richard Williams cycle*. She refuses to let her son grow up with bitter pain. Pain from witnessing his parents troubles, the way his father had done up until age 7. That's the main reason she had been seeking the divorce. But 1 thing is for sure. Through all of the pain and drama she had with Rich during their 13 year relationship. She never once thought he would ever be *completely* out of her life.

"He's dead and buried. *Oh my God*. Oh my God. I didn't even get to see him before they buried him. I didn't get to say goodbye," she whispers to herself as she continues to cry.

Lil Rich climbs up onto her bed and she wraps her arms around him. He tells her, he went to the funeral and his daddy looked good.

"I touched him. His face was cold, mommy. His hands was cold. His suit. He had on a *tight* suit. He was dressed up. He was clean, mommy. His face was happy. He laid down and went to sleep," he says innocently.

She tries to fight back more tears. When she can speak, she says,

"I loved your daddy a lot, Richie. He loved me too. Until death did us part. And we both loved you. I don't want you to *ever* forget that. Okay?"

"I love you too, mommy," he says, "And I love my daddy."

T-baby hugs him tight. Then she looks into his innocent little eyes.

She says, "As soon as I can walk and drive. We're gonna go to his grave so I can say goodbye. Okay? Then I want you to meet your sister."

"I do have a *sister*? For *real*?" he asks with bright eyes and a smile, "Some of my friends at daycare, said I did. But I didn't believe them."

"Yes you do have a sister," T-baby says, "Her name is Richaunda and she's two years old."

"Cool!" he yells and smiles, "Can I see her?"

43

TIME TO FEEL-RELOADED-Time Will Reveal part 5

"Yes Richie," she says with a smile as she gives him a kiss, "It *is* cool. And of course I'm going to do whatever I can to help you see her. I want y'all to know each other and play together too. Your daddy would've like that. A lot."

It's the last day of the year. The crew are going to have another huge New Year's eve party. They haven't had a celebration since Rich Jr had taken his own life. It's 3 months later. They need to release some stress.

This New Year's eve, Ajay and Ebony have been married for 5 years. They keep with the traditional gift giving just as their elders do. Paper is the traditional 1st anniversary gift. Ebony had given Ajay the title to his Jaguar and the car. For their 2nd anniversary where gifts of cotton are traditional. They gave each other new wardrobes. The 3rd year it was leather. The gifts was desk sets for the home and work offices. Full length coats, luggage and wallets for both. Plus 4 Marc Jacob handbags for her. And she gave him a leather whip but hasn't allowed him to use it, in the 2 years he's had it. The 4 year anniversary traditional gifts are fruits and flowers. They went all out last year and filled the house with flowers of all sorts. Even house plants. They did new landscaping and a facelift for their entire property. They also shared a life size fruit bowl. It was large enough for *them* to fit in. It was a sticky mess of fun and healthy eating too. This year, they've arrived at anniversary number 5. Ebony is excited because they went together this year and got something the entire family can enjoy.

"I've been married for five years to my one and only. I want my gift of wood, right now," Ebony says as she laughs.
It's the early morning of their 5th anniversary.

"I've got your wood right here, baby," he says, returning the laugh and holding his rock hard dick in his hand.
Some of the gifts are being used already. They've bought new furniture for their home. They haven't discussed Rich's letter in detail yet. So they make sure and do that this morning.

"I've noticed how distant you've been since Rich's death," she says.

"You know what baby? The way I feel about Rich *lately*. Is *fuck* that nigga," he says, "He was foul, all along. To say shit like he said in that letter. He had a lot of hatred towards me and for *what*? Because I didn't take *no* shorts and *no* losses from *no* one."

"I think he wanted to leave us with bad feelings," she says, "Knowing we couldn't confront him about it."

"He wrote that shit back during the summer time," he says, "He

44

could've said what he wanted to say to *me*. But he knew he would've had to hold up for it."

"He said some really *evil* things," she adds.

"He said he was going to *'catch you here while I was on the road and rape you. Then beat your ass real good because that's what you needed to have happen'*," he says, "And baby girl, *I* would've killed him. He wanted to die. *Obviously.* And he didn't have *anymore* passes left with me. I would've beat him to death."

"Anthony, he was just jealous of what we have. He knew I never even thought of looking at another boy. That bothered him a lot. Because he knows T-baby messed around with Craig."

"And then she's feeling Wes now," he says, "That's the surest sign that he was never handling his personal with her."

"She once told me, he use to tell her things like, *'I don't have fourteen inches like Ajay. If you want a bigger dick. You'll have to fuck my cousin.'* She told me that when we was in the tenth grade. That's when him, Bre, Tank and June was juniors and you was a senior," she says, "That was before Craig was even in the picture. So it really wasn't about him."

"Rich wanted to beat me since we was five and six years old," Ajay says, "And he never beat me at *shit*. That was his problem. Not you and me. Or T-baby. Nor any muthafucka she was fucking with. It was just his low self esteem having ass."

"Anthony I don't want you to be mad with him," she says, "Because he's gone now. He needed you more than you ever needed him. But he didn't know how to say that to you. He admired you. People usually judge whether they view themselves as successful or not. Based on how the person they look up to is living. And you were always number one in each division. The All-star at every basketball event. Football too. When you was playing. You beat him at his sport. He felt inferior."

"Because he was and he was always gonna be," he says, "I should've fucked him up when he hurt you and my twins."

"Don't say that."

"I should have," he says again.

She wants to change the subject. It will take some time for her husband to forgive his 1st cousin. She'll slowly get him to where he needs to be. But it's not going to happen this morning. She decides to talk about something she knows will bring a smile to his face.

"The twins are gonna be so happy with their new furniture."

"They got big kid rooms now," he says with a proud smile.

45

TIME TO FEEL-RELOADED-Time Will Reveal part 5

"They'll love them," she says, "So what are we gonna do for today? You told me not to plan anything."

"How about we stay in bed until New Year's," he suggest with a smile.

"That sounds good to me," she says, "The twins are at mama's. Kim's got Ike and Tina."

"Yes and they can keep her company today," he says, "I just want to make love to my wife all day. Are you wit that?"

"I'm wit that."

They go back to bed. For the most part, that's where they stay until a couple of hours before midnight. Then they join the crew, T-baby included, at their club to ring in New Year 2003.

Jan and Rob have brought Robert Jr to Cleveland to celebrate his 3rd birthday at Granny's House. Rob's label *Bringing the Noise Records,* which Reaper and Brittany J own a percentage of, has gone major. Atlanta turned into the Mecca of Hip-Hop by the turn of the millennium. Rob had gotten the right contact and moved there, at the right time. Reaper has a top 10 album and invitations to this years *Vibe Awards, Bet Awards*, the *AMA's* and *the Grammy's.* He's even nominated for a Vibe and a Bet award for best new artist and best dance video, respectively. His big sister Rebbie had choreographed his video and shares in the nomination for the Bet award. The crew are very proud of them. They're going to sponsor their trips to the shows, later in the year. Some of the crew are going to attend with them too.

Big John's trucking company has picked up more clients. He has been offered contracts for interstate driving. He's keeping his word to Pearl. He won't personally accept the offers to drive long distance. What he does is hire 4 commercial drivers to take the long hauls for his company. Pearl retires from East General officially, this week. She takes an office at Jackson's Real Estate and Investment Banking which is her daughter Ebony's office. The office for CrewLand Trucking is housed within Ebony's side of the split level duplex, just as T-baby's father Greg Jr's construction office is located on T-baby's side.

"Y'all have to work your way up to getting your name on the marquee," Ebony says as she laughs with her parents.

They tell her, they'll be building their own office within 24 months.

46

"Make me proud then," Ebony says as she speaks the words they had said to her, not so long ago.

Before Kim will be ready to build a law office and by the time Jan is ready build her pediatric office. John and Pearl are guaranteeing they'll be taking up a space in that new strip for the trucking company office too.

"I believe you guys. I really do," Ebony says, "I had to get it from somewhere."

"We're gonna have strip after strip out here by twenty ten," John says.

There's nothing this crew feel they can't do. John only wishes his mother, the deceased Pearline known to all as *Granny*, had lived long enough to see how well her grandchildren have done. September will be 12 years since her untimely death. This past Christmas was 12 years since Stoney was killed. Last August made a year since grandma Sally had passed away. It's been 3 months since Rich killed himself.

Still T-baby finds herself waking up thinking he must be out at the mansion in Mentor. She wants to move on with her life and yet, still hold on to his memory. But she's finding it impossible to shake her guilt for missing his home going. To help her with this, Arthur gave her the service on DVD. She watched it for nearly a month straight. *Everyday*. She doesn't want to live without a mate and a love of her own. Still she needs the support of her entire family before she can be open to dating again. She calls mama Anna to see if she can meet her for lunch. Her support has to start with Rich's parents before she can bring it to the rest of the crew.

"Hello," Anna says.

"Hi mama Anna. It's Trisha. How are you today?" T-baby asks.

"I'm doing okay, I guess," she answers, "How are you and my grandson?"

"We're okay. I'm about to take him to school. Then go back in to work. But I was wondering if I can talk to you about something today?" she asks.

"Sure you can, Trisha," Anna says, "*Anytime* you want."

"You wanna meet me for lunch at Crew's House? Say, *noon*?"

"I'll meet you there after I finish my last massage," Anna says, "My last client before lunch is at eleven."

"Perfect. I'll stop in the Spa on my way down to the restaurant. Alright?"

"Alright."

It's 6 days into the new year. T-baby is going back to her office today. With all the other drama she already has going on. Now Katrina wants a tryout with the *Shock*. She had the nerve to ask her for help. She knows Katrina has violated her 1st cousin's man. That's where her loyalties lie. She tells Katrina she'll have to find her own way and leaves it at that. She's ready to get back into her regular routines and just get back to work. She isn't going to be distracted by Katrina. Ebony had told her as much.

"Her day will come, cousin. You do *you*," Ebony had said.

And T-baby is taking Ebony's advice. She's going back to doing something she enjoys. Which is helping her clients find tax relief. Anything other than sitting at home and being consumed with guilt and shame. She needs to feel busy. Sitting around grieving over the lose of a husband who had tried to take her with him, isn't doing anything positive for her recovery process.

Wes is happy to see her come back to work. He had made dinner for her and Lil Rich, nearly every night while she recovered at home. They had become even closer during her recovery. Lil Rich and Jada are already calling themselves sister and brother. T-baby is smitten with Wes. Just as he is with her. But she tells him, she needs the blessings of Rich's parents before she can start another relationship.

"I'm gonna talk to my mother-in-law about a *couple* of things. Today at lunch," she tells him.

Her and Wes are becoming more serious. They both feel like the family will think it's too soon after Rich's death for her to be in a relationship.

"I understand," he says, "I think it's great that you're gonna talk about it with his mother."

"I know most of the family was all for us getting together before he died," she says, "But I just wanna show mama Anna respect. By telling her, *personally*. You know. I'm also gonna talk to her about Rich's daughter Richaunda."

"Okay," Wes says, "You want Richie to know her, don't you?"

"Yes. I told him I knew about her and I promised him I would make sure they meet and be apart of each other's lives," she says, "I wish Richard had done it. But he wasn't in the right frame of mind."

"That's so noble of you, Trisha," he says, "You're an amazing woman. That's why I love the time I spend with you. You're so strong and just beautiful. Inside and out."

She smiles and thanks her new suitor for his compliments. They work all morning as he brings her back up to speed on all the business that transpired during her recovery.

She teases him, saying, "I can keep my name on the building *now*."

TIME TO FEEL-RELOADED-Time Will Reveal part 5

They laugh. It's lunchtime and T-baby heads off to meet Anna.
They meet up just outside of *Crew Spa and Health club*.
"Shall we eat?" Anna asks with a smile.
"We shall," T-baby replies.
They go into Crew's House of Soul Food, take a seat and order lunch.
"So Trisha," Anna says, "What do you need to talk about?"
"Well as we all know. Rich has a daughter."
"Richaunda. Yes," Anna says, "But I haven't really seen her."
"None of us have," T-baby says, "But have you tried too?"
"No."
"Why not? She's your granddaughter."
"She's an...., well, you know, Trisha. I don't know really. I guess I had a few reasons."
"Like?"
"How she came about," Anna says, "And how you would feel. Plus my own memories of an outside child. Honestly that last reason may be the first one. I was so disappointed with Rich Jr for doing that. The same thing that had hurt me so much about his father. He did to you."
"With Corey, right? Because you did know about him, correct?"
"Correct. I knew about him. But Richard denied him. Just like our son did with this little girl, in the beginning."
"Her name is Richaunda, mama Anna. Let's say her name."
"Richaunda. Okay you're right and I do wonder about her. It's easier with Corey because big Richard's parents was already passed on when he came and my parents was supporting my decision at the time."
"Which was to deny it and move on?" T-baby asks.
"Yes."
"I want that to change, mama Anna," T-baby says, "I don't wanna do that. I want my son to know his sister. I think if Rich had grown up with Corey. His life would have been fuller. He would've had someone who looked up to him. Richard had low self esteem. He always felt like no one had faith in him to do better than the next person," she says, "That, *I* think, is where a lot of his problems stemmed from."
Anna listens intensely as T-baby continues, "We talked about a lot of things during our fourteen years. It wasn't always bad. Richard loved me. Only because I loved him more than I loved *any* other person. *Ever*. He was the only one to have that and that made him attach to me and need me."
"Oh Trisha. I do believe you," Anna says, "And I wish you had come to me years ago. Because this might would've saved him."

49

"I agree. That's why I want Richaunda in Richie's life."

"I'm listening," Anna says.

"She's apart of Richard. Which means her and my baby have the same blood," T-baby says, "I want them to know each other."

"You *do*?" Anna asks, rather surprised.

"I really do," T-baby says, "I don't want another Rich and Corey situation. Farther down the line. You *know*?"

"I see," Anna says, "You're definitely more open than I was about him, Trisha. I think you may be right too. I really do."

"Well Rich isn't here to do it," T-baby says, "And I would just rather not hide that from my son. I wanna break that cycle, if I can. I would love your help in doing so."

After some discussion, Anna agrees with T-baby that they should arrange a meeting with Regina, for Ritchie and Richaunda to meet.

"I'm also still thinking of moving on with my life as well," T-baby says, "You know Wes and I are still seeing each other. And though it's not physical. I really do like him."

"I know that Trisha," Anna says, "And I understand that completely. You and my son was separated and filing for divorce. You don't have to feel bad for still wanting to move on."

"I just wanted your opinion, mama Anna," she says, "Because, well you know. Rich *just* died. That's still hard for me to even say or believe."

"Trisha you gave my son your best. The best years of his life," Anna says, "He didn't appreciate you for it and you all didn't make it. Even if he was still living. You two was over. You should go on with your life. With someone who loves and appreciates you. I understand. I *truly* do."

"That means everything to me," T-baby says, "Because I don't want you to be upset about it."

"Trisha you have my and Big Richard's blessings," Anna says, "We've already discussed this very thing, as a matter of fact."

"Y'all *did*?"

"We sure did. Even before Rich died," Anna says, "We love you like our own daughter because you are. You're his first and only girlfriend, that we knew. And it will always be that way. But we want you to be in a healthy relationship for our grandson's sake. So he don't fall into that pattern, like his father and grandfather. By not having a man in his life, *full* time."

"Wes is great with him," T-baby says with a smile, "He encourages him to tell him how good his daddy was in football and all of that."

50

"He sure is," Anna says, "I've noticed how he interacts with him at your games. And just around the mall too."

"He stepped in and did things with Richie that Richard wasn't able to do because of his addiction," T-baby says, "Richie is crazy about Wes. And Wes never tries to take his daddy's place either. He has an ex-wife who treated him similar to what I was going through with Richard. So we bonded as friends, from that. And now, it wants to grow."

"He's a wonderful young man. You should be open to seeing him because he seems to adore both of you. That's all I care about. Okay?"
T-baby is relieved. She thanks Anna for having lunch with her. And for the talk. Then Anna asks, "Do you know how to find this *Regina*?"

"She use to work at the juice bar. But after the crew found out she was Richard's mistress. She never returned," T-baby says, "But I know she was working at the Medical Complex, back then too. So I'll start there."

"Okay. I hadn't seen her since Rich's funeral. She was living in some shelter," Anna says.

"I'll find her and make sure my son and her daughter know each other as sister and brother," T-baby says, "This is something I have to do before I can move on with Wesley or anything else."

"You set up the meeting and I'll be there," Anna says, "If it's something you're okay with. Then Richard and I will support it and get to know our granddaughter as well."
T-baby says she'll let her know when the meeting is set. They finish their lunch, pay the check and walk back to their jobs.

****

Marvin Huntley has managed to get some footage of Farah with another man, over the past year. The nigger he taped her with, works at CrewLand mall but he isn't the same one he met at the club. He had followed them from the mall to this other guy's home, on 3 occasions this year. And on each occasion, Farah stayed until morning. That angered Marvin beyond words. He just hasn't been able to catch her alone. She always stayed on school nights. Or on the mornings when they left, she would go into Crew's House to get breakfast before work. Marvin would lose her then because he'd been banned from the property or near it. Officer Deloris Miles, who now works security at the mall, remembers him stalking Jackson Heights when she worked the gate. He's 1 month from opening his insurance and carpet store in Brook Park. But his focus isn't on the opening the store, as much as it is on getting his girl back. He wants her to share in his new venture. He doesn't know she already is and neither does she. The grand opening is 1 month away. He wants to win her back before then. He plans to approach her after her job and tell her about the business. Then convince her to become a partner. He has given himself a week to get this accomplished.

Mya Dean had moved back home from Baton Rouge, back when Greg Jr found out her son wasn't his. They haven't messed around or even spoken since the paternity test which proved he hadn't fathered her little boy. Since being back home, she has enrolled at Cleveland State. The winter following the birth of her son, she was in school at CSU and still up to her old ways. Only with a little more dangerous flair. She has met and become interested in Corey Grey. Corey turns out to be more bisexual, then straight out gay. He still dates women, from time to time. Mya knows about his sexuality and she's open to it. They began dating officially, this month. Because of her lack of education on the subject, her mother isn't crazy about having a gay man around her 2 year old grandson. Mya has always been rebellious and stubborn. So naturally her mother's concerns, she takes minimally. She dates Corey regardless. She's has history of irresponsibility. And that's partially because her mother isn't responsible either. When Mya's son was a newborn, Mya had left him unattended many times. Her mother fought her for custody last year and won. After being stripped of her rights to her son, Mya moved in with Corey and Tameka. They've taken an apartment at the U. Mrs. Dean has her son. Mya still gets supervised visitation.

Greg Jr had been home for Rich's funeral and to visit T-baby when she was in the hospital. He and Jesse don't come home from Southern University very much. They're expected to be drafted this March. Then they'll graduate in May. In the meantime, Greg Jr has been trying to win Erica back. Since he and Mya's split, he has sent many cards, letters and gifts to Erica at Oklahoma University. She wasn't interested then. Certainly not now. Erica got engaged to Eric McNair at Christmas. They're very much in love. Greg is disappointed with the engagement but he has no other choice but to accept it. With Rich's suicide and nearly fatally shooting T-baby, the bad memories of their abusive relationship resurfaced for Erica. Eric is nothing like Greg Jr had been. He treats her like a princess and he doesn't cheat. After signing his NFL contract, he had flown her to every game she could attend without missing her drill team performances.

And Eric keeps a new piece of jewelry in the mail for her. They're always going off to spend private weekends in the most exotic places. Greg Jr let go of it because Erica wasn't coming back to him. *Ever.*

T-baby manages to contact Regina at the medical complex. Regina isn't open to having the kids meet. Not initially. But after talking with T-baby, Anna and Richard Sr, she realizes their desire for the kids to grow up as family is from the heart. So she accepts the idea of them meeting each other. In Regina's own way, she loved Rich dearly. She agrees to let Richaunda and Lil Rich meet.

They all meet up at Granny's house and the meeting goes well. Lil Rich and Richaunda become fast friends. That makes T-baby happy. Just knowing she has already broken 1 part of the Richard Williams cycle. Lil Rich and Richaunda will grow up having a sister-brother relationship, instead of being strangers. Anna will become active in Richaunda's life as well. She enrolls her in preschool at Granny's house, where she'll do drop off and pick up duty with her now. Just as she had done with Lil Rich before he was school age. Further, her and big Richard keep the 2 of them at their house every other weekend. Ruthie is overjoyed to come home and have a nephew and a niece to spoil. With that done, T-baby is open to having her relationship with Wes. Everyone in the crew are supportive.

It takes Marvin 2 weeks but he finally does catch Farah in her classroom after school. He arrives on the MLK campus just before the end of all classes, bell rings. He walks up to her open door, walks in and straight up to her desk.

"What are you doing here?!" Farah asks in shock.
This is her 1st time seeing or even knowing that he's been in Cleveland.

"Wow. Hello to you too, Farah," he says.

"What are you doing here, Marvin?"

"I just came down to see how the new job was going," he says.
He acts as if he has come straight in from Pittsburgh. But the more he talks. The more she realizes he's probably been here a few other times, at least.

"How did you find me?" Farah asks.

"You told me you had a job here. Don't you remember?"
She remembers when her and Alana was doing the virtual tour of the home they now live in. And he'd walked in and surprised them.

"I do remember telling you I got a teaching job. But I don't recall telling you *where*. Or inviting you to visit me here," she snaps.

"You never invited me to visit you. *Period.* I was wondering why that was? After all, we were engaged when you took the job," he says.

"We're not now, Marvin. And I would like for you to *leave.*"

"I just wanted to see you and say hello. I figured the safest place would be here, at school," he says, "And I wanted to let you know about the new office we're opening here."

"You should have waited on an invite," she snaps, "And what new office?"

"It's in an area west of here. Just off interstate seventy one. The area is called Brook Park?"

"Oh *really*? Who's gonna maintain it?"

"I do believe I am."

"Marvin I didn't want you to look me up. I moved here to get away from you and your mentality of *other* people."

"I don't have a mentality of *others*. It's more like a *reality*."

"You're reality is racism to me. Face it Marvin. How did you come to find this, ..area? Brook Park?"

"It was suggested to me by a nice looking black woman. She runs a Real Estate and Investment office. Not to far from the University."

"Oh it's a black woman now? Not a nigger bitch?"

"Farah we all have to grow at some point," he tries.

"You haven't. Did this black woman have a name?"

"I don't recall. It was set up through our agencies. I never met her. I just got a wireless business card and email," he lies.
She doesn't believe him.

"What's the name on the card and email?"

"I don't remember. *Why?* Are you interested in an investment? I was gonna ask you about becoming a partner."

"Hell *no*! Who set this up? I believe you do know and you're just not telling me."
She's a bit more impatient now and growing frustrated. She's feeling like she has invested in a business with the very guy she was trying to get rid of and away from. All while she had focused on trying to get with a new guy who hasn't even given her *his* attention. She feels like *that's* only a temporary problem though.

"Honestly I don't have the info with me. But I can email it to you, if you'd like," he says. Then acting as if it had been a mere oversight on her part. He says, "But you forgot to give me your contact information for here. I'm sure that was a mere oversight, right?"

TIME TO FEEL-RELOADED-Time Will Reveal part 5

"No I didn't forget. I don't want to be contacted by you. Nor do I wanna be any partner of yours. Please leave and leave *now*."
She has heard all she needs to hear. She needs to call Chill. She wants Marvin out of her sight immediately. She gets up and pushes the intercom button. The office comes over the P.A. system.

"Yes, miss Benson?"

"Can you please send security to my classroom. Please? My ex fiancée has shown up. I don't feel safe with him here!"
She tries to sound *especially* desperate. Marvin begins to move toward the door quickly. Within seconds, he's outside of the room. Then the hallway and heads to his car. He had thought time would've eased over whatever had brought her the tension she had about him. But he can see that it hasn't. He hops in his Porsche and leaves quickly. Farah gives security a full report and description of him and his car. They suggest she file a restraining order. She says she will. But right now she wants them to leave so she can call Chill. No sooner than the officers are out of her classroom and out of earshot, she dials Chill's office.

"The Chill Spot. May I help you?" Courtney Freeman says as she answers the main line.

"Mr. Kenneth Payne Senior, please," Farah says while breathing heavily.

"May I ask who's calling?"

"It's top investor, Farah Benson. And I have a problem with my last investment. Put him on the phone. *Now!*"

"I'm sorry ma'am," Courtney says, "Jackson's Real Estate and Investments handles all of those matters for the family. I'll transfer you-"

"Put Chill on the goddamn phone! He's the one who got me into this shit! And he's the one who will need to fix it!" she shouts.

"Hold on, ma'am."
Courtney calls Wayne over to the reception booth. They giggle as she tells him Farah is on hold and how angry she is about her investment. They all know the background and why she's upset.

"Call Chill and see what he says," Wayne suggests.
She does and Chill tells her to transfer the call to Ebony. She does that.

Farah is upset that she didn't get to talk to Chill. She orders Ebony to withdraw her funds and cancel her contract. She says Marvin had been abusive when they were together and was her reason for leaving Pittsburgh. Ebony tells her she'll freeze her shares and do a reversal of fortune, so she can get her capital back from the company's first profits.

55

Or she can see if the primary has a desire to buy her out. Farah doesn't like either option. Because then Marvin will find out it was her. She decides that since she has partner sized stock in the business. She also has the power to hold up the opening until she's either reimbursed or bought out. This will cause Marvin to lose money or be forced to sell his shares. Ebony sets the plan in motion. The opening of *Huntley Insurance and Textiles* isn't going to happen 12 days from now. Ebony has to inform Marvin immediately that his chief investor has put in a stop order. Then offer him the opportunity to buy her out or continue to spend money down a hole. She finds it hilarious that Farah thinks she gives a fuck about her being upset. Her entire crew loathes this pushy bitch. She should've taken their advice and got the hell out of their lives. But instead, she became more of an infestation. Setting her up with Marvin's stock has only sent her further into their business. Because now she can play cat and mouse with Marvin and refuse his offers. It won't cost the crew anything. And if they play for too long, Ebony will dump the stock. She isn't going to baby sit an option that won't pay her either. She calls Marvin Huntley.

As she figured, Marvin is pissed about the delay. She still can't give either of them contact on the other because both invested anonymously. The fun is over now. So before she'll allow them to waste her valuable time. Ebony will set up an appointment with them together and relieve herself of their drama. Marvin has purchased 1 of their condo's as his Cleveland address. She fax the notice to him and sends it to his blackberry. She knows he'll come calling, sooner than later and definitely heated. She laughs to herself.

T-baby and Wes announce they're an *official* couple. The news takes Ebony's mind off of the undesirables of the stalled Brook Park deal. The crew celebrate the new relationship on the same night they give T-baby her going away party. She's going to the *Detroit Shock* camp on Monday, where she has leased a condo. Terrell's wife Chrissy had a luxury condo there and all it needed was a resident. They did the deal. Before she leaves for camp, T-baby gets 2 tattoos to cover the scars from where she was shot. She puts Richie Rich October 1, 2002, over the scars.

"He'll be with me forever," she says and Wes likes the idea.

"He was your first love, honey. Now he's gone," he says, "I think it's a great way to pay him respect."

By March, Marvin is livid. He has lost a great deal on the failed opening. He shows up at Ebony's office without an appointment. Ebony has Farah in her office giving her an update on her potential returns, when he shows up. Claudia alerts Ebony of Marvin's arrival. Ebony can hear him from her office and so can Farah. She tells Farah that the primary is in the lobby and asks if she'd like to have a face to face.

"Fuck no! I don't!" Farah yells.

Ebony stays calm because she knows her husband will be there in minutes, to secure her office. She knows he's already alerted security too.

Ajay was already on the way after hearing that Farah had shown up, being unreasonable. Farah, who hadn't been sure of whom the primary was until now, storms to the lobby and comes face to face with Marvin. Ajay comes into the lobby just as the argument ensues. There is no way Ajay is going to let the argument get off the ground.

"Get the fuck out of my wife's office with this country bullshit," Ajay says calmly. He continues, "Before you both get arrested. Or worse. And don't either one of you muthafuckers *ever* come back around my wife with any type of stupid shit. Or you will have to deal with me. *Understood*? Now get the fuck out."

Before Marvin can leave, Bronson and Joiner enter and apprehend him for trespassing. Plus Farah had already signed a restraining order from when he came to MLK. Marvin is taken to the county jail.

He posted bail within minutes. People with money don't have to wait for the hands of justice to unfold. They have people.

CHAPTER 50

BACK ON THAT STREET SHIT

In March a newcomer to the national scene named *50 Cent* signs his *Gunit* label to a major deal with *Shady/Aftermath records*. Shady is run by *Eminem*. *Eminem*, 1 of the best lyrical MC's in the game who just happens to be white, was discovered by *Dr Dre* originally from *N.W.A*. The crew's favorite group during the days when they just ran heavy in the streets of Cleveland. These days, they just run Cleveland. *Aftermath* is run by Dr Dre, who has grown into the label of best producer in the business by many. The crew are apart of that many. 50 Cent grabs everyone's attention with his hit on the soundtrack to the movie *8 Mile* titled *Wanksta*. His whole persona is about beef, sprinkled with a few tracks to females. Much like the other rappers of today, who glorify street crimes and the usual. The crew like some of his hits. His label known is Gunit which includes *Lloyd Banks, Tony Yayo* and *Young Buck*. And it will take the world hostage by years end. Because of 50 cent, 2003 is billed as the year of the beef. Many labeled 50 Cent, a snitch right out of the box. The crew don't buy that nor do they bother to research him because he isn't their main focus. Not from that collective. They remember *Young Buck* from the *Cash Money Millionaires* and *UTP, s*o he quickly becomes their favorite *Gunit* member.

"He's the rawest," Rob says.

"The realest too. Watch what I tell you," Chill says, "Dude is sincere and humble. That counts for everything with a true and crew."

"I can't believe how much weight fifty cent lost," Jan adds.

"I guess that's why he raps to women now," Renee says and laughs.

"But wait, that's what he's going at *Ja Rule* for," Ced offers, "For singing songs and his *R n B* collaborations. It's the same deal, just slower and less raspy. Kind of like *Mase*."

"His money will surely bring the insecure women out for him," Bre says.

"The prostitutes, you mean?" Rob ask as he smiles.

"Six of one," Jb says and laughs. He adds, "But he has to get rich to get them. That's what he's saying. He'll get the gold diggers, just by wearing that spinning chain."

"I think he's insecure too, to a certain extent," Lynn says, "He already knows and admits it."

"Ebony don't trust him," Chill say as he laughs.

"No she don't," Renee adds, "She said he's insecure and has to make the world see him as a ruler. She said he's gonna topple over like the Empire state building in a King Kong movie too. In other words, he'll fall hard or sell out and everyone will see it coming." They all laugh.

"But then, y'all know Ebony will never support a Cain and Abel type," Jb says, "She's all about taking care of her people. Not beefing with them."

"The way we were raised," Lynn adds, "So are we."

"To Ebony," they all say as they toast.

They're enjoying a family dinner at their Southern Exposure Restaurant in Atlanta. Chill and Renee are down on a visit.

"You know some contacts from NYC seem to think that the five oh in fifty cent's name, stands for five oh as in *po-po*," Chill adds.

"You heard that too?" Ced asks, "I'm from the same Borough, man. That's been out there for years. But his name really comes from a real drug kingpin from the N-Y streets."

"Who cares?" Renee says as they all laugh. She continues, "Look, Ron and Carolyn called us last night. They have a few homeboys who got some serious ass time this week. Big Tony's gang."

"Double life, Capital murder and Death penalty type of time," Chill adds.

"Damn!" Jb offers.

"It was some real heinous type of shit, they was doing too," Chill says, "But for the homie Ron, it's opportunity. He's coming to Cleveland to visit. We'll talk more on it then."

"I know where this is going," Jb says with a smile.

"Somewhere solid as a muthafucka, sounds like," Rob adds, "These the dudes with the interstate charges? Big Tony and them?"

"The same ones," Chill says, "Texas to Cali. Michigan to Florida and then some. They're contract killers. They're the same ones who found Raymond's ass, so they're family too."

"Yes and we're already partners with their crew," Renee says, "Money exchanges have *been* going on, you know? These dudes are the truth and Big Tony brought this new info to Ron."

"We'll get the actual when Ron and Carolyn come up," Chill says, "But we'll be back on that street shit, to a certain extent."

Renee says, "Or taking care of old street shit, is more like it."

Chill raises his glass, "To family and business and again, to Ebony," he says with a smile, "We have legal money."

TIME TO FEEL-RELOADED-Time Will Reveal part 5

"And we've got people too," Renee adds.
The others repeat it, toast and add a smile as well. They understand fully which cases they can soon wrap up. And for mere financial support to the offspring of the men who may never again see the light of day. The more things change for the crew. The more things stay the same. Sometimes familiar is lucrative. And in other times, just plain convenient.
Chill and Renee return home on the 1st day of April.

****

The year of the beef for this 3 month old New Year, is a fitting title in the crew's opinion. Not only is the 50 Cent and Ja Rule beef notable. But even some magazines get on the beef wagon for the year 2003. *The Source Magazine* with *Benzino* and *Mays* have taken the position that *Eminem* is a phony and a racist. It's been said that they stopped featuring him favorably in their issues. So since The Source hates him, they refuse to print favorable articles on Dr Dre, 50 Cent and his Gunit team too. Largely because of their associations with Eminem. Or that's the meal that they put out there for the masses to gobble up. In a lot of the crew's opinions, the Source had never given significant and ample coverage when it came to artist from the West Coast. Nor labels from the West, Mid West and the South either.

"Hey, I remember we use to wonder why they never really put *Niggaz wit Attitudes* in their shit," Chill says, "They covered *Cube* when he went solo. Mainly because he was fuckin with *Public Enemy*."
He had voiced that opinion to the crew, back when Bre and Ced where at McClellan AFB. Ebony remembers when she stopped her subscription to the Source magazine.

"It was right before *Tupac* got killed," she says, "They were taking sides, instead of trying to defuse the East Coast, West Coast beef. I wasn't about to be apart of that. *No Way*. I've been mad at them and *Vibe Magazine* since then."

"Yep. Baby Girl stopped subscribing to the source before those Bone Thugs *individual* covers came out," Ajay adds with a chuckle.

"And I had to go out to every store until I found all four of them too," Ebony adds with a giggle, "Then they didn't even give *FleshNBone* one. I was even madder about that. The reason I bought the fifty cent one is because of *Dr Dre* and *Young Buck*."

"That's the reason we bought the CD from fifty cent," Tank adds, "Because of *Blood Hound*."

60

TIME TO FEEL-RELOADED-Time Will Reveal part 5

"I just don't like how fifty always sound like he's got a mouth full of spit," Nina says and laughs.

"Uh uh, the iron influenced body," Tonya says.

"We know you like your man *lean*," Jr adds and chuckles.

"I feel like lifting weights takes away from the southern exposure," T-baby says as she laughs.

"It's not the weights," Rebbie offers, "That's the steroids. Because my baby didn't lose anything. Isn't that right, Brian?"

"That's *damn* right," June agrees, "Them steroids will draw your shit up like a cocktail weenie."

They burst into side splitting laughter.

"Rich didn't have that problem either," T-baby offers, "I have to admit. He was packing and proper. Even if he didn't think, so in the beginning." They laugh again, as she continues, "But I do remember Ebony had all of us out at the bookstores and supermarkets trying to find all of those Bone covers."

"Then she made all of us stop buying most of those mags and rags," Rebbie says as she giggles.

The whole crew agree on that being the reason for not reading Vibe anymore. They all stopped reading it by the end of 1998 and invested in a new magazine known as *The XXL*. They all subscribed. The XXL is set to take over as top Hip Hop magazine and since taking such a negative stance against some of the hottest artist, labels and regions of 2003. The Source lost popularity, in the crew's opinion, for printing their personal opinions in issues. Instead of covering the hottest artists and labels in Hip Hop.

"How can you say you're Hip Hop and you don't give a legend in the game, like doctor Dre props?" Chill asks, "If they're not down with Dre. Then we're not down with them. Point blank!"

The crew agree and the issue is closed.

Subsequently, XXL and The Source do beef with each other about who is the top Hip Hop magazine. XXL features Shady, Aftermath, Gunit and *Interscope* artist in nearly every issue for the coming year.

The crew have also taken issue with another group that split in 1999. After dropping their 2nd album, *Destiny's Child* breaks up. Sort of. To say they were rearranged, would be a more accurate description. The foursome hadn't quite warmed up to them but they were getting there. They had each purchased *The Writings on the Wall* CD, just before the unraveling. The foursome, much like most of the world, blames *Beyounce* and her father Matthew Knowles for the "dismembering" of the group.

61

TIME TO FEEL-RELOADED-Time Will Reveal part 5

They feel like it was all about her solo career from the beginning. And with her father managing all 4 members individually plus the group. It was bound to turn out in the lead singers favor. They were right. This year, *Beyounce* drops her solo CD *Dangerously In Love* and takes over the female R&B scene. This only helps to fuel the already burning suspicions.

"I knew she was gonna go solo," T-baby says, "I just think they should have kept the original group in tact."

"I know that's right," Rebbie agrees, "They grew up together, like we did."

"How can you just drop your sisters like that?" Ebony asks.

"That would be like us breaking up," Nina adds solemnly, "But if cash rules everything around you. Then you're gonna go for the money."

"Money over your family?" Ebony asks, "They're not like us, Ree Ree. We wouldn't do that to each other. Not for fame, money or *anything*."

"So true," Rebbie agrees, "I guess there goes that prostitution word again."

"Or sellout," Nina adds, "There's a contraction that fits."
The foursome agree that is the primary reason that neither of them are buying *Beyounce, Kelly* nor *Michelle*, the remaining new members to the group. They won't purchase either of the 3 remaining members efforts, if and when they are released.

"I just can't support something that I feel is wrong," Ebony adds, "But Beyounce is very talented. She'll do great."

"Yes she is and will," Rebbie says, "But all of them are."

"Yes and the other members just wanted the freedom from their contracts. Plus *their* time to shine too," Nina says, "But that wasn't Matthew's vision."

"He's pushing his oldest daughter," Rebbie says, "That's going to come back on them. Because *Solange* is gonna be in that looming shadow. She won't ever be large. And watch, she'll be the tantrum throwing sister of the two."

"The other girl who was added was named Farah," Ebony says, "And she's already gone. I just hope the original two get to shine."

"They will," T-baby says, "If *Latavia* and *Letoya* ever drop CD's. I'm buying them."

"We all will," They all say and agree on that point.

****

TIME TO FEEL-RELOADED-Time Will Reveal part 5

There has been rumors about a movie detailing *Tupac's* life. The crew regret that neither of them had ever gotten a chance to meet him or that he didn't get the opportunity to perform at their clubs. They have spent the years since his death, grabbing up every piece of information, knowledge and release from or about him. They're collecting his memento's for their children.

"Tupac was the closest thing to a revolutionary soldier for our generation," Ebony says, "Much like *Malcolm X* was for our parents crew. And *Mandela* and *MLK* was for big mama's crew."

"MLK was it for the world," big John says, "Still I feel like *Suge Knight* was involved in Tupac's death. He may not have orchestrate it but-"

"-But he played a part in it," Al adds, "I believe that too."

"We all do and I am so ready for that movie," Ebony says, "It's coming in November."

"It's been almost seven years since he died. But it doesn't seem like it," Nina says, "This must be the Machiavelli theory of the seven year thing. This movie."

"I suppose so," Ebony says, "But I'd settle for the real him, any day. I know we'll go and see the movie though. That's something to look forward to in November, along with the holidays."

"You and Ajay are hosting Thanksgiving again this year, by the way," Al says suddenly.

"Oh yea. We heard that last night," John reveals with a smile, "Did you?"

"No not until now," Ebony says with a smile, "I guess that's why mama was blowing up Anthony's cell phone."

"He was blowing up hers *first*," her father says with a chuckle, "And don't you break up the party this year, baby girl."

John and Al laugh loud. Then Al says, "Not unless y'all have to make some more of those grandbabies. The kind that just can't wait."

Al, John and Nina laugh and Nina says, "Uh oh Ebony. This sounds like a caper. What else have y'all heard?"

Their fathers laugh and go on with their work.

"A set up is more like it," Ebony says, "Anthony's biological clock is ticking, so loud. That he thinks I should be able to hear mine at the same time." They all laugh.

Ebony and Nina are seated at Stoney's having hot wings and conversation with their fathers, on this chilly Saturday afternoon. Nina had finished with her clients early and took a break before she has to be at *The Spot II*. Her and Ebony are enjoying laughs and good conversation with their fathers. When all of a sudden, they hear chaos outside. They look in the direction of the disturbance. Over at *Crew Cuts and Styles,* they see the source of the noise.

"Oh my God! When did she get out?" Nina yells as she runs out of Stoney's and toward her salon with Ebony close behind.

John and Al trail them. Ellen has been released from jail and she still has a score to settle with Matt. His daughter Kelly has intervened again today and this time, a fight breaks out. Kelly and Ellen had tied up inside of the salon and now, it has spilled out into the parking lot. Nina and Ebony reach the fighting females before security gets there. Ebony and Nina try to break it up with help from Matt, Tonya, Justine and the other 2 barbers from the shop. Coincidently, Alana, Darlene and Farah have their appointments today and they're outside as well. Suddenly, Farah gets involved and she's on Kelly's side. She starts swinging on Ellen. Ellen's 2 friends Rudy and Dorothy jump into the fray. They grab Farah and begin handling her. Alana and Darlene join in. The fight is 4 on 3 advantage Kelly. Nina and the crew pull and yank bodies until they get the situation near control. Security arrives and takes over. By now, Alana seems to have lost her mind. She starts yelling and screaming with the focus of her outrage aimed at Nina.

"I think y'all set my girl up!" Alana yells as she looks at Nina.

"What the fuck did you say?" Nina asks cursing Alana before she thinks about it.

"Y'all not right and I know y'all not," Alana continues, "Why would y'all schedule them to come up here *together*?"

Tonya is about to correct Alana, when Nina stops her. She wants her to continue to advance toward her, so she can knock the ever loving shit out of her. Tonya eases back and tells security to watch and document. Because if Alana poses a threat. Then they're going to whoop her ass. And they don't want her to get a lawsuit out of it. Just as they figure, Alana keeps advancing and keeps talking shit. Ellen is slinging similar accusations at the crew, at the same time.

"Nah ho! They're helping that white bitch get closer to Matt!" Ellen screams, "Don't try to change that shit up! They're on *her* side!"

"Ellen, you're wrong," Tonya says, "I've told you that before. Both of y'all are wrong. Ellen doesn't have an appointment. She's banned from the property until after her trial. I'm gonna say this and make sure all of y'all listen. Don't ever bring this mess back to our businesses again."

Then she insist to Matt that he get his personal life under control. Or he'll

64

have to leave their employment. Ebony cosigns her immediately.

"We're not gonna have this drama going on here," Ebony says, "We're doing business and this isn't a good look."

Meanwhile the husbands out at Jackson Heights have been alerted of the disturbance by security. They're arriving 2 by 2. Each of them find their wife and get the details. Al and John have managed to create enough space between Nina and Alana. Plus Ebony and Darlene. They want to prevent their daughters from pouncing. Still, Tank and Ajay say their peace. Tank is heated. Ajay is calm.

"Bitch don't say another word to my wife," Tank oozes at Alana, "She might think it's okay for you to work for us. But I don't. Besides, she's above you and this petty shit you're trying out here anyway. Fuck up again and you're out of here. I don't care *who* hired you."

Nina likes that a lot. The way he let Alana believe that she was the 1 responsible for her working for the crew. Ebony has goose bumps from the statement, as she stands with her chest stuck out and chin raised. Ajay puts his arm around her and merely makes eye contact with Darlene. *No words.* After the look he gives her, nothing close to words is even needed. She had thoughts about advancing toward Ebony when Alana was putting on her show. But she never actually got close enough for contact. She just made comments that could've been taken out of context. She knows Ajay well enough to know that's more then enough to get her contract cancelled. If this had happened 14 years ago. She would already be seeking a new zip code. Or possibly on her way to be buried in one. But today, neither of the crew see any physical action.

All of this happens while former trespasser Marvin is near the scene. He stays far enough off of CrewLand property too witness the mayhem. Rather he knows it or not. He isn't completely out of everyone's site. He has his binoculars to spy through. The rest of the gear he had purchased from Que Psi Phi Studio's is hooked up and rolling too. He recorded Ellen threatening to kill Matt and Kelly. That was music to his ears because he has some of the same ambitions. He hadn't thought about taking out the daughter. But now, she can be collateral. He can make it look like a domestic situation. A lovers quarrel. Something that spilled over from today's events. He knows plus it's already documented that Ellen had shot at Matt, once before. So if he were to come up dead. Ellen would be the *prime suspect*. There are plenty of witnesses out here today. They can testify to hearing her threaten Matt. Security holds all parties involved until Cleveland Police show up and arrest them. Joiner suggests to Tonya that the crew sign charges as well. In the event something does spur from today's actions.

"The report can go a long way towards ruining any lawsuit that young lady may try to use as grounds later," Joiner says with a smile. "We've got plenty of real good documentation already."

Tonya takes his advice and they file charges. Most of the fighters receive only fines. But Ellen's being held. She'll have to bond out. Because of her priors, her bond is set at $75,000. Matt feels comfortable with that amount.

"She'll have to sit awhile, just like before," Matt says. "Her hood rat friends don't have that kind of money," he adds and laughs.

"She don't have no people?" Chill ask as he laughs too.

He's about to go open up *The Chill Spot* when he looks way over Matt's shoulder and sees Marvin across the way. He makes Ajay and the guys aware of him too.

"I don't trust that muthafucka, man," Ajay says, "He's up to something."

"Him and his billionaire boys club looks and polo shirts," Tank says with a smile.

"Those kind always are," June adds, "They use their money to buy the law."

"I'm sure he's up to something," Wes adds.

They all go help Chill and Tank get the clubs open and running. Then they check on Allen Saul's complex. Steven, Ally and Jamal have it open and flowing smooth already. They've heard about the commotion.

Alana and company do manage to get back and get their hair done. There's no more mention of the altercation in the shop. Tonya makes sure of that. Matt doesn't even say anything to Farah today.

Meanwhile, Rudy and Dorothy get a call from central lock up. It's Ellen Barnes and she needs a ride home. She made bail and has no idea how. Her bond had been paid by cashiers check through an anonymous source. She's free to go. She doesn't ask anymore questions. She gets her court date from the bondsman and leaves with her girls. They're going home to strategize. Their fighting is done for today. But their beef with those 4 females is far from over. They fought 3 against 4 today. But they have somehow picked up a mysterious sidekick who has bailed Ellen out and who they count as number 4. Her friends suggest it may have been 1 of the pro athletes who was out there on the scene. They tell her that they seem to like the girls they were fighting, a lot less than they like her.

"Maybe whoever it was, will contact me," Ellen says, "And as long

66

as it ain't for his money back. Then that's fine, cause I'm still broke."
They laugh and head home.

All parties stay in their proverbial corners, for awhile. Marvin uses this quiet time to seek some help in disposing of the parties who are a problem for him. At the same time, he keeps Ellen engaged in a game of cat and mouse while she tries to figure out who bailed her out. So far, every mission he has sent her on, supposedly leading to this mysterious 4th person. She's shown up for, only to find some other monetary token there. She's loving the game because she's winning and getting loot to boot. Marvin plays on the stereotypes that he believes to be true about black women. They're working on Ellen.

****

In Akron, there is a high school basketball player named *Lebron James*. He has received a lot of attention in the past 2 years. He has surpassed Ajay's high school build up, by a mile. This kid is marketed as being ready for the *NBA*, after high school.

"He's ready right *now*," Chill says, "They're coming at him, the way they were coming at you, cuz and at Kenny too, for the *NFL*."

"The *Cav's* are gonna get him, if he goes into the draft," Ajay says.

"Shit, that's gonna be a lift for us," June says and they all agree. Lebron James is the truth. He's getting just as much or more press, then the NCAA players who are going into the draft in June.

Greg Jr and Jesse get drafted by the NFL. Greg goes to the *Bengals*. Jesse goes to the *Lions*. Both of them want to play with the Browns eventually. Jb tells them he'll make it happen, as soon as the opportunity comes.

While home for spring break, Greg Jr meets Matt's daughter Kelly. He likes her and she likes him. He asks her out and she accepts.

But the most notable event in March, unfortunately turns out to be the so-called war in *Iraq*. Bush had been threatening to go to war against Saddam Hussein since his presidency began. This month he declares *Operation Iraqi Freedom* and troops are deployed to the region. The crew are not in support of this conflict. But nevertheless it happens and Bre's platoon is called up. Bre will leave for Iraq in April. What's worse is Wes is on standby. Even worse then that, Lynn has been placed on standby too.

"We have to get Bush's ass out of the white house," Jo says, "Our

babies are going to die over there, in butt fuck Egypt and for what?"
"Oil," Al says.
They're both still disgusted with this administration as are all of their crew.

****

Brina James is only a sophomore at MLK but the girl can play some basketball. She's already got the attention of not only the NCAA but the WNBA too. As a 10th grader, she's already ranked in the State, just like her 1st cousin Ebony was. She still gives Ebony credit for teaching her the game and sparking her interest in it. She comes out to their home to play basketball with Lannie, weekly.
"I'm just giving back to my little cousin," Brina says to Ebony, "Because you did that for me."
Her and Ebony play basketball together a lot and they teach soon-to-be 4 year old Lannie, all of the fundamentals she'll need to surpass them both.

****

In April, Katrina Dobbs tries out for the Shock again and this year she makes the team. T-baby isn't happy about it and she lets her know that, on every chance she gets.
"I will never forgive you for what you did to my family," she tells her, "We'll never be close. So don't even try it. Outside of this team's business. Don't even speak to me, bitch. You better understand me when I say that too. You still got a beat down coming, if my crew wants it."
Katrina says she understands and they leave it at that. Still tensions are high with them. Tension that will eventually boil over and explode. But that will all come much, much later.

****

Marvin finally has the grand opening for his new store. His father bought out Farah and found a new investor. He called Marvin incompetent for not handling the deal better than he had.
"Never mix emotions with business, son," he'd said before putting a home office liaison in charge of watching Marvin and the new business.
Marvin sulks as he has done many times. But he's a slave to his family's money, so he takes it in stride. He takes the unit he'd gotten at

TIME TO FEEL-RELOADED-Time Will Reveal part 5

CrewLand Condominiums fulltime. In his years of stalking Farah, he has become very familiar with the city of Cleveland. He had also become more familiar with a few inner city thug types too.

Marvin has been shopping around for a hit. Someone who will kill Matt and Chill. He was referred to a guy with the street name of Pac Man. Government name; Oscar Wells. Pac Man is from west Cleveland. He's the guy to hire if you want to snuff somebody out. Marvin sets up a meeting with some of Pac Man's people. They meet at a little diner in *Brook Park* known as *The Landmark*. The crew already have history there from their beef with the Johnson family. They also have allies there too. Marvin still has no idea of how connected the crew are. Much like big Jake Johnson had done in the past, Marvin feels as if he has the element of surprise. He shows up and waits for 10 minutes without anyone showing up.

Finally 2 guys walk in, see him and introduce themselves. 1 of the guy's name is Woody. The other is Joe. Marvin is about to learn a very valuable lesson. In his own mind, his parents wealth has made him invincible. For him to underestimate the power of the crew is idiocy. But he's a 4th generation rich kid, who was raised completely the opposite of *anyone* in the crew. Often times, those who come from old money don't have the benefit of knowing *real* loyalty. Only the type of loyalty their money pays for. Those who are loyal to the dollar, more so than to them. But in the case of Chill and his crew. *Loyalty has no price.* Long before they had money, they had loyalty, trust and respect. From and for each other and many others, outside of their family. They had strategically placed their resources and good will, throughout the years. That's strictly because of a lesson Chill and his crew learned from their parents and grandparents as they grew up. *Money may come and go. But true friends are eternal. Nurture those friendships and keep them viable. Take care of your family and friends.*

Take the situation with Andre and Joe from the Westside. Over 13 years ago, they committed a lewd act against 2 girls who had come up with Ebony from Houston. Back when big mama and poppa still lived in the house, they have since sold to Ron. The crew nurtured the relationship with Ron and Carolyn. When big mama and poppa offered them the Houston home. Ron, knowing how special the home is to the crew, knew they viewed him as family. The bond became cement. Andre and Joe have been in and out of jail. The crew took care of them and their families legal matters. When Ajay got shot in 1994 and was falsely charged. He spent a few hours in a holding cell with Joe. Joe had given him the skinny on Tim and his posse.

69

TIME TO FEEL-RELOADED-Time Will Reveal part 5

That information put the crew onto them *correctly*. And eventually, the crew took them down. When Andre and Joe committed rape against Sonya and Shuntay, even though the crew didn't agree with what they had done. They never rolled on them. That left Andre and Joe feeling as if they owed the crew. They became and still remain loyal, to *this* day. That's when their loyalty to the crew really started and because the crew had looked the other way then. They're about to get a payment. *Tenfold*.

Andre was in prison when Ajay got shot. While in there, he met and befriended Pac Man. Pac Man was known as a severe killing machine and became Andre's cellmate and friend. Andre shared his commissary and all contacts from home with Pac Man. Something Pac Man took to heart. His reputation for knowing how to kill a person 100 ways with his bare hands, is well known. Thus he had no real troubles in jail. Maybe a few enemies but for every enemy he had. There was 25 friends or those who just wanted to be loyal to him for their own protection. He had no family, outside of prison. However through Andre, Pac Man found out him and the crew had a murderer in *common*. A murderer by the name of Danny Washington. Danny was 1 of the guys who had helped kill Stoney in 1990 while working for big Jake Johnson. Danny Washington had also killed Pac Man's mother, 2 years prior. Pac Man was only 9 years old, at the time. Danny had looked young Pac Man in the eyes and promised him, he would come back for him if he ever snitched. Pac Man didn't tell because he was afraid of what Danny would do to him. With no mother or any relatives to claim him. Pac Man was placed in foster care. That's where the real horror began. He had learned to kill as a means of stopping abuser after abuser from ravaging him. Killing became a way of life for him. By age 15, he was a pro. He dreamed of growing up and killing Danny Washington, the man who had raped and killed his mother. But Danny had been killed in 1991 when Pac man was 11. He heard Danny's killing had been professional. That's what made him strive to be a professional killer. The man's life who had taken his only security was taken by a professional killer. He never knew who did it until years later, while he was incarcerated and sharing a cell with Andre. In confidence Pac Man had shared his plight with Andre, for he had no family. Andre's family was huge. Pac Man needed real family and Andre needed real protection. Pac Man told Andre if he ever found out who had saved him from Danny. He would owe them his life. Andre gave him that revelation when he told him the story about Chill and the crew and the reason they had taken Danny Washington's life on that rainy Tuesday night. They had killed Danny because Danny and his boys had

70

TIME TO FEEL-RELOADED-Time Will Reveal part 5

taken the life of their brother Stoney. Only because they could never get close enough to kill Ajay or Chill. Andre also promised to put Pac Man in touch with the crew as soon as they touched down. From that day, Pac Man protected Andre from any harm. They were both released 2 weeks ago. Andre hooked back up with his lifetime friend Joe, to see about scheduling a meeting with Chill and the crew. They wanted to introduce Pac Man. This just happened to be during the same time this Marvin's hit request came through to Joe. It's also when that certain recipe in loyalty for Marvin Huntley started to simmer. Andre is like a manager or an agent for Pac Man, who has spent so much time in the system that he has no contacts on the outside. He only has a talent for killing. That's all he knows. The crew have become professional business people now. They aren't into the street game, not like prior to Andre's prison time. But Andre knows old habits diehard and real loyalty, never does. So when Andre heard about Marvin's contract. He knew exactly what he was going to do. Get paid. Get at Chill. And get this foul mouth white boy taken out of the game, in the process. Being the person who'd heard someone saying they wanted to have Chill killed. Pushed Andre's stock through the roof with the crew. The fact that he had the contract in his hands was money in the bank. Not from Chill and the crew. But from Marvin. For Andre managed a killer who was loyal to Chill by default. But he held the contract which had been shopped by a filthy rich racist white man, who was angry only because he had lost his pussy to a brother or 2. Neither of which really wanted his pussy for the long haul. The racist part was enough to insure that Andre wouldn't do shit in Marvin's favor. Knowing it was against Chill, made Andre and Joe happy they had stayed glued to the streets. They wouldn't have wanted to miss this chance to pay the crew back. Not for the world and everything in it.

Andre sent Joe and Woody, a young trainee, to meet Marvin and set up the terms of how the money will be transferred. In this meeting in The Landmark café, Joe and Woody become familiar with exactly what Marvin wants done and how much he's willing to pay. For Matt, the cost is $40k. But for Chill it's high six figures to the tune of a half a million dollars. Because Chill has people, who have people. And in *this* case. Even the people who are hired to kill him are his people. So to go after him isn't going to be cheap. Marvin agrees to pay whatever to get rid of the 2 niggers whom *he feels* are screwing his debutante. He's none the wiser to the fact that he has opened up a can of worms that will bait him good. Marvin's only concern is that they aren't cops. Joe is appalled at being questioned

71

about being a police officer. He curses Marvin instantly, for the accusation.

"I hate muthafuckin cops, fool," Joe says, "Don't you *ever* come at me wit that shit. Do you see these tats, right here? I've done more time in jail then I've done *out* here. You ever heard of a cop with prison tattoo's, fool? Or one with blunts in his pocket and on his breath?"

Marvin lets that go and goes on with setting up the hits. He's so focused on getting rid of Matt and Chill. That he has already started the preparations to get the down payment transferred over.

"I want that Matt guy killed first and *quick*," Marvin says.

"Hold on," Joe says, "You wanna say *how* they get done? That'll cost you extra. And our guy is gonna do them on the same day to avoid heat. Think about it. If he kills a guy from *CrewLand* mall. Don't you think they're gonna beef up security?"

"Okay. I suppose you're right," Marvin says.

"I *am* right," Joe says impatiently, "You haven't been on this side of the law before, have you?"

Marvin tells him no and he won't be after this hit.

"That's a bet," Joe says, "Then you should just let me handle *how* and *when*. But to go at Chill. You'd best be serious about it and be ready to pay. We need half of both contracts, up front before we move *anything*," Joe adds while reeling him in.

"How do I know it's really gonna happen," Marvin asks, "And that you're not just taking my money?"

"You *don't*. But still you took the meeting," Joe says, "Our guy loves his money. If I go back and say there's no deal. Then he'll think you're a cop. That'll be *my* neck. Which mean it's yours too. Cause you knowing me, makes it hot for him. Don't put shit down if you're not serious about it. He'll come to see you, if you bullshit from here on."

Joe shows him articles of some of Pac Man's work. It's obvious to Marvin, Pac Man has a real reputation but no *real* convictions. At least, not for murder. Just for everything else.

"He's good and he don't leave no traces," Joe says, "But it's up to you."

"I want it done during the holidays," Marvin says, "When I'm away, visiting my family."

"He'll let us know *when* he can," Joe says, "If you wanna call the shots. That's extra, like I said. It's like this. Once you transfer the down payment. He sets his shit in motion. It happens when it happens. Could be sooner. So stay protected from any drawback. If you can. The five hundred and forty thousand is just for the hits. It don't cover extras like surveillance or any travel he'd have to do to get to the marks. But if he's able to get them here in Cleveland. Then there's no extra for travel."

"I have equipment for tracking them," Marvin offers, "I've gotten their daily routines down pat. I've got all of that ready for him."

"Get the money ready first. Bring me back what you got," Joe says, "He'll let you know if he needs you to provide anything else. But he's gonna have to see the money before he'll even meet with you."

Woody doesn't speak. He only observes. Marvin assures them he wants the jobs done. He tells them to give him a few months to get his alibi solid. Then when he transfers the funds, they'll know he's ready.

"Say by October," Marvin says, "I'll have the fall guy set up good by then. My trip will be booked for months. Then I'll transfer the funds."

"It's *May*," Joe says, "We need two hundred and seventy thousand to get started. That's half. When you're ready to move forward. Use this phone and call this pager number."

Joe gives him the throw away phone and pager number. They shake hands. Then Joe and Woody leave.

Marvin is going through with the hits. By this being the end of the school year. He's sure Matt's schedule will change some. He needs time to get the new 1 and also he wants Farah in Cleveland, when Matt and Chill are killed. He figures she'll be devastated and will need someone to lean on. He has plans of being there for her when she needs someone to bring her grief too. But the school year is ending and he still doesn't know where she lives. He needs to wait until the fall, to have time to find her residence. He thinks he has the move to have both the niggers who have Farah's attention, done away with. He believes everything is going to work out perfectly. By the time these hits take place. He feels he'll have all of his bases covered and no traces will lead back to him. Once again, he hasn't taken into account, the major pull and savvy the crew have on the streets of Cleveland.

May 2003 is graduation time again. Ebony, Nina and Rebbie finish Grad school at CSU. Then they all go see Erica graduate from Oklahoma. Her and Eric are having a home built in Jackson Heights. It'll be finished and ready for occupancy in October. They haven't gotten married but the date has been set for October 10th, 5 months from now. Greg and Jesse graduate from Southern University in Baton Rouge this month, as well. They've already been drafted and will join their respective teams this summer for rookie training camps. Sam graduates from The University of Cincinnati and begins employment at Brown's Sports Agency at CrewLand Mall. He's Jb's partner. He'll manage and run the Cleveland office which

TIME TO FEEL-RELOADED-Time Will Reveal part 5

will leave Jb freer to manage the southern businesses. Erica is going to partner with Tank at The Spot II, starting in June. This will free up Nina's schedule so she can concentrate on the upgrades and new additions for Crew Style's hair salon. Her and Tonya are still partners. They've given Justine a vested interest in the salon as well. Kilo helped Justine to get stock in the salon. Her uncle Jason is so proud of her progress since she's moved to Cleveland. Her and Kilo are also talking marriage and kids.

Brittany James graduates from Clark-Atlanta University and goes full force into her music career. Reaper is still doing well. He's close to making his award show appearances. He's also taking online classes, something which has just become available. Now he can get his degree while he tours the country, at the same time. His parents were very pleased when they got that news. He's going to be featured on Brittany J's 1st CD also. Brittany's CD is set to drop in 2004.

Charlotte is the lone high school graduate from the crew this year. She isn't enrolling in college at this time. She opts to work at Granny's House with her mother Jackie. Her boyfriend Brandon and his twin sister Brina won't graduate until 2005. Their mother Brenda is still partners with Jackie at the preschool. Charlotte plans to enroll in college in the fall of 2005. When the 1st twins from the crew, Brandon and Brina graduate high school and enroll. She's going to wait so her and Brandon can be freshman together. Thus they can graduate college together too. Charlotte wants to be an elementary school teacher. She's going to get her job experience while working at the daycare center as a work study job.

Kenny or Lil Chill as he's called, won rookie of the year honors at Ohio State for this past season. He's still being courted by the NFL but he's promised his parents Chill and Renee, he will stay in school and graduate before going to the league. Renee is thrilled but Chill is split on the decision. He wants his son to get his education. But he longs to see him playing in the NFL.

****

Rebbie and Ally are at Crew's house having lunch with Nina and Erica. They just left *Crew Gear and Alterations* where they were doing the 2nd fitting for Erica and Eric's wedding. Rebbie and Ally are flying to Los Angeles in a week with their parents. They'll meet Reaper at the AMA's. While enjoying lunch, the 4 ladies strike up a conversation about TV reality shows and the awards while they pass time until they have to go back to

74

their perspective jobs. They spend time grading the most popular shows of 2003.

"Do y'all like that *Making Da Band* show on *MTV*?" Ally asks.

"With *P. Diddy*?" Nina asks as she laughs.

"Uh huh," she answers.

"Yea I watch it," Erica says, "For the *drama*."

"Me too," Rebbie says, "I wish Diddy would audition some dancers. I'd go and take Jerica with me."

"Tank likes *Who got Game*," Nina says, "He watches it *every* Sunday Night."

"I like that too," Erica says, "Eric watches it with Tank."

"My favorite MTV shows are still *Real World and Road Rules*," Rebbie admits.

"I like the challenges better," Ally says as she laughs, "They're some cut throats, man."

They all agree as they laugh and Erica changes the subject to AMA talk.

She says, "I just hope Reaper gets the best new artist award. Our crew is going to outdo, y'all crew."

"For real," Ally agrees.

"Dream on," Nina says, "Chill's crew is going down in history as the crew that set the family up and set it off too."

"Word," Rebbie agrees as they laugh more.

With the 1st pick in the 2003 NBA Draft. The *Cavaliers* select *LeBron James* on June 2, 2003. *Paul Silas* is named the 15th head coach in the teams history. Ajay has a new coach and a superstar kid who is going to be a huge impact player for their team. He's super excited about the possibilities for the 2003-2004 season.

T-baby's 1st season with the *Shock* gets underway in mid-June. Wes attends each and every game and brings Jada and Rich III, just as he'd done when T-baby played for the Rockers, who are now in their last season. This season Wes brings along Richaunda too. Greg Sr and Sandy come and so does Anna and Rich Sr. The tension with Katrina Dobbs is still very much there. It's still bubbling under the surface. It just hasn't boiled over yet. Many of the Shock players know the source of the tension and they don't like it at all. They've taken T-baby's side. They agree that what Katrina had done was very greasy and grimy. They feel like T-baby should whoop her ass.

TIME TO FEEL-RELOADED-Time Will Reveal part 5

Archie Wilson Jr is being highly sought after by every division I college in the nation, as well as the NBA. He'll be a senior at MLK, this fall. Brandon and Brina are looking forward to their junior year. Brandon is being heavily recruited for basketball by Division 1 schools. Brina is also and she's already receiving interest from the *WNBA*. Her and Archie Jr are still an item. They're going to sign with the same college and they both plan to play basketball professionally. They hope they can get professional contracts in the same city. Jb already has Sam Jr working on that for them. Brina still credits Ebony as her reason for taking interest in the game of basketball. She still calls Ebony her role model. But she's going to follow in T-baby's footsteps and play professionally after college. Archie Jr has developed into an awesome basketball player, much to Ajay's credit. Ajay was the first person who put a basketball in his hands. These days, he plays pick up games with the Cavaliers, at every opportunity.

"Cuz you're gonna go higher in the draft than I did," Ajay tells him after they'd just finished a pick up scrimmage at the Allen Saul Williams facility.

"I wanna play with you and Lebron," Archie Jr tells him.

"Keep working, man," Ajay says, "It's gonna happen."

Even though they aren't *blood* relatives. They still carry on their kinship. This is something that was started by Ajay's paternal grandparents, Allen and Bertha Jackson Sr and Archie Jr's maternal grandparents, Jeb and Jessie Mae Johnson-Baker Jr who still live in Europe. They've considered themselves cousins since before Archie Jr's mother Rena was born. Nina and Rebbie will argue that with anyone who tries to draw on blood lines.

****

Charlotte and Brandon are sticking it out as a couple. He's going to be a junior this year. She's going to wait for him before she enters college. He's leaning toward Cincinnati, where his big brother June and their 1st cousin Tank had gone. His twin sister Brina is going to sign there too. Senior-to-be, Archie Wilson Jr is a shoe in. He's going to attend UC, just as his big sister Rebbie had and Ajay too. Parkwood has already promised them a crew house, if enough of them sign and attend UC. Or if Archie comes alone, he'll have a nice pad just for himself. But Parkwood is familiar with this crew. He knows they *rarely* go anywhere alone.

}*JULY 3*}
76

TIME TO FEEL-RELOADED-Time Will Reveal part 5

The crew are preparing for tomorrow's 4th of July celebration. They'll be in Jackson Heights again this year. It's where they've spent all of their holidays since Jackson Heights existence. This is a changing of the guards, so to speak. The mothers and daughters prep food today. Jerica, Destiny and Jada are helping and learning their roles as females in this crew. Orian and Lannie are here too. The *very young* girls think it's funny. They prep at T-baby and Rebbie's homes while all the fathers play cards, share party flavors and brag on who's the best grill man, at Ajay's home.

After the prep work is done, Ajay steals his wife away for a break and a little private time. The day before the 4th of July is still a *very* special day in their relationship. She walks out the backdoor with him. They head down to their gazebo, hand in hand. They walk and talk about their family traditions and how important all of those traditions have been in their lives and their relationship. This is the anniversary of the day she gave him her virginity. They reflect on their 1st sexual experience together.

"It was fourteen years ago today," she says with a smile, "And I still don't have any regrets about giving you, *all* of me."

"Yes it was," he says and returns the smile. "It was so good on that early morning. And it's still off the damn chain *today*. We've been together for a minute, baby."

"Almost sixteen years," she says, "It's been worth it, Anthony."

"It's been all our lives, really. And yes baby girl. It's well worth it," he says as he pulls her to him and gives her a sweet kiss. He adds, "I've watched you go from being totally scared of me *sexually*. To a straight up freak."

He chuckles. Before she asks, "I'm a freak now?" she's still laughing.

"Yes indeed. You're *my* freak, baby," he says, "And still all mine."

"We've been through it all Anthony," she says, "And I still love you with all of my heart. You're everything to me. After the twins, of course. They come first. Even before me."

"I'm alright with that, for *sho*," he says as he holds her close. He adds, "I had those same dreams. I use lay in my bed and think about what our kids would look like. What they would be like. I don't have one regret. I'm so glad I got it together for you and me. I knew it wasn't gonna get any better than you, Ebony. I always knew that. I just had to learn how to be what you needed and deserved."

They reminisce on the many events they have experienced over the past 16 years. There have been many. Both good and bad. But memorable, nonetheless.

77

TIME TO FEEL-RELOADED-Time Will Reveal part 5

On the morning of the 4th, Ebony has to go to *Shaker Heights* to pick up the twins. After her and Ajay started the reminiscing session yesterday out on the gazebo. Pearl and Jo had suggested they "get a room" and told them they was taking the twins home with them. In other words, Lil Ajay and Lannie had spent last night with their grandparents. They're still there with big John and Al. Pearl and Jo have already returned to *Jackson Heights* to get things set up for the 4th of July celebration. Ajay and Ebony are preparing to leave and go pick up the twins. But not before they stop by Nina and Tank's house to joke with their mothers.

"Why didn't y'all bring my children home?" Ebony asks as she walks into Nina's kitchen where Pearl, Jo and Nina are getting an early start.

She laughs because she knows they're going to have a few jokes for them.

"We wasn't sure if you two would be up," Jo says as her and Pearl laugh.

Nina cosigns her mother and they all laugh.

"I guess I need to go pick them up *first*. Ha?" Ebony asks, "Before I can start to help y'all?"

"And bring your daddy back too," Pearl says.

"You mean her father, right?" Ajay corrects her as he walks into Nina's kitchen chuckling, "Her daddy is already here."

They all laugh again.

"Then bring both of your father's back," Jo adds as she rolls her eyes. She adds, "I don't know if we need to let Ebony leave with you. Because we may not see her again until everything's done."

"I'll drive you, baby," Ajay says as he makes a weird face at his mother. He adds, "I was about to go and pick up the kids by myself. But since you said it like that. I'm taking my wife with me."

They head back out to her Caddy truck and head out. As he's driving her in her Escalade, he gets an idea for another gift for her.

"It's time for me to upgrade this one," he says suddenly.

"Upgrade what?"

"The Escalade," he says, "I'm getting a two thousand four model."

"Why?" she asks.

"Because I can," he says, "And I want too. Plus you deserve it. That good pussy is gonna get you everything I *think* I can afford."

They laugh before she says, "Anthony this one is still new."

"My wife and kids are not gonna ride in nothing older than five years. Unless it's an antique. That's my final answer."

78

He looks at her. The look on his face tells her, he doesn't want to hear anymore about it. He's going to trade her 2000 model in for a 2004. She says nothing more as they ride out to their parents homes. They get there, pull into the double driveway and park.

When they go inside of Pearl and John's house, they find big John and the twins in Ebony's old room helping Lannie finish making her bed. Ajay, John and Lil Ajay leave Ebony and Lannie in the room and go downstairs to the living room. Al has arrived from next door. He's sitting on the couch watching TV.

Ebony and Lannie talk upstairs while they finish making the bed, in what was Ebony's childhood bedroom. It's her daughter's room now whenever she spends the night. Lannie tells her mother she has a boyfriend at preschool and Lil Ajay has a girlfriend.

"You two are too young to be talking about having *anybody*," Ebony tells her. "I want you to always talk to me when you think you like a boy. You can always tell me. Okay?"

"Yes mommy," Lannie says, "I don't like him though. His name is Reggie. Ajay's girlfriend's name is Jamela but he has more than her."
Like father, like son.

Ebony doesn't approve of the subject, so she changes it quickly.

"This use to be my room," she says, "Now my daughter sleeps here. I can remember when I use to lay up here in this bed *dreaming* about the day when me and your daddy would be married, have our own house and kids. Lannie you like my old room. Don't you?" Ebony asks.

"Yes," Lannie answers, "Papa John said me and Jerica can have this room and come live with them."

"Well your daddy is going to have something to say about that," Ebony says as she laughs. She adds, "He's not gonna let daddy's girl leave his house to stay with nobody else. Not until you know, without a doubt that you are daddy's girl."

"I know," Lannie says, "I don't wanna leave my house anyway. I'll spend the night with Nana Pearl and papa John so they won't miss me, too bad. But I love my house and my room. And we have our own ponds and a big playground to play with our crew," she adds as her and Ebony laugh.

Meanwhile downstairs, Ajay is watching TV with Lil Ajay, John and Al. When Ebony and Lannie join them, after they finish straightening up the bedroom and cleaning it up, she finds out Lil Ajay has a revelation for her too.

"Mommy I have a friend girl," Lil Ajay says suddenly.

"I already told her that, Ajay," Lannie reveals.

"You can't be telling all my business, sis," Lil Ajay says and giggles.

Obviously the guys had been having the same conversation downstairs, that Ebony and Lannie had been having upstairs.

"Oh yea?" Ajay asks with a smile, as if he's hearing it for the 1st time. He asks, "What's her name, son?"

"Jamela Bryant," Lil Ajay says and giggles.

Ajay looks at Ebony and smiles.

"Is she pretty?" Al asks.

"Uh huh," Ajay Jr says, "But she not really my girlfriend. She just wanna be my girlfriend. She want me to kiss her everyday. I'm not doing that. Not to her, I'm not."

"Here we go again," John says and the men laugh.

Ebony doesn't. She says, "Son you're not old enough to have a girlfriend or a friend girl either. You're not even four years old."

"Maybe he's gonna beat out my record," Ajay says and laughs hard.

Everyone knows Ajay became sexually active around 8 years old.

"Not if I can help it," Ebony says, "Not my son."

"He's my son too, baby," Ajay says, "And he's got my blood in him and a legacy to live up too and fulfill. It's in him, baby."

"Not at four years old, he won't," Ebony insists, "I don't even want him talking about girls in that way, Anthony. Not right now. It's *way* too early."

"That's a sign of the times, baby," Ajay tries.

Him, John and Al think it's cool. They're giving dap to Lil Ajay and each other while chuckling and laughing.

"I have a boyfriend," Lannie says.

Ajay's smile disappears and so does the rest of the males. Lil Ajay included.

"What?" Ajay asks his daughter.

"His name is Reggie Ford. He goes to my school," Lannie says.

"No way in hell," Ajay says.

"I know that's right," John says and Al agrees.

"Wait a minute," Ebony says, "It's cool for Ant to have a girlfriend at almost four. But it's out of the question for Lannie to have a boyfriend at the exact same *age*?"

"Yea," Ajay says, "My daughter is not gonna have any boyfriend at four years old. At fourteen years old. Or at twenty four years old," Ajay declares sternly. "Now when she's done with college. If she wants to bring someone for me to meet. I'll meet him. Before then, I'm not gonna have it."

John and Al laugh initially. They knew the double standard of their crew would win out with this generation too. That's how it's always been. Their daughters were only allowed to mingle and date within the crew. For their grandchildren, the crew will have to have new blood. That's really the part they hadn't looked forward too. But they trust that they've raised their children right. And they'll guide their own children in the right direction too. They'll have them to mix with the right type of people.

"We tried that same thing with you two, Ajay," John says pointing to Ajay and Ebony, "Did it work?"

Ajay has to laugh, "No it didn't. But this time it will. I *mean* that."

"That's a double standard, Anthony," Ebony says, "It's not fair."

"What did you call me?" Ajay asks Ebony, "I haven't heard you say my name in years."

The men laugh but they're still on Ajay's side. He knows Ebony only called him by this government name because she's perturbed.

He continues, saying "It may not be fair but that's how it is, has been and that's how it's going to be. *Still.*"

Al and John agree with Ajay. They're cool with Lil Ajay talking about girls. But not with Lannie talking about boys.

"Men," Ebony says in a disgusted tone.

"That's *man* as far as you're concerned," Ajay corrects her, "One man for you. It's not men. Just *man*. This one. *Yours.* Your one and only." He laughs as he stands up and gives her a kiss. She doesn't say anything. She just stands there with a displeased look on her face.

"That's just how it is, baby girl," Ajay says and laughs, "Don't be mad."

"I'm not mad," Ebony says.

But she is, as she looks at her daughter who's looking back at her with a questionable look about her face.

"We'll talk about his later, daddy," Ebony tells Ajay. Then she turns to her daughter and says, "Remember what I said. Anytime you wanna talk to me. You can. Maybe not your daddy but with me, you can."

"Except for boys," Ajay says to his daughter, "If it's about boys. You have to tell me. Not mommy. Do you understand me?" he asks looking directly at Lannie, then picking her up and kissing her on the cheek.

"Yes. Okay daddy," Lannie says with a giggle. Then she looks at Ebony and says, "It's okay mommy. I can talk to you too."

Ebony forces a smile for her daughter's sake. But she's noticeably irritated as they all go out of the side door and pile into her Escalade. She's definitely going to finish this conversation with Ajay.

The 6 of them get into her Escalade and head back to Jackson Heights to celebrate the 4th of July. She doesn't say another word as they drive. Their fathers are too busy interacting with the twins to notice any tension. But Ajay notices it right away. He chooses not to bring it up. Not until him and his wife are alone.

TIME TO FEEL-RELOADED-Time Will Reveal part 5

CHAPTER 51

FOR THE GOOD TIMES

JB and the Atlanta crew don't make it home for 4th of July this year. They're staying in Atlanta because of the Iraq conflict and the fact that Bre is over there in the middle of it. Also the southern businesses are booked solid for the Holiday. They have *Ludacris and Disturbing the Peace. Lil Jon and The Eastside boys,* all performing for the 4th. *Usher Raymond* had performed to a packed house, the night before.

In Cleveland the entertainment portion of the holiday features 4 generations of crew, with the 4th generation taking 1st prize. 6 year old Orian, 9 year old Jada, 8 year old Jerica and Destiny who will be 10 tomorrow, are the stars *this* year. They do a rendition of *Bills, Bills, Bills* by the original *Destiny's Child* and receive a standing ovation. Wes is so proud of his daughter. She has gotten right in with the rest of the crew kids and she's utilizing her talents.

Later in the evening, Ajay and Ebony go see *Bad Boys II.* Then they join the rest of the crew at The Chill Spot. Ajay notices Ebony seemed preoccupied most of the day since they'd left Shaker Heights. Each time he'd asked her, *'what's wrong'* she'd said, *"Nothing's wrong."* But he knows better. He knows her moods and tendencies, very well. He knows they need to talk. He decides he'll wait until they return home from a night of dancing at their nightclub. Truth is, she didn't spent much time with him at the spot. She'd gone over to the Spot II with Rebbie and T-baby. That's where Nina was working. She'd left Ajay in the VIP with June and the rest of the guys. They were making plans for his 29th birthday party which is a week from tonight.

Even after leaving the club and arriving home, Ajay still can't get Ebony to talk about what's bothering her. She tells him, she isn't ready to talk right now.

"Just make love to me and let's go to sleep," she says, "If that's what you wanna do."

He doesn't like that answer at all. Nor the way she delivered it. He tries enticing her to talk to him anyway. She isn't willing too. She isn't in the mood to talk, so he lets it go. *For now.*

The week leading up to Ajay's birthday, all of their parents in

Shaker Heights are remodeling the rooms in their homes where their children slept. They're remodeling and redecorating for their grandkids. Pearl and John are fixing up Tank, Jb and Jesse's old room for Lil Ajay, Tank Jr and John III. Jesse stays out in Jackson Heights when he does come home. He either stays at Ebony's house or at T-baby's with Ruthie. His home will be completed soon. He has already bought the site for it. John and Pearl make sure Greg Sr and Sam Sr have whatever they need whenever Jesse is away on a football excursion.

In Shaker Heights, John and Pearl have put 2 new sets of bunk beds in the boys room, plus a desk and 3 chest of drawers, a *Playstation 2*, *Xbox* and game chairs. Ebony comes by to help with her old room.

"I might have some stuff in here I wanna save," Ebony says as her, Pearl and Lannie clean out her closet.

Ebony retrieves a lock box full of old letters from Ajay and the crew. It contains many photo's she'd left stored here for safe keeping.

"These will come in handy for my scrapbook," she says.

"What's this thing for?" Lannie asks as she holds up a cast, "It's got my daddy's name inside of a heart, on it."

"That's my cast. From Houston," Ebony tells her.

"Houston?" Lannie asks, "What's Houston? Texas?"

"Yes. That's the city where you were *almost* made," Pearl says as she laughs.

Ebony jerks around and looks at her mother. Then she shakes her head and smiles. Lannie smiles and looks at her.

She asks, "Is it true, mommy?"

"No baby girl," Ebony says, "That's a city down south. In Texas. You got that part right," Ebony says with a smile, "That's where big mama and poppa use to live. I went to live with them when I was thirteen."

"Why?" Lannie asks.

"Big mama use to get *real* sick," Ebony tells her, "She had breast cancer and she needed someone to come stay with her and help her out. I was the oldest granddaughter, so I went. Your daddy and me. We've been together all of our lives. That's why your nana is saying that. You was made right in our bedroom at *our* house. But Houston is where your Godmothers, April and Yolanda are from. That's when I met them. They helped me to *not* miss your daddy and home, so much. April died when you was a year old. I got pictures of her in your baby books. She's holding you and your brother. And you know that's her big picture that's on your wall and in our downstairs family room and library too."

84

TIME TO FEEL-RELOADED-Time Will Reveal part 5

"I saw her and she was *so* pretty," Lannie says. Then with a frown, she asks, "Big mama bought you this thing?"

"No. Not exactly," Ebony answers, "It's a long story, Atlantis."

"Will you tell me?" her daughter asks.

Pearl looks at Ebony and says, "I think you should tell her."

Lil Ajay comes into the room to see what Lannie is inquiring about. Ebony decides to tell them the story about her life altering night with Raymond White. She tells them enough details for them to understand that it was an awful thing to do to someone. She also tells them she had fought with everything she had and she had gotten away.

"I bet my daddy beat him up," Ajay Jr says, "My daddy can fight good."

"Oh yes, Ant. He beat him up. That's for sure," Ebony says, "Everybody in our crew beat him up. And his mean girlfriends too."

"Did you?" Lannie asks.

"Not exactly but he's not gonna ever do that to anybody else again," Ebony says as she looks at Pearl. "Our family got their point across. He won't bother me again."

"No he sure won't," Pearl adds, "Maggots are his friends now."

By now Ebony knows her mother is aware of the whole story of Raymond's demise. All of the parents and grandparents know he's gone for good. Even though the fathers hadn't told them about the video tapes they have buried in Al's yard. They still know Raymond is dead and buried. And he isn't coming back. That's all they're concerned with.

"I don't want a cast like this," Lannie says suddenly.

"And you won't have one either," Ebony states bluntly, "Or your daddy would do more than just beat that boy up. If you have to have a cast for the reason I got mine. I would kill whoever did that to you."

"And me too," Lil Ajay says, "And I'm gonna beat them up first. Me and my daddy. The *man!*"

They all laugh. Ebony feels comfortable after she tells her kids about that traumatic experience down in Houston, in 1991. She'll tell them the full story someday, later on. For now, they're content with the explanation she has given them.

"I wanna boyfriend just like my daddy when I get bigger and older," Lannie says.

"Hmm. Well your daddy said you can't have a boyfriend, baby girl," Pearl says with a laugh.

"I know. He told me that too," she says as she laughs, "But he was

85

talking to me about Reggie Ford. I don't like Reggie Ford anyway. He's a big cry baby."

"I know *my* daddy not a cry baby," Lil Ajay says, "My daddy is the *man*."

"No Lannie. You don't want a cry baby," Ebony says with a laugh, "And yes, Ant. Your daddy *is* the man. I really need to talk to the man too," She adds and laughs with her twins.

"Nana Pearl. If you get sick. I'm gonna come and stay with you," Lannie says.

"Me too," Lil Ajay adds.

"I know you *both* will," Pearl says as she smiles, "Ajay and Ebony sure have some smart kids."
She hugs and kisses her grand twins. Then she says, "You two are getting on out of the way for the next baby."

"The next baby?!" Lil Ajay yells and frowns. Then adds, "Yuck!"

"It's not nasty, Ajay," Lannie informs him. "Don't make that kind of a face. It's the same way we got here."

"Your daddy and I *have* been talking about it," Ebony says, "We're gonna try again real soon."
Pearl and Lannie are happy to hear that news. Lil Ajay doesn't seem sure.

"Well I've got two granddaughters and three grandsons," Pearl says, "It's time to even it up. You know that's a real feat for Ajay's family. To have more than one son."

"I know it is," Ebony says, "We're gonna *shatter* that legacy."
They all laugh. Within the next few minutes, they have Lannie and Jerica's room set up. They have added matching princess twin beds, dressers, a desk and a vanity to match.

"Now if the next grandbaby is a girl," Pearl says, "John and I will only need to put another bed right here," Pearl says as she points to the empty area and laughs, "And a dresser over there."
They are finally done with the redecorating.

"I *kinda* miss my old room," Ebony says before they all leave the room. "I have a lot of good memories in here."

"Uh huh," Pearl says, giving Ebony that mother's look. "I'll just *bet* you do."

"No comment," Ebony says as her and her mother laugh.
When they're all done, Ebony drives them in her Escalade to the restaurant so they can eat.

TIME TO FEEL-RELOADED-Time Will Reveal part 5

It's the evening before Ajay's 29th birthday. Ebony is done with all of the preparations for his party. *Nelly* will be the entertainment. He'll be performing songs like, *Hot In Herre* and Ebony's favorite song on the CD, *Dilemma* with *Kelly Rowland,* from his newest hit CD; *Nellyville.* Up until now, her and Ajay have been moving *around* each other. They haven't really talked in their *best friend* kind of way. Ebony still has discerning thoughts about the double standards under her family tree. She's been wanting to confront some of these issues with her husband. The vibe she has gotten from him lately, tells her he wants to do the same. He wants her to get whatever is on her chest. Off. And he seems to want it off *now*. So they can get back to the passion, when they make love and stop going through the motions.

Tonight they're relaxing in the family room, after putting their twins to bed. Ajay is very impatient with the distance between them. Ebony feels lonely. She doesn't feel like their relationship is on the right path either. She knows tonight has to be the night for the discussion. She's ready to put it all on the table and let him know what's made her so distant lately. Before she can figure out where to start the talk, he opens the conversation.

"What's on your mind, baby?" he asks, "Talk to me."

She's hesitant but he presses. "Don't just sit over there quiet," he tries, "The twins are sleeping. Now is the time to get *whatever* is bothering you. Out in the open. I can tell there's been something on your mind for awhile now, as *Floetry* say it," he says and smiles flirtatiously, "So let's go on and get to the bottom of it. So I can get to......." he pauses and slides closer to her. "...*to your bottom.*" He whispers, smiles and she smiles too.

"Come on out wit it baby," he insist. "Because our relationships is solid. And you know we can talk about *anything*."

"Why does there have to be one rule for Ant and another rule for Lannie?"

He picks up the remote and turns the volume down on the home theatre system. He kisses her cheeks before he answers.

"Because Ant is a boy and Lannie is *daddy's* girl," he says with a slight frown.

"Why do we have two sets of rules when it comes to,...." she pauses and he finishes her thought, asking, "....talking about boyfriends or girlfriends?"

"Yes," she answers.

"Because that's how it is, baby. That's the way we were raised," he tries. "The crew girls are *above* average. Morally correct and *special*."

87

"It's a different time now," she tries.

"Not for the crew, it's not. And not for *our* children," he says, "Our upbringing has worked for us. I don't see a reason to change it."

"Do you feel it's okay for Ant to date a lot of different girls?" she asks.

"Not *date* them. No," he says, "But he's gonna fuck them ho's. Because he's a handsome fellow and they're gonna come after him. So as long as he can handle himself," he says with a sly smile, "He can *get* it."

"I don't want him with a lot of different girls. Kissing them and-"

"He won't kiss just any girl. Just like his father," Ajay says, "He's only gonna kiss, *one* girl. The *one* girl that he really likes and *wants* for his future. Just like his daddy and his grandfathers did it. We go over that every week, baby. He knows there's gonna be *one* special girl who gets that. Not all of 'em. We're already talking about *all* of that type of stuff."

She catches him peeking down in her shirt.

"Daddy this is serious," she says, "Focus. *Okay?*"

"I *am* focusing," he says, "But Ebony. I'm gonna be looking at your body even if we're at a funeral." They laugh and he continues, "That's what my eyes are trained to do. I can't control that. But I'm focused. Ant is only gonna kiss one girl. That's his legacy and his daddy is always gonna have eyes for his mother. No matter what the situation is. I'm always gonna want you. Every *fuckin* second of every day. I can't turn that on and off. Ant is my son. He's gonna have that same passion one day. And he's only gonna have that kind of passion for that one *special* girl."

"Then he should only be with that *one* special girl *too*," she tries.

"He will," Ajay says, "But not until he meets her."

"Then teach him to look for that one girl. And not spread himself around to all the others," she tries.

"That's not realistic," he says with a chuckle, "He's crew."

"So is Lannie," she says.

"*Exactly*," he says, "And she's gonna conduct herself in the same way that her mother did. And her grandmothers and so on. She's only gonna be with one guy. Just like the crew women before her. Period," he says. Then he smiles and mumbles, "When she turns thirty five."

They both laugh but this talk is far from over. He has a special mix CD playing. Rob had sent it to them. The volume is on low. He can hear *Anthony Hamilton* singing his new single, *Coming from where I'm from.*

"His CD drops in October, baby," he says, "He's smooth as a muthafucka. I need to turn him up, up in here. So he can help me beg."

He smiles and his eyes are filled with lust. He's licking his lips too. Ebony tries to keep her composure. She wants to finish this discussion and get everything out in the open. Because she knows they have to get back to the real loving that they've both *trained* each other to crave.

"I loved him on *Thugz Mansion* too. And you don't have to beg," she says, "I just want you to treat our daughter the same way you treat our son."

"I know you do, baby," he says, "But I can't do that."

"That's why I didn't bring it up," she says, "I knew it was gonna be a double standard."

"Could you stay at the crew parties as late as Tank and Jb did? Or go to the places I was going too?" he asks.
She smiles and says, "No. No way and you know I couldn't. I had to be home at eleven."

"All the girls did. Until y'all got to senior high school," he says, "Or until y'all had a steady man. A *crew* type man, that is. You know all of this was arranged and set in motion *way* before we got here. I know you remember the talk we had with granny and papa?"

"Of course I remember. But Lannie is very smart," she says, "We should give her the benefit of the doubt."

"What doubt? Benefit *what*? She's *my* daughter," he says, "John and Al's *granddaughter*. Allen Saul, Allen Sr, Jackson and Percy's *great*-granddaughter. I can't afford to slip up. I don't have that option. I'm not giving her the benefit of anything except everything a daddy can give her," he says, growing impatient, "The ground rules have already been set. They're not gonna change for her."

"*See*. That's why I was scared to say anything to you," Ebony says, "I knew you would fuss about it."

"I'm not fussing," he says, "And I've told you before. You have no reason to be afraid of me unless you plan to harm me. And I know you're not. You can talk to me about anything that's on your mind," he says, "What makes you scared is that you wanna be able to tell me what my opinion is. And you know I won't allow you to do that."

"I just thought we was gonna be responsible for raising our *own* children," she tries.

"We are. Along with our entire village," he says, "Our elders, baby. Just like our parents did it. Who do you give a lot of credit for teaching you how to deal with me and how to please me? Who taught you what it takes to get and keep a husband?"

She smiles. She knows it was big mama. She knows that even if she was to have this discussion with her big mama. She's going to get the same answers he's giving her now.

"Who is it?" he's insisting that she answer.

"Big mama," she giggles.

"Right. Even when mama and mama Pearl didn't like us being together, back in the day. *Still*, they didn't try to change it," he says, "Why do you think that was?"

"Because they knew big mama knew what she was doing," she says, "I get it. I get it, daddy."

"Okay, good," Ajay says, looking deep into Ebony's eyes. "Now baby, let me tell you this. Lannie is my heart. *She's* the girl who'll be giving me *my* chance to learn the father's side of dating and relationships. When I first saw her come in this world. I could understand everything big John ever said to me. I felt him, right then and there. That fear of failing. I also knew he loved and trusted me, one hundred percent. Because he allowed me to see you and never tried to harm me. *Ever!*" He laughs and adds, "Because I know now what a *real* father feels for his daughter. What he demands for her and that he will *not* compromise. Not even one percent. She's gonna take me through it without even trying too. I'll sit up nights. Worried, wondering, waiting and hoping that boy knows how much I love her. How much she means to me and how precious she is. So he'll keep her from harm, like I did with you. My daddy made sure I knew what my job was, year after year, once he accepted that I was gonna cherish you. That's what I want for Lannie. A boy who knows what's expected. And if he hurts her. I'll kill him."

Ebony smiles and says, "That's how I feel about both of them though."

"It's different for a father and his son," he says, "Ant is my chance at a do over," he laughs hard and says, "He's single. So he can get all the pussy he wants and I won't have a problem, as long as he's not married."

"I would," she says.

"Yes you would because you're his mother," he says with a smile, "You want him to like, just one girl and bring her home so she can cook with you and shop with you. Like you did with my mama. She will be best friends with his sisters," Ajay says and smiles, "There will only be one girl that's gonna get that privilege. He'll find her, in time. And even after finding her. He's still gonna fuck other girls. That's just what we do when we're growing into men. He will too because he don't wanna fuck only one girl in his *whole* lifetime. Males don't want that. That's what wholesome

90

females want because y'all are in love, with *love*," he says, "Males. We love to fuck, first and foremost. But fucking somebody we love is a *huge* thing. It makes us vulnerable. It's just like the vulnerability I have now, as the father of my daughter. I know that fear now. My heart is on display and my ego is at stake. As males, we can't claim a girl who we think will fuck over us. Not if we're trying to love her. That's why we go through more girls. Good girls are harder to find. Or rather to believe in, that is. Not when we don't believe we can be faithful ourselves. So we're thinking, how can a girl do it? And then we convince ourselves they can't, just to satisfy our own insecurities. Plus that gives us the excuse we need to keep fucking around. Still we want our main girl to be faithful. If we really like her, then that's what we want her to do. I had a whole family to assist me. Then God blessed me by putting the perfect girl for me, right next door. And no matter how much of a dog I was. I never ever wanted to share you. I knew I wanted to spend my life with you before I even had peach fuzz. I knew that. But still, I wanted to get all the pussy that was available to me."

They both smile. She feels good. This is the Anthony she has learned to love. The 1 who had his flaws when it comes to fidelity. But he never lied to her. He's always said he had been in love with her since Kindergarten. The way he use to look at her 2 decades ago, his eyes said he'd do anything to make her feel good about him and her. And he would do anything to make her smile and be happy. And he would never allow anyone to do damage to her virtue nor hurt her. That look never changed. That look he had when she gave herself to him in 1989, is the same look he had when he came to get her from Houston after Raymond attacked her. It's the same 1 he had after Angel killed their unborn child. He even had it when he asked her to marry him, at their elaborate engagement party. She instinctively knows how to recognize that look because it's always there when they make eye contact. It's the same 1 he had when their twins were born. The one he has when he looks at them. It's the look he has right now. He had promised her if she gave him her heart, she would love him in amounts immeasurable. And it's all true. He can never really do any wrong in her eyes. She loves him so much, she has risked life, limb and freedom to shelter that love. And she knows she'll do it again and again, if the need arises. She can't imagine the measures he would go through to protect their girl child. But he's trying to explain it to her.

He continues, "Now if Lannie finds a boy like me. I'll have to watch him close and his family too," he says, "Because I won't be able to stop her from liking him. The same way big John wasn't able to stop you from being with me. He would go to my pops, most of the time. Because mama and mama Pearl would be nagging him to stop us. You're gonna do that when Lannie has a boyfriend too. Especially because he'll be like me."

"I want her to fall in love with a boy who's *just* like you," Ebony tells him, "I want her to be with a boy who's just like her daddy because that's what I did. I just hope I see that and I hope I know I'm *suppose* to like him. Like my parents and grandparents did with you. That's what I'm worried about. Will I be able to tell."

"You will and you'll like him. But you won't wanna give up your little girl," he says, "She's not gonna fall for a guy that's not somebody she's use to or trained to like. So he'll be just like me and she'll like him because that's what she's being raised around. She's gonna learn what to look for based on what she sees from you and me. Then she'll turn into a young *you* and she'll defy me and you if we try to interfere with it. Same way you did it. Because it's in her blood. But Ant, he's gonna fuck around with a lot of the wrong ones. But eventually he'll find and fall for the right girl because he's watching you too. He's gonna want a girl who's just like you. That's how it was for me. Lannie watches me and how you treat me. Ant watches you and how I treat you. They're both watching, *both* of us. That's why I keep it one hundred percent with you, baby. That's in order for our children to see what it's suppose to be like. We want them too mimic us. Ant don't and won't see his father fucking around. So he won't fuck up on the girl he likes, once he's committed to her. Because *that's* what he sees from *his* father. But he is gonna fuck around until then because that's just what boys do."

"He'd better not see his father messing up," she says, picking up on that part rather quickly.

"He won't see me fucking around. Because I'm not gonna fuck around," Ajay clarifies, "But to think he won't have more than one girl after him or at his whim. Is not realistic," he says, "That's in his blood. A long line of it too. On *both* sides," he laughs.

"Okay I understand it," she says, "I want Lannie to marry her only love, like I did. That's like mama, big mama, mama Jo. All of the women before her," she says, "And yes, all of the men *was* players before y'all settled down."

"See baby. All I was saying at big John's, the other day, is I want my son and daughter to have what we have," he explains, "That's just how it is. And we turned out alright, didn't we?"

"Yes we did," she says.

"Only Anthony Hamilton could help me get through *that* one," he says and they both smile.

"Those Anthony's *are* smooth," she says and smiles, "But sincere." She's still smiling as she leans in and gives him a big kiss. He knows the tension is over.

He says, "Now that *that's* done. How about some *fuckin*? Since you *now* understand that's something I love to do to you too."

They both laugh again as they slip under the huge comforter she keeps on the couch for cuddle time. They slide out of their clothes.

"I need some of that *real* loving, Ebony," he whispers, "I knew you had something on your mind since the fourth. The loving is always good. But with you, I'm use to better than just good. You got me spoiled on you giving me *all* of you. So come here."

He kisses her with fervor and she kisses him, just as hard.

"I missed you," she whispers, "I knew you could tell I wasn't a hundred percent. But I just worry about our babies."

"Uh huh. I understand," he says, "That's your first job and you do it well. I'm here to make sure you do that job, baby. I'll never do anything to sacrifice our kids. I'm just learning what a father feels when they have a daughter," he says and chuckles, "It's a scary thing. I have to admit. I worry about Lannie and she's not even in grade school yet."

"Ant isn't either," she whispers back, "I know he's just like you already. He's very protective of Lannie. She's got to go through him and you. So she may never date because her daddy *and* her brother will have every boy in the world scared to even speak to her."

"That works for me," he whispers as he smiles.

He begins to rub his hands through her hair and all over her body.

"I love the way your hands feel on me, Anthony," she whispers as they trade passionate kisses.

"My hands love to feel on you too," he whispers and they both chuckle.

She moves to his neck with her kisses. Then to his chest. His breathing pattern changes. She knows he likes it. She wants to turn him on. She wants to make up for all the days they haven't ravished each other. She moves back up to his ear for just a few seconds.

She whispers, "Uh I need to taste you, daddy. I want you to have every inch of this girl you molded into your freak."

With that, she moves down to his dick which is rock hard after that statement. She shows him, she's all his. She takes him into her mouth.

"*Oh!*" is all he can say.

She sucks the head of his dick as if she's starved while she gently massages his balls. She moans. She's enjoying the way his body jerks and tenses up, then relaxes each time she pulls on his dick. She deep throats him and he gasps for air.

"*Mmmm*. You taste *so* good," she whispers as she deep throats him again. She whispers, "I'm gonna keep working on this dick until I can swallow it all."

"*Shiiiiit*," he oozes, "You're working that bone, baby."

"Uh huh," she says, "I love this big dick, Anthony. My pussy may can't handle it all. But I'm gonna get my mouth *trained* on it."

"Ah baby," he whispers, "That shit is *so* good."

From her southern position, she whispers, "I got to be good to my baby. That's my job."

"I need to taste this sweet nectar too," he whispers.

He reaches down and grabs her by the thighs and spins her around. Putting her pussy in reach of his mouth. He dives in. Sticking his tongue as far into her moist tunnel as he can get it.

"Ooooh!! Yes baby," she moans.

Her body jolts from the sensation. She's on top of their *69*. She grinds against his mouth and continues giving him champion head. He can feel his nut rising. He goes to work on her clitoris. He refuses to be the 1st one to cum. He's always insist on giving her, *hers* first. He goes to work on that immediately. There's a lot of heavy moaning and loud breathing. Ebony is on the edge but she refuses to let go of his dick. Her orgasm comes like a rushing race horse, as she screams, "Oh baby! *Anthoneeeeeeeee!*"

"Sing it baby!" he demands.

"Ooooh Anthony *baaabeeeee*! It's *soooo* good daddy! *Oooo!*" she sings. "I *missed* this baby! *Mmmm!*"

The twins must be sleeping solid tonight. Because some of her screams would be heard by anyone within 30 yards of them.

"Get that shit, baby," Ajay orders, "Get it! Get my pussy wet! Come here baby. Come *here*."

She's out there. *Spinning*. He takes this opportunity to turn her around and pull her down on his throbbing dick.

"*Ooooh!*" she screams as he starts to push up into her pussy immediately.

"Oooo," he moans and whispers, "This sweet muthafucka stays tight, baby."

"Oh baby. *Ssss*," she moans, "Oh God! Ugh!"

"Anything you need Ebony," he whispers.

"I love you so much, Anthony," she moans, "I love you baby."

"I love you too, baby," he says and gets on his job of pleasing her again, "I love my pussy too."

She leans down and grabs his face in both hands. She gives him a passionate kiss, as she says, "Baby I can feel that you do. You're taking it easy on me."

She smiles and he smiles back before saying, "I'm learning to let you work me when you're on top. I gotta make you love this position too. I'm getting old. I need to reserve my strength for when I'm on top. And when you put it on me."

She leans down to his ear and says, "My dick ain't getting old. It's getting better. So you can't be. You're way to pleasing to be old."

"Well let me roll you over then," he says, "So I can put my back into it."

"Oh *Lord*," she says and giggles, "I done wrote a check my pussy can't cash."

"It's been cashing them for sixteen years, baby," he says, "I ain't never been up in this and didn't get paid."

They both chuckle and get back to the work of pleasing each other. He's so happy to have that discussion behind them. He can tell by her participation tonight, that she's glad too.

"Let me see can I wake my twins up," he whispers and moves in for the long haul.

"Not until we've finished with this, daddy," she whispers, "I wanna get all of this in. Even if I can't handle it. You still make love like you always did. Damn good. *Shoot*. It ain't nothing old about this. It still feels like it did in room one eleven. I just try to hang on as best I can. I'm always gonna please my man."

That turns him on even more. He starts to stroke her with precision. She's loving it. In between the kisses and sucking on her neck and nipples, he's whispering sweet shit in her ears while he's working her wet pussy. She's on her way to ecstasy again. There's no other place he wants her to be.

"I can feel a payment coming on," he whispers as he chuckles.

"Oh baby!" she screams.

Her 2nd orgasm is on deck and he knows it. He's watching her facial expressions.

"You're so fuckin sexy, woman," he oozes, "Is this dick good to you?"

TIME TO FEEL-RELOADED-Time Will Reveal part 5

That did it. As *Earth, Wind & Fire*'s hit song *Reasons* plays. She's getting another one and he's drilling her as he's watching her enjoy him.

"*Ooooooooooooo yesssssss*, daddy! *Anthoneeeee! Ooooooooooooo!* Yes! *Yesssssssssssss. Ooooooooooooo!*"

"I Love that song the best, baby," he whispers.

Which takes her further out there into the abyss of satisfaction. He's pulling on her nipples with his mouth. He's letting his tongue roll around them while they stand at attention.

"I feel *soooo* good! Anthony! Oh *God*! Yes daddy. Do it! *Do it!*"

"Hmmm baby," he whispers. As he feels his climax nearing, he whispers, "That's some sexy shit to me, Ebony. Ugh! I love you baby! Take this dick for me. Please. *Please*," he whispers through heated breathing.

He's churning into her now as he's about to blow. Even though he's trying to hold it and go longer. He knows he's never been able to do that. Not after watching her cum. They're both sweating like they've just run 2 full 24 minute halves. She knows he's about to get his because he's so deep into her flesh and the pain is present. But she loves the look on his face. It's so intense. She knows he's loving the feeling he's getting from her.

"It's something deep off inside of you that feels so good to the head of my dick," he utters.

She knows that's her diaphragm. She'd gotten it after she'd stopped taking the pills. He'd asked her if she was ready to add to their family back in April. She uses the diaphragm until he says he's ready. But she knew if he really went deep, he'd shoot right past it. Or his huge dick would move it right over out of the way. He moves it every time. Sometimes he pushes it further into her then it's suppose to go. He's headed to the abyss and she feels like he's going to push her through their overstuffed sectional.

"Oh baby!" she screams because the pain is very prevalent.

He's *Cuming* and he's *Cuming….*, hard.

"Oh *God*! *Yes*!" is all the words he can form.

He bites down on his lip so hard, she's afraid he's going to cause it to bleed. His face is more intense than ever. He's loving this feeling. He cums. *Hard.* Then all he can do afterwards is flop down on her and lay there. She's kissing him. He's trying to kiss her back but he has no strength left. If they didn't make a baby tonight. Then it's going to be because her birth control methods was able to withstand her fertile man. They sleep on the sectional for the remainder of the night. Holding each other very tight.

Ajay turns 29 the next day. He has a large party at the Spot. All of

TIME TO FEEL-RELOADED-Time Will Reveal part 5

his crew are having explosive parties and both clubs are filled to capacity.

"Ajay, man you're getting on up there, cousin," Rebbie says as she laughs.

"Yes and you are too," he laughs, "I don't get older, cousin. I get better. Ask your home girl."

"That's right, Anthony," Ebony agrees, "My man ain't old by a long shot. Not with the way he was working me last night *and* this morning too." She smiles as they finish their slow dance with a kiss.

"You still feel *so* good in my arms, baby girl," he whispers into her ear.

"And in your arms is still the only place I wanna be," she tells him with a bright and sexy smile.

"What do you say we start on that new baby when we get home tonight?" Ajay asks.

"That's cool," she says, "I think we already started. We're not on the pill anymore. Remember? We've been off of them for months and I think we scored last night."

"The time is right for another Anthony and Ebony union, ha," he says as he chuckles.

"I hope so," she says.

Ajay's party last until 4am. In keeping with their word and their plan. They head home and work on their family planning some more. Just in case they hadn't scored the winning shot, 24 hours ago.

****

By the twins 4th birthday party, Bre's platoon in Iraq has come under heavy fire. 2 members of her squadron have been killed. Her sister platoon had been taken hostage back on April 13. They've been held for just over 13 weeks. *SPC Shoshanna Johnson,* whom Bre had been partnered with in basic training is 1 of the hostages. As if that isn't enough to keep the crew on edge. They get some more bad and then some good news from the conflict. Bre has been injured but her injuries aren't life threatening. The army is sending her home. She'd caught some shrapnel in her left leg. She has experienced the type of injury that'll cause her a lot of pain, from here on. She will have to use a cane to walk, early on. But the crew are just happy she's finally coming home. Lynn and Wesley haven't been sent over yet but they're still on standby.

TIME TO FEEL-RELOADED-Time Will Reveal part 5

It's August and the crew are busy with preparations for Erica and Eric's, October wedding. Rena, Belinda and Sandy have all the gowns cut. *Crews House of Soul Food* has the food list. Erica has chosen Ajay's, *Allen Saul Williams All Sports and Recreation facility* conference hall for the reception site. The after party will be at *The Chill Spot* and *The Spot II*. Eric and Erica's wedding will be the largest of all the crew weddings, thus far. Erica chose Nina, Lynn and Ebony as her Matrons of Honor. Pam will be her maid of honor. They've planned her bridal shower already. It will be held at *The Spot II.*

This month *Reuben Studdard,* a black man from Alabama, is named as the 1st winner of *American Idol.* They book him to sing at the wedding. His nickname is the velvet teddy bear. He has a soulful sultry voice, similar to *Luther Vandross.*

"But there's only one *Luther!*" Brian Sr says.
Luther Vandross had fallen ill, earlier this year due to a stroke. He's still the reigning crooner of R&B and everyone knows that to be a fact.

"I know that's right," Archie Sr agrees, "Luther is gonna surely recover and come back for his title. All the crew who was born in the eighties. Was made while his music was playing."
The fathers have a big laugh at that comment. It's the apparent truth and the mothers have to cosign them.

G-Unit reigns supreme in Hip Hop this year, which isn't a surprise to the crew. 50 cent's album sold more than 7 million copies and he raked in awards from *BET* and *MTV.* But the biggest talk of the month of August is his appearance at the *VMA's* with *Miss Vivica Fox.* They look stunning as a couple. Ebony and Ajay are watching *50 cent, Snoop Doggy Dogg, Lloyd Banks* and *Young Buck* perform Ajay's favorite song at the award show tonight.

"P.I.M.P. is the shit, baby girl," Ajay says as they watch the performance in their 2nd story family room and Ajay recites the lyrics.
"I don't know what you heard about me. A bitch can't get a dollar out of me. No Cadillac, no perks, you can't see? That I'm a muthafuckin P.I.M.P," he sings as they both laugh.

"I know a bitch can't. But I get *plenty* of dollars out of you," Ebony says.

"Oh baby," he adds, "You're the *wifey*. You get it all!"

"G-unit dropping their group CD in November, right?" she asks.

"Yea. It's gonna feature *Yayo* too," he answers, "He's still locked

98

Up until January. But he's still, *G-g-g-g-g-g-unit!* To the bone gristle. As Buck would say it." They laugh at his *G-unit* call.

"All those gee's before the unit. Yea, right," she says, "We know Young Buck is gangster. We've seen him in action. But how do I know the rest are even as gee as *we* are?" she asks, "I think this union is a bad move for Young Buck. A southern gentlemen signing a contract with an insecure beef loving New Yorker. A recipe for disaster."

They crack up laughing at her wit.

"Why fifty cent gotta be an insecure New Yorker?" Ajay asks.

"It's obvious he is. Because he's been made fun of so much. That's all he knows how to do. Can't you tell? His whole angle is gonna be trying to bring down others and beefing whenever somebody doesn't take his side or kiss his ass. He wants to be loved. But he doesn't know how to show love. Like DMX said, *'Don't know love. Can't show love'*."

"Hip-Hop was built on beefing though," he tries.

"Beef for the sake of competition. Not redemption or degradation of your own people," she shoots back, "He'll disrespect an elderly person or a pioneer, if he thought it would boost his career up," she says and they laugh again. "He's gonna be like Shuntay and Sonya. He'll be friends with you, as long as he can use you to get over. But once he see that, *that* person disagrees with his ways. He'll turn on them."

"*Damn!* Sonya and Shuntay? That's cold, baby. I think dude is a pimp though. But we'll see."

"He won't be *that* bad," she says, "Nobody can be as bad as them. I think he has a brilliant business mind. That may be why he's doing it this way. But we *will* see. We'll see if he's insecure or if he's just a better con then the rest of the rappers." They laugh again.

As usual, they don't get through the entire broadcast without a love session. They had put the twins to bed early, then relaxed in front of the upstairs family room TV with Hennessy and party flavors from their bar. Ajay starts undressing her with his eyes and she returns the look.

"That pussy hot for me, baby?" he asks.

"Yes indeed. It's on fire," she giggles.

"Well let me help you cool it off," he says as he smiles.

He starts kissing her. Gently at first. Then, very aggressively. She starts to remove his clothes quickly. He smiles. He's liking this action from her. When she has him completely nude. She gives him some oral gratification. She's become quite good with her new weapon too. She takes him into her mouth. Sucking him hard instantly, like she's been starved for a taste of him. She takes him to her throat. He moans. He sounds so good to her, that she repeats it, again and again. She sucks on him hard, again and again. He rubs his hands through her hair and down her body. Pulling her head to him and to his dick.

She whispers, "You love how this feels. Don't you daddy?"

"Fuck yea," he says in a whispered exhale.

She sucks him harder. Faster. She takes him deeper into her mouth, then to the back of her throat. He gasps for air. Then he takes in a deep breath. He's ready to unload. She wants his feast but he isn't going to let her have his juices, just yet. Not without getting a taste of her sweet nectar first. He rips her clothes off so he can return the oral favor. He tears her blouse and as he's promising to replace it, he slings it to the floor. They pause long enough to smile at each other. He pulls her up on his chest, positions his hands under her bottom while he lays on his back. Finally he lifts her bottom up and sits her on his face. It's time for his feast. He doesn't sneak up on her pussy like he wants to tease her. He captures her button instantly. She moans and trembles, as his tongue draws circles around her clitoris. He holds her hips in his strong hands while he tongue fucks her. She rolls her hips in a symphony. He rolls her over onto her back and licks her clit in rhythms. She arches her back. Ecstasy is on deck. Cuming is in her *very* near future. Ajay lets her yell and roll and gyrate but he keeps his grip. After that orgasm, her chassis is *well* lubed. He slides right in and begins fucking her hard. He's turned on. His dick feels like a lead pipe has been shoved into her pussy. Thirteen and a half inches on a teenager was hell to handle. But he's a full grown man now. With another inch plus he's well conditioned and cut from his NBA training. He's a pussy terminator, these days. Everything about her that turns him on, he's whispering it to her. It's taking everything she has to keep from screaming to the top of her lungs with every thrust. The closer she gets to her next orgasm. The more he demands that she *"get it!"* And the harder he fucks her too. Their not even midway through the award show and they're bumping and grinding on the couch. She gets hers, twice. Then he gets his. They finish the 1st session and lay in each others arms as they watch the remainder of the *VMA's.*

"Anthony let me go to the bathroom real quick," she says, feeling instantly nauseated.

"Alright," he says, "And I'll go check on the twins."

He does, after letting Ike and Tina outside to go the bathroom.

In the master bathroom, Ebony is over the toilet. She vomits for more than 5 minutes. When she feels strong enough, she returns to the family room. She finds Ajay seated on their sectional with the twins. And Ike and Tina are on the floor in front of the sectional. All of them are waiting for her, like they already know what's up.

"They don't even try to sleep all night anymore," she says, managing a smile.

"I know," Ajay says as he notices she's a little green around the gills. He asks, "Are you okay?"

"I don't know. But I was throwing up, just now," she says.

"Oh *yea*?!" he shouts, nearly scaring her and Lannie.

Then he smiles and says, "You'd better make an appointment with Doc Weston. The man done scored again!" He laughs.

"My daddy is *the man*! Lil Ajay adds.

"Uh huh. He's the man, alright," Ebony agrees.

They all cuddle on the sectional. Ike and Tina jump up on the sectional with them and they watch the VMA's together.

****

Jarvis, Gwen and Lil Jarvis go for a walk around Jackson Heights on a lovely Saturday afternoon. They walked up CrewLand drive passed the guard booth and are now making their way back down the street, heading home. Tank drives through the gate, speaks to Jacobson and continues. He spots Jarvis and his family. At that same moment, Gwen turns around to see who's approaching from the rear. Her eyes meet Tank's. It's still awkward for both of them. And it has been since their days at the UC. Jarvis throws up his hand and waves for Tank to stop.

"Ah shit," Tank whispers but he does stop.

"What's good, man?" Jarvis asks him with a bright smile.

"Just heading home, man," Tank manages.

Immediately Gwen can tell he's having the same recollection she's having. She's feeling equally awkward too. Jarvis doesn't pick up on it at all. He continues his casual conversation.

"So the crew meeting has been scheduled, right?" Jarvis asks.

"Yea, man," Tank answers, "It's tomorrow."

"I'm nervous, man," Jarvis admits.

"I don't blame you," Tank says, "It's time for the big vote."

"Every member has to approve it too, right?" Jarvis asks.

"Yep," Tank says, "All or none. That's how it's always been for non blood crew. Arthur, Wayne, Justine and Kilo got in like that too."

TIME TO FEEL-RELOADED-Time Will Reveal part 5

"So how do you think it'll go?" Jarvis asks as Gwen fidgets.

"It should be good," Tank says, "We do a silent vote. Everybody puts a piece of paper in the plate. We vote yes or no. It's that simple."

"I've been telling Gwen to relax," Jarvis says, "She's been so nervous about it. She don't think we'll get in but Ajay feels like we will." Gwen is quiet the entire time. She's gazing up the street toward the curve which leads to the *cul-de-sac* where they live. She wants the conversation to hurry and end so they can be on their way home.

Suddenly, 5 year old Jarvis Jr has a question for Tank.

"You my uncle?" he asks.

Tank is caught off guard by the question from the tike. But he does manage to answer him, saying, "Yes indeed, Lil man. You can call me, uncle Tank."

"Okay!" Jarvis Jr yells and giggles.

Big Jarvis laughs and says, "He's ready to be crew too."

"I wish y'all luck, man," Tank says, "I think y'all will get it too. If Ajay feels confident then I do too."

Noticing Gwen hasn't spoken a word during this conversation, Jarvis Sr turns to her and says, "Baby you're not gonna speak to Tank? He's gonna have a vote too."

"Ah yes," Gwen says, rather nervously, "How are you doing Tank?"

"I'm good," Tank answers quickly as he looks toward his home. Then he says, "I need to get on to the house. Nina's waiting on me."

"Well alright, crew," Jarvis says with a smile, "We'll let you go. I'll get at you later."

"Alright," Tank says, "Y'all be easy."

He pulls away heading to him and Nina's home. He glances in his rearview mirror. He can tell Gwen isn't comfortable with him and Jarvis even having a casual conversation. She's been that way since 1993. Since the night him and her hooked up at the mansion in Natty. Tank has never told Nina about it. It obvious Gwen hasn't said anything to Jarvis either. Tank thinks to himself as he pulls into his driveway and on into his garage. He closes the automatic door immediately.

I can't go on being uncomfortable around them. Damn! I hate this secret shit! I needs to call Ajay. We need to talk. Today.

Rebbie is leaving Nina and Tank's home from their front door. She's heading back to her own house. She spots Gwen and Jarvis at the same time they see her. Gwen smiles big and waves her hand. Rebbie waves back but she picks up her pace. She wants to get inside. Gwen seems to have other plans, as she yells," Rebbie, how are you doing today?"

"I'm doing fine," Rebbie yells back, "How are you?"

"We're doing fine," Gwen says, "We're just out for a family walk."

"Okay," Rebbie says as she reaches her garage and starts in, "Y'all have a great day!"

"You too," Gwen says as her, Jarvis and their son continue walking. Suddenly she says, "You didn't even speak to Rebbie, *Jarvis*."

"She didn't speak to me either," he says, "But I thought it was just girl talk. You know. I wasn't trying to butt in."

"You embarrassed me when you said *'Oh you not gonna speak to Tank.'* But then you didn't speak to Rebbie. So how is *that* right?"

"It's not a big deal, Gwen. Don't make it one," Jarvis says, rather annoyed, "I just didn't want to be rude, honey. I figured it was just a little girl talk, that's all."

"Right," is all Gwen says as they make it to the curve and head on toward their house.
I should've been asked him about that rumor, I heard. I wonder did they go as far as Tank and I did.

Once inside of her house, Rebbie takes a deep breath as she leans against her closed door. She closes her eyes and thinks.
Oh God! That kissing session is gonna catch up with me. I wish they hadn't moved here. Especially not in Jackson Heights. Now I have to see him. He's my darn neighbor. I keep telling myself that nothing happened but kissing. And my husband has done way worse than me. But if Brian wouldn't have called me when he did. I can't say that it wouldn't have gone farther.

Satisfied that she's comfortably in her home, she exhales and with her eyes still closed, she says aloud, "I don't know how I'm gonna hide this."

"Hide what?" June asks, as he walks into the kitchen and startles her.

"Oh! Ah! Hey baby," she says, "I didn't know you was there!"
She's caught off guard and doesn't have an immediate answer for her husband. But he's persistent.

"What is it that you don't know if you'll be able to hide?" he asks.

"That I'm in the mood, Brian," she lies and smiles seductively, "That's the reason I rushed home. I was hoping you was done watching your game film because I need some sex."

103

TIME TO FEEL-RELOADED-Time Will Reveal part 5

"Well hell *yea*," June says, "I can watch game tapes *anytime*."
He walks over to her and they kiss passionately. He's more than ready and
he can tell she's hot too.
"Orian's at mama's, baby," he says with a sexy smile, "We can get naked
right *here* and go for it."
That's exactly what they do. Only problem is. Rebbie is thinking about her
sighting of Jarvis as she ravishes her husband.

Ajay has just heard Tank's confession about the early morning
he'd spent with Gwen at the mansion in Cincinnati. Ironically, he learns the
incident happened on the same night Katrina Dobbs had assaulted him.
"Well *now* I know why you didn't see that bitch when she snuck in
my room," Ajay says in a disgusted tone. He continues, "Damn Tank!
Where was Jarvis?"
"He'd left after we carried you to your room," Tank answers
somberly, "He said he was going to look for June. Rich went with him the
first time but they didn't find him. And Rich had to get back to the house
for his own rendezvous. Rebbie came while the two of them was looking for
June. She was coming as a surprise visit. She'd snuck down in Ebony's car.
But after he wasn't there, she said she was going back home. Ebony didn't
even know she'd come down there. She was suppose to stay at mama Jo's
with Nina and T-baby while Ebony was at your apartment at the U."
"June was off somewhere, Fuckin off too. I suppose," Ajay says.
"He was at the hotel with Diana Keyes," Tank reveals.
"This is some fuck shit, Tank," Ajay says, "Did y'all find him?
What happened with Rebbie? Because she wasn't there when I came too."
"Jarvis brought Rich back but he went on the second run by
himself, to look Ree. That took awhile but when he made it back the second
time, June was right behind him. Rebbie didn't come back to the house
though. As I said, Jarvis went back after her while Rich stayed at home.
Rich called and told June to hurry home so he'd be there in case Rebbie
came back. She never did. When Jarvis came back 2 hours later, he said he
talked to her and she said she was leaving. She was gone back home."
"And?"
"And she must have. She didn't come to the house once I was up
and back in the living room. By the time June got back to house, me and
Gwen was done. She had gone to her dorm. When Jarvis got back, he
seemed distracted. I thought he knew something happened because he said
he needed to talk to me about something *really* serious. But he wanted to

104

wait until all the shit that was going on then, had calmed down. I thought he knew about me and Gwen but he didn't. That wasn't it, at all."

"Well. Did y'all ever talk?" Ajay asks, "And what did he say?"

"It was three days later when we talked," Tank admits, "He had some shit of his own to tell. It wasn't about Gwen. It was him and Rebbie."

"*What*?!" Ajay asks in shock.

"He said she was real mad and she knew June was fucking around because he wasn't answering his phone," Tank says, "And when she first came to the house. She said June had cut off his phone after she'd called him over ten times. Jarvis said she came onto him. I don't know how true that is. He said they didn't have sex because she didn't wanna go that far. But he said they made out and he did oral sex on her too."

"Oh my God," Ajay whispers in disbelief, "Ebony was right. We don't know none of y'all asses like we think we do."

****

The next morning, the same morning of the vote, Gwen's sister Nickeia is expected to arrive for a visit with Gwen and Jarvis. While the crew convene in Ebony and T-baby's offices, the morning before CrewLand Mall opens. Gwen and Jarvis pick up Nickeia from *John Hopkins Airport*.

"I'm so glad to be back to see y'all," Nickeia says.

"We're glad to see you too, Nic," Gwen says, "It'll take our minds off of this vote today."

"So y'all are gonna get to be in Ajay's crew, ha?" Nickeia asks. She's jubilant and hopeful, as she adds, "When y'all make it. Y'all have to vote me in too."

"One thing at a time, Nic," Jarvis says as he smiles, "We'll have to learn how the process goes before we can even think about adding anybody to it."

"Well okay," Nickeia says, "Just so y'all know. I wanna be down too. I've decided to attend Cleveland State. I hope y'all will let me stay with y'all while I go to school."

Gwen and Jarvis look at her. They had no idea she was planning to stay in Cleveland *indefinitely*. Not until just now. But Nickeia has a plan of her own. She's planning to get closer to Ajay. She knows with her sister living right across the street. She'll have the best seat in Jackson heights to keep her eyes on his comings and goings.

"I think it's the bomb that y'all live across the street from Ajay Jackson," she says with a giggle, "He's a damn celebrity in my book and *hella* fine too. Oh my God!"

Jarvis says, "We live across the street from Ajay and his wife *Ebony*."

"And their twin son and daughter," Gwen adds, "Plus they're working on another baby. They want a lot of kids. I think that's awesome. I think they're going to have a big family one of these days. They both want a lot of kids."

"Uh. Whatever," Nickeia says as she thumbs through her phone's photo gallery, ogling at the pictures she'd downloaded of Ajay.

****

The crew vote is taken and counted. All voted yes except 2. Ebony is shocked they didn't get a unanimous outcome.

"Wow," she says, "I didn't realize some of you didn't want Jarvis and Gwen to be crew. This changes things. How are they gonna live in Jackson Heights and not be crew?"

"They can't," papa Brown says, "That's a rule *your* crew set."

"Maybe we should've voted on their *living* arrangements first," Poppa Jones says.

Big mama surveys the room. She's looking for the 2 negative votes. She knows she'll be able to see it in their faces. The rest of the crew start to ask questions immediately. No one owns up to the negative votes. Ajay sits in silence. He knows who 1 negative vote came from. He's pretty sure, Rebbie was the 2nd. No one else has a clue. Nor do they know the reason they would've voted negatively. The crew rule has always been, no one had to say *how* they voted or *why* they voted the way that they did. In a way, Ajay is glad that rule is in place. However he's tormented by the fact that his wingman had been intimate with his play cousin. Also that his wife's *closest* brother had been sexual with Gwen. He knows he and Ebony have to be apart of the announcement meeting and he's not looking forward to it. The only thing to discuss now is what time to have the meeting for Jarvis and Gwen to come in and find out the results.

"I say we do it right away," Grandpa Charles says and Grandpa Joshua agrees, "There ain't no sense in wasting time and letting them have to sit and wait on it."

"We've always respected and honored our crew's decisions on who gets in and who doesn't," Grandpa Joshua says, "That won't change today."

"I know crew," Ajay says.

Ebony can tell Ajay is conflicted because he has that familiar frown above his brows and his nose is turned up.

"Are you okay, Anthony?" she asks as she gives him a hug.

"Not really," he says, "I need some good news. *Soon*. Something to take my mind off of this vote."

"I think you'll have some *real* soon," big mama adds with her usual charming smile.

"Good," he says, "I'll call Jarvis and get him down here."

He does.

The matrons and matriarchs wait with Ajay and Ebony, for Jarvis and Gwen to arrive. They come into Ebony and T-baby's office smiling nervously. That doesn't last very long. Gwen can see the look on the elders faces. She can also tell that Ebony and Ajay aren't in a great mood.

"Y'all didn't make it in," Ajay says, before they're even adjusted in their seats.

"I wished the vote had gone better but it didn't," Ebony says sadly. Neither Jarvis nor Gwen say anything. They sit there with Ebony, Ajay and all of the 1st generation. But to Ebony's surprise. Neither of them look shocked. It's like they expected *not* to get in. This changes everything. No way the elders will approve of a courtship between their kids if the entire crew aren't in favor of them even *being* crew.

"I'm sorry man," Ajay says to Jarvis, "But it's how the family stays together. Stand as one and never divided."

"That means we have to sell the house and land back to you and Ebony too, right?" Jarvis asks.

"Yea," Ajay says, "I had no idea it would turn out like this. I'm really sorry."

"Hey it's okay," Jarvis says which surprises Ebony too. "At least we'll get to be teammates again. Maybe we can get a better vote in the future."

"We'll see," big mama interjects, "We'll have to see how it goes, from here on."

"Exactly," poppa Jones adds.

Within minutes the meeting is closed. Jarvis and Gwen make an appointment with Ebony to deal with the real estate and to find a home outside of Jackson Heights. Ebony is sad about the circumstances. She has no idea this is probably the best thing that could've happened for her and Ajay. Because Nickeia is definitely planning to be a problem for them.

TIME TO FEEL-RELOADED-Time Will Reveal part 5

Ebony contacts Trina Yvette Sloan-Wheeler to reside over the closing. It's way to personal for her to even deal with it. Trina takes the wheels and promises her, she'll have the deed completed. Plus have them in a nice new home, somewhere in Cleveland within 30 days.

****

On September 1st, Ebony and Mr. Parkwood continue with their deal to acquire some property in the state of Michigan. Mr. Parkwood has been looking to expand his business which would be an automatic expansion for Ebony too. They're acquiring land in the Ann Arbor area. He sets up the acquisition through her firm, *Jackson's Real Estate*. She stands to make a high 6 figure commission when the deal goes through. Her take will be $750,000. Ajay has always been proud of her business savvy. He's even happier when that news comes, this late morning.

"I needed some good news," he says as he and Ebony sit in the kitchen while big mama makes breakfast.

"That's not all the good news you'll get," big mama says and smiles.

Ebony and Ajay leaves, taking the twins to Granny's House daycare before heading on to their jobs.

Later that day, Parkwood finds out him and Ebony had gotten the large piece of property for a great price. He calls Ebony at her office.

"I'm going to put an office complex there," Mr. Parkwood says, "And I want your agency, along with Trina Yvette, to handle the sale of my office spaces. I also want you to open a branch office there, in the future."

"That sounds *great* to me," Ebony says, "It's all set, for the clearing and the construction permits to be drawn up."

Trina Yvette and Mr. Parkwood will handle the rest of the deal. The land is his now. Ebony makes her commission and is done with that part of it. It will be cleared for construction in a week.

With her commission, she invests some of it in G-funds for their twins. She also purchases a vacation package for her family to go to *Disney World*. That's where they'll celebrate Ajay's 30th and the twins 5th birthdays, in July 2004. They'll spend 2 weeks in Orlando. In the back of her mind, she feels like their family will be a bit larger by then. So the package includes a 16 member deal. They're taking Pearl, John, Jo, Al, big mama, poppa, Ashanti, Jarvis Jr and papa with them. The 2 extra tickets are just in case she's pregnant and another set of twins come. If it's a single

108

birth, she's going to invite Ida Mae Graves to go as papa's companion. She'll be sure and talk it over with her father before she does *any* inviting. Because she knows he's still not comfortable with Ms. Graves dating his father.

****

The NFL preseason camps come to a close this week. June, Bruce, Eric, Greg Jr and Jesse are prepared to start their 2003 NFL regular season schedules. Ajay's preseason camp will start next Monday. He's happy to still be on the home team.

Today is Friday September 5, 2003. Ajay and Ebony have an appointment with Weston. Nurse Tenischa comes out to the reception lobby and she's smiling big.

"I see y'all are at it again," she says with a huge smile, "I'm starting to see y'all as job protection."

They all crack up laughing as they head back to the examination room.

Ebony says, "I hope so."

"She knows her stuff, baby," Ajay says.

"You're right," Ebony agrees with a smile, "She said we looked different when we came in and found out about the pregnancy that brought us the twins."

"And y'all have that same look again today too," Tenischa says as she continues to smile very brightly, "I could be Miss Cleo."

They all crack up laughing again as she takes Ebony's vitals, over cheerful conversation. Then she gives Ebony a cup and says, "You know the drill by now."

"I sure do," Ebony says as they share another laugh and Ebony heads into the bathroom.

A few minutes later, as they're all waiting on Weston to come in with the results, Ajay has a surprise question for Tenischa.

"We're gonna have to get you to be a Godmother pretty soon," he says and smiles, "Since you're turning into our good luck charm."

Tenischa smiles pleasantly and says, "I would love too. But I can't take credit for being the reason you two are getting pregnant. You guys adore each other and you have a very active sex life as well. I expect to see you in here a lot. Like I said earlier. *Job protection*."

They're all laughing when Dr. Weston enters the room with a huge smile on his face.

"Well, well, well," Dr. Weston says, "We didn't have to go through the doubts this time. *Did we*?"

She tells Ajay and Ebony their pregnancy test results are positive.

"I *knew* it. I knew I hit it right," Ajay declares as he chuckles, "The man can't miss *no* more."

Ebony laughs and says, "He has been a bit much too take these past couple of weeks."

"Well he has a right to be proud," Dr. Weston says, "I remember you thinking you guys would need fertility to have kids."

"All we need is opportunity," Ajay gloats as they laugh.

Tenischa laughs and says, "That's what I was saying to them. It's not luck. All you two need is opportunity. I'm so happy for you guys. *Again!*"

They laugh all the way back to the reception desk. Their due date is May 27, 2004.

"This won't be a summer baby," Ebony says, "More like late spring. Just in time to go to Disney World in July. We got this one in here quick, Anthony."

"The twins are gonna be making five next year," Ajay says, "That's not quick."

"You're right," Ebony says, "But it don't even seem like it's been that long since they were born."

"I wanted the kids to be closer in age. But I know we agreed to let the twins get a few years old before we tried again," he says, "I don't wanna wait another five years though."

"That's easy for *you* to say," Ebony says and laughs, "You're not the one who has to deliver them."

"And you'd better not clown on me this time," Ajay tells her with a very serious face.

"I didn't wanna say anything," Tenischa comments, "But that delivery was hilarious. It took everything I had not to laugh. Ebony, I know you was in pain. But your comments had me running out of the room so I could laugh and you not see me."

"It was rough," Ebony says as they all laugh, "But I'm gonna have to learn how to deal with it. Because my husband is *so* fertile. as we can all see."

"I've told you *and* Ant has told you, baby," Ajay says, "You're married to *the man*."

"*Apparently*," Tenischa adds and they all laugh again.

Marshel sets their next appointment and they leave the medical complex.

TIME TO FEEL-RELOADED-Time Will Reveal part 5

Ebony and Ajay head to CrewLand mall to share the news with their family and crew.

"Another May baby!" Nina yells, "Now Jeremy junior, John the third and Orian are gonna have another cousin to share birthday parties with."

"Yes and I get to be pregnant during cooler months this time," Ebony says, "By the time it gets hot. This baby or *babies* will be here."

****

They all have to go for their 1st fittings at *Crew Gear* today, for Erica and Eric's wedding. Everyone shows up on time and finishes early.

"Baby we have plans tonight," Tank says.
He and Nina are going sailing on Lake Erie. Tank has to find a way to tell her about Gwen. He feels the best time to tell her will be while they're on the lake. That way, she can't storm off. Jerica and Tank Jr are staying at Pearl and Jo's. Ajay hasn't told Ebony but he plans to tell her soon. Her and Nina are talking while at Crew gear.

"Our mother's have our kids and Ajay said he's taking the twins over there," Nina says to Ebony, "So what y'all got up?"

"It's no telling, Nina," she answers, "He hasn't said nothing to me."

"Well I know preseason starts Monday," she says, "You know he always puts it down before he starts training."

"But sis. I'm pregnant *now*," Ebony laughs, "I'd say he's already put it *down*."

"Good point, sis," Nina says and they laugh as they leave the store.

}September 7, 2003{

Ajay has been doing all sorts of romantic things for Ebony this entire week. Tonight is no different. He has candles burning and soft music playing. He has arranged for their restaurant to make dinner for them. He draws Ebony a warm bubble bath in their Jacuzzi.

"Now baby. You sit in there and relax while I go get the food. Alright? I'm gonna bathe you when I get back. I have something very important I need to tell you."
She says, "Okay."
He leaves her listening to the smooth grooves CD he has playing on the stereo. While he heads out to pick up their dinner.

111

TIME TO FEEL-RELOADED-Time Will Reveal part 5

"This is the life," Ebony says aloud, "This is another lovely evening with my man, my lover and *my* best friend. I love the way Anthony spoils me. He always has. I know he always will."

Ajay returns shortly with the food. He sets it up in the formal dining room, then he comes back to Ebony's side. He bathes her thoroughly. And though she's in the mood right now. He tells her, she has to have her dinner while it's still hot. He has her outfit already picked out. He dresses her, then they head into their fancy dining room and take a seat at the table. He pours wine for him. Milk for her. They do a formal toast. He raises his glass to her and she reciprocates.

"To sixteen years *today* with my one and only love," he says with a smile as she realizes what today is.

"Oh Anthony! It's our anniversary!" she yells in surprise, "I've been so busy at the office that I hadn't even thought about it in weeks."

"Baby I remember a time when you would never have forgotten this date," he says, "But I'll just say you forgot it *this time* because I've given you so many more memories, over the years."

"Yes Anthony, you have," she says, "I love my life with you. Even the bad moments. It's all been worth it because I'm truly happy *now*."

"I am too, Ebony," he says. Then catching himself immediately. He says, "I know I hardly *ever* call you Ebony." They both laugh.

"It's okay," she says, "As long as you don't forget that it's my name."

They laugh again, as he says, "There's no way I can *ever* forget your name. Even when I get Alzheimer's."

She's laughing hard. He chuckles too. Before telling her, he knows why the crew vote for Jarvis and Gwen wasn't unanimous. But he wants to discuss the reasons why *this day* is so important for them first. Then they'll get into the crew vote fiasco. They reminisce over their past 16 years together.

This is the date he 1st asked her to be his girlfriend. It was September 7, 1987. He had already asked John, Jb and Tank. Lynn was all for it when he asked her if he should ask Ebony out. Both sets of her grandparents was approving of it, so he went for it. She was 11 going on 12. He was already thirteen and crew initiated.

"I will never forget how I felt that day," she says.

"Not again, ha?" he says as he chuckles.

"Never again," she says and laughs too.

"Neither will I," he says.

They go even deeper into their relationship memories and smile a lot.

112

TIME TO FEEL-RELOADED-Time Will Reveal part 5

They talk about their first kiss. The first time they had sex. His 15th birthday. Her leaving for Houston. His incarcerations. Christmas 1990. Stoney's death and when she 1st found out he'd killed someone.

"I remember thinking I could never do that," she says, "But I found out later, that I could. Which also helped me to remember that I already had. That was crazy how I had suppressed all of that."

"When you was in the hospital in Houston. You said you could do it," he says, "I always hoped you could, if you had too. But I was more than willing too and I still will, to take that burden off of you."

"I remember how mad you got when I was asking you if you had ever killed anyone," she says.

"Because you was my good girl," he says with a smile, "My naïve little princess. Me having you in my life is what made me stay safe, thorough and on point. I never wanted what I did in the streets to come back to haunt you. And at the same time, with me not wanting to bring trouble to your life, is what made me leave those streets alone completely."

"You got mad at me for asking about Eddie," she says, "But really, I didn't have a clue that you could kill someone. *Then*. But later *on*. Yes. I knew you could when I saw how you changed after Raymond White attacked me. I knew you would kill him in a heartbeat. And after he hurt me, I wanted you too."

"I wasn't mad when you asked me about Eddie," he says, "I was disappointed in myself. I didn't want you to see the bad in me. I didn't want you to be scared of me. I could never hurt you, baby girl. I would hurt myself before I would hurt you."

She smiles and says, "I remember wishing you had gotten mad enough to hurt Anita and Darlene. Only because I wanted them to know you would hurt them to keep me. I wanted you to hurt Angel too," she admits, "But then I knew you would go to prison. I couldn't let you go out like that. I couldn't allow that to happen. So I just kept demanding that you put all of them out of your mind. That was only so I could let it go too. If you was upset about something. I was just as upset too. Even if you brought it on yourself. I was always on your side. No matter what or who." He smiles.

"I just don't want our son to ever deal with any psycho ass girls," she says. They laugh and continue rewinding over their relationship, the other girls in his past and the many fights Ebony and her crew had with them.

"You was a fighting ass girl," Ajay reminds her.

"You was a P.I.M.P," she reminds him as she smiles.

He smiles and agrees. They talk about when she met April and Yolanda. His first car. Ray's assault on her and when granny Pearline died. When Ray was killed and buried. And also when he got shot and Chill and Renee too. Her car accident that took their 1st child. Her remembering Neal. Him admitting he had used cocaine. Lynn competing in the Olympics and winning. They even discussed all of the Hip Hop stars they lost during their relationship. Plus all the stars who have performed at their clubs.

"But after I came clean with you, things started to look up," he admits, "Our crew was marrying each other."

"And having babies," she adds, "We all graduated high school and college on time."

"Most of our crew went pro and we have our own businesses in two states," he says, "Just like we always said we would do it. And you know, I miss Rich, baby. Even though he was an *asshole*. I'm just glad I didn't get hooked on that shit and fuck up my dreams. I want you to know that you are the *biggest* reason I wanted to stay on point and not fuck up."

"I'm glad you got clean and stayed clean too," she says, "I thought about you every time Rich had a relapse. It's strange to think about it now. Him, granny, grandma Sally, Stoney and April are never coming back."

"Remember when you and your girls tried to go out dressed like video ho's?" he asks with a chuckle.

"I don't wanna remember that," she laughs, "But yes I do. I also remember how you handled that situation. You were so much of a man about it. I knew then that you was ready to stay with me and take care of me. I knew you was a man then and mature too. You reminded me of my father, the way you handled that whole thing."

"Oh yes. I was maturing," he says and laughs, "I knew what I wanted for my future, for sure by then. I wasn't a scared little boy no more. No more worrying about if it was gonna look cool to have a main girl or not. I knew I wanted to look out for you and take care of you. I'm doing that too. But you know I was steaming inside, at the same time. You was out there advertising *my* goods, baby. Those fools in the club was acting like wild dogs, trying to get at you."

They talk about when they first moved into their home and their wedding. Having *Mariah Carey, The O'Jays, Bone and Mo Thugs* perform. The honeymoon and them starting oral sex. Him being on the road with the *Miami Heat*. The day he bought Ike and Tina home. Her thinking she needed fertility drugs. Then finding out they were going to be parents.

"My best memory is still the day the twins came," he says with a warm smile, "Out of all the getting drafted to the NBA, making millions and all of the successful businesses we have. Still the day they came into my life is the sweetest. They changed me *forever*. I could never take a chance on losing my credibility. Not when I have to take care of them and the one on the way."

"I agree," she says, "They topped it all."

Suddenly he says, "But I have to tell you this. Tank and Rebbie are the two crew members who didn't vote for Gwen and Wingman."

"They told you?" she asks.

"Tank told me before the vote," he says, "Him and Gwen had sex in the Natty house. That same night Katrina Dobbs took advantage of me. And Rebbie had drove your car down there and found out June was out cheating. Jarvis was the one who found her. Apparently she was mad enough at June to make out with him but they didn't have sex."

"You knew this all this time?" she asks in shock.

"No," he says, "I didn't find out until the day before the vote. Tank called me and spilled it. He's suppose to try to tell Nina while they're on the lake. June don't have a clue but with the shit he was doing. I can't be mad at Rebbie. I just wish none of it had happened."

"Oh boy," she says in disbelief, "I'm glad they've moved out to the condo's then. I remember Nina telling me that Gwen better not call him Jeremy, no more. Like she's privileged. I must be the most clueless soul in this crew. Because I would've never guessed *any* of this. I thought it was two of the elders. I figured it was because they didn't want us to allow our kids to date theirs because Jarvis' parents aren't married."

"They got a house, out east and very near Mentor," Ajay reveals, "Gwen don't even know about the condo. That's just for Jarvis."

"Are you *serious*?" Ebony asks.

"I think he really likes Rebbie," Ajay says, "Since Tank told me. I've been peeping *both* of them. There's something still there, I think."

"Oh my God," Ebony says, "She hasn't said *anything* to me. Wow! I'm shocked. I was sure it was our grandparents that voted no."

"Nah," he says, "It was our crew who voted them out because of their *own* skeletons."

"You know baby," she says, "I'm not even gonna stress over any of it. Tank never told me. He wouldn't have told me nothing like *that* anyway. Not when he's married to my best friend. But Rebbie hasn't said a word either. I know she didn't want to help with their move. She didn't even think they would get married, now that I think about it. That must've been one hell of an early morning. I still haven't forgiven Katrina for her

115

assault. I don't plan to either. But *wow*! My girls have secrets that they haven't told me. You know what Anthony? That's fine. If they want me to know. They'll tell me. It's all about our life as far as I'm concerned. I've always felt like you and I would be the most *in love* couple of our generation, with no flaws or secrets. And we are. I'm not even gonna think about them and their secrets and affairs. This is *our* night and *our* anniversary. I want to spend it with us and our memories, as the discussion. I'm so proud that we was open and honest with each other, from the start."

"You *was* the perfect girlfriend. Now you're the perfect wife and mother," he says, "I'm the most blessed man in the world. At no point in our entire relationship did I *ever* worry about you being dishonest or cheating. I don't know any other man in our generation, who can say that. You've been mine forever. That means the world to me, baby."
Just then, *Prince*'s *Adore* comes on the stereo.
"This was our first song as husband and wife," he says, "May I have this dance?"

"Yes you may," she answers with a sweet smile.
They dance through the song. Kissing and groping each other, same as if they were 16 years younger, all over again. They close the subject on their crew's infidelities and vow to focus on themselves from here on out.

"Oh God. I still love it so *much* when you hold me," she says as she looks into his eyes, "You have a way of making me feel like I'm the only other human on the planet. I love the way you spoil me, Anthony."

"That's daddy to you," he says as he chuckles, "And I still love touching you so much and spoiling you too. I can't think of anything I'd rather do then to touch you. You're still the only female I've ever slow danced with or tongue kissed."

"And you for me," she says, "We were meant to be together, daddy. I knew you loved for me to call you, daddy," she giggles, "I love you, daddy. I have no doubts. No fears."

"Then *I am* the man then," he says as he smiles, "Because that's all I've ever wanted to hear you say."
They kiss and retire to bed.

TIME TO FEEL-RELOADED-Time Will Reveal part 5

CHAPTER 52

A LOVE OF HER OWN

Nina wasn't happy to hear that Tank and Gwen had slept together. Even if it was *over* 6 years ago. She told him she now knows why Gwen was calling him Jeremy, instead of Tank. It's been a couple of weeks since they went sailing. Nina had gone full stride in assisting Trina Yvette and Ebony, in getting Jarvis and Gwen's home sold back into the family and crew. Ajay and Ebony now own the house and property again. And even though Tank assured Nina that he had no feelings for Gwen. Nina still insisted he should've told her back when it first happened and not left that secret lingering. He agreed.

June and the crew are still in the dark about Rebbie's make out session. No one is ready to tackle that yet. Ebony is going to make Rebbie aware that she knows about it. But she'll do that at a later time. Jarvis and Gwen have found a new home, closed on it and will be moving into it in a few weeks. Both tried to apologize to Ebony and Ajay but neither Ebony or Ajay wanted to discuss it. They prefer to let those involved, deal with it.

Meanwhile Nickeia has finally registered at CSU. Still no one has a clue about her plans to get Ajay's attention.

****

T-baby and the *Shock* win the 2003 WNBA title. T-baby wins the MVP title as well. She's very excited about it. The crew are all on hand for her big night and team victory.

"I wanna do this *same* thing," Brina says, "I wanna play with T-baby when I come out of college."

"You're gonna be awesome, Lil sis," June says, "I'm gonna try my best to make it to every game too."
That brings a big smile to Brina's face. She knows her oldest brother is proud of her and he wants to see her name in lights, just as his name is.

"It's possible that all of mama and daddy's kids will be famous," Brina says, "You're in the NFL. Brittany got an R&B contract. Now me and my twin brother can get professional basketball contracts!"

"Brandon's game *is* tight. He can make the pro's," June says, "Imagine all of us on *Real Sports with Brian Gumbel* or *Costas now*. Then Brian Sr and Brenda James won't miss seeing us as much. Right?"

"No," Brina says, "But they'll still want us home every weekend."

"She's right, Brian," Rebbie says, "Mama is already making Archie Jr *promise* he'll come home on the weekends. Like she did with me."

"*Co-rect*," Archie Jr says with a chuckle, from where he sits.

He's in the back seat of June's Lexus with his arm around Brina. They, along with the rest of the crew, are heading home from Detroit after watching T-baby's game. They all laugh at Archie's comment. They arrive back in Cleveland within the next few minutes. June and Rebbie drive Brina and Archie home. They tell them to break up all the kissing as Brenda and Brian are pulling into the driveway too. Brina hops out and heads inside. June drops Archie Jr at home before he and Rebbie head to Jackson Heights.

Down Payne's lane, T-baby and Wesley make their intimate relationship official. After the championship game, she wanted a sex reliever. Tonight, she's spending the night at Wesley's home.

"I am twenty seven years old and you're only the second man I've had sex with," she says as they cuddle in bed.

"I hope it was memorable for you," he says smiling, "Because for me. It was off the *chain*."

"Oh yes baby," she says, "It was well worth the wait."

"You don't have to wait anymore, Trisha," he says, "I wanna marry you baby. You do know that, right?"

"Yes I do," she says, "I wanna marry you too."

"We'll make it happen," he says, "I have to keep you an honest woman. I'll propose for sure, after I speak with big Greg again. I'll do something romantic like the crew do it. You know. Then you can tell me when you're ready to say *I do*. Okay?"

"Okay Wes," she says, "I will."

They make love several times throughout the night. T-baby has been celibate for more than eighteen months. For Wes, it had been longer than that. But tonight, they *more* than make up for lost time. He was very thorough when he made love to her. They both survived abusive relationships to find each other. His wife was mentally and emotionally abusive. Rich was all of the above. And though she had real love for Rich. She'll never forget what he put her through over all of those years. Her and Wes deserve happiness in their lives. They vow to be that for 1 another.

The next day everyone drives back to the Detroit for the Shock victory celebration and parade. Then again, they all head back to Cleveland

TIME TO FEEL-RELOADED-Time Will Reveal part 5

for the nighttime celebration party, the crew are throwing for them. This is the party where things *finally* come to a head between Ebony, her girls and Katrina Dobbs.

It's already been revealed that Katrina had been a conniving and underhanded snake while they was in college at Cincinnati. She'd forced herself on Ajay while he was in an alcohol and drug induced, coma-like sleep. Everyone knew Ajay was Ebony's man. *Then* and still is now. Ebony was T-baby's closest 1st cousin and 1 of her 3 best friends *then* and nothing has changed there either. When the crew found out about the Katrina assault on Ajay. His sister Lynn, after returning from Afghanistan, had jumped Katrina at Ebony and Ajay's dinner party. Still T-baby has been promising Katrina an ass whooping for those same actions, for over a year. Katrina had slowed her role and minded her manners for this past year. She had stayed away from Ajay….., until *tonight.*

As the Shock attend their party at *The Chill Spot,* Katrina makes another 1 of those wrong moves. She spots Ajay getting on the VIP elevator. She rushes the doors and jumps on with him, just before the doors close. Leaving Ajay no time to exit. On the way up, she tries to pitch her story to him about how she really wants him to fuck her, just once while he's conscience and in his right mind. He declines instantly. He orders her to move to the other side of the elevator but she doesn't. Instead she moves closer to him. She can't resist her urges. All of sudden, she grabs his dick and attempts to massage it. Ajay shoves her so hard, she slams against the opposite side of the elevator wall. Banging her head hard enough to dazzle her and leave a crick in her neck. The thud was so loud it could be heard outside of the elevator. Even if it couldn't have been, the foursome are in Renee's office where the club audio and video camera's are routed. They witnessed the entire incident. Instantly they go into attack mode. For Ajay, this is the longest elevator ride *ever*! But he isn't done.

"Bitch! I told you to stay the fuck away from me! I don't want yo *dumb* ass!" he yells which is something he *rarely* does but he's panicked.

He can be heard outside of the elevator. Just as it's resting on the VIP floor where the foursome are heading to meet it. Ajay is livid and wants to beat her ass but that goes against *everything* he believes in. His wife would gladly do it but Ebony is *with child,* so it isn't going to happen by Ebony. He's thinking of getting his sisters to beat her ass because once again, she's violated his space. There won't even be a need for him to tell them. He had pushed her so hard that it was heard by everyone outside the elevator as it taxied to the VIP floor. The foursome had seen it on camera too. When the

119

doors open, he's still cursing at her. The foursome are standing there waiting for her ass too. When their eyes meet Katrina's, she knows they're onto her. Just by the look on their faces, it's obvious to her that their temperatures are at *400 degrees*. Ebony charges at Katrina immediately. Ajay grabs her in the nick of time. He pulls her to him. At the same time, Nina, Rebbie and T-baby pour all over Katrina and take her down to the elevator floor. They drag her out of the elevator and into the hallway where they have more room. They want enough space and an ample amount of room to kick her ass *properly*. Ebony squirms to get free from Ajay but he reminds her that she's pregnant and he isn't going to allow her to fight.

"Anthony please! Let me hit that bitch! Please!" she yells as the tears well up in her eyes.

"Your crew got that bitch covered baby," he says, not willing to let her risk anything requiring excessive physical force.

In the meantime, Nina, Rebbie and T-baby are royally whooping Katrina's ass. She doesn't stand a chance. Even if Ebony was to get loose, she wouldn't be able to get an angle to make contact with Katrina. Her girls have her covered like flies on shit. One of the assistant coaches makes it up the hallway as the fight is going into stage 2. The girls are now stomping Katrina. The coach is aware of the situation between T-baby and Katrina, as is the entire Shock team. T-baby is their marquee player and they've tried to keep things smooth. Finally the coach, with the help of Chill, Jr and a few of the other players, brings the situation to a slow simmer. But it takes a few more minutes for the foursome to stop clawing for freedom and from the clutches of those who have pulled them away.

"She had it coming, coach!" T-baby yells as she still struggles to get free. "She tried it again! I saw her do it! We *all* did! She went at him on the elevator. We all saw it and heard it too. On the office camera!"

Eventually the coach gets T-baby to calm down. The foursome and a few of T-baby's teammates who had witnessed the incident on camera, quickly confirm T-baby's accusations. Katrina is still on the floor unconscious. Renee has already called the paramedics in from outside. Jacobson's security keeps a unit stationed. The assistant coach attempts CPR but Katrina doesn't respond. Paramedics arrive as security takes statements from everyone. They tell Ajay to press charges. Initially he declines until Chill and Renee help him to see the proprietary side of it. It is not only to protect his family but his business property as well.

"It won't be in the press, superstar. Don't worry about that part," McDaniel says, "We've already arranged to have a fictitious name used."

TIME TO FEEL-RELOADED-Time Will Reveal part 5

After hearing that, Ajay files charges of sexual harassment and improper sexual contact. He also files a retraining order prohibiting her from coming within 100 yards of him or his properties. This is to include The CrewLand Mall. Katrina's aunt Deloris is on hand as the Cleveland police take statements and record charges. Deloris apologizes to the crew, once again. She promises them that her niece will no longer be around. Deloris is both embarrassed and uncomfortable. She doesn't know if she'll have a job after what her niece has done tonight. Renee assures her, they aren't going to hold her responsible for what another adult has done.

"You do your job, Miles. We haven't had any complaints on you," Renee says to her, "You're good. Just keep Katrina away from here."

"I will do everything in my power to make sure she doesn't come around," Deloris says, "Do you mind if I accompany her to the hospital? I'm her only family here in Cleveland."
Renee tells her, she can go with her family. Deloris leaves and the party continues.

CrewLand mall is building quite a ban list. Something the crew had never anticipated. The list includes; Ellen Barnes, Marvin Huntley and now Katrina Dobbs. These 3 people are never allowed on the property again. Unless *otherwise* noted by the board.

After the fight is over, Ajay nor Ebony feel much like being in a party atmosphere. They go pick up the twins from Shaker Heights and go home.

Katrina's injuries aren't life threatening but it'll be awhile before she'll play basketball again. The right wrist of her shooting hand and her left arm are both broken. Her right knee which she has already had ACL surgery on, has been twisted out of place and her left ankle is broken too. Her jaw is broken in 2 places. She has a severe nose sprain. She also has a bloody nose and 4 missing teeth. Other than that. She's fine. The girls had worked her over pretty good. They still want to do more. When Lynn, down in the Atlanta finds out. She has to have her say on it, at least.

"Good y'all whoop that ass," she says as she laughs, "We still got it ladies. All of these bitches out here better recognize. The female crew don't hold back on no scandalous ass ho's."
Katrina will remain at East General for 3 weeks. On the bright side, her family owns a flower shop outside of the UC campus now. Her hospital room stays loaded with gifts and flowers. Not 1 gift, get well card or memento was sent by the crew. They don't give a damn if she heals or dies.

TIME TO FEEL-RELOADED-Time Will Reveal part 5

On the last day of September, Rich III turns 8 years old. Him, T-baby, Richaunda, Wes and Jada go visit Rich Jr's grave. Tomorrow will be a year since his suicide. Rich III and Richaunda have grown close in this past year. They carry on like siblings do. Rich III is very protective of her. His aunt Ruthie tells him that's exactly the way his daddy was with her. Rich Jr would never let anyone harm his little sister. Rich III takes that to heart. He decides that's how he wants to be with his soon-to-be 4 year old sister. He's a straight A, 2nd grade student. He gets along great with Wes, who is going to officially become his stepfather next year. Wes keeps Rich Jr's name alive with his son. He has gone as far as having the *New York Jets* to send both of the kids pictures of Rich Jr. Most of them, the crew hadn't even seen so that was a delight. The Jets make a scrapbook for Rich's kids and sent them all of his original jerseys, helmets, cleats and even his practice gear too. The Jets organization has been kind enough to let Rich III have his father's original game helmet. Rich III's playroom is close to being a shrine of his father. All because Captain Wesley Stewart thought he needed to see the better side of his dad. He doesn't want the last day of Rich's life to be the only thing his son has to remember him by. T-baby loves Wes even more for being so thoughtful.

"I'm a man, baby," Wes says, "If somehow I wasn't able to be in my daughter's life and I left her tragically. I would want someone to do this for me and make sure she knows that her daddy wasn't always like that."

"It would never be hard to find the good things you've done, Wes," T-baby says, "You're a treasure. I really mean that. You saved my life, *so* many times and in so many ways since you came into it. I love you."

"I love you too," he says as he thanks her with a sweet kiss while they're working together in the office at *Williams Accounting and Finance*. T-baby finally feels like she has the kind of love she's always dreamed about. The kind of love that her 1st cousin Ebony has, in Ajay.

Minutes later, Ajay pulls right up into the fire zone in front of the dual office doors of *Jackson's Real Estate Banking & Investments and Williams Accounting & Finance*. Only thing is, no one recognizes it's him. Security is rolling up in the trolley cart to ask the driver to please vacate the fire zone. That's when Ajay jumps out with a huge smile on his face.

"What's good, Joiner?" he asks while still sporting a huge smile. "I know y'all didn't know this was me because you're looking like you was about to give me the business. I know y'all was," he says, "Was you about to write me a ticket? Because if you was. This baby here is in my wife's name. Not mine."

TIME TO FEEL-RELOADED-Time Will Reveal part 5

He laughs as they shake hands and the security guys acknowledge him.

"Ah man. This is *gorgeous*," Joiner says, "Did she know this was coming?"

"I told her I wanted to upgrade her but she didn't know *when*," Ajay says, "And I haven't mentioned it anymore since fourth of July."

"This baby is crowning, man. Pearling paint job. Platinum package. All leather and.., Are those the new heated *seats*?" Joiner asks.

"Air conditioned too," Ajay tells him, "She's got navigation in it, six DVD screens, Reverse camera so she can see behind her. It might be a bathtub back there too. I don't know."

He has a grin on his face like the cat that swallowed the canary. He has bought an extravagant surprise gift for his wife. This morning he'd asked her if he could drive her Escalade and he would take the twins to daycare while she drove his Mercedes to work. She agreed, though she suspected he was up to something. She'd asked him as much but he wouldn't give her a clue. What he'd done was took the twins to Granny's House. Then he went directly to the Cadillac dealership to trade in her 2000 model for the 2004 model which he'd had lots a extras added to, back when he'd paid for it.

"What size wheels are those?" Bronson asks.

"Twenty two's. They're going bigger now, man," Ajay says, "Only the best for my Queen. She *is* married to the man. *Alright*?!!"

Wes has walked out to see what the commotion is and sees the new SUV.

"Uh oh. Do I need to step my Cadillac game up?" he asks with a chuckle.

He has a 2001 Escalade, powder blue with 3 monitors and a gold package.

"It's twenty two's and platinum now, man," Joiner says.

"And Navigation without the Navigator," Bronson chuckles.

Ajay goes in to get Ebony while T-baby and Claudia come out to check out the new caddy. Ajay goes into Ebony's office and tries to pull a fast one.

"I need to pick up my car and get to practice, baby," he says as he walks around her desk to give her a kiss and she frowns.

"Is my breath humming?" he asks with a smile.

She laughs and says, "No but you was driving my car. How are you gonna take your car?"

"You don't have a car. You have an S-U-V baby," he says, "You and my babies ride *big*."

"Well whatever," she says with a smile, "You know what I meant. What am I suppose to drive?"

"Your S-U-V. It's out here. Come on," he says.

She follows him out into the lobby. She notices Claudia isn't at her desk. Before she can ask a question. Claudia, T-baby and Wes come back in and they're grinning like the guilty.

"What's going on?" Ebony asks, "What are y'all up to? All of y'all grinning. My husband is grinning. Security is outside grinning."

"Go outside, cousin. You're gonna be grinning too. Big time, boss lady!" T-baby yells and laughs aloud.

Ebony walks out the door and gazes at the Escalade parked in the fire zone. It's the same color as hers but that's it. Everything else looks different. She already knows it's hers, as she smiles.

"Daddy it looks great. What all did you have done?" she asks.

Ajay and security laugh.

"That's not the same Escalade, misses Jackson," Joiner says.

"No ma'am, it's not," Bronson adds, "He upgraded you to the two thousand and four model. He got you sitting fat on the first day these came out, miss lady. You got yours before most did because he had to have gotten it a few months back to have all this stuff added by release day."

Ajay nods. Ebony loves her new vehicle.

"My *new* caddy from daddy, ha?" she says as she grins too.

She laughs as she puts her arms around Ajay and gives him a big kiss. She says, "Thank you, daddy. It's beautiful."

"Nothing but the best for my wife and kids," he says, "I told you that. Now can I get a ride?"

"Sure," she says as she reaches for the door.

"No. Not that ride," he says.

She smiles. He wraps her up in his arms.

"Why don't you grab what you need for today," he suggests, "And let's head home."

"You don't have practice?" she asks.

"Not until seven," he says, "So what's up?"

Without hesitation, she heads back inside to grab a few files from her desk. She grabs her purse and her keys to his Benz and heads back out the door.

"Claudia can you lock up today? I'm going home, ear-"

"--Big boss lady. You know I got you," Claudia says with a snazzy smile. "Go get your naptime in," she says as she bats her eyelashes.

Ebony grins. She leaves her office and returns to Ajay's side. He has made preparations with Bronson and Joiner to get his Benz to Jackson Heights. She finds him waiting on the passenger side of her new Escalade, with bedroom eyes. She puts her set of keys to his Benz in her Attaché case and

124

hops into the drivers seat of her new caddy truck. Ajay hits the wireless key remote and starts the vehicle up. Then he puts the key in the ignition. It has to be in there before the truck will go into gear.

"This is *so* neat," she says, almost dazed.

"New anti theft system," he says, "You're worth it baby."

His stare which is fixed on her, is one of *anticipation*. She smiles, knowing this look *too* well. They head home. He slides the passenger seat to the center position and starts kissing on her neck while he finger fucks her, all the way to Jackson Heights.

She's so turned on by the time she pulls her new caddy truck towards the garage, that she wants to go for it right there on the driveway. He'd remembered to get the garage door opener out of the 2000 truck. He lets the door up to the bay where she usually parked the old one. He isn't ready to get their kind of moisture on her state of art seats. The seats are wired for heat and air. No doubt too much moisture can electrocute them both. He isn't willing to chance that. Not with the way he knows her waterfall of orgasms to be. Surely that would be their lovemaking swan song. He kills the engine for her and demands that she leave everything in the SUV. Then he meets her around at her driver's door and carries her inside. They make it as far as the kitchen before he rips away her clothing and sits her on the low end of the counter. He lays her back and lets her hair swing down to the inside of her crescent shaped kitchen island.

"I had this counter put in for this very reason," he whispers as he pulls her up and nibbles on her ear.

She purrs. He lays her back again. She thought he had designed the counters this way for when they had kids. So the kids would be able to reach up and place their dishes on the counter. But with what they've done on this counter since the house was built. Surely he wouldn't let them near it. The counter comes up even to his groin. *"Perfect for fucking,"* he'd said. He pokes his fingers in and out of her pussy. She purrs louder. Her voice is impatient. She needs to unleash her churning honey that his actions are causing to brew inside of her. He gets up on his toes so he can watch her facial expressions to what he's doing. Her head still dangles to the inside of the crescent shaped countertops. Satisfied that she's good and ready, he moves her thong to the side, goes down on his knees and sticks his tongue in nectar alley.

"Oh *God!*" she screams.

She feels a rush of heat move through her body like a riptide. Pushing everything out of the way and opening her all the way up to her man. He

125

flings her legs over each of his shoulders. Rips her thong off and dives in deeper. He can sense that she's *so anxious*. Ajay is on a mission of pleasure and it isn't even noon. Ebony knows this is going to be another wonderful day in *Mr. Raw Dick's* neighborhood. When she's pregnant, her hormones are always overactive. Her senses more keen. Her sex drive full on and her body temperature stays slightly higher than normal. Her breast swell to the size of casaba melons painted caramel brown. Her nipples which he thoroughly wets, stretches to the size of small dollies. Or the antique coasters that use to sit on granny's coffee table. Diameter reaching 3 inches easily. He simply devours them on a daily basis. Rather it's during sex, when she's driving or when they're just watching TV. Which eventually leads to sex. He loves the extra thickness of her pregnant body. Right now he's busy at her south end. He's making her moan in harmonies that turn him on even more. He sucks her clitoris until she explodes. He quickly sops up all of the evidence. Then he stands to his feet and rushes his rock hard dick into her. It's like he has a schedule to keep. He isn't allowing time for the slightest break.

"Ooooh daddy," she purrs.

"Uh huh," he grunts, glad to hear that she's enjoying him.

Her sweet sexy whispers of approval give him the energy to pump his ass like he's on automatic. She's speaking many more words than what's coming out as coherent words. In her mind, she knows how good she feels. But his rhythms won't allow her to translate it. At least not in English. In Tibet, perhaps her speech could be deciphered.

"Baby this pregnant pussy is *extra* good," he says, "This shit is so hot. *Oh!*" He isn't going to tire anytime soon. *The man* can lend out 2 inches of dick and still be working with 12 *solid* inches. The slightest hint that she's protesting or complaining about pain. Will only cause him to pick up the pace and fuck her harder. She just dangles there. *Purring*. Gasping and yelping until she feels climax number 2 approaching. She could never understand how he could be hurting her and making her cum at the same time. Maybe she likes pain in the pussy area. That *has* been her sexual norm. This big dick man she's married to is the same man who, as a boy started her on this sexual journey. He has only grown an inch more since that beginning. And there have been no other passengers for her ride, in between. He's the lone rider. The *Lone ranger* to her *Tonto*. The answer to her prayers. Still she can't throw her ass back to him against the pain he's delivering right next to the pleasure. She can't slang her hips against this dick. Not the way he demands her too. He knows she can't now and never could. But he gets more aggressive because she can't handle his giant and acts like she's afraid of it. It's a game he always wins. That's the rouser in this *fucking* rebel. He's going to fuck his wife well. He'll get his nut some 5 to 10 minutes later. After she's cried and tears have rolled up her forehead into her hair and dripped onto the kitchen floor. Since she's afraid to test her limits. He pulls her hips to him as he stirs in her pussy with his 14 inch spoon. She's always down for pleasing her man. He knows he can have his way with her by this stage in their lives. He's given her 2 fully loaded orgasms. She's his playground now and he rules the monkey bars at this park. He beats the insides of her vagina relentlessly. As he talks *much* shit.

"My baby's gonna know who daddy is," he says, "Ain't that right, my sweet ass baby."

He's down right arrogant with it. He knows she isn't going to answer. He just drills her harder and says she's being disobedient for not answering him. But he knows she's got nothing left. Not even the strength to speak. This is her life. The same man who spoils her, protects her and loves her. Has something to prove when he fucks her. And whatever it is he's seeking. He's certainly deep enough in her pussy right now, to find it.

"There's something inside this pussy…, that feels so *good* to the head of my *dick*, baby," he growls, "What's that? Ha? What's that? What's that? Cause I know it ain't no diaphragm *now*."

He asks her over and over. She can't answer. It feels like he's going into her womb. The womb which his unborn infant is presently occupying. The head of his dick is actually poking her cervix but he's loving the feeling. She's trying to back flip over the counter just to get away from his steel rod. If she was being held hostage in a terrorist prison camp and she had secret government information like her sister-in-law Lynn. She would sell America out to get this dick to cum. Or just pull out. But in daddy's prison, there is no reprieve. He pounds her until his nut crawls up the back of his legs. Over his ass. Up his back and leaps over his shoulder. She holds his arms and pulls herself up enough to see his face. She can tell his climax is toying with him at *her* expense. He's grimacing like there's a spot inside of her which is reserved for him and he's trying to get to it. His nut is moving down his chest. He starts to chop his words and gasp for breathe.

Oh God! I think he's found his cranny!

That nut has just crossed his navel. It's easing down to his groin area and finally, it creeps into his hard as a steel pipe dick. Then it slides aggressively into his nut sack.

"Oh *shit* yes!" he yells out as he feels his nut pushing to escape. He's all in and ready to blow. She lets her head fall back to dangling. It's all over now except for the big bang of the explosion. She had been a casualty of daddy's sex war, 15 minutes ago. All escapes had been blocked off. She has to hang on until the high tide of cum comes, washes her down stream and lays him down on top of her.

"Damn! *Oooo* shit! Ah yes!" he yells.

His nut had taken the long *fucking* route but it finally finds it's way to the tip of his whipping rod and escapes into her tunnel. Taking his pounding and hard thumping of her pussy walls with it. He kisses and suckles her nipples. As he descends slowly back to the man who cuddles with her and protects her from any hurt or harm. His nut is offloaded. She feels heavier as if his nut weighs 10 pounds. She's spent and is ready for a nap. But she has no energy left to make it to the bedroom. She thanks God Ajay has enough energy left to carry her to bed. Because she certainly doesn't feel like she can move. Not even a muscle.

Now that they no longer hear bombs dropping. Ike and Tina jump back through their doggy doors and follow daddy down the hall while he carries mommy, cradled like a baby. They're use to this scene and well trained for it by now.

God. Don't ever let them learn to speak human. Because they would have much to tell.

He lays her down on the bed.

"Are you thirsty?" he asks.

"Yes."

He gives her a bottle of apple juice from their wet bar's mini fridge before going to get her things from her new truck.

He puts her work things on her desk, in her home office. He gets her some ice chips from the sub zero, then joins her in bed.

"We can nap now," he says while kissing her lips, "I'll go get the twins from school before practice. You sleep, baby."

Sir yes sir!

Okay to that. He faces her with 1 arm bracing her neck. The other draped over her waist. She buries her forehead in his chest to hear his heartbeat. She drifts into dreamland. He holds her. Planting sweet kisses from her lips to her forehead. She doesn't know what the rest of the world are doing. But it's a wonderful and satisfying day in *Mr. Raw Dick's* neighborhood.

128

TIME TO FEEL-RELOADED-Time Will Reveal part 5

The next day is the anniversary of Richard Williams Jr's death. In his honor, the crew hold a special candlelight ceremony for the entire day at CrewLand mall. Each guest who patronizes is asked to light a candle and place it out on the wall under the crosswalk.

Today is also the day Chill and the guys in the crew will meet with Joe, Woody, Andre and Pac Man. At Chill's 34th birthday party back in June, Andre and Joe had made him aware of the contract purchased by Marvin Huntley. He knows Marvin has plans of taking him out of the game of life before his namesake turns 20 years old. Marvin wants Matt killed before Thanksgiving. Chill before Christmas eve. Chill had called him the holiday contractor and laughed.

"What it is though Chill? This dude is worried about his bitch spending time with you and Matt," Andre says, "He figures she got plans with one of y'all for the holidays and he wants to spoil it."

"He won't be spoiling shit for me," Chill says, "I don't fuck wit her. *Period*. That bitch fucked my son while she was still his teacher. We got her on tape, giving him head in her car right out there in the parking lot."
The guys from the Westside, shake their heads and laugh.

"He's gonna be back home in Pittsburgh when it happens. He hopes she'll come running home when the first dude gets popped," Joe says.
Woody has finally gotten enough rank that he can speak now.
He says, "Dude don't even have a clue that we're loyal to you and crew. I've been admiring y'all all of my life and didn't even know it until this summer. My granny use to live in the point before she died. We lived with her. My mama got strung out on crack after my little brother was born. Then she went to jail and got killed while she was in there. So we stayed on with grandma, after that. Junior, Stoney and Rob use to come to granny's house and bring all of us a plate on the fourth of July. He'd come all the way from Shaker Heights. But after grandma died and we couldn't pay the bills. The state sent us to live with relatives in Toledo."

"I had got crewed up by then," Jr says, "Daddy started letting me drive back when I was like eleven. That's cause I was tall and could see over the steering wheel. Stoney was fifteen and Rob was fourteen. You're the same age as the foursome, right? Our grandparents use to send us out there to feed you, your sister and brother. And your grandma too. You use to have that fucking *Freddy Kruger* mask and shit. It was nowhere *near* Halloween. Little Woody would be running around scaring people like *Nightmare on Elm street*. He had all the kids out there, calling him Freddy."
They all laugh.

"And we lived on Elm street too," Woody says and smiles, "I wanna say thank you though man. Cause all that food you use to bring us. We would make that shit last for like a week or two. And then y'all granny and her husband, the music teacher, fed us most of the rest of the year."
The guys in the crew nod. They know there are many folks in Cleveland loyal to them for doing things that came natural to them. Things they were reared to do. *Love thy neighbor and harvest your village.* What Woody is grateful to them for. Is nothing out of their character. It's basic survival and taking care of your own. What had helped the 1st generation of their crew survive. Had been past down to them. That's what the Cleveland crew are best known for. Not the street game which they managed to perfect while not becoming a victim of it. Chill tells them a bit more about Farah.

"She's a trifling muthafucka, black. As *Baby* would say it. 'We had to bake a cake for her ass,' a long time back. Damn near since the day she got to Cleveland. My wife's been wanting to kill her, about our son anyway. That just might be possible. She might get her chance. But I wanna make this Marvin *muthafucka really* feel me. We're gonna need Farah, in order to do that. I'm talking about what the crew calls, *Crew Thangs.*"
He begins to tell them the game plan and how it will play out. His plan will reel Marvin Huntley into their trap and give them reason to revisit;
The Chamber.

"*Cake already been baked, Whoadie,*" Tank adds, imitating the *Cash Money Millionaires* as they all chuckle.

"Let's get it *poppin,*" Ajay adds, "I'm sick o' his bitch ass."

****

Archie Jr turns 18 on October 4th and registers to vote like all of the crew before him had done. Voting is a must for the crew. Their elders had instilled this in them from birth. The right to vote was the thing which had initially brought them all together. Each time a new crew member registers, it's something to celebrate. Archie Jr heads to *Crew Gear* to see his mother and let her know he's registered. They're on the subject of politics when he starts asking them who he should vote for in next year's Presidential election. Though *Mosley Braun* and *Al Sharpton* are in the race. *Howard Dean* is the early front runner for the Democrats. There's still over 8 months to go before a final nominee will be picked to represent at the DNC. *John Edwards* and *John Kerry* show a lot of promise. As does *Richard Gephardt.* But Archie Jr has a problem with his name.

"Gephardt is not a Presidential name. Not to me," he says.

"The name has nothing to do with the ability," Rena says.

"And what name *is* presidential?" Belinda asks.

"Bush hasn't been a people's president so the name doesn't matter," Rena adds to stress her point to her son. "Him nor his father was the type of presidents who made strides for *all* Americans. We want these republicans out. The sooner the better."

"You never know what kind of name our president will have by the time Bush gets through messing up," Sandy says, "We would elect a Dikembe Mutumbo or a Hector Ramirez if they came with something hopeful. As desperate as we feel nowadays. Anything is better than this rubber stamp government we have now."

They laugh hard. Rena and the ladies at Crew Gear are finish with the dresses for Erica's huge wedding which is 6 days away. They have their hands full with all the items they have to inventory and deliver to the church on the 10th. Every member of each generation will do something in this crew wedding.

Two days later and all of the final preparations are done. The flowers arrive and the mothers decorate *First Baptist Church*, for Jo and Al's 4th child and 3rd daughter's wedding. She's the 1st member of the crew to marry outside of the blood crew family since Chill, Jr and Bre. Eric's family have come in from Chicago to help get them settled into their home in Jackson Heights. They're next door to Nina and Tank but on the opposite side as T-baby, who's behind Ajay. Eric and Erica's house is directly across the street from Rebbie and June's. Their homes are the 1st ones along each side of CrewLand drive. The 1st to be seen after coming into the entry gate. This has been a busy week for Erica already. Tomorrow is her bridal shower. All of the ladies are anticipating the fun while the guys are planning to spoil it. Which is *still* a long standing crew tradition. It's a usual crew ritual that takes place before each wedding. Venitia is thrilled to be a bridesmaid and to participate in her 1st crew wedding. She's walking with Jarvis. Gwen wasn't asked to be a bridesmaid. Nickeia wants to make a big deal out of it but Gwen doesn't allow her too.

****

Marvin is spending the majority of his days trying to figure out how he'll approach Farah in Cleveland for the 3rd time. Satisfied that he

TIME TO FEEL-RELOADED-Time Will Reveal part 5

has killers in place to remove his competition. He's moved on to phase 2 of his plan. Which is to get his girl back. But first, he has to find her residence. He decides to wait for her to leave MLK, then follow her home.

On the 1st day he tries to follow her. He gets caught at a red light and loses her. He had to stay at a safe distance because she knows his Porsche. The next day he follows her from 4 cars behind. She turns into CrewLand mall and ruins his plan again. He isn't permitted on the property since his last altercation. He tries staking out her car from a neighboring property but it's too far to get a good visual. He gives up and goes back to his condo. He had rented from the newest condominium complex in the city. Which just happens to be the same condominiums that are owned by the crew. He isn't going to give up looking for his lost love's home. He'll follow her at every opportunity he gets until he's successful.

****

Kenny drives home from school today. It's the Tuesday before Erica's wedding. He isn't home to stay. He only came to show his crew the gift he'd gotten and to have his father drive him back to Ohio State. Kenny Jr comes home driving a brand new 2004 *GMC Denali*. He pulls into CrewLand Mall and up to the front of The Chill Spot. Before security can asks him to move. He jumps out and quickly lets them know who he is. He had called his father in advance and asked him to meet him outside. Chill joins them within seconds. He looks at the new sport utility vehicle his junior is driving and shakes his head. Then he smiles initially.

"Farah is pulling out all stops, ha?" he finally says.

"How did you know?" Kenny asks.

"How could I *not* know?" he answers, "She's gonna make your mama hurt her *real* bad, if she don't back off."

"This truck is *for* my mama," Kenny Jr says as they all laugh.
Farah had gone down to Ohio State over the past weekend. She went to deliver the 2004 Denali she'd purchased for Chill. She put it in him and Kenny's name. Chill didn't know his name was on the title until now.

"Oh hell no!" he says, "She's really trying to push my wife over the edge. But you know why? To make my home *unhappy* and slow down my ability to get good loving. I'm gonna bake this cake a bit faster. *Shit*."
Chill adds an option to the plan he has for Marvin Huntley. But the plan still calls for Marvin to know where Farah lives.

"Come on in, son," he says, "Gotta get some things finished first.
132

Then I can drive you back. But only if your mama says it's okay."

They laugh as they go inside the club to find Renee.

Renee is on a phone call with Chaundra, who is still at Ohio state. She's upset and crying to Renee that Kenny has to be seeing someone else. According to Chaundra, the word on campus is that Kenny has a new girlfriend.

"Everybody is saying they saw him driving a new S-U-V with a white girl in the passenger seat," Chaundra tells Renee in between sniffles.

"I don't know who it is, Chaundra," Renee says, "But Kenny is still with you. He hasn't told me about any other girl. So there *isn't* one."

"He's not answering his phone," she tells Renee, "And he left the apartment early this morning, for class. I haven't seen nor heard from him since. I'm so tired of him messing around on me."

Renee talks to Chaundra until she's calm. Just about that time, her husband and son knock on her office door. She tells them to enter. They come in quietly and Renee continues her call with Chaundra.

"He's not off with no white girl," she tells Chaundra, "He just walked into my office with his father."

"Ask him why won't he answer his phone," she says to Renee.

Renee tells her to hold on while she checks things out. She puts the line on hold.

"Kenny this is Chaundra on the phone," Renee says, "What's going on with you?"

"I got a new S-U-V, mama," he says, "And I didn't have to pay nothing for it."

"Son *nothing* is free in this world. I told you that," she says, "Now who did you get the vehicle from? Because I know you're not allowing those alumni to ruin your future."

"Alumni didn't buy it, ma. It was one of my fans who bought it," he says with a chuckle as Chill looks at the floor.

"Kenny," Renee says as she gives him an impatient look.

"Honey," Chill breaks in, "Farah bought this boy a two thousand and four G-M-C Denali."

"*What*?! Oh hell no, Kenneth!" she yells, "I've told you. I don't want that grown ass woman messing with my son."

"She's not ma," Kenny Jr tries, "She's been promising me a car since I graduated."

"Kenny I don't want you sleeping with…., with,…*her*," Renee says as she tries to slow her breathing and not use foul language.

"I'm *not* mama, I promise you," he says, "I told Chaundra I wasn't messing round with Farah. But she don't believe me."

"I wouldn't *either*. She bought you a S-U-V," Renee says, "If she ain't getting with you anymore. Then she's gonna want too."
Chill is still trying to get a word in but Renee has barely stopped fussing to breathe. She's so irritated she forgets Chaundra is on the phone. She storms out of her own office and heads to the elevator. Chill follows her. Kenny grabs her phone and takes Chaundra off hold.

"Hello," he says.

"Kenny why didn't you ask if I wanted to go home with you?" she asks, "I've been calling you all day."

"I figured you would be mad if you knew I had the truck," he says, "And if you knew who bought it. I didn't want to argue all the way home."

"Who bought the truck, Kenny? Are you still *fuckin* Farah?" she asks as she yells into the speaker phone, "I thought you said that stopped in High School?"

"It did."

"Then why is she buying you a Denali?" she asks.

"Baby she wants my pops," he says, "She *always* did."

"How are you gonna do that to your mama?"

"I ain't doing nothing to my mama," he says, "We got a plan and I can't let you in on the crew plan. You just have to trust me baby. I'm giving this truck to my mama, if she wants it."
Chaundra wants to believe him but her heart is aching. She feels betrayed. While Kenny is calming her down, Renee is coming back up the elevator with Chill, hot on her trail. She's just seen the new Denali outside. But not only that, Chill has told her what motivated Farah to buy it.

"She wants me, Renee," Chill had told her, "She wanted me from jump. You knew that. I told you. We're baking a cake for her. We're gonna get all the bread out of her, she wants to spend in the process."

"Kenneth I'm not going along with you fuckin that bitch!" Renee screams as she heads back into the office.

"That bitch bought you a truck so she could fuck with your father, son?" Renee yells, "Is that what you was coming up here to tell me? Are you really okay with something like that?"

"No ma'am. Daddy's not either, ma," he says, "You know I would never allow *no* junk like that. It's just all in the plan. I wouldn't even speak to pops if he was really going after her. Or any other female. Mama you know that. Don't you?"

"I don't know either one of y'all no more," Renee says, "I'm not going to be okay with neither of you fuckin that tramp. I don't care *what* the plan is."

"And neither am I," Chaundra says from the speaker phone.

"It ain't nothing, Chaunny," Kenny says, "I told you the truth. My mama just found out what she was up too. That's why she's screaming. I just came to Cleveland to bring the vehicle to my parents. So she can't try to take it back once she knows me nor my pops don't want her."

"Who's name is it in?" Renee asks.

Kenny Jr shows her the title. It has both he and his fathers name on it.

"And daddy said we was gonna put it in you and Destiny's name," he says.

"Exactly baby," Chill adds, "Or we can sell it if you want too."

"No don't sell it," Kenny disagrees, "I wanna drive that truck. Me and Chaunny going out in style on that white bitch's purse."

"Watch your mouth, son," Renee and Chill say simultaneously.

Chill wouldn't have said anything, had they not been in Renee's presence. And Kenny was doing what came natural around his father. He wouldn't dream of letting his mother hear him talk like that. It's just that his adrenaline is pumping right now. He wants to keep the 2004 Denali and he's trying to talk upon that as fast as he can. Renee finally tells Chill to get their son back to college in time for his evening practice. Chill calls Wes and ask him to ride with them. He says yes.

They leave for Ohio State while Renee and T-baby stand outside watching them as they pull away.

135

CHAPTER 53

THE EXTRACTION OF SWEET RAY

It's 3 days before Erica and Eric's wedding. She's so nervous, she's having trouble breathing. Tonight is her bridal shower. Everything for her wedding day is ready and waiting for her to walk down the aisle. The dresses are done. The tuxedo's are rented and the crews from Atlanta, Boston, Oklahoma, Chicago and Houston have arrived. Tonight the mothers have to usher the guys away from The Spot II so the ladies can have Erica's bridal shower in peace. The guys aren't going to be able to crash this bridal shower either. Thanks to Jo and the ladies who also introduce Eric McNair's mother Jillian, as the newest crew mom.

"It's ladies night!" Lynn yells as they kick off the bridal shower for her 2nd youngest sister.
Lynn, Nina and Ebony will be matrons of honor for Erica this Friday. While Jo and Al's youngest child Pam will be the maid of honor.

Ajay and the guys go to Stoney's for drinks and fun. They tease Eric for most of the evening, about his upcoming nuptials. Eric isn't phased by it at all.

"I'm ready, man," he tells Jb, "I'm *definitely* ready."

"I know you'd *better* be," Ajay says as he laughs. "Because Erica is *no* joke. She's spoiled just like the rest of my sisters and my mama too. All the crew women are spoiled, brother-in-law. They have to be though. That's how we do it in this family."

"Amen to that," Sam Jr agrees.
He and Pam are planning to be the next in line to get married. Their taking the house across the street from Ajay and Ebony. Jarvis and Gwen's 1st home. Steven and Ally, Reaper and Brittany are also talking marriage but neither have proposed or bought rings yet. They're just *talking* about it.

"Well I'm happy with my life," June says with a chuckle. "I'm doing things the right way now man and I miss my homeboys."
Ajay doesn't comment. He knows about Rebbie's kissing session with Jarvis. He suspects it's been more. He also knows June had an affair which started before he'd even married Rebbie. So he feels all is fair at this point. Chill knows it too. He decides to keep the homeboy talk going.

"Ah man me too," Chill says, "It's not a day that passes that I don't think about Stoney and Rich."

"Yea man," Jb starts, "I think about all the dirt we did over the years too. We did some major damage around these parts."

They all laugh as Kilo adds, "I definitely think about that shit."
Him and Justine are still living in Jr and Tonya's old house on Union street. Which was originally Stoney's house, across the street from Mrs. Green. They've made plans to get married, sometime next year.

"I will never forget all the times y'all came to Houston," Ron says, "None of em! We just clicked from day one, Fam!"
They agree with Ron and laugh.

"We hit it off like we was family, from day one," Jr adds, "Shit don't get no realer than that."

"Like brothers," Rob adds.

"We're gonna go on forever as family go," Ajay says, "We're all successful and got families. Well, most of us."
They all laugh again. That was a stab at the brothers who aren't married with children.

"It won't be long before all of us are settled down," Corey adds.
He has become more of a fixture with the crew, at gatherings and all. Him and Mya are still dating. Mya was even invited to Erica's bridal shower.

"Though I was against this whole relationship at first," Greg Jr finally says to Eric. "After getting to know you Eric. Man you're a good dude. I think Erica will be happy with you."
He proposes a toast. As the glasses clank together, they all cheer and yell, *"Bottoms up crew!"*
Al and John serve up the drinks and food as the other fathers stroll in, 2 by 2.

"Is this the pre-bachelor party?" Bradley Sr asks with a loud laugh.

"Yea!" they all yell back.

"Then pour me up one!" Sam Sr yells, "I ain't driving."
The guys are rowdy early. They pretty much forget about their plans to crash the bridal shower. They wouldn't have gotten past big mama and Annabelle anyway.

"Forget about trying to break the shower up, *this* time," Ajay says, "Let em have their fun. We're having our fun too. We ain't never got into *none* of their showers and y'all know why."

"Because Eloise and her crew are the bodyguards," poppa says.
Stoney's is packed with the crew men and they're very jolly. From papa Jackson Brown, the oldest. Right down to the twin, Brandon. The youngest of the active crew. The youngest kids are at the shower with the ladies.

"Man I can't believe my son is old enough to party with me," Chill says as he laughs. "My son will be twenty years old this Christmas!"

Kenny holds up his drink to toast his father and all the guys join in. Afterwards, big Al has to get off a joke.

"Damn Chill. It's about time for you to join *our* crew," he says.

There is a huge burst of loud and rowdy laughter. Chill grabs his side as he laughs. He has been expecting 1 of them to say that since Kenny left for college.

"Yea I know," Chill says as he still laughs. "But y'all don't get down like my crew."

"Man y'all just took up where we left off," grandpa Joshua says, "Each generation just went with the times."

"And went a little farther too," grandpa Charles adds.

"Yes indeed," poppa says, "Now you watch how this next generation is gonna jump off."

"Yes sir, "Jr says, "Because my junior will be crewed up by this time next year."

"Man you're getting old too," Ajay says to Jr.

They erupt with laughter again. The guys are having a wonderful time. There is no more mention about crashing Erica's bridal shower.

Meanwhile the females are having a great time too. They have gotten pass the traditional gifts and the gifts for the home. The male strippers just left and their party is getting more rowdy as Lynn, Bre and Kim dance on the tables, imitating the strippers. The ladies are laughing nearly as loud as the men next door. Big mama and Annabelle had taken up all of the cell phones from all of the ladies. They're determined nothing but emergency calls are going to get through. Big mama has alerted Ebony that if Ajay tries calling her. He won't get through either.

"Not unless he's in one place and one of his limbs is in another," Jo adds as they all laugh.

"I don't even wanna think about nothing like that," Ebony says.

Suddenly a call comes in which qualifies as an emergency. Ebony receives an urgent phone call from Mr. Parkwood. Big mama allows her to take the call. She walks out of the 1st floor dance area and out into the hallway near concessions, so she can hear.

"Hello," she says, still giggling from big mama's teasing.

"Hi Ebony. This is Parkwood," he says.

"Yes I know. How are you?" she asks, "You got another *great* deal for me?"

"Not exactly," he says, "I have a situation with the land we acquired in Ann Arbor. I don't wanna alarm you but I think it's something you should hear from me."

"Yes. What is it?" she asks, "Is there a problem with clearing it?"

"Yes I'd say there is," he says, "They dug up three bodies, two days ago out there."

"Oh my *God*, mister Parkwood," she says, at a lost for more words. He continues, "They ran test on one of them. They say it's that kid. The one that's been missing from Ann Arbor State since nineteen ninety one. Raymond White. The kid from Houston who tried to assault you, twelve years ago."

Ebony feels weak. She can't speak another word. Parkwood continues to share the news, feeling she had no idea Raymond was already dead.

How can this be?

She never knew what had happened to his body. Nor where it had been taken and buried. None of the guys had ever revealed that fact to her. The guys who had taken the body to dispose of it. Never mentioned it again. Of all the land in all of the United States of America. Her and Mr. Parkwood had purchased Raymond White's *gravesite*! She passes out and falls to the floor in the lobby of The Spot II.

At Stoney's the guys are partying it up. They're drinking shots and chasing them with beer. It's almost like the real bachelor party but that's still 2 nights away. Their designated drivers are on hand. Corey is 1 of those picked to drive his crew family home. So is Steven, Archie Jr and soon-to-be 17 year old twin, Brandon James.

"Hey Brandon. Have you been driving for a year yet?" Ajay asks as the others prepare for his humor and Brandon tells him yes.

"I'll take my chances getting home, man," Ajay says, "I've driven drunk more times than you've driven. *Ever!*"

They all share another laugh. Brandon goes to Ajay and puts his hand out. He says, "Give them up, cousin-in-law. I've been waiting *all* year for this."

Ajay hands him the keys to the Benz and shakes his head.

"Try to wreck it so baby girl will let me upgrade it," he says as he chuckles.

His cell phone rings. It's from Ebony's phone. He answers to someone who sounds like big mama on the other end. There is panic in her voice. He heads out the door and towards The Spot II without even hearing what she has called for. She talks. He walks then runs. He runs to the door, flings it open and spots his wife sprawled out on the floor with at least 6 ladies trying to revive her.

"Ajay. Ebony fainted," big mama says, "We don't know what happened. Doctor Weston needs us to move her to a comfortable place."

Before she can finish talking, Ajay is inside the lobby and runs straight to the pile that is his wife. Several of the men have followed him over. Ajay picks Ebony up and takes her on the elevator and up to Tank's office. She comes around as he's laying her down on the leather couch, inside of Tank's plush office.

"Are you okay, baby?" he asks.

"No! Raymond's back! He's back, Anthony!" she yells, sounding as if she's just awakened from a nightmare.

"Raymond's back?! *What*? Baby he's dead. He's not coming back," Ajay tells her as he props a pillow under her head.

Chill, Ron and Rob stand by the door. They can hear the talk their having.

"The new project in Michigan is where they found his body. Mister Parkwood just called to tell me," she says as her eyes well up with tears. "He said there was two other bodies with him. I must've passed out after hearing it. I'm scared, Anthony. I'm gonna go to jail if they find out what I did!"

"Be quiet," he orders, sounding forceful but really he wants her to snap out of it and right now. "Don't ever say that again. Don't talk about it unless we're at home. *Alone*. Do you understand? You're not going to jail baby. I promise you that. Okay?"

"Okay Anthony," she says, "I wanna go home. I wanna take our babies and go home. I don't feel well."

"Okay," he says, "I'll get the kids. We'll get Brandon and security to get us and our vehicles home. You just calm down while I take care of things. Don't stress my baby out. Okay?" He adds and smiles.

"Okay Anthony. I love you," she says, calmer now.

"I love you too." he says, kissing her. Then he asks, "Are you hurt? Did you hurt yourself when you fell?"

"I don't feel any pain. But I'm dizzy," she says.

"I'll see about getting doc Weston to drop by the house," he says, "And she can check you out, once we get there."

"She's at the shower and probably waiting to check on me now."

"I'll get her. Then I'll find Bronson and Brandon," he says, "I just need for you to rest here and don't talk about Raymond. Alright?"

"Alright," she says as she lays back and closes her eyes.

He sends Dr. Weston to check on Ebony. Her girls follow Weston while Ajay goes to get Bronson. Brandon has already gotten word that Ajay is ready for him to take the Benz to Jackson Heights. Tank hears the news and runs over too. It's time to open the doors to the public, for tonight. But first, he has to check on his sister. He comes up to his office just as Weston is finishing up her exam. He sees that Ebony is okay. Then Chill, Rob and Ron tell him about her call from Parkwood. They step down the hall until Weston comes out and goes back down the elevator with Nina, Rebbie and T-baby.

"They found him, ha?" Tank asks.

"He was never lost," Rob says, "I just didn't know they had bought *that* land. Or I would've told you he was there. Maybe we could've moved him before the clearing started."

"No. We wouldn't risk that," Chill says, "We'll work it out. We always do. We got a back up plan just in case them folks come sniffing around."

"You've got people too, Chill," Ron offers with a smile. "Don't forget what I told you. My crew got that handled. No problem."

"Oh yea. We've got people. We'll get with Ajay later and tell him about that plan," Chill says, "He'll be glad to know about *these* people."

"The guys who was up here with you when he went in the ground?" Rob asks, "Big Tony and them interstate killers?"

"The same ones," Ron says, "They're in a position to help and we'll help their families. That bastard fucked with one of my crew's family members too. She committed suicide after he raped her. Big Tony still ain't over that shit."

They're all pleased to hear Ron speak. They have people and an absolute way out of this, should the need arise. Chill feels secure over the Raymond issue, with only 1 exception. He doesn't need this to break at this particular time. Not with Marvin's contracts open and the need to get rid of him, sooner than later. If the police start surveillance, it will be harder to move as they've planned. Going to the chamber will be out of the question.

Ajay returns to carry his wife to the SUV. John and Al have Lil Ajay and Lannie. Lannie is sound asleep. Lil Ajay isn't. It's only 8pm.

"Chill don't forget we have a treasure we can dig up," Al reminds him, after hearing of Parkwood's call.

"We have one already above ground. Just locked down," Chill tells him with a smile, "And this one will keep y'all out here and running the crew's businesses. *And* cooking at Stoney's."

141

"Right where we need y'all," Ron adds.

Big Al and big John are eager to hear about this new treasure.

"Let's make sure Ajay and Ebony get home safe," Chill says to John and Al, "Then Ron and I will drop into Stoney's and give y'all the scoop."

Bronson drives the Escalade with Ajay and his family. The shower is over and the clubs are opening for business.

Ajay gets his family inside of their home. Bronson and Brandon head back to CrewLand mall with Jr, who had trailed them. Ajay calls Mr. Parkwood as soon as they leave. He needs to know what's going on. Parkwood answers on the 2nd ring. He was expecting the return call, after hearing silence and then ladies making a fuss over Ebony.

"Hi Ajay. How's it going?" Parkwood asks in his usual, glad-to-hear-from-you tone.

If it has been nearly 3 days since they recovered Ray's body. Why hadn't they contacted us or Wheeler? Is it because we aren't suspects. Or are the police watching us and building the case against our crew that they've wanted for years?

Ajay believes the latter. Parkwood tells him, he has been in touch with Hardin. Hardin is his friend and the lead detective for Cuyahoga County and the North Ohio district. He has been following the Raymond White discovery since it came down the wire, 60 hours ago. Hardin has actually followed the case since becoming familiar with Ebony and her crew. Ajay asks Parkwood to give Hardin a call. He wants to hear what he has to say, *firsthand*. Parkwood calls Hardin. Hardin answers and gives them the up-to-the-minute information on the Raymond White situation. He tells them there isn't a search on, to go after the crew.

"They haven't tried to tie the crew to him," Hardin says, "Not as far as his murder. They know better than that."

"In what way are we tied to him?" Ajay asks, "Hopefully the right way."

"Actually yes. First they identified him through DNA. Then Ann Arbor contacted Houston and told them they had their missing person. They asked for his jacket so they could try to put together a scenario which could've landed him dead in their district. Houston was the ones who gave them his history. Including his criminal history. His DNA is being used to see if it matches the young suicide victim from ninety one. Her name was Ayesha Robinson. She committed suicide in ninety one, down in Houston.

142

His criminal history includes the assault and attempted rape of Ebony. Thus he is tied to the crew for the assault of Ebony Brown. Who is now Ebony Jackson, the wife of an upstanding, outstanding NBA player and businessman. She owns the largest real estate agency in these parts. And she works with the *heart* of the land when it comes to investments and Real Estate. Mister Bert Parkwood. That's what we have."

Parkwood chuckles and says, "I'm not sure if that last part will help or hurt."

"It definitely helps to have your name on their team," Hardin tells Parkwood, "Then they're pillars of this state too. Not just the community. Precincts won't wanna try to build cases like that. District Attorney's find it hard to win cases against prominent citizens. So they usually don't press for it unless it's a slam dunk, high profile and a sure win. This wouldn't be. Especially when the victim didn't have the same stature or status. According to Michigan, they can't find anyone willing to vouch for him. There was members of his family slain. His ex coach and his family was slain as well. This guy was most likely involved in some heavy drug trafficking, for this to be interdepartmental and interstate too. The focus is still on the fraternity. Just as it's always been since he was first reported missing. Reports say he was headed there but the frats said he never arrived. He hadn't been heard from since. My bet is, this'll be wrapped up as drug related before long."

Ajay is thinking of the day they set Raymond up. He wanted to pledge Omega Psi Phi at the Ann Arbor University chapter. Jr got his frats to help. They set up a fake meeting. The crew drove to the Ann Arbor frat house and waited in the garage. Ray showed up, the crew grabbed him and brought him back to *The Chamber*. That's where he met his death by a .357 magnum and Ebony Brown. His body was cleaned thoroughly, leaving no traces to them. Then he was driven back across the Michigan state line and buried. Ajay doesn't want any part of that story to be discovered. Even though he knows Parkwood could call in favors to make it go away. He just doesn't want this case on his girl. *Ever*! He'll cop to it and do the time himself, before he'll allow his wife to be charged. If it came to that. He'd plead to it in a heartbeat.

"Can you keep us or our Attorney updated with the latest, please?" Ajay asks, "Because just hearing his name has my wife upset."

"I can and I'll do that," Hardin says, "I know Wheeler and his wife Trina, *well*. I worked close with him on the Angelise Taylor case. Raymond is another person who violated Ebony. I get to defend her and her families

143

honor again. I look forward to it. Bert would disown me if I didn't."

"And you know this, *man*" Parkwood says, imitating *Chris Tucker* from the *Ice Cube* movie *Friday*.

Hardin and Parkwood laugh but Ajay can't allow himself to be quite as jovial as they are. He knows how the system has always tried to get something solid on his crew. He remembers how Cleveland police use to jack them up on sight. So he isn't taking anything for granted. For now, everything is going in the best way possible. But he knows it's only a matter of time before something will shake out. He just hopes all of his family can still remain free, when this is done. The crew have Wheeler, who will stay on Hardin and stay up-to-date on the newest Raymond information. Ajay will talk to his crew in person tomorrow, as they pick up their tuxedo's for Erica and Eric's matrimonial event. He wants to talk now. But they'll never risk text messaging anything this serious and he's not about to leave Ebony's side. Not until this is gone *completely*.

No paper trail. No Phone trail. No digital trail.

After Ebony is resting and the twins are sound asleep. Ajay drives his Benz back up to CrewLand Mall. He finds Chill and Ron at Stoney's, talking to his father and father-in-law.

"I knew you'd be back," Chill says to him, as they exchange dap.

"Hell yea," Ajay says, "My baby *fainting* blew my buzz completely. I'm sober now. What's the business? Because this NBA shit is gonna be over for me, if they come after Ebony. I'm going in, if they come-"

"It's no need for all that," Ron says.

Chill and Ron give him the low down on the new treasure they have. The 1 that's going to clear the crew before the crew even become clogged up with more of this Raymond situation. After hearing what they have, Ajay smiles and relaxes instantly.

"*Damn*. That's right," Ajay says, "We've got people."

He smiles at Ron and gives him some dap. Ron smiles back.

"The crew have made me, my wife and family very rich with all of this good business y'all been bringing our way since we met," Ron says, "I told y'all, way back. I would always have something to offer the crew. From watching over Ebony, big mama and poppa. To sending my crew to Atlanta to keep upper management in house. This is my *family*. Ebony is like another sister to me. Not to mention big Tony's niece, Ayesha. Raymond *did* rape her. I know he did. I don't have to wait for Houston to run no fucking DNA. He did it. Big Tony told me he did it. That's all the confirmation I

144

needed. I told that bitch ass nigga he was gonna be a maggot buffet, if he didn't get his shit right."

"My man," Chill says as they give each other dap.

The 3 men say goodnight to John and Al, who are about to start preps for their 10 o'clock opening. Chill and Ron head back over to the club. Ajay heads home to his family. He's not allowed to tell Ebony the plan yet. But he's going to reassure her so she doesn't worry herself sick. Everyday since her attack from Raymond and even since the attack from Angel. Ajay has promised her, he would never allow any harm to come to her. Not at the hands of anyone. And certainly not Raymond White. He's going to keep his word to her, *by any means necessary*. Even if that means doing the time for Raymond's death, himself.

He makes it home and parks in the garage. He hurries inside where he finds Ebony laying on the couch, watching TV.

"I thought you went to bed, baby?" he asks and gives her a kiss.

"I tried but I couldn't sleep," she says.

"You didn't wanna watch TV in our room?" he asks.

"I did for awhile," she says, "But I wanted to be out here. In case our twins got up. Ant finally went to sleep too."

"Okay. You lay right there. I'll go up and check on them," he says, "I'll be right back. Okay?"

"Okay. Thank you baby," she says.

He smiles at her, then hurries up the stairs. After finding his twins still asleep, he descends the stairs and goes right back to his wife's side.

"They're sleep for the night," he says, "Can I take you to bed?"

"I wanna be wherever you are?" she says with tears in her eyes.

"You definitely get that wish, baby," he says, "Anytime."

He lifts her cradle style and carries her to their bedroom. He lays her down on her pillows and kisses her again.

He says, "I'm gonna be right next to you, baby. I came back home to take care of you."

He smiles at her as he's removing his clothes. She has a stressed look on her face. Once he's undressed, he slides under the covers and pulls them over the both of them. He pulls her to him and adds another kiss. He smiles but she doesn't. "Where's that beautiful smile at Ebony?" he whispers.

"I'm worried about the call from Parkwood, Anthony," she says, "I just don't feel as confident about it as you do."

"If you knew what I know. You would," he says with a smile.

"What do you know?" she asks.

145

"I can't tell you that," he says as he chuckles, "But you're not going to jail. Okay? That's the most important thing."

"I don't want you to go either."

"I'm not going," he says, "No one from our Cleveland crew is going," he says, "We've got people, baby girl. Just remember that. We have people and it's all because of you, that we have them."

"All because of me?" she asks, "I don't understand."

"Baby I can't tell you the particulars. But the most important thing is *none* of us are going to go anywhere," he says, "Raymond had raped a girl from Houston before he tried to rape you. She had family in Ron's crew. She never told on Raymond, just like them rats didn't. But she ended up committing suicide because of what he did to her. Her family is still pissed. They wanted him *dead*. One of her family is a member of Ron's crew. His name is big Tony. That's how Ron got the info to Chill, about Raymond being at Ann Arbor State. That's how we knew where to go and get him. Nobody is willing to let anyone who was violated by him, go to jail. Just know that. We can discuss the other case later. When I know more about it. But just know this sweetheart. You are safe. Your life is set and it's not gonna change."

She looks doubtful as she cuddles close to him. He wants her to relax her mind. He lifts her chin and gives her a kiss while demanding she gives him her tongue too and she does.

After the kiss, he asks, "Have I ever lied to you or steered you wrong?"

"No you haven't baby," she says, "Even if the truth broke my heart. You always told me and you've never steered me wrong Anthony. Not at all. Even when you was going somewhere to do wrong and I wanted to go with you. You would say no."

"Because you was *always* my baby, Ebony," he says, "I *knew* you was gonna be my wife. The mother of my children. I never wanted a scar on your record. I could have them but not you."

"But I've killed two people. That's more than a scar."

"That's not written down anywhere baby," he says quickly, "You're not a murderer. You're a person who believes in self defense."

He laughs. She can't help but smile too. He hugs her tight as he continues, "I do have one regret about Raymond and Angel," he says.

"What is it?" she asks.

"That I didn't kill them both," he says, "I wanted to find him myself. Do you know I went to Ann Arbor *twice* before the crew went?"

"I remember a few times when I couldn't get a hold of you," she says, "That was before we all had cell phones. You had yours then. With the same number you got now. I just figured you was out with one of your many…., ho's," she finally says as she rolls her eyes.

"Nah. Ho's didn't get that kind of time with me," he says, "Not where you couldn't contact me. Hell no." They both laugh.

"I'm not sad that I did either of them," she says, "I just wished I had got that gun from Raymond and shot him *that* night. Then there would be nothing to worry about."

"There's nothing to worry about *now*," he says, "You don't even know where the body was or in what condition it was in."

"I know he was shot up," she says.

"Yes but there was no bullets in him," he says, "They got them out. So there was no traces to our guns when they found him. Baby if it was anything leading back to you, they would have called you already. He's been out of the ground for damn near a week."

"I know. Mister Parkwood told me," she says, "I just wanna know how you can be *so* sure."

"Because we've got people. People who was going to kill him on sight," he says, "Way before he ever went and bothered you or went to Michigan. Now that's gonna have to be enough. There's history there. Threats on his life. They've already copped to his coach and his family. They've already been asking them what they knew about his disappearance. I'll just put it like this. Ron's crew is our crew and our crew is Ron's crew. When it comes to taking a charge for murder. He's got dudes who have already said they'll cop to it."

"The guys who came with him when we was at the chamber?" she asks.

"I wasn't suppose to tell you," he says as he chuckles.

"You didn't. I guessed it," she says with a bright smile, "They was already trying to make Ron tell Chill to let *them* do him. April and Yolanda told me that. They was almost as bad as you."

"Yes but Chill and Ron said he was *your* kill," he says, "And that was that."

"They're gonna go to prison for *me*?" she asks.

"They're already in prison serving multiple sentences. They're never getting out," he says, "We're gonna take care of their loved ones. Just like they're taking care of mine."

She looks up into his eyes. He's looking at her. She can see the sincerity. He really wants her *not to* be bothered by this. She can see that he isn't

147

anymore. Not since he came back from talking to Chill and Ron. She knows Chill has always got a fix for whatever the situation. She settles her nerves and relaxes in her husband's arms.

"I feel better knowing you're on the case, Anthony," she says, "And I know Chill will never let anything happen to us. I'm so blessed to have so many people who love me."

"I'm blessed to have you to love," he says, "And I don't take it lightly Ebony. I don't take you for granted at all. I know you're a prize. I know I'm the lucky one in this relationship. You could've had *any* boy you wanted from every school we've been too and you chose me. I'll never stop paying you for that one."

"You've paid me, Anthony," she says, "By loving me in return and giving me those smart and beautiful twins. And now we've got another bun in the oven."

"Yes and this is a girl," he says as he rubs her stomach. "I can just tell it's a girl. I get to be home in the mornings with this one. I'm so glad I got a trade to Cleveland."

"I am too. I remember how hard it was for you when the twins were babies," she says, "You never wanted to leave us."

"Hell no I didn't," he says, "You was my reason for living, Ebony. Until they came. They took over that void that I use to have where I didn't give a damn how the world turned out. Now that I'm a father. I want shit to be nonviolent and peaceful. I can't even imagine the shit I put my parents through."

"Oh my God," she says as she giggles. She continues, saying, "You were bad in elementary school. Mama and mama Jo says Ant is doing to same things you did when you were single digit in age."

"That's that Jackson male ego. That shit is gonna drive us crazy," he says, "Until he gets some pussy on the regular, he's gonna be hell to deal with. I'm just letting you know that."

"Oh yea. His daddy started at eight. His papa Al started at ten," she says, "His other papa and uncles were all having sex by age twelve."

"And he'll beat all of us," he says as he laughs.

"No *way*," she says, "I've told you. I don't want those older girls messing with my baby. I don't even wanna hear about *any* of that."

"Okay. We won't tell you," he says as he still laughs.

"*Anthony*," she says with an impatient look on her face.

"What? Okay come here," he says, "Give me something else to do besides talk about sex. I'd rather be *having* sex then talking about it."

TIME TO FEEL-RELOADED-Time Will Reveal part 5

She gives in and lets him caress her tender breast. He has to put 1 in his mouth, of course. He looks up at her and smiles, before saying,
"I've had henny and penny back for two years. I was so happy when my twins turned two and could drink regular milk from a cup. But I know I'm gonna lose them again when this little girl comes. So I'm taking advantage."
He smiles at her, then heads south. They turn in for the night. Making love is on the agenda at the Jackson's estate, each and every night. They don't know who's hornier since the pregnancy, her or him. But they make sure and take care of both.

****

October 10, 2003. It's time for Erica and Eric's *huge* wedding. Alana, Darlene and Farah received invitations by design. Darlene's youngest son Jamal and Holly Stevenson, the mother of his 2 children are in the wedding. The entire event is exquisite. Erica is radiant. Eric's parents, Eric Sr and Jillian came in from Chicago 2 days ago with his 3 siblings; Leilenne, Alan and Kimmie. All younger than Eric. They brought a host of uncles, aunts, cousins and both sets of his grandparents too. They're all apart of the wedding. 3 year old Kimmie is 1 of the flower girls. During the ceremony she cuts up with 4 year old twins Lannie and Lil Ajay and her 5 year old brother Alan. They almost steal the show. Lannie as the miniature bride and Lil Ajay as the ring bearer plus flower girl Kimmie, draw a lot of attention. 5 year old Alan, who has a 1st name similar to Lannie's papa Al. And the middle name of her father and brother Anthony is the miniature groom. Lil Ajay keeps a strict eye on him, just as his father has trained him to do since birth. Lannie keeps asking Alan Anthony when is she suppose to get her ring. While Lil Ajay tells her repeatedly, she isn't getting a ring from no boy and he's going to tell their daddy if she doesn't stop talking to *that* boy. On the other hand, Kimmie keeps telling Lil Ajay,
"Let Lannie have the ring from my brother, right now."
Lil Ajay just smiles at her. He tries to be charming with her but he remains insistent with his twin sister. The miniature wedding party is hilarious. All the guest enjoy them. Ebony and Ajay have to keep reminding their twins that this isn't *their* day. But they never manage to convince either of them of that fact.

Erica cries throughout the entire ceremony while Eric Jr keeps her comforted. At one point, Ebony catches Greg Jr crying as well. Erica will always be his 1st love. He tries to be supportive of her on her big day. But

149

he has never stopped longing for them to get back together. He never will but he can see that she's happy. That's what's important to him.

Alana, Darlene and Farah are just happy to be in attendance. They had been hinting around for months, that they wanted to attend the wedding. Darlene's son is a member of the party. That was the crew's excuse for inviting her. When really Darlene and Alana was invited because of their friendship with Farah. Chill wanted Farah invited because it's time for the crew's plan against Marvin to begin implementation and Farah is a huge part of it.

In the plan, Renee's role will be identical to what Nina's was back when Tank had to reel in Alana, in order to smoke Angel out of hiding. Renee has to pretend her and Chill aren't getting along and are heading for a divorce. And she doesn't care that Chill is meeting Farah on the low, is the signal they're trying to pull off. At 1 of his meetings with Farah, she told him to let her know if Renee failed to do her job as a wife because she would be more than happy to fill in. The crew have to make her feel like her opportunity has come. They know she'll bite. Matt is just the chocolate on a hotel pillow. The fill-in for the Chill buffet, Farah has wanted since the 1st night she entered the club and laid eyes on him. Alana had fallen for this same plan when Tank had unveiled it to her back in 1994. So it's nothing new for the crew. They just use the infatuation factor these women have to be with them, as the honey. Honeybee Alana bit hook, line and sinker. Farah is slower than Alana. But the crew knows she'll show up anytime Chill summons her. Chill knows wherever Farah goes. Marvin is sure to follow. And he's right. Because Erica's wedding day is no exception.

Marvin had been banned from CrewLand mall and all crew properties. But that doesn't include the roadways. In true stalker fashion, Marvin rides back and forth by the *Allen Saul Williams recreation center* during the reception. This Pittsburgh native has been busy since his last meeting with Andre. He'd managed to find Farah's Parma home in the past week. Primarily because that was part of the crew's plan. However he hasn't found the nerve to approach the door. He has pulled stakeouts on the nights Matt visited. During his off time of planning Matt and Chill's demise, Marvin used the information he had on Ellen to employ her at his business. He had sent an application out to her. She filled it out and sent it back. He called her in for an interview and hired her on the spot. She has an associates job in his carpet outlet store. She'd asked him to give her girls Rudy and Dorothy a job. He did that too. After all, having her friends employed there, *keeps* her there and that helps him to keep her close. In no time, he had her talking about Matt and his *"white bitch"* and how much she can't stand her. Marvin had also made sure the information about Matt spending nights with Farah had gotten back to Ellen. Anonymously, of course. Ellen has been obeying her restraining order since her fight at the salon, the last arrest and the new charges. But she's been baking a cake of her own. She has to get rid of Farah Benson. She doesn't have a blueprint. Nor does she dare reveal any of it to her new boss. She doesn't want him to think she's some crazed lunatic who kills people.

"White folks get scared when black people talk like that," she had said to Rudy and Dorothy.

She hasn't told Marvin about her shooting incident at *The Spot* either. She had lied on her application. She's a felon now and isn't allowed to purchase a gun. But Marvin already knows her history. He's playing her and she's none the wiser. She's his backup plan for Matt's demise. Just in case Pac Man gets cold feet or doesn't go through with the hit. With Ellen angry enough to kill, he can get that hit on Matt for the bargain price of $7,500 and a gun. The $7500 is what he had paid when he *anonymously* bailed her out of jail, after the salon fight. The bail money and gun cost together, is a lot cheaper than the $40k Pac Man and his *thugs* are asking him to pay. Plus if Ellen kills Matt, Marvin couldn't be implicated in *any* way. Ellen doing it would look more like a crime of passion. Like an *NBC movie of the week*, in the making. Marvin has all of his bases covered and a plan B. Matt and Chill are going down and he will finally be able to woo his woman back. Free of interruption from either to those *niggers*. Ellen doesn't know that her boss is also her anonymous sidekick. She hasn't told him about the free bailout she'd gotten because she would have to admit her history. Or she feels he might do a background check which is why she'd lied on her application. But in Marvin's thoughts, if she'd turned out to be useless in his plot to have her kill Matt. Then later, he would use that false application to fire her. For now, he figures her fatal attraction to Matt is going to help him, more than she'll *ever* know. Until it's too late. Ellen has no plan of how to get a gun. But that all changes Halloween week when she receives another *no obvious strings attached gift* from her anonymous source. Or *mysterious* sidekick.

****

Erica and Eric aren't able to take their honeymoon because the Browns are in the middle of the NFL season. That's also the reason they had their wedding on a Friday and not on Saturday. That way Eric wouldn't be exerting all of his energy the day before a game. They'll go to Barbados in the spring of next year.

Seeing Gwen at the wedding, brings up those feelings in Nina about Tank's revelation while they were on their sailing excursion. She has to let her know that she knows her secret. She takes Gwen into Ajay's office to speak with her, in private.

"I need to let you know that I know about you and Jeremy. And y'all one night stand at the Natty house in ninety three," Nina says with a dry wit tone to her voice. "But just so you know. It's not gonna happen again and you still don't get to call him Jeremy. Now unless you want this info shared with your husband. You'll back the fuck off and keep your sister in line too. She'll never get with my brother."
Gwen doesn't say a word. But she does have a shocked expression to Nina's comment about Nickeia.
"Yea Gwen. Crew comes like that," Nina oozes, "My brother don't even have to tell me about females who are after him. I can recognize it better than my sister-in-law can. We got enough. With Alana and those ho's hanging around. Neither one of you wanna go on that list and I know it. So both of y'all best stay in your place. Or you can feel my crew, for *real*."
With that, Nina goes back to Tank and they continue to enjoy the reception. Gwen and Jarvis leave early and take Nickeia with them. Jarvis has no idea why but Gwen just told him, she felt sick. Rebbie was in a much better mood after Gwen and Nickeia left. But Jarvis could've hung around longer.

****

It's the last week of October and the Jackson Heights community is preparing for Halloween. All the wives, along with their holiday décor company, decorate their community with ghost, goblins, spider webs and jack-o-lanterns. They go about Saturday morning, carefully placing lights up and thinking of the safest way to make their neighborhood look spooky. For the candy seekers and at the same time, keeping the safety of all those kids who visit Jackson Heights at the forefront. The fathers are going to take the children out trick-or-treating, this evening. Venitia comes out to pass out treats with the Jackson Heights wives. Gwen comes by and so does Nickeia. Nickeia's eyes are trained on Ebony, the entire time. Gwen can't shake her nervousness around Nina but Rebbie doesn't notice that part. Because she's still uncomfortable, just being around Gwen. These inconveniences are going to have to come to a head and to the light, *soon*.

Across town, just off Euclid Avenue, Ellen receives 2 packages delivered by USPS. In one, there's a brand new *Ruger* 9mm handgun. There are bullets in the other package. Inside the box with the bullets is a free membership to the shooting range in North Olmsted. Ellen searches through all of the papers and finds no hint of who had sent her the gifts. Rudy and Dorothy witness as Ellen takes the empty gun out of the box, points it at the mirror and pretends to shoot Farah Benson in the head. Then she pretends to stand over her and unload the imaginary clip.

"I'm going to the range and get good with this thing," Ellen says, "And the next time that white bitch or muthafuckin Kelly say some shit to me. *Boom, boom, boom, on your ass, bitch!*"

"I wonder who sent it?" Dorothy asks.

"Must be someone who knows you, El," Rudy adds.

"It's probably the same person who bailed you out," Dorothy says.

"Probably someone who wants that bitch gone, just like me," Ellen says, "It might be the crew. Because they don't like her either. I know that now. They just have to be professional about it. I'm going to the range. It says I can bring 2 friends with me. Y'all wanna go?"

They say sure, they would love to learn to shoot the gun too. Ellen is so busy thinking of how convenient someone is making things for her. That she doesn't even phantom for a second, that this is *too* coincidental. That mysterious source is coming through for her, again and again. But she has no clue of who it is. When all the time, that person is none other than Marvin Huntley, her new boss.

****

The site for the crew's Thanksgiving dinner has been set since late spring. Everyone will gather at Ajay and Ebony's house. It is now, the 1st Thursday of November. They have 3 weeks to prepare. Jamal and Holly are invited this year too. But the crew don't invite Darlene, Alana and Farah, as they'd done for the wedding. No one wants them in Jackson Heights whether there is a plan in motion or not. Ajay had hired Holly at the sports facility, after she had Jamal's 2nd baby. Nickeia has been trying to get Gwen to help her get a job there. It hasn't happened, thus far. Gwen is just trying to remain as inconspicuous as possible. Venitia works at Big Mama's House and Granny's House, with the crew mothers.

TIME TO FEEL-RELOADED-Time Will Reveal part 5

At Allen Saul Williams facility, Holly and Jamal arrive for work. They wait for Steven and Ally to come to unlock the doors. They show up just after Jamal and Holly arrive. While they get the Sports complex ready for the day. Jamal tells them he has come in to work with some news to share. He tells them what *he'd* witnessed the night before.

He says, "Y'all know I go to that range in North Olmsted, right?"

"Yes," Ally says.

"I saw that chick there. The one that shot at the dude from the salon that night at the chill spot," Jamal says, "What's her name? The one who had the fight at the salon."

"Baby you're talking about Ellen," Holly says, "That crazy lady who bust the windows out of Matt's car, Ally. That's who he's talking about." Holly is laughing.

"Oh yea. That's her name," Steven says, "She's a felon. What the fuck she doing at a shooting range?"

"I was too. Remember?" Jamal asks, "They don't care. You just can't bring nothing in *loaded* and they got strict security too. She has to have someone bring her weapon in and leave with it. Just like I do. She had her two girls with her. But once inside, she can handle it and shoot targets. She had a brand new *Nina*."

"Somebody had to buy it for her, ha? If she's a felon?" Holly asks.

"One of her girls probably purchased it," Steven offers.

He wants to listen now. More than talk.

"Why is she going to a shooting range? Ebony told me she's working for that white guy," Ally says, "The one who use to date Farah, the loony school teacher. Is she ready to shoot his weird ass already?"

They all laugh. Steven offers a little more on the subject of Ellen and the shooting club. He offers nothing on Marvin at all.

"She might be doing it for her *own* protection," Steven says, "She did get her ass whooped in that fight."

They all laugh again as they get the facility opened by noon. Then Steven grabs his cell phone and ducks into the equipment room. He calls Chill with the latest news. He knows Marvin is up to something sneaky. He wants Chill to know about Ellen and the brand new 9mm she has in her possession.

The next day as Ebony goes about her day, in her office. She gets a call on her office phone, just as she's preparing to take her lunch break.

"Jackson's Real Estate," she answers.

"I need to speak with misses Jackson, please."

"Only if this is *mister* Jackson," she says and smiles.

"This is daddy," Ajay says in a matter-of-fact tone.

"Same deal," she replies while smiling, "Hi daddy. What's good?"

"I was hoping you could tell me. I'm trying to find a lunch date."

"You just did," she says, still smiling.

"I'll be there in five," he says, "We can check out Crew's house."

"Sounds perfect," she tells him.

"I'll see ya."

"In a minute, daddy."

****

After Chill talked with Steven yesterday. He called Farah to set up a meeting in his office for 1pm. Renee is going to be there as per their plan and no recording devices will be on. Chill has a true 1 listening on the speakerphone. Renee didn't want it recorded because they don't know how far things will go while pulling this whole scenario together. Today's meeting will start with Chill and Farah. But someone else will join them before it ends.

"Good afternoon, miss Benson," Chill says with a fake smile.

"Are we still *that* formal? When are you gonna call me Farah?"

"Good afternoon, Farah. How are you?"

"Better now that we're *less* formal," Farah says, "And best, because your wife is not in the building. Correct?"

"No she's not. I figured you would feel a lot more open to talking to me about some personal stuff. If she wasn't around," Chill plays.

"Are you two splitting up?" she asked suddenly, "The word is out there, you know."

"I don't know. But that's not what I wanted to talk to you about," he says, "That's nothing that concerns you anyway and you know it. I wanna know what plans you have for me."

She smiles then blushes openly. Finally, an *opening*. She's waited *years* for Chill to give her a sign or a hint that he's the least bit interested in her. She feels he just did, as she says, "I can show you, better than I can tell you."

"Tell me first. I'll decide if I wanna be shown," he says.

She spills it, when she says, "I wanted to fuck you from the first night I saw you. I wanna suck that sweet black dick of yours, so bad. And I know it's sweet. Angie has told me. Nicole has told me. Samantha, Gloria, Anita. Darlene too. Even a few other girls from your past, claimed to have been

155

to heaven too. I figured, *damn*. If all of them can have some. Why can't I?"

"I wasn't married *then*."

"Seems like you're not now either. And for a change, I'm here and she's not."

He says, "I don't fuck nor get head without a condom. Unless it's my wife."

"Fine. It's an even bigger turn on that she still gets respect like that. Even though you two are on bad terms," Farah says, "That's the sign of a *real* man."

She stands up and is about to walk around his desk.

"Not here," he says, "I've got your number. I'm gonna call you later. We're gonna hook up. *Hell*. We might even swing an episode tonight. I'm feeling horny as a *muthafucka*."

"Oh shit. I can't *wait*," she says bubbling with energy and anticipation.

Just then, Kenny walks in the door on cue. Just as they'd planned it.

"What's going on?" he asks, "Hey Farah. What's *poppin*, baby?"

"I was just finishing up a meeting with your father."

"Are you leaving?" Kenny asks.

"She is, son. For now," Chill says, "But we're gonna hook up later. I think you should come. I'd like to know *which* Kenneth she likes better."

Farah is shocked at first. But game, nonetheless.

"I'll be waiting for your call," she says to Chill, "I guess the Denali was the key. Someone should've *been* told me I had to come *big* to get you."

Then she winks at Kenny and walks toward the door.

"I already know who she thinks is better," Kenny says, "I use to leave chalk dust all over that ass. I got the title and the keys to the Denali. Didn't I hit that shit right?" he asks moving up behind her.

Farah smiles and says, "Yes you did. I really miss that too."

Then she leaves the office and heads to the elevators. Chill and his son go out and catch up to her. They ride down the elevator with her too. Kenny feels her up, just as they'd discussed he would, as they ride down to the ground floor. She's more than ready to suck him off before they reach the bottom floor. But Chill promises her that'll all come later. They walk her to her car, in the parking lot. Chill surveys the area and surrounding properties. Just as he had counted on. Marvin is in his surveillance duck off hideaway. Watching and recording. It's just a matter of time before Chill gives him *more* film footage than he can bear to view. The cake has been baking. It's just about done and from all accounts, the ingredients have been added and blended perfectly.

Ajay walks Ebony back to her office after lunch. When they step inside the lobby, they notice Mr. Parkwood, Wheeler and Detective Hardin standing there. Ebony freezes in her tracks. Her stomach ties up in knots instantly. She feels as if she'll lose the southern style lunch she had just devoured.

"Hello mister Wheeler. Mister Parkwood. Detective Hardin," Ajay says, "What can we do for you guys?"

"I was hoping I could speak with misses Jackson about Raymond White," Hardin says, "Just some minor things. We need to gather our responses."

"Uh sure. What is this about?" Ebony manages.

"We need to discuss this in a more private setting, misses Jackson," Hardin says.

"Is this a formal thing?" Ajay asks as he looks at Wheeler and Parkwood.

"No. It's just your representation getting ahead of this thing," Wheeler says, "Like I always do."

"If it's not formal. Then call her Ebony," Ajay demands as he tightens his grip on his wife's midsection.

"Okay Ebony," Hardin says, "Can we do this in private?"
Claudia is at her desk trying to appear totally busy. It isn't working.

"We can use her office," Ajay offers, "It's right though here."

"I think it would be better if we did it in *my* office," Hardin says.
Ebony looks at Ajay and he puts his arm around her shoulders. He leads everyone into her office anyway and closes the door. He looks from Hardin to Parkwood. Then he asks, "Is she under arrest for something?"

"No she's not," Parkwood says, "I just want him to get her official statement now. Get it out of the way, so they can go on and finish this case up. Hardin says it would be okay to do it here. But I thought you two would be more comfortable if you didn't conduct this kind of interview at your place of business."

"I would rather stay here," Ebony says to Ajay.
Wheeler conveys that to Parkwood and Hardin.

"That's perfectly okay with me," Hardin says, "See Bert. What did I tell you? Nobody ever wants to go downtown," he chuckles and says, "That's hardly a voluntary thing anyway."
Ajay can feel Ebony trembling. She's nervous about having to talk about Raymond. He escorts her around to her desk where she takes her seat. Still very nervous about having to answer *anything* about Raymond White.

Hardin begins his questions as soon as they're all seated. Wheeler never even has to speak because Parkwood isn't going to allow Ajay nor Ebony to go any farther than this office.

"When is the last time you saw or heard from Raymond White?" Hardin asks.

Ebony thinks about that day at the chamber in November 1991, when she emptied the .357 magnum Colt Python Revolver into his body. But she knows she isn't suppose to tell him *that* side. Still she wonders does he know about it already. She thinks about her twins and the baby she's carrying. Her eyes well up with tears. Ajay can't stand to see her in distress.

"She's pregnant," he says, "Her hormones keep her emotional all the time. I don't want her to be stressed out with this again. What he did to her. It took me a long time to bring her back from. She doesn't need to relive it."

"I won't ask her to relive it, Ajay," Hardin says, "I just told the lead detective from Ann Arbor that I'd conduct whatever questioning of her that's going to be done. That's why we're here. To make sure no one stresses her out. You have my word on that."

"I wanted him to get a statement today and get it done," Wheeler clarifies.

"Have you seen him since he attacked you?" Parkwood asks.

"No sir," she says, "I was in the hospital when he went to court for arraignment. The judge sent him away until our court date. I was back here in Cleveland on that court date. My grandparents went to it. But he wasn't there. My big mama told me his lawyer had continued it until the next year, in May."

"And before that court date, she called us back and said the news in Houston was saying he was missing," Ajay adds, "And that went on for awhile. That's when I got heated because I felt like they was hiding him out. Just like they did the day that he bonded out. I've felt like that for the longest time. It's been some years ago and my girl was getting on with her life. Without any thoughts of that attack. For me, as long as he didn't come near her again I was able to let the thought of him go too. As long as he kept his distance."

"Until they finally closed the missing persons case and said he was presumed dead," Parkwood says, "I remember all of that. Ajay was at Natty by then."

"And still I wanted to find him and kick his ass," Ajay adds, "That didn't change until about a month ago. When I found out he was dead

TIME TO FEEL-RELOADED-Time Will Reveal part 5

already. I have to be honest with you. I'm damn glad to know that he's dead. It saved me from going to prison for killing him. Because that was my plan since nineteen ninety one."

Everyone is silent for several minutes. Ajay has spoken with conviction and they can tell he's angry and has no love for Raymond White. That's expected. But he's also convincing. Wheeler likes that part and so does Parkwood. That's all they need and want, is something that sounds convincing. They give less than a damn about *how* Raymond White died. Just as long as no one in law enforcement can charge the crew with it.

"That's what I had and that's what I thought," Hardin finally says, "Was you angry that you wasn't able to confront him in court, Ajay?"

"You don't have to answer," Wheeler advises but Ajay wants too.

"Honestly. I'm angry still that I can't kick his ass, Hardin," Ajay says, "I wasn't convinced he was dead when it was announced that he was *presumed* dead. I told Ebony that his coach probably had him in protective custody somewhere. But then, I heard that someone had killed the coach. I wanted to kill Raymond *myself*. And I'm pissed off right now that I never got a chance to get him back for what he did to my girl. It makes me angry that I wasn't the one who got him. *Yea*. Yes it does. Because for years, the only hurt Ebony knew about was the emotional pain from my cheating ass. But then she goes to Houston to take care of her big mama and he attacks her because she loves me and wouldn't talk to him. She came back home as only half of the girl that left here. To add to that. She gets pregnant for me and then Angel tries to kill her and *does* kill my baby. *Why*? Because she loves me and wouldn't leave me so Angel could feel better. The only pain she had in her life was because of me. I wanted to assure her that the pain was over with. Hardin you know I tried to kill Angel with my bare hands. I wanted her and Raymond dead. I had plans of killing them *both*. Somebody beat me to Raymond. But Angel, she's still living. And if she comes back out here and I see her. I still will kill her, just like she killed my first baby. Now you can make of that whatever you want too. But I'm not sorry he's dead. I'm just sorry that I didn't get to kill him."

"My whole family thought his high school was helping him to get out of it. Until that coach and some of his family was killed," Ebony says, "Then it went in a whole new direction. Like they was into way more than assaulting girls and covering it up."

"Yes. It was ruled drug related," Hardin says, "That's strange because there *is* proof that Raymond White dealt drugs, smoked pot and that he had assaulted other girls too. Some who had never come forward.

159

And one who committed suicide because she wasn't able to live with the pain. But there was never anything on the coach at all."

"So he was most likely killed *because* of Raymond," Parkwood offers.

He's trying to close this case quicker than Wheeler, Ajay and the crew are. He continues, "That drug game is deadly. They don't care who they take out, just to send a message."

"So you think whomever killed him, killed the coach too?" Ajay plays along.

"And some of his family members and friends as well," Hardin says, "Yes. That's my statement on it."

Parkwood shakes his head. He seems to know the crew are involved some how and some way. But he's determined it will never be found out. The more Ajay talks to them. The more he realizes Parkwood is willing to risk it all, to save him, Ebony and their family. After all, Cincinnati is about to get another blue chipper from the crew, in Archie Wilson Jr. The alumni are all in as far as the crew go. Ajay continues to massage Ebony's shoulders as they finish up the meeting.

"It's gonna be okay, baby," he says, "He's never gonna hurt you again."

He kisses her and puts her head on his shoulder. She cries. It looks to Hardin like he has upset her by bringing back the memories of the assault. That's what Ajay wants it to look like. So does Wheeler and Parkwood.

"I'll go now," Hardin says, "I didn't want to upset you. I'm sorry. Just doing my job. And part of that job is keeping you in the clear too."

"She'll be okay," Wheeler says as they stand to leave.

Parkwood rushes Hardin up.

"Let's leave them to their day and go over to that fine restaurant they have," Parkwood says.

"Do you think they have some of that peach cobbler in there today?" Hardin asks.

"They do," Ajay says as he walks them out, "Sweet potato pie and chocolate cake too."

"That will conclude our meeting then," Hardin says and laughs, "If we need anything else. We'll call Wheeler and he can contact you all."

They all bid each other farewell.

After the 3 gentlemen leave, Ajay sticks around Ebony's office just to make certain she's going to be okay.

"I thought you was gonna cuss them out when you started talking

160

TIME TO FEEL-RELOADED-Time Will Reveal part 5

about how bad you wanted to get Raymond and Angel," she says, "It made me feel scared for you. I thought they was gonna say you killed him. Because you was saying you wanted too."

"Baby everybody this side of Tibet, know I wanted to kill that bitch ass nigga," he says, "Wheeler, Parkwood and Hardin know it too. I told them I wanted too. So yes, they know I wanted too. I *still* want too."

"I knew you was on the edge when you was massaging my shoulders," she says, "It felt like your fingers was gonna break my skin. But only when you was saying his name and Angel's name."

"I'm sorry baby," he says and gives her a sweet kiss. "But like I told you then. I would confess to it and do the time too. Before I'd allow you to go to jail. And that's on everything I love."
He smiles and rubs her belly.

161

CHAPTER 54

THE MIGHTY BLACK MAN....AND WOMAN

Chill has Joe and Woody to meet with Marvin in the late afternoon, while he meets with Andre and Pac Man. This is so Marvin can't be spying on him while he's meeting with the guys who are suppose to kill him, for Marvin. Chill wants to make Pac Man aware that Marvin is trying to double cross him by using Ellen.

"He bought the gun for this girl?" Andre asks.

"Who else got that kind of bread and is around Ellen?" Chill asks, "She's working for him. She's a felon. So you know she didn't buy it. Then one of my employees said he heard her and her girls at the range. Saying it came in the mail to her home."

"She was at the range? Olmsted, ha?" Pac Man asks.

"That's the only one that'll let just anybody come in there," Chill says, "As long as you can pay."

"Sounds to me like he's trying to get out of paying that contract to me," Pac Man says.

He isn't happy. He was already going to kill Marvin Huntley but he wanted to get the full amount of the agreed upon money first.

"We need to go on and move this along," Chill suggest, "Y'all need to make it happen faster. Like, before Thanksgiving for both of us. They'll be a change in plans."

Chill tells him the changes, then they part. He has to get back to CrewLand to open the club. He's looking forward to seeing Renee, since he hasn't seen her since he left home this morning. They've been spreading the word that he's living with Ajay and Ebony until the divorce is final. So outside of Jackson Heights, him and Renee have to play the role. That lie alone is enough to make him want to tear Farah's pussy, completely off. And not with his dick either. He also has visions of putting Marvin's face in it. Only his head won't be attached to his body at the time. The crew need to get on with their lives in *Sugar Hill*. In order to do that, these nomads have to be removed. *Somebody's got to die.*

Joe and Woody's meeting with Marvin ends as soon as Joe receives the text message from Andre which reads; "Holla at ya boy."

They part ways with Marvin and head off to hook up with Andre and Pac Man.

}*West Cleveland*{

TIME TO FEEL-RELOADED-Time Will Reveal part 5

Andre and Pac Man meet up with Joe and Woody at *The Landmark café*, off West 150th street.

"That muthafucka is low down dog," Woody says to Joe.

He's speaking on Marvin and how he had just bragged about the fact that they can use his employee Ellen as a *scapegoat*. They recorded him saying it. He had even talked about them using the same type of gun to kill Matt and Chill, that she has. Saying she'd told him what kind of gun she owns. She did tell him. But she didn't realize he was the one who'd bought it for her. Nor that he was just using her. Her whole employment happened because Marvin needs a fall guy. Or girl, in her case.

"That evil muthafucka is gonna get his," Joe says.

****

GUnit's *Beg For Mercy* CD drops on the 14th. Two days before Tupac's tribute movie, *Resurrection* is released in theatres. On it's opening day, the 16th, all of the crew go to see the movie together. All 4 generations, that is.

The movie was well done. What the crew didn't like is that in the theatre where they viewed the movie, there were cops posted up at the door and inside the theatre too. Thing is, there was no violence at that movie. Everyone was there to show their love and respect for *Tupac Amaru Shakur*. Nothing more. Nothing less. So Cleveland PD looked like some suckers, for hanging around there.

Later at both clubs, the DJ's plays all of the new CD by *GUnit*. It bumps hard body. They play a lot of Tupac's music and every GUnit song that Young Buck is on.

"*Buck* shining like a muthafucka on that shit, Cuz," Jr yells as he's bobbing his head to the track; *Footprints*.

"*Banks* bussin' heads too, man," Kilo says, "He's kind of witty wit it. But his shit is nice. *Young Buck* raw as a *muafucka*, bro."

The ladies in the clubs are feeling, *I Wanna Get To Know Ya* which features *Joe*. But the fellows throughout, like *Salute you*. The CD gets major play, all night.

"I'm supporting both of them," Ebony says immediately.

She liked *Young Buck* and *Lloyd Banks* from the beginning. Every since the remix of *P.I.M.P.* Nothing has changed with that.

"Me too," Chill says, "I'm trying to get GUnit to perform at The Spot pretty soon too."

TIME TO FEEL-RELOADED-Time Will Reveal part 5

Renee adds, "We're buying those also. I like the two of them more than fifty cent. He was better on his solo CD."

"And we're gonna buy that Pac movie too," Ajay adds, "As soon as that DVD drops. And crew don't buy bootlegs. That shit touched me, man." They all agree on that point as well.

}*CrewLand Mall*{

Farah's crew are allowed in VIP tonight. The plan is still on and in full effect. They have to have this entire plan done in 11 days. So if Marvin would've shown up or gotten close enough to CrewLand tonight. Security would've allowed him to party too. Or spy or whatever he would've really been there to do. Ellen and her girls show up. Ellen is allowed to come to the club as long as she doesn't cause any problems. She promises she'll behave. Her and her girls have a great time. Matt is at his wife's house tonight and not at the club. Which helps to keep things calm. Tonya had advised him to lay low for awhile. Eventually, he'll need to disappear completely. Ellen notices Farah being chummy with Chill tonight. She knows how close the crew are, so she isn't buying it. She knows Renee as a black woman, isn't going to give up her life with that beautiful brother. Not for some white bitch. She figures Renee has to be plotting on something. That's when it hits her. She turns to Rudy and Dorothy.

"The ladies in the crew are my anonymous source. And now I know why," she says.
She isn't right about the crew ladies buying and sending her the gun. But she's on the right track. Someone did send her the gun to get rid of someone else. That part of her guess is correct. But the crew ladies know nothing of her having a gun or an anonymous friend. They just want it to appear that they're amongst friends because shit is about to move around in Cleveland. And pretty damn quickly.

}*Operation Messy Marvin*{

Time to push the plan into overdrive. First they have to get Matt in the news. The plan calls for Woody, Joe and Andre to grab him when he leaves Genia's house, *this* Monday morning. As Matt says goodbye and walks out to his vehicle, the van pulls up. They slide the door open, grabs him, sacks his head and speeds away. They put hand cuffs on him while they ride. Genia, Kelly nor Matt know about the plan. It looks real enough

TIME TO FEEL-RELOADED-TIME WILL REVEAL 5   Black Coffee

enough to them, as well as all the neighbors who witnessed the kidnapping. Immediately Kelly calls 911 and reports his abduction while her mother screams and gets comfort from the neighbors.

Matt's kidnapping hits breaking news just in time for Marvin to catch it. The teary pleas of the wife and daughter, gives him a real sense of power. He watches the coverage and gloats as he eats his takeout dinner from *Sizzlers*. He counts 1 down and 1 to go. Before 5 o'clock, Joe contacts him for the balance on Matt and the down payment on Chill.

"We want it just like we discussed," Joe says, "Same spot as before. Up the block from Farah's house. The same way you did the first payment. And like I told you before. The only reason I showed you where *your* woman lived. Is so *you* know that *we know* where she lives too. If we don't get our money or you double cross me. That will be the last place she lives. Are we clear?"

"We're clear," Marvin says, "I'll be there. At nine tomorrow night. Please don't harm Farah."

"Don't give me a reason too," Joe says and he hangs up.
Marvin goes about securing the balance for Matt and the deposit for Chill. Once he gets the money counted and safe in the drop bag. He gets dressed for a night of spying on Farah. This is something he has done often since finding her abode. But tonight, he wants to see how she deals with the abduction of her *nigger* lover. He arrives at his surveillance spot, just down the street from her house. Where he spies from, gives him the full view of her home and the comings and goings, in and around it. He puts his night vision goggles to use as he scoots down in the drivers seat of his rental car and waits for something to move.

In the meantime, Matt is at the motel with the guys who had taken him. They keep him in the hand cuffs and blindfold. They've barely spoken to him since they grabbed him. They make sure he eats and drinks plenty of fluids but they haven't allowed him to see their faces. They wait there as he begs, not to be killed. That when the crew arrives.

When Chill, Tank and Jr show up, they have Pac Man with them. They remove the blindfold and the cuffs. When Matt looks up and sees Chill's face, then Tank and Jr's too. He look's confused as he starts to ask many questions. Quickly they make him aware of what's going on and why they had to do this, like they did it. He's instantly relieved. Then he recalls what Tonya had been hinting to him about, in the previous weeks.

"Ah man. I've never been so happy to see y'all motherfuckers in all my *life*," Matt says with a chuckle. He adds, "Can y'all let my wife and daughter know I'm okay? I've been hearing them on the news all day."

"No Matt, we can't. Not until the plan is done," Chill says, "They have to think you're really kidnapped and in danger."

"It has to look real until we put this dude away," Tank says, "He paid to have you killed and Chill too."

"So you know we've got to get in his ass, crew style," Jr adds.

"Why? Who is he?" Matt asks.

"He's Farah's ex fiancée," Tank says, "Dude came from Pittsburgh and from a wealthy family. He's obsessed with that sleazy bitch that you've been fucking with."

"He's a racist piece of shit too," Joe adds.

"He was willing to pay forty grand to have you killed," Pac Man says to Matt, "He put down the first twenty and has paid the balance."

"He watch Farah's house every night," Woody says, "But she don't even know that he knows where she lives."

"We showed him where she lives," Andre says, "That way he knows that we know where she lives too. That's in case he doesn't pay us or tries to back out of his contract. But the hits was already ordered by the time he learned where she lives at. So he knew you was fucking her. But it's really about more than that. We know he'll show up there, if he thinks he has to save her."

Chill says, "And tomorrow night, he'll show up out there to pay and no doubt, to watch her every move. That's when we'll grab his ass."

"We're gonna do him in, Matt. Just so you know," Jr says, "Can you handle that and not talk?"

Matt looks up at Jr and sees that he has a serious look on his face. Every guy in that room has a similar look. He knew then that his own life would not be spared if he didn't keep his mouth shut.

"I understand and I want say anything," Matt says, "After all, y'all saving my life in the process. I owe y'all, *big* time. But how did y'all know he hired someone?"

"Because he hired us," Pac Man says, "I could've killed you and made that money *legit*. So you're right. We saved your life."

"Twice," Andre says, "Because we didn't know you. We know big Chill," he says, "If he would've just asks for you. Then you'd be dead already."

"But once he said my name. They reached out," Chill says, "And the crew let them know that we knew you too. After that, we rearranged the contracts on his ass. And they're gonna be carried out, real fuckin soon."

"All of this. For *Farah*?" Matt asks, "She gives some good ass head. But damn! That bitch ain't worth dying for."

"Well I'll find all of that out tomorrow," Chill says, "We'll give him a show before he leaves this world. I figure that's the least we can do."

"So you and Renee aren't breaking up?" Matt asks.

"Not for *any* reason," Chill says, "That was part of the plan too."

"Farah told me she was done with me," Matt says, "She said she wanted you, all along. She said I was just her excuse to keep coming around so she could watch you. Did you ever fuck around wit her?"

"No. Not at all," Chill says, "And I never wanted too. I'm not into white girls."

"None of the crew are," Tank says, "It's about a girls *mentality*."

"Then why does Marvin wanna kill you?" Matt asks.

"Paranoia, I guess. Or maybe she told him she was moving here for me," Chill says, "I don't know. But that's beside the point really. There's nothing between us and never has been. Never will be. He should've been a man about it and just came to me. I would've met with both of them and showed him that I didn't have nor did I wanna have, his bitch. It's all in her head. She stays in her lane with me. But him. He acted on it. Spying on my businesses and shit."

"They both do a lot of fuckin watching, don't they?" Tank asks. They all chuckle briefly.

"Maybe that's a white thing?" Andre asks.

"That's just a dumb ass thing," Chill says, "A money thing. People who have had it easy all of their lives. Think they can play others like puppets. They feel like their money can get them *anything* they want. Or out of any type of jam. Just by dangling some money at them and pulling the strings."

"It's working," Joe says with a huge grin, as they all laugh.

"Damn sho is though," Pac Man says, "Until he asks for the crew boss. Then there was no fuckin way."

"I've always heard that the crew had power," Matt says, "I'm just glad I'm on the good side of that power. And I'll make sure that I stay there. You got my word on that. I am on the good side. Right?"

"You're straight," Tank says.

"Stay where you're at too man," Joe says "It could mean saving other peoples lives that you care about. Because we're loyal to Chill's crew. For life."

"I understand," Matt says, "I got a woman who worries the hell out of me. How much would y'all charge me to get rid of her?"
Though no one gives him an answer. They do laugh at his comment. Chill informs him that he'll have to stay in kidnap status until further notice. He doesn't have to stay blindfolded or handcuffed. But he can't contact anyone except the folks who are in the room with him right now. He's okay with that. They tell him they'll stage a fake escape for him. After they get Marvin to the chamber.

"So it'll look like it's random? Just something that's happening in the area?" Matt asks, for clarity.
Again no one answers him. But Tank winks and nods. Woody and Joe stay behind while the others head to CrewLand. They have to get set up for the following night. Then watch Monday night football at Stoney's, like they normally do. And they'll update John and Al on the progress of the plan.

}*Jackson Heights*{

It's morning and Ebony is up with the twins. Lannie is helping her make breakfast when she gets a call from Gwen.
"Hello Gwen," she says, "How are you, this morning?"
"I've been better," Gwen says, "I was wondering if we could meet and talk today?"
"Can you come by my office?" Ebony asks, "Maybe around *noon*?"
"Okay," Gwen says, "I'll be there."
They hang up.

Renee wakes up to *Frankie Beverly and Maze* on the radio, singing *Happy Feelings*. She sings along as she gets Destiny up for school and makes breakfast. Chill gets up and calls Kenny. They review tonight's plan again. Then Kenny tells him, he'll be driving home immediately after class to get things kicked off. He speaks to his mother and his little sister. They're riding in the Denali, these days. Kenny felt like that was the only way he could feel better about keeping it around their house. After saying goodbye to his little sister, he heads off to class. Chill is dropping Destiny off at school today. She turned 10 years old this year. Chill and Renee often reminisce with her about the way she came into the world. She finds it amazing that both her parents was shot and survived. She says she's an angel. That's why they all lived. Her parents and her brother agree with her. She *is* an angel. She's now in fifth grade at *Abe Lincoln Middle school*.

168

TIME TO FEEL-RELOADED-Time Will Reveal part 5

A few minutes later, Wes and T-baby show up for breakfast. They bring Jada and Rich III, just as Chill and Destiny are preparing to leave. Jada and Rich III catch a ride to school with Chill and Destiny. Wes sits down and T-baby fixes both their plates. Then she sits next to her man. Renee had invited them over. She wants Wes to see that Chill is still living at home before their mission happens. Also she wants to bring him up on what's really going on *with* the mission. This will be his first. T-baby came with him to help Renee give him the crew history. She knows Renee and Chill aren't breaking up. But she isn't really informed on what the latest and entire plan is. Renee sits down with them at the table and fills them in, as best she can while they eat breakfast. With T-baby's help, she explains to Wes what the crew mean to each of them and how they have moved over the years. This is to help him understand that her and Chill aren't really breaking up. But sealing their bond even tighter, by getting rid of a mere obstacle. He's amazed and proud, all at the same time. He now understands the closeness he's been witnessing for the past 5 years. *Solidarity*. He also understands why she'd stayed in Cleveland with Chill and the crew. And severed ties and her relationship with their mother. This crew family is thick, loyal and completely self contained. His big sister wouldn't have gotten this kind of support from their family. He never has. Neither of them have. That's what made them depend on each other all of their lives.

"I see why you moved here and stayed, Renee," he says, "This is some real *Mafioso* type of shit."
He smiles broad. T-baby kisses him and smiles too. She has been bringing him up on the connect since their courtship started. But she hadn't been permitted to give him all of the information. Not until Chill and Renee felt he was ready to hear it from them. Once he was fully aware of what the crew is and what he would be expected to do as a part of the crew. Wes feels honored to be invited in. He's more than willing to do his part. He's always been down to follow Renee since he was a toddler.

"I want in on this crew thing," he says, "Hell yea I do. Sis, I knew you had some loyal people around you. But I never knew you all had this type of commitment plus strategy too. The crew is damn near it's on political party. Except y'all sponsor candidates instead of running for office yourselves. So far."

"We're a self contained unit which was the plan since the eighties," Renee says, "That's true. But we support democrats as long as this republican bullshit is reigning. But we're moderate and progressive independents, politically. Gangsters, as far as street shit goes. With no tolerance for dumb shit. We hold each other down. No matter *what* it is."

"With covert actions when necessary," Wes says, "I'm definitely able to help out in that area."

"Every year we step our game up to another level," T-baby says, "That was the plan from day one, when our girls went into the armed forces. That's apart of the crew plan as well. Big Brad taught his kids, Brad Jr and Bre. Then they trained us."

"You, Bre and Lynn will be our Military operations team," Renee says, "You three are in charge of making sure the future generations are properly trained and keep all of us toned too."

"Got it, sis," he says, "I'm honored."

Wes is all in now. After breakfast, they all go in to work at CrewLand. Wes will be accompanying the crew men on their mission tonight.

}*CrewLand Mall*{

Ebony's line is ringing as she arrives at her office. Claudia patches the call through and she answers it. She thinks it's Gwen calling her back. But it isn't. It's Wheeler calling her, 1st thing this morning to tell her there has been movement on the Raymond White case.

"They're focusing on the *Omega Psi Phi Fraternity* angle," he says.

"Okay but you're calling me, *why*?"

"I need to bring Brad junior in," Wheeler says, "Ann Arbor is looking at the possibility that he could've used his membership to influence the chapter there to do harm to Raymond."

"*What*? That's ridiculous," she plays it off, "We have *ques,* all through our family tree. That's just crazy to even suggest that. Omega men are honorable. They're not schemers."

"That may be. But that's the latest word," he says, "Can I get you to set up a meeting with him and I, at your earliest convenience?"

"Why is it for *my* convenience?" she asks.

"I need you to come too," Wheeler says, "I need to know what part, if any, the crew had in his demise. If you come. Then Ajay will come too. Because they're going to work this lead. Ann Arbor had big expectations for that kid. Plus some of his family and the coaches family have a lawsuit. The school is trying to clean their noses."

"I don't see why they're bothering my family though," she says.

"It's their only lead. Once we kill and bury this. Everything else will go away."

She doesn't believe him. She feels like there's more to it that's not being said. But Wheeler has always shot straight from the hip with her crew. So she trusts what he says.

"I'll call junior and Anthony too," she says, "We'll call you back and set up something for later this week. Is that gonna be soon enough?"

"That should be okay. I just wanna get something solid before Thanksgiving."

"Okay. We'll call you back soon," she says.

He says okay and they hang up. Ebony calls Ajay immediately. He's still at *Big Mama's house,* where he'd dropped the twins off for preschool. He was going to hang out until time to open his sports complex. He has practice at 3p.m. He calls Jr and tells him to meet him at Ebony's office. Ebony calls Gwen back to tell her they'll have to postpone their meeting.

"Something else came up," Ebony tells her, "I'm not avoiding you at all. I want you to know, I know all about what happened at school and I do want us to talk about it. But I have an appointment to make with my husband. And you know he comes first, okay?"

"Okay," Gwen says, "I understand. We can do it later. Just let me know."

"I will," Ebony tells her and they hang up just as Ajay is coming into her office.

"Who was that?" he asks.

"Gwen," she answers, "I had to let her know we had to cancel our noon plans and we'll get together later."

"Is she still on that Natty shit?" he asks.

"I suppose so," Ebony says, "I told her I know about it. She didn't seem shocked. I guess because Nina confronted her at Erica's reception. But it just seems like it's more than that."

Ajay shrugs his shoulders and says, "Jarvis hasn't said shit about it. So I don't know. Right now I don't care. I wanna get this Raymond shit over with."

"So do I," she says.

When Jr arrives, Chill is with him. They come into her office and get right down to it. Chill tells Ebony to call Wheeler back and tell him they're all on the way now. She does. Wheeler is pleased they're coming on in so soon.

The 4 of them go in. Jr gives his statement. Then Wheeler tells him Ann Arbor is looking into whether or not he used his influence to get the

TIME TO FEEL-RELOADED-Time Will Reveal part 5

Omega fraternity to do harm to Raymond. Jr tells him that isn't factual. "I was against Ray joining the fraternity. That much is true. And when I got the ninety one fall pledge list. I looked for his name on the Ann Arbor's sheets. When I saw it. I called all of the Omega's in the crew. And we all sent votes of *no,* to that Chapter. The Chapter was gonna meet with him and let him know they wasn't gonna extend a membership offer to him and why. But he never showed up."

"How did you know to look for his name as a potential pledge?" Wheeler asks.

"Two of our business partners from Houston told me they'd heard word he was planning to pledge, *Q Dog.* Actually, we met them when Ebony and Tank was living down there. We became fast friends. Now they're part owners in our businesses in Atlanta. Charles Washington and David Jones. We've known them for fourteen years now. We met them before the assault happened and remained friends. They was keeping an eye on Ebony, down there *because* Raymond was always harassing her. Anything they heard about him since the assault. They kept us informed of. So in that aspect. Yes I did use the crews influence to keep him out of the frat. I didn't want him in because he wasn't Omega material. He had to go to trial for attempted rape and assault on Ebony. A prominent citizen plus business owner, community organizer and volunteer. Add on that big mama Jones learned that Ebony's assault wasn't the first time he'd done something like that. I didn't want him in the purple and gold. And once the brothers found out about his criminal history and drug selling. They didn't want him in the frat either. I did influence it, in that way. I would have to say yes. But he could never fit in anyway. We don't get down like that. But after he didn't show up. We figured someone from Houston had told him we had black balled him. Because I told them I had plans of black balling him."

Wheeler's paralegal takes notes as Jr talks.

"Who was the Chapter President at Ann Arbor, at the time Raymond disappeared?" Wheeler asks.

"Aaron Stubbs. He arranged the meeting but when I called back the next day to see how everything went," Jr says, "He told me Ray never showed up. Then later on. He called me and told me that he was missing. But the Houston guys had already told us about him missing."

"This Aaron Stubbs was killed in a car accident, two years ago?" Wheeler asks.

"No. Aaron lives in Flint with his wife and kids," Jr says, "Michael Mallard was killed in the auto accident. He resided in Ann Arbor and was

172

in his third year of residency, when he was killed. Actually he was riding his motorcycle home from the hospital when it happened. He was one of the three who was gonna meet with Ray."

"Did you guys have close contact before and after Ray went missing?"

"Sure, on fraternity matters. All chapter presidents do. I had been president at CSU and Aaron use to pull my coat whenever he needed too. But other then that. We never got to hang out. Aaron and I talk more now since Michael died. We hated we all never got together like we'd plan too."

Then Wheeler tells him, he had already spoken with Aaron and he gave him the same statement. The 3rd guy, Rashon Dunnings is an assistant football coach at Ann Arbor. He had talked with him and gotten the same statement also. Jr knew their stories were solid. He also knew Wheeler was only interested in making sure his crew had their statements together. Any guilt or innocence, he could manipulate. But the crew knows Wheeler very well. This is the dress rehearsal. Just in case things get thick.

"I just wanted to make sure everything would flush," Wheeler says, "I *will* need to talk with David Jones and Charles Washington too. Can you guys hook that up for me? Ask them to give me a call, here at the office?"

"For sho," Jr says.

Then Wheeler bids them a good day. They leave and head back to work.

They drop Ebony back at her office. Then use her Escalade to pick up Ron from Cleveland-Hopkins International Airport. He has come in for the chamber meeting tonight.

"Right on time as always then. Ha brothers?" Ron asks after hearing Wheeler wants to interview his homeboys.

"Right on time," Jr repeats.

"Charles and David already know the script," Ron says, "Ann Arbor and Houston are looking at the case as drug related. We're gonna send them back on that route. Wheeler will wanna talk to me next. I got what he needs to move any implications from the family."

"You said it would shake out to where you could get your hands in it again," Ajay says with a smile.

"And so it has," Ron smiles, "I got four gee's waiting to hold this one. Like I told Chill. All they need is for me to look out on their love ones. Big Tony's cousin Ayesha committed suicide behind Ray's assault on her. That was right after I met y'all. Ray attacked her after Tank and Ebony moved back home. Ebony came back to H town alone and that bitch nigga wouldn't let her be. But Ayesha left a box full of info. Right down to the conversations that went on before *and* during her attack. And all the shit that happened afterwards," Ron continues, "He told Ayesha, she was going to take Ebony's place. Ain't that about a *bitch*? Then Sonya, Shuntay and Tina, his nasty ass hood rats as we all call them. Kept the nightmare going *for* him. They kept threatening that little girl and telling her they was gonna kill her mama and Raymond was gonna rape her, again and again after her mother was dead. Because she would be alone. Big Tony still got that box of information. That and *then* some. He was gonna kill that nigga before he ever got to fuck with Ebony but he couldn't prove it was him. Ayesha never told because she was scared to death. *Literally*. Big Tony got them rats strung out on crack now though. They a fuckin *mess* these days. He still has plans of them dying. He just got sent up on that interstate killing before he could off them. I told him I'd make sure it got done because he got double life. All of them got at least one life sentence. So you see. They know they'll never touch down again. Fifth ward always gave them work. Y'all was a big part of the work they made huge profits on. This is just how they pay homage. By keeping their folks out here. People keeping people safe from prosecution."

"We've got people," Ajay says with a smile.

"Oh yes indeed, Cuz," Ron assures him, "We've *been* people, man. Since the eighties and shit don't change when it's true."

"See how that shit come back around here?" Chill says, "Real recognize real."

"And big Tony wanted to thank y'all personally for doing away with that crumb," Ron says, "We could never get everybody together before they caught those bids. But my killers did that work in Houston. The coach and all those family members. They was doing that for us *and* y'all. For family. *Period*. Real recognize real."

"All the time," they all say as they head back to CrewLand Mall.

Gwen and Ebony meet in her office after 2pm. Ebony invites her to sit. She can see that Gwen is tormented, so she starts the conversation.

"Gwen, I don't want you to feel that we can't talk or be friends," Ebony says, "What you and my brother did. Happened in college before you knew how tight our crew are. Tank is responsible. Same as you are."

"I wished it hadn't happened, Ebony," Gwen says, "Jarvis still doesn't know about it. He's thinking we didn't get voted in because of him. I don't know how to tell him, that it's all my fault."

It's not all your fault. It's his fault too. You just don't know what he did.

174

Ebony knows neither Gwen nor Jarvis have been forthcoming with each other about that fall night in Cincinnati. She also knows she isn't going to be the one to tell it.

"You just have to find a way to tell him," Ebony suggests, "I don't know how to advise you because I'm not familiar with that kind of thing. I've only been with Anthony and I know I'd never wanna keep a secret from him, of *any* kind."

"That's not the only reason I came, Ebony," Gwen says.

Ebony surfs carefully. She wonders now if Gwen does know about Jarvis and Rebbie. She needs to get this conversation done, so she can get back to work. She asks, "What else is it?"

"My sister," Gwen says.

"Nickeia?" Ebony asks with a rise in her voice. She asks, "What about her? Don't tell me she messed with crew too."

"No she hasn't," Gwen says, "She's still a virgin. But...., but she has her eye on someone she'll never have."

"Who?" Ebony asks, "A crew guy?"

Gwen shakes her head affirmative.

"Who is it?" Ebony asks but not really wanting to hear or so she thinks.

"She's had a crush on Ajay since meeting him at Natty," Gwen reveals.

"Oh well she can definitely get over that one," Ebony says, "Anthony is mine. My husband. I can't even pretend I would be okay with her *ever* going after him."

"I told her as soon as she admitted it, last night," Gwen says, "That was her whole reason for enrolling in school here. She was planning to live with us. You know. When we were *right* across the street. That's how I was able to get it out of her. Because she was more upset than we were about the move. I kept after her until she came clean. And yes I told her, I would never be okay with her ever saying anything to him or trying to make a move on him."

"That makes two of us," Ebony says, giving Gwen a very stern look. "I was sad about the move too. But I can't say I am *now*. And Gwen, Anthony isn't gonna like hearing this at all. Not even that you told me. But I don't keep anything from him. So I'll have to tell him. I'm gonna to tell him tonight."

"Just make sure he knows we aren't gonna allow her to impose," Gwen says, "I've done enough already."

"Oh I will," Ebony says, "That's for sure."
Ebony has to get some work finished before she can pick up her twins. She tells Gwen, they'll talk later and excuses her from her office.
Once Gwen is gone, Ebony sits at her desk and replays their talk in her head. She has to comment aloud.

"My man is on every woman's mind. I *swear*," she says, managing a slight smile. "But those are my goods. I'm not even thinking about sharing him. Besides, Trina Yvette has already said she would be honored if I ever needed a substitute after the baby comes. *Hmm*. It's something about her asking my permission that doesn't piss me off like knowing some woman is trying to get at him and acting like I'm not even here."
She smiles to herself before dismissing it all from her mind and getting back to her work files. She smiles and thinks to herself.
Maybe I should write a book, so these hot women can get an inside glimpse of how my man puts it down with me. Hmm.

Down by the clubs, Kenny arrives at the CrewLand mall just as Ajay is about to leave for *Gund Arena*.
"Hey uncle Ajay," he says, "What's good, man? Tell Lebron I said what's up," he chuckles.
"Alright. And I'll be back for the chamber meeting," Ajay tells him.
"Word? I ain't never been on a hoot ride with my uncle Ajay," he says, "This here is one for the journal, bro. *Legendary*. I'll be sure and take notes too."
They laugh as Ajay hops into his Grand Cherokee, his work truck. He heads to practice. He calls Ebony to chat while he heads downtown.
I don't know what they're expecting. But I'm not fucking over Ebony. Not even for a crew thang. And definitely not to fuck Farah.

Kenny had just left from visiting at MLK. Something he does every time he comes home from Ohio State. But as per his part of the plan, this time he went by to visit Farah Benson. She was surprised and thrilled, to say the least. Before the Denali and the meeting with Chill last week, Kenny had been avoiding her. He wouldn't have seen her today if it hadn't been apart of the recipe for her cake. He reminded her that they have a date tonight. She confirmed it. She assured him, she hadn't forgotten. He could tell she was looking forward to being shared by father and son.
Kenny is in Chill's office now, going over the confirmation.

"So that bitch is ready to taste the rainbow, then ha?" Chill asks with a chuckle.

"She stay ready," Kenny says, "I could've got it waxed at MLK. But I told her to save it up. She's anticipating getting her knees dirty. I see a lot of ho's, pops. But I ain't never seen a ho that's *proud* to be a ho, like that bitch. She has no shame." They laugh.

They laugh and Chill adds, "She's gonna need all the energy she can get. She needs to be able to show Marvin how much she loves dark meat."

"And how much of it she can take," Kenny adds with a chuckle.

They had gone into the club by the time Farah shows up at CrewLand mall. She comes by Crew Cuts and Style's as soon as she leaves work. She wants to see if there has been any word on Matt's kidnapping. Tonya tells her they haven't heard anything. Her number is already on file, as a customer. She asks them if they'll let her know when they hear something. Nina tells her they will and she leaves.

Minutes later, Ellen and her girls come by. They're worried about Matt too. Joiner and Miles escort them to Crew Cuts. Justine, Tonya and Nina tell her they'll inform her as well. Security sees them back off the property immediately. Ellen is being a lot more civil, these days or so it seems. It may just be the calm before the storm. The heaven before hell. The drought before the high water.

The work day has finally come to a close. The crew wives are conducting their normal daily routine. Ebony and T-baby are closing up their offices and are about to head home. Ebony has to go by Granny's house to pick up the twins before heading to Jackson Heights. T-baby has to get Rich III from Big Mama's house, where the school bus drops him off each day after school. He's in 2nd grade at Beachwood Elementary. That's where the crew had all attended elementary school after the families migrated to Cleveland. It's where all of their children go for elementary school.

"We've all got things *so* convenient, cousin," Ebony says, "I absolutely *love* my life."

"Yes we do have it convenient," T-baby agrees, "We're a big part of that convenience *to* though, cousin."

"Yea you're right about that Tee. We made the right moves when and where it counted," Ebony says.

"And now our children are in the care of their grandmothers. But for *pay*," T-baby says and they both giggle. She adds, "Our mothers and grandparents are so proud of us. Can't you tell?"

"Oh yes indeed. But they gave us the blueprint," Ebony says, "By making us so close and teaching us to be loyal to our own. And to stay to our own. Together we *all* made this happen. But we couldn't have done it without their guidance."

"And now it feels so good and pays good too," T-baby says as she smiles.

"Our kids still get to attend the same public schools, like we did but they get aftercare from the matriarchs of the crew," Ebony says as she smiles too, "That's progress."

"No. That's the icing on the cake," T-baby says and they laugh. Then T-baby heads down the walk to meet Rebbie at *Big Mama's house* and get Rich III. They're also picking up Jerica, Orian, Destiny and Jada. Ebony heads across the street to meet up with Nina at *Granny's house*. Together, they pick up Tank Jr, Donovan, Ashanti, Richaunda, Lannie and Lil Ajay. The foursome bring all the under the age of 13 children to Jackson Heights, every weekday, where they have evening study groups, TV time, snacks and play time at their park. They make sure the children have dinner too, if necessary. The other parents work jobs in the evenings. And since the foursome are off by 5pm. They was selected to make sure all the other children do their chores and homework, so their parents don't have to find additional childcare after *Granny's house* and *Big Mama's house* closes by 7pm. Chill's crew decided to do this so their mothers and grandmothers at the daycare centers could have an evening break and spouse time too.

The foursome meet in the parking lot before they leave. After all the children are secured in their vehicles, Ebony has an issue she wants to discuss with her girls.

"I wanna ask y'all something," she says, "I need to know if y'all have noticed something different with your husband lately?" she asks.

"Something different, like what?" Rebbie asks.

"Like they're tip toeing around us?" Nina asks.

"Yes," Ebony says, "Like they've got something going on. Like another *Raymond* situation."

"Well they did just dig him up, cousin," T-baby says, "Maybe their planning a strategy in case the cops come after the crew."

"No. We've got people, cousin," Ebony says with a smile, "That Raymond thing was cured and settled the first time Ron was up here. Trust me. Anthony went straight at it. He wasn't gonna allow me to be worried

178

about it. He had things working during Erica's wedding week. But like I was saying. There's something *new* going on. I can feel it. Y'all haven't noticed *anything* different? Am I the only one that's picking up the signs?"

"I have," Nina finally says, "And Jeremy only gets like this when the crew have a mission to carry out."

"*Exactly*," Ebony says, "Okay and y'all know with the whole disappearance of Matt thing? Anthony hasn't even mentioned anything about him *missing*. Nor has he acted like he's worried about his kidnapping. Not even once. I find that strange. Especially with him being our *employee*."

"Oh *wow*! Okay. *None* of them have said anything about it," T-baby says, "I hadn't really thought of this, until you said it. But Wesley is going on his first crew caper, sometime soon. Renee had us over for breakfast to tell him that he's expected to go along with the men. But she didn't have the info on *when* it was taking place. Chill was gonna fill him in farther. I didn't put the two things together though."

"I've been around this crew shit, all my life," Ebony says with a giggle. "I've learned what to look for. And Anthony, oh my *God*. My baby loves me so much. He tries to hide his feelings but I can always tell when something's on his mind. He may not tell me the *particulars*. But I know when he's distracted. It's that street shit too."

"I *have* noticed Andre and Joe has been coming back around too," Nina says, "That's a sure sign of that street shit," she laughs.

"Brian is on the phone with his brothers a lot more, lately," Rebbie says, "So yes. I do believe they're planning something. I just didn't wanna seem like the nagging wife. But I sure did want to mention it to him. A couple of times."

"I do too," Ebony says, "I just had to see if it was going on in several houses. We can't be like our mother's crew was. Mama told me they missed out on stopping a lot of their males activity because they would feel a certain way or see something they didn't feel was *all* together cool. But they wouldn't say anything because everyone else *seemed* okay. And didn't say anything either. So I figured I'm gonna be the wife to *say* something."

"Ebony you're always the one to notice something and demand changes," Rebbie says.

"Yep and she got it for all of us because she was *so* spoiled," Nina says as they all laugh.

"Like *you* wasn't," Ebony says and laughs, "We all was. Because we was always so close. Y'all got everything I got because I demanded it. I couldn't have the best baby doll and y'all not have to same type. How in

the world was we suppose to play together, if got it and y'all didn't?"
They all laugh again.

"Yeah but you played with them dolls *way* too long," Nina says.

"Until Ajay started tearing em up," T-baby says and laughs.

"He use to put 'em in the fireplace and melt them so Ebony would grow up," Nina says and they all laugh hysterically.

"Oh yes Ebony you was still playing with your baby dolls, up until the night before you lost your virginity," Rebbie adds as they all laugh again before T-baby gets back on the subject.

"And she ain't played with one *since* either," T-baby says, "But do y'all think it's gonna be the typical crew type of stuff?" she asks, "Like, are they gonna be fuckin off too?"

"If so, I'm not okay with that part," Ebony says, "I know Anthony better remember that he's married to me. That's all I have to say on that. Because him and everybody else should know by now, that I will kill if I have too. Now let's get these kids to Jackson heights. We can talk about it out there."

"Let's go hold this family thing together," Rebbie says as they all giggle.

"That's how the crew do it," Nina says, "We're gonna make some more changes."

"The awesome foursome strikes again," T-baby adds.

"Let's head out crew," Ebony says with a laugh as she double checks the kids in their car seats and seatbelts.
She hops into the drivers seat of her Escalade and the other 3 jump into their Navigators. They convoy to Jackson Heights.

Bradley Lee Wilson III or Lil Brad is 12 now. He and CJ will be initiated to crew, next year. Jr and Bre are already planning to have their party together. Brad III stays at *The Spot II*. He does his homework there and he works his after school job as well. He plays basketball for his league team at *Allen Saul's Recreation center*. His father Jr was a good player and so was his aunt Bre. But he isn't planning to play basketball as a career. He has more of a business mind, like Jr does. He wants to be a CEO.

}*Chamber Time*{
It's finally Tuesday night and time for *the crew* mission. The mission is starting with Chill and Kenny's date, with Farah. While out at the CrewLand Condo's, Marvin is leaving for another night of staking out Farah's home. But first, he has to pay the balance on Matt and the down

payment on Chill. He meets Joe and Woody at the opposite end of Parma Heights. They complete the transaction. Marvin leaves the area as if he's gone for good. Only to give Joe and Woody time to leave. Once they're out of sight, he goes back, parks at the opposite end of Farah's street and watches her house. The guys already know about the watching. They have a plan for that too.

By 9pm Kenny and big Chill pull up in Chill's 2004 Chrysler 300. He and Jr have both bought new cars. Again they get the same models of a different color. As Chill pulls up and parks, Marvin looks on. He's isn't familiar with the new car, so he watches through his night vision goggles as Chill and Kenny get out. He recognizes them immediately.

"Ah fuck me," Marvin whispers to himself, "She got two of those thug ass niggers coming to her place. This shit will end soon. I'll just have to get his bastard son too."
He squirms in his seat as he sees them go up to the door and ring the bell. Farah answers the door wearing very sexy attire. She's all smiles as she hugs them both. Chill and Kenny know Marvin is watching but Farah doesn't. Chill and Kenny ham it up for his cameras, by grabbing her ass when they hug. Farah has her purse, in hand. They're picking her up because their date will take place, *elsewhere*.

"Where the hell is she going?" Marvin asks himself.
He's so busy watching them, that he doesn't notice Andre and Pac Man as they ease up to his driver's window. Pac Man points a 9mm with a silencer, at him. Then Andre taps on the window. A startled Marvin, jerks and looks out of his window, only to see that he's staring into the wrong end of an automatic pistol. He freezes as Andre pulls the door handle. The door is unlocked.

"Unlock it fool or die here," Pac man says and Marvin pops the locks.
While Chill, Kenny and Farah drive away in Chill's 300. Pac Man and Andre escort Marvin to the van they'd parked just around the corner. The same van they'd used to grab Matt, on the other side of town. Joe and Woody are in the van.

"Good to see you again, sir," Joe says to Marvin with a chuckle.
They handcuff Marvin, hogtie him and duck tape his mouth. Andre goes back to get the rental car. They all head to CrewLand Mall where they'll meet up with Chill, Kenny, Farah and the other guys at Arthur's video store. They have a plot to play out there, before going to the chamber. It's time to formally introduce Marvin to how the crew gets down, on his type.

}CrewLand Mall{

Ajay arrives just outside the front of *Que Psi Phi studios*. He's the front door man. He has to make sure no one notices anything peculiar, before he can unlock the front door and go inside. He parks his Jaguar in reserved parking. He hops out and locks his doors. He hears the familiar click of high heel ladies pumps, from behind. They're approaching quickly. He puts his hand on the handle of his 9 and whips around to see, *Nickeia*.

"Hey Ajay. What's up," she says, out of breath.

She had run all the way to his car when she saw him pass *The Spot II*.

"How are you?" Ajay answers but not really wanting to know.

He's relieved to see it's only his wingman's sister-in-law. He still doesn't know about her crush yet. Ebony's planning to tell him about it when he makes it home tonight.

"I'm good *now* that I see you here," Nickeia says, batting her eyelashes. She adds, "I was just hanging out at the spot two. It's a nice spot. But you know I'm old enough for the main club now."

"The main club don't open on Tuesday night though," Ajay says.

He's caught off guard by her demeanor and the way she's dressed.

"Do Jarvis and Gwen know you're dressed like that?" he ask with concern.

"I'm a woman now, Ajay," she says, "I'm ready to do *big* girl things too. I saved myself for you. I heard you like virgins."

"Ah hey. Nickeia I'm married to *my* virgin," he says as he chuckles, "I'm alright with that one."

"She's not a virgin anymore though," she says, "She's had twins and she's pregnant now."

"Oh I know that Nickeia. Those are my babies," he says, growing slightly irritated. "All of them are my kids and *she's* my baby. For life."

He could never stand for anyone to be salty about Ebony. That hasn't changed and it won't. Not to mention, she seemed to be throwing off on his children, as if they ruined his queen, in some form or fashion.

"I want you to have *my* virginity," she says suddenly. "I've dreamed about being with you since before Jarvis even signed to Natty. I begged him to go there. Just so I could meet you."

Ajay knows he needs to get her away from down here on this end before the plan starts to unfold. He decides to treat her nice and convince her to leave on the pretense that he'll meet her later.

"I can't do that," he says, "Not tonight. I have a meeting to attend. There's no way I can be late for it. Maybe we can meet later and I can find out what you're really trying to do here. What do you say?"

TIME TO FEEL-RELOADED-Time Will Reveal part 5

"Oh yes!" Nickeia squeals as she throws her body against his.
She hugs him tightly while rubbing her pelvic against him. He looks around to see if anyone is paying attention to them. Thank God no one is. Being that they're down on the end by the photo store and the spot II is 40 yards away, none of the other patrons seem to notice. He hugs her back. But he isn't about to grind on her. He's not going to give her the impression that he's going to fuck her because he isn't going too. He loves Jarvis like a brother. This is his wife's sister. He'll find a way to let her down easy. But cheating on Ebony with her or anyone else, isn't an option.

"Okay you got your hug in," he says, "Write down your number and I'll have to call you later."

"I can text it to your phone," she suggests.

"Write it down," he says, "I'm not about to put another woman's number in my phone. You'd better learn that now."
He has no patience for this, at all. She writes her number down and hands it too him. Then she moves back up on him and asks, "Can I have a kiss?"
He knows he isn't going to do that either. If it wasn't for the murder mission they're on. He wouldn't have even taken it this far.

"You can kiss my cheek and I'll kiss yours," he says, "Then you have to head back to the spot two, so I can get on to my meeting. Cool?"

"Cool!" she says as she giggles.
He lets her kiss his cheek. He gives her a kiss on the forehead. He's out of patience.

"Go," he says, "I'll call you."
She leaves in a hurried pace. He watches her as she makes her way back to the spot II and goes back inside. He checks the far entrance and sees the van when it turns in. The van that has Marvin in it. He hurries to get to the front door of the photo store, as the rental car turns in too. He opens the door quickly. He goes in, hit's the alarm, then locks the door behind him. He rushes through the store to the back door. He knows Joe will be backing up to it shortly.

The van arrives and parks behind the studio and video store. Arthur is at the back door, waiting with Ajay to let them in. He'd locked himself in the store to set up the video equipment. Joe, Woody, Andre and Pac Man bring Marvin in and into the storage room. Arthur has set up a video screen for his viewing pleasure. He has video cameras in the upstairs apartment loft, which are tied into the storage room screen. Once they have Marvin inside, Bruce and Eric handle car duty. They take Marvin's keys to his Porsche and the rental. They have to get out to CrewLand condo's and

183

get the Porsche for the latter half of this caper. They leave in the rental car.

After Bruce and Eric pull out of CrewLand Mall, Chill turns in and drives his 300 to the back door of the photo store. Him and Kenny escort Farah up the outside stairs entrance and on into the loft apartment. She's bubbly and anticipating this night. Their date is going well but it's about to go into overdrive.

Downstairs in the storage room, Marvin has been cuffed to a steel bench which is welded to the floor. It's directly in front of the 52' TV screen. He has the best seat in the house. They leave the duck tape on his mouth, keep him in cuffs and cuff his ankles to either leg underneath the bench. Arthur turns on the screen. They're all able to see and hear Chill, Kenny and Farah upstairs.

"Are you ready to do this?" Chill asks Farah.

"Yes I am, baby," she says, "I've waited *so* long for this night."

"Oh you're calling me baby *already*?" Chill asks as he chuckles, "You don't even know if you're gonna like how I taste yet."

"Ain't that a bitch? I thought you was missing me," Kenny says with a chuckle too. "We ain't been in the apartment *five* minutes and you're calling my pops, baby. Right in front of me."

"I *have* missed you but I was trying to get at your daddy before you took my attention," she says, "You're so good. I have imagined your father fucking me since the first night I saw him. I hope that's not wrong."

"Let's get it on then," Chill suggests.

He takes her by the arm and leads her over to a portrait viewing table, Arthur has set up in the middle of the floor. The camera's are trained on the whole room. But the motion 1 is particularly focused on the table where the motion will be. Chill leans against the table, undoes his pants and puts on a condom. He looks at Farah, then Kenny speaks.

He says, "Serve my pops. Show him you're a bad bitch with that mouth."

Immediately she goes down on her knees, puts Chill in her mouth and sucks him like he's a *Jell-O pudding pop*.

"I've wanted this big ass juicy black dick, for years," she confesses. She takes him to the back of her throat. It feels good to Chill, as he leans his head back. He hasn't been unfaithful to Renee in years. This feels strangely familiar but weird, at the same time. Banging on a whore is something he's done with his crew, many times in the past. Him, Ajay and Stoney, more times than not. Stoney is nearly 14 years gone but Ajay is downstairs viewing the live action. This is only the 3rd time Chill has turned a bitch out with his son present. Not since turning Kenny on to his 1st time and his 1st

TIME TO FEEL-RELOADED-Time Will Reveal part 5

ménage trios, have they shared a woman. Chill has no desire to fuck Farah. He's just giving Marvin the ultimate heartburn. He grabs the back of her head and shoves his dick as far into her throat as he can get it. He demands that she suck it like she's been waiting on it for years, as she claims. She does. At that moment, Kenny reaches down and pulls Farah. He tells her to stand up and then he brings her to the table. He tells her to lean across it, face down. She does. Knowing what his son is about to do, Chill moves to the other side and faces the table. The table is only 3 and a half feet wide. So when Farah leans across it, her face is right in front of Chill's groin. He puts his dick back in her mouth. Kenny pulls up her dress and pulls her thong to the side. After strapping on a condom, he enters her. She purrs.

"How is it bitch?" Kenny asks, as he pounds into her pussy from the back.

She lets out a sound that almost makes him shiver. His father keeps her mouth full of hard dick. She's cumin already. This is something she's really into. Though it's a bore to Chill, these days. He knows his son's crew still tag team girls often. Him and his crew had done it too. Call it maturity or whatever you want to call it. But Chill is bored with this act already. He wants someone else to take his spot.

"Maybe I'll come back later and fuck you," he says as he pulls her hair back. "But right now my namesake got you filled up. One of my brothers might wanna know what you're working with."

He grins as he pulls out of her mouth, discards the condom in the trashcan and zips up his pants. He heads for the door, stopping to look back over his shoulder, at his junior. He's working Farah over like the man he is. Chill sees visions of himself, 15 years ago. He smiles as Farah makes pleas for Kenny to fuck her good and make her cum again. Chill leaves them in the room alone and goes downstairs. Jr heads upstairs to join Kenny and Farah. Ajay turns to Marvin.

"Since you wanted to fuck my woman. I should go on up there and fuck yours. I need her to tell me if you're as good as I am," he says, "My wife would kill my ass if this dick ain't proper. Because that's what she's use too."

"This muafucka ain't *slangin* dick correctly," Ron says of Marvin, "That's why his bitch floating. And that's why he wants to pay muafuckaz to kill *niggers*, as he calls us."

"She done went black," June says as he laughs.

"And she'll never go back, Marv," Tank teases, "She's gonna get each and every hole, she's got. Entered into by some big black juicy dick

185

TIME TO FEEL-RELOADED-TIME WILL REVEAL 5   Black Coffee

tonight. So face the facts, Marvin. She'll never want yours again."

"And crew don't do ass," Ajay says to Marvin, "So you ain't gotta worry about *that* hole."

They all laugh. Marvin squirms as he watches Farah. She's now giving Kenny head while Jr fucks her from the back. Bruce and Eric are back by now. They're standing on the stairs but they don't want a turn.

"I don't like how white girls smell," Bruce says.

"I just don't fuck wit em," Eric says, "I love brown skin."

"We all do too," Bruce says, "The bitch up there, just happens to be white. This ain't about her color or his. This is about getting to a whack motherfucker before he can get to us. That muafucka just happen to be white. This ain't happening because of their race. It's to avoid two of ours dying because of *our* race. While showing him that the bitch he's losing his life over. Ain't shit but a whore who wants a brother, who don't want her."

They're waiting to accompany Marvin to the chamber while Ajay just seems to enjoy taunting him, more than anything.

"My wife is pregnant right now," Ajay says to Marvin, "So she's hot all the time. But see. I don't allow her to give head when she's carrying my seed. I'm gonna need to let Farah wet this fourteen, in the meantime. Are you okay with that?"

He laughs at his own taunt. The crew enjoy it too. Kilo and Wayne go up.

Marvin seems drunk with anger, by the time they're done. He can't believe Farah isn't resisting *any* of them but she isn't. As a matter of fact, when Kenny, Kilo and Wayne are about to leave. She even inquires about how many more are waiting, *"to sample this sweet woman?"*

Farah, just like her friends Alana and Darlene, thinks this is the way to crew hearts. She thinks it's the way to Chill's heart. He kicked that bullshit to her and she fell for it. That's typical of a female chasing a crew man. They always think with their mouths and pussy's. So the crew men give them hard dick. Because they're usually fresh out of bubble gum.

Tank, June and Wes go in as Kenny, Kilo and Wayne are leaving. Tank and June tag team her. Then they step back and introduce her to Wes. He gets some head for his 1st crew night out. He's still mesmerized by the whole atmosphere and how much leverage and power his crew has.

Chill goes back up and takes Ajay back with him, when Tank, June and Wes finish. Chill and Ajay are going to be the last 2. Or so they let Marvin think. Joe, Andre, Woody and Pac Man had all declined a turn initially. They just want to get rid of Marvin and keep his money. They had said that would be enough to get them off.

Up in the loft, Chill gets behind Farah this time. She *thinks* he's going to fuck her. And she *thinks* she's going to suck Ajay's dick. She's pulling on Ajay's waistband but he won't allow her to unzip his jeans. He teases her. Because he knows Marvin is taunted too.

"This reminds me of my first time," Ajay says to Farah, "He use to bring me in when I was little and let me score a piece of pussy and some head. I've been fucking since I was eight years old. So I should be pretty good at it, by now. Chill said I can have some of this. Are you okay with that?"

"Sure. I don't wanna make Darlene angry but after hearing her talk about you. I *am* curious. Yes." Farah says as she smiles and sips from her wine.

"Darlene ain't got shit on this. This dick has Ebony Brown Jackson's name on it," he corrects her, "Darlene knows that too. She's been angry and ain't shit changed. Shit won't change either."

He spins her around on the table and puts her mouth on the side, he's on. He continues, "I don't even want no head from you. I don't wanna fuck you either. I'm absolutely solid in the pussy and head department. But I am gonna coach my crew through this round. You'll like it. Don't worry about that."

He calls for Pac Man and Woody to come upstairs and they both come.

"I want y'all to fuck this bitch. I'm gonna tell y'all what I want y'all to do to her," Ajay says as he smiles while Chill chuckles proudly.

He remembers doing that for Jb and Ajay, back in the day. He tells Pac Man what to say while Chill coaches Woody.

"Turn on around here and put this in your mouth," Pac Man says, "I don't wanna talk to you for *too* long. Because you might start to think we're on a *real* date or something."

Ajay and Chill laugh. Ajay is playing in Farah's hair while Chill massages her breast.

She sucks Pac Man's dick while Woody fucks her *doggy style*. She's in heaven right now. She still wants to have Ajay and Chill, *actually* doing it. That's not going to happen. But at least she can hear their voices while she's *being* fucked. She tries to close her eyes and let Chill's voice set her mood but she can't focus on Chill like she wants. Because Pac man is giving her more than she can swallow. Pac Man has about 11 inches of dick and he's rushing it into her mouth at a heated pace, over and over.

"*Damn*. You've got a big ass dick," Farah says.

"Come on. White girls are suppose to be the best at this shit," Pac

Man says and Ajay has to comment, "My wife would put your ass to shame."

Then Chill and Ajay tell Pac Man and Woody to switch. Now Farah is giving Woody head and Pac Man is fucking her, doggy style. Pac Man is hitting it so hard, the table is raising up. Farah starts to yelp which interferes with her ability to suck Woody correctly.

"Pac Man you're killing this ho," Chill says as he laughs, "She can't even suck Woody's shit right. You go ahead and finish it off, Pac Man. So we can go on and handle the *real* business."

Him and Ajay leave Pac Man and Woody in the loft with Farah and make it back downstairs where Kenny has a request.

He's smiling as he says, "Uncle Ajay. I ain't never got to trick no ho with you, man."

"Kenny I'm married to your babysitter," Ajay says with a chuckle, "That's more pussy than I can handle, as it is. But we can go up there. I'll play wit her while you turn her out. How about that?"

"Cool," Kenny says and they head back upstairs.

While Pac man is still killing it and Woody is trying to get head. Kenny plays with her breast. Ajay straps on plastic gloves so he can play with her clitoris. It isn't long until she begins to beg Pac Man to cum. The thrill was fun for awhile but she's worn out.

Ajay starts to rub up and down her body, as he says, "See if you can get my dick hard so I can go home and fuck my wife."

Farah yelps. She's exhausted.

"Uncle, let her make it," Kenny says as he laughs.

"No shit, nephew," Ajay says, "She can't even make me hard."

Pac Man doesn't cum but he does stop and discard his condom. Farah is spent as her limp body remains across the table. Woody pulls off his condom and jacks off, all over her.

"*Damn*! You nasty muthafucka," Ajay says while they all laugh.

Farah is worn out. Still she's asking for Chill and Ajay to fuck her. Kenny tells her, she's done for tonight. Him, Woody, Pac Man and Ajay help her up and sit her in the recliner, across the room. Ajay tosses her, her clothes which had been removed from her body during the night and tossed about the room. While Ajay and Kenny see to Farah. Andre and the other guys are moving Marvin back to the van for his trip to *The Chamber*. Farah never even knew he was there. If the crew's mission goes correctly. She never will.

After Jr, Joe, Andre and the rest of the guys leave with Marvin.

TIME TO FEEL-RELOADED-Time Will Reveal part 5

Chill goes back upstairs to accompany Kenny, Ajay and Farah downstairs.
"Did you have fun with my crew?" Chill asks her.
"Yes. Oh my God. I don't have enough energy to walk, hardly," Farah says, "But next time. I wanna fuck you and Ajay. *Please*?"
Neither of them answer her. They know it isn't going to be a next time.
"Let's get you home *until* then," Kenny says just to get her moving.
Chill gets in the drivers seat of his 300. Ajay rides shotgun while Kenny sits in the back with Farah. He has her to give him head, all the way to Parma Heights.
"You've been bugging the shit out of me for this," he says, "So lap it on up."
Chill and Ajay look at each other and smile. They drive Farah home and wait until she's inside. Then they drive to the chamber so they can finish the business.

}*The Chamber*{

At the chamber, Marvin has been hoisted up in the chains. Only after realizing he isn't going to make it out of there alive. He starts to beg for mercy. They shut him up, each time. Chill talks to him which should've been a hint to him that nothing he said was going to change his fate.
"We've got Ebony running trace on the large withdrawals you made this month," Chill says to Marvin. "We got the balance you paid to have me killed, out of the trunk of your rental car. All of your surveillance shit, we got that too. The tapes you had in your condo? We got them. All the money you withdrew is suspect. That shit is going to look real interesting to the feds when they find your body and start piecing shit together, trying to figure out why you got snuffed," he says, "And your store is another business that's gonna go to the crew."
"They're gonna figure you had gambling debt or you was being extorted," Ron says, "Since you was always making large withdrawals."
"If we was sloppy, we would let them have the tapes of you buying a hit," June says, "And the nine you bought to set up Ellen too. Just bogus."
"But instead we're gonna act grateful that we inherited another business from some wayward asshole," Tank says, "One who owed somebody a lot of money and couldn't get the cash up to save his life."
"That's right. *Jackson's Real Estate is* the new buyer," Jr says as he acts surprised.
"My baby is about to own this fuckin city," Ajay brags.

189

"We was expanding out that way, anyway," Tank says, "That'll be the first, of many."

They've gotten audio on Marvin admitting he was trying to set Ellen up to look like Matt's murderer. They'll figure out how they can use that later, if necessary. But for tonight, they torture Marvin while the tapes of Farah fucking members of the crew and their entourage, play in front of him. That's another form of torture as well. But the crew will not prolong his chamber stay. The mission is that Marvin will die tonight at the hands of big Chill. But before Chill can do him in. Pac Man asks for the honor.

"I would like to kill him for you since you took a serious threat from my life, years back. I've been wanting to square up wit you," Pac Man says, "I would be honored to kill this muthafucka on your behalf."

Ajay smiles. Chill hasn't lost it. He's still a boss. Not only of the eastside, where he started. But now, much of west Cleveland has his back too. That's going to serve as a feather in his cap when his crew takes care of old big Jake Johnson, for good.

"I'll give you that honor brother," Chill finally says, "With incentives to come."

"Guaranteed," Ron adds.

With that, the crew lower Marvin's feet onto the plastic which they have spread underneath him. Pac Man takes out his knife and stabs Marvin, just above the groin. He pulls the knife straight up towards his chest. Then he steps back and watches as Marvin's insides spill out over the floor like a pig at the *slaughterhouse*.

"That's some nasty shit," Ajay says with a frown.

"Damn you're vicious!" Ron yells in excitement, "I know I got some work for you, brother."

"Dude got his training with prison shanks," Tank says, "A real knife made it *child's play*."

They all chuckle. It's time for the cleaning and the disposal. They wrap Marvin up in the plastic and duck tape him into a neat package. Kilo, Jr, Wayne and Tank leave with him, headed for the pier.

When they arrive at their boat ramp, Kilo hops out and runs to untie the yacht.

"This muthafucka is gonna sleep with the fishes in Lake Erie," Tank says with a chuckle.

They load Marvin onto their 90 foot yacht, named and owned by *The Spot* nightclubs. Within minutes, the 4 guys are cruising towards Canada.

Back at the Chamber, June has the tape of Marvin admitting to trying to frame Ellen. They decide to use this 1 which had come from his condo and has only Marvin's voice on it. June, Bruce and Eric gift wrap it from Marvin and drop it in the mail. It's addressed to Ellen as overnight express to the Insurance and Carpet store. Ellen is sure to see it tomorrow before the close of the day. She'll be the 1 to open up the store.

Chill, Kenny and Ron head to CrewLand while Ajay and Wes head to Jackson Heights. Joe, Andre, Pac Man and Woody go to Stoney's for hot wings and drinks. *The Spot* is closed tonight. Renee and Tonya maintained *The Spot II* while Tank was on the mission. Chill and Ron show up to help out. Kenny kisses his mother goodnight, after going by Jackson Heights to say goodbye to Destiny. She's still at Ebony's with Ashanti and the twins. Kenny heads back to Ohio State. Renee had told him, he can drive the Denali back to school and keep it until he comes home for Thanksgiving.

TIME TO FEEL-RELOADED-Time Will Reveal part 5

CHAPTER 55

NO MORE *CREW THANG*

T-baby welcomes Wes home from his *first* crew caper. They're staying at *his* home tonight. He takes a shower, 1st thing then he has a late supper which T-baby warms for him. She sits at the table with him and they talk. She wants to know details about the mission but just as he'd been trained, Wes doesn't discuss the mission. T-baby will only be told as much as the guys agreed to share with their wives or woman. No particulars will be offered by *any* man who participated. T-baby has learned not to ask about things she doesn't want the real answers too. For while married to Rich, she'd forgone *many* opportunities to confront him just to keep peace. That isn't the case tonight. With Wes, she has no desire to know if he had gotten his full initiation to the crew. Initiation for the guys, *always* includes some type of sexual act. Once they're passed the initial one. They have the option of turning down any other crew pussy that's offered up afterwards.

"So you made out okay?" she asks.

"Yea it was cool," Wes says, "I think the crew are very well organized and very loyal."

"We are that," T-baby says, "Renee is the head female in our crew. She kept our heads on straight and she's always here when we need her."
Wes is barely talking. He knows he'd gotten oral sex from Farah. He's not sure how much T-baby knows but he isn't going to volunteer any of the indiscretions. That includes the murder he witnessed too.

At Ajay's house, things are going a little bit differently. He had come home and taken care of his daddy rounds as he usually does, after placing the number from Nickeia on the kitchen counter where he would be having his dinner. But tonight, *he* has to get his *own* plate out the microwave. He thinks it's strange because Ebony had always put his plate down in front of him whenever he came home, after her and the twins were done with dinner. But not tonight. Tonight he has to get it himself. He grabs his plate from the microwave and sits down at the kitchen island counter to eat. Ebony walks back into the kitchen and glares at him. He looks at her and smiles that sexy smile he always gives her. She doesn't return 1. As jovial as ever, he asks, "Hey baby. How are you feeling?"
He can sense some tension from her but he isn't sure. Not until she speaks.

"I'm fine," she says, "Ah and one of us is not sleeping in the master bedroom. As for sex between us tonight? I'm not gone be able to do it. Nor am I sleeping in the same bed as you. So since you've already been through

TIME TO FEEL-RELOADED-Time Will Reveal part 5

our room. I'll take one of the guest rooms. *Goodnight Anthony."*
Before he can speak, she exits the kitchen. She smelled the hint of sex in every area of their home which he's been in since returning. When she'd placed his plate in the microwave minutes ago, the kitchen reeked of a perfume that wasn't hers. That was just from him passing through it. Before his plate was half warm, she was heated. She left his plate in the microwave and left the kitchen to escape the foul odor he'd come home wearing. She isn't even ready to hear him try to explain it away if she brings up a discussion about this scent that smells nothing like the fine fragrances he's bought for her. She finds the smell in her bedroom, her bathroom and their children's rooms. Every room he had passed through. Now smells like someone else has been in her home. She *had* to say something. Once she'd said her peace. She left him in the kitchen alone and began to light candles in every room where this new scent was detected.

Ajay sits on the bar stool, his plate in front of him and a mouth full of food. He looks dumbfounded. Her statement has rendered him paralyzed and caught off guard. He isn't even able to deliver a smooth line to feeble her strong recommendation. He feels caught red-handed when he hasn't even had sex with anyone. He's off his and she knows it because he hasn't come behind her with *any* kind of explanation. Not even a question as to why she's angry with him. In her mind, he has had sex outside of his home. *Their* home. She feels he has cheated. That thought hadn't even crossed his mind once, until right now. And no matter which crew rule he would later cite and recite as his permissions for promiscuity. He's in the dog house with the woman he loves. That's his reality tonight. Being a male member of the crew makes heartless and mindless acts, like the 1 he and his boys committed tonight. The norm or the acceptable, in his mind. However when they were boys, the repercussions wasn't as they will be after tonight.
Back then there *was* no repercussions. He wasn't married to Ebony. The guys were always raised to sew their wild oats. Back in the days, she wouldn't have had any support from the matrons if she'd gone to them to complain. The matriarchs would've *only* been able to give her *their* familiar. In other words, they had lived through it until they got married and the crew thang shit, something which was passed down and tolerated, was out of bounds. But the last time Chill's crew had a chamber meeting with a female involved. Was years before the success of the CrewLand mall. At least Ebony hasn't been told of any others since. That was years before the professional contracts, the southern expansion and fine dining restaurants. They weren't head of households, back then. Back in the days when they

would make a mockery out of the doomed by sexing their favorite girl, while the doomed man watched. But back then, Ajay wasn't coming home and kissing their babies in the mouth. Tonight, Ebony believes he's strayed. There will be repercussions for him. Tonight's dismantling of Marvin will tear down a whole lot more than Marvin would ever have felt if they had allowed him to live. Unless Ajay can find a way to explain to Ebony that a young girl with a long time crush had hugged him. And than later he was in the room while a crew thang was going on but he didn't have sex in *any* form or fashion. Then his happy home life shall remain interrupted.

Damn! I touched that bitch's clit! But I had on gloves. What the fuck!

Tonight's chamber meeting will eventually set a new precedence for the crew. Ebony may not know what the details of the mission was. But she knows for damn sure that her man has been in the company of a another woman. If that came as a result of the mission. Then his participation in future missions will have to be curtailed. Crew is important to the entire family. But matrimony trumps crew!

Period! Over! End of story!

Ebony takes a room upstairs next their children and locks the door. She cries every emotional tear that can be shed. She's hurt and angry. She feels deserted and cheated on. Something Ajay *vowed* he would *never* allow her to *ever* feel again. Tonight's course of action by her crew is 1 that she has never agreed with. She remembers back when Lynn, Renee and Tonya use to talk about their guys gangbanging the enemies girl, if she was down for it. They were doing that during Ebony's wonder years. And even in her parents and grandparents crew's, this was overlooked or allowed. That's the excuse Chill, Jr, Jb and the males in her crew had used back then.

"It's a crew thang. She don't mean shit to me," They use to say.

She understood it then. That was the 1 thing about the crew's ruthless mentality that she didn't like and wouldn't stand for Ajay to *ever* do. She still doesn't like it to this day. It's like giving him an excuse to fuck another female and call it, *crew business*. That's a fucking double standard, is what that is. They can fuck around and their woman is suppose to take it and stand by her man.

What?! Hell to the nah! What is a <u>written </u>rule for the gander. Isn't even a <u>possibility </u>for the goose! That same double standard that caused me so much pain in my young life is still lurking! So I'm suppose to just accept that my sacred marriage is suppose to be only a doomed muthafucka away from my husband cheating on me!?! No fucking way!!!

TIME TO FEEL-RELOADED-Time Will Reveal part 5

Actually Marvin and Farah's demising night had been high tech and even considerate. It was done through video because they didn't want Farah to know Marvin was present. In the past, all parties had been in the same room and the girl had died too. Marvin was doomed to death. The crew didn't see the same fate for Farah. Not just yet. That's why they went through the trouble of setting up a video relay. But fucking another man's woman in front of him, wasn't a new or unusual scenario for the crew men. Ajay had stood around and watched what had come natural. Something that was the norm. He had been unfaithful to Ebony before, when he was a boy. But not since taking her as his wife has he strayed. When his focus was more on street credibility then on his future. Fucking another woman was seen as *Don status*. It was an image builder. But he's a husband and a father now. No longer a recluse, a street hustler or a player type. Those were the things he had vowed to her before _God_ that he was done with. But 1 night at the chamber and suddenly it's 1989 again, in Ebony's mind.
Why did he not even think about his vows? Can't he be just as loyal and faithful to me and our marriage as he is to the crew?

She devoted her love and loyalty to him, a long time ago and she hasn't looked back. As a matter of fact, she has never even thought about having a substitute for Ajay. He's all she needs and wants. And he's suppose to be *all* hers too. Matrimony is before God. The crew are God fearing. Yet the men refuse to see that *no matter* what wrongs have been done to them and how much they want to stick it to the doomed fellow. It still isn't a pass to fuck another woman. She wonders why none of the other crew women have put a stop to it before now. Renee and Tonya are her oldest sisters.
Why didn't' they check Chill and Brad junior years ago? Even before that. Why didn't my mama and the females in her crew change this action? I never even wanna imagine my daddy, poppa or papa would do some shit like this. But I know they have. I wanted my husband to put me and his kids before that bullshit. But no! He comes home smelling like a bitch! I'm not having it!

The crew men are great providers and protectors. But they have a double standard about what they can do as men, that the women have lived with up until now. Ebony isn't going to live with it. In the past, crew women would just pray that their man would grow out of it or get tired of it or bored with it. But they haven't. Not really. Nor have they tried to change it within themselves. But at this moment, Ebony is only concerned with 1 man in her crew. 1 man in the *world*, for that matter. Her husband, Anthony

Devante' Jackson, Sr and the fact that he fucked around tonight. It doesn't matter whether it happened during the killing of a marked man or a rendezvous with some groupie bitch. Fucking someone other than her is *cheating*! She isn't going to let it pass without using it to make a change in her family values. That's the only way she can see them getting through this for her daughter's sake and her son's sake too. Already the tension in their home can be cut with a knife. That's not a suitable environment for children. Certainly not for *her* babies. She knows Ajay feels the same way when it comes to their twins. She knows he'll want to try and make it better with her *tonight*. So the tension will be gone by the time the twins wake up for preschool. But she isn't ready yet. Not this soon. He has to have the rest of the night without her, to know what he's really missing. Besides, she's way to emotional. She wouldn't be able to make her points without blubbering. But as soon as she can bare to speak to him without crying. She's going to make him understand that she will never live with him and that type of behavior. She paid her dues before the marriage. All of that bullshit is suppose to be a thing of the past.
I can't believe he cheated on me!

      Ajay knocks on the door of the guest room and calls her name. She doesn't answer. He dials her cell phone over and over. She doesn't answer. She doesn't want to talk tonight. That shit poppa told her, back in the day about him coming to her as soon as possible. Isn't going to work tonight either. She's not letting him in. He might convince her to come to bed with him. She doesn't want to fuck behind some whore. That's why she's honest and faithful and *married*. He's going to know the ledge after tonight's actions. If he wants a faithful wife. Then he's going to have to be a faithful husband. They'll have to have that conversation when the hurt has eased up. She needs comforting but her comforter is the guilty one. She has never thought of another man *sexually*. In the words of *Barry White*. Ajay is her first. Her last. Her everything. And that is how it shall remain.
Damn right!

She isn't going to chance her virtue. Nor change her values. Just the rules of her family.
Anthony senior is gonna be faithful to me. Period. Over. End of Story.

      "Baby *please* open the door," Ajay tries, "Please let me talk to you. I haven't cheated on you Ebony. I promise you I haven't. Please just open the door and let me come in and talk to you. I love you. I wouldn't have sex with nobody else. I promised you that. I haven't broken that promise." But she's steadfast. She feels sure that he's been unfaithful. *How else does he come home smelling like a woman's perfume and of sex too? He can kill that noise and get away from the door. Oh God! What am I gonna do without my man? I can't even sleep without his arms around me.*

She's made up her mind but Ajay isn't going to sleep on this. He has to see her eyes and explain to her what happened. He's ready to tell her every damn detail about the mission, if that's what it takes. But he isn't going to suffer a night without his better half when he hasn't been unfaithful, they're in the same house and it is *their* home.

"I'm calling Chill, right now," Ajay finally says, "Fuck it. He's gonna have to come around here and vouch for me. I'm calling Jarvis too. Make him bring his fast ass sister-in-law over here too. I ain't going out like this. Fuck no! I didn't *do* shit!"

He's yelling which is *definitely* not him. But the thought of having Ebony refuse to see or talk to him, hasn't ever been a reality for him. But it is tonight. She thinks he's cheated and he has to make her aware of the truth.

He dials Chill's cell number and gets no answer. He knows he's at home, so he grabs his Benz keys and heads to Payne's lane.

Ebony can hear him leaving. She jumps up and heads to the window at the far end of the 2nd floor hallway. From there, she can see his car as it turns on Chill's street. She watches as he pulls up to Chill's garage doors, hops out and runs to the door. He's banging on it until Renee and Chill open it and he rushes inside. Within minutes, her cell phone is ringing again. It's Chill's number. She doesn't answer for him either.

"He can't explain this shit away," she says to herself as she takes her phone with her, back to the window.

She sees Chill get into the passenger seat of Ajay's Benz 2-seater. They're heading back to her house. She stays in the window. Her phone rings again. This time it's Jarvis and Gwen's new home line.

"Oh hell no!" she screams, "I know he didn't fuck with that girl! Now she's calling my house phone?"

She burst into tears. She's definitely not going to answer to neither 1 of them either. She can hear Ajay tear up the driveway and stop suddenly. She hears his doors close and soon, she can hear him and Chill come into the kitchen door. She heads back into the guest room and secures the door.

"Ebony!" Chill yells as he's running up the stairs.

197

She can hear Ajay pleading his case to Chill. She can hear desperation in his voice as well. Chill is knocking on the door now and still calling her name. Ajay has gone to the safe to get the door keys. He isn't going to wait any longer for her to open the damn door. She's going to hear him and she's going to hear him tonight.

Meanwhile at Jarvis' house, he has Nickeia and they're leaving for Ajay's home in Jackson Heights. The suburb him and Gwen has just recently had to move out of. Jarvis is heated because he knows he wants no negative flack with the crew. That could ruin his chances of being inducted.

"Why the fuck would you do that Nikki?" Jarvis asks, "Ajay is happily married. He ain't gonna fuck around. *Damn.* He's like a brother to me. I wanna be apart of his crew and you fuck me up like this?! *Fuck!*"
He drives to Jackson Heights. Bronson is at the gate and he's expecting him. He waves him on through. Jarvis acknowledges him as he passes. He heads down CrewLand drive, around the curve and past the home that use to be his. He pulls into Ajay's driveway and parks his Benz 4-door right next to Ajay's car, which he can tell wasn't carefully parked.

"My big brother on a tear, over this *dumb shit*," he says as he meets Nickeia at the passenger door and all but pulls her out of the car. "Let's go in here and straightened this with his wife. I'm gonna tell your parents about this, if they tell me too."

"You gonna tell them what you do too?" Nickeia asks with a smirk.

"If I have too. *Yes*," he says, "Hell I'm gonna tell Gwen about some things anyway. As soon as we finish here. Now let's go!"
The kitchen door is still open. Jarvis enters, dragging Nickeia behind him. "Ajay!" he shouts, "I'm here with Nickeia!"

Upstairs Ajay has opened the bedroom door. Ebony is laying across the bed, refusing to move. Ajay tells Chill to go downstairs and seat Jarvis and Nickeia while he tries to get Ebony to come downstairs. Chill leaves, leaving them alone in the guest room.

"Ebony I got all of these people here because I need you to know what happened tonight," he says, "Will you *please* give me a chance to prove to you that I haven't cheated on you?"

"You got her to come here and lie for you?" Ebony asks while still in tears.

"I've never lied and I'm not gonna start now," Ajay says, "I want her to tell you everything that happened. Then after they leave. Chill and me, we're gonna tell you why I said what I said to her. Just please. Come downstairs so I can make you understand, I *haven't* cheated with her or

198

anybody else. *Please baby girl?* Just please. Do this for me. I love you Ebony. I don't want another woman. I haven't wanted another woman since you gave me your heart. That's my word baby."

She looks at him. Though apart of her is still angry and hurt over this evening. There's no way she isn't going to confront this young girl who wants her man and has probably had him. Ebony gets up. She's already wearing her maternity bed clothes. She slips on her large robe and slippers too. Ajay reaches for her hand.

"I got it," she says as she passes by him and heads out of the guest bedroom.

He follows close behind her. His impulse is to place his hand in the small of her back and hold her elbow. It's what he's always done.

"Let's take the elevator baby," he says, "I don't want you on the stairs. *Please?*"

She heads to the elevator. They go down and join the others on the 1st floor of their family room. Ajay doesn't even wait for Ebony to ask anything. He starts to explain what happened outside of the photo store.

"I pulled up and parked. Out of nowhere, here she comes," he says, "She came up to me, telling me she had a crush on me and how she's been saving herself for me. I had no idea about any of that, baby. At first I thought it was a prank. One of those test that me and Jarvis use to pull at Natty."

"I knew about the crush," Ebony says suddenly, "Gwen told me today. That's what she was calling me for, this morning. That's what she told me when she came to my office today. Now I know it was you," she says to Nickeia, "Because I smell that damn perfume."

Ajay looks at Nickeia and says, "Tell her how your perfume got on my clothes."

"I put it on there," she admits, "I hugged him and I was rubbing on him too," she says trying to be confrontational. "I sho was and I sprayed some on his back while I was hugging him too. What of it?"

Jarvis steps in and says, "What of it, is this man is married and he's not interested in you." Then turning to Ajay, he says, "Ajay I have never *ever* tried a test like that and I *never* would. I know how you feel about Ebony. I know you're not interested in Nickeia or any other female."

"That's not what he said," Nickeia says, "He asked for my number and said he was gonna call me later."

"Here's the number right here," Ajay says, "I had it on the kitchen counter to show to you, baby," he says to Ebony. "I was gonna tell you how I came to have it. But you left without giving me a chance to say anything."

"Why did you take her number?" Ebony asks.

"That's the only way I could get her to leave," he says, "I was late for our…, chamber meeting. I had to get the doors open for the guest of honor. I had to get rid of her. She asked if she could kiss me. You already know what that answer was. I let her kiss me on my cheek. I kissed her forehead. Same as I do Pam, Erica or any other *little* sister."

"I'm not your little sister though," Nickeia tries.

"And going this route, you never will be," Ajay states, "I'm not a virgin connoisseur. Regardless of what you was thinking." He points to Ebony and says, "This is my virgin. She's my wife and the mother of my twins. And yes, we have another baby on the way. So you see, I have my virgin already. I would never go there with you. I just tried not to hurt your feelings because Jarvis is like a brother to me. I was gonna get with him and have him to set you straight."

"I don't need to be set straight," Nickeia says, "I said what I meant to say."

"Get out of my house," Ebony says, as her voice starts to rise a bit. "If I wasn't pregnant. I'd put my foot in yo fuckin ass. You'd better know that. Don't come into my home thinking you're gonna disrespect me because I am *not* the one. I know you know me well enough to know that. I am not a pushover. And though I'm usually a mild person. I'm not when it comes to my children or my man. I don't share either of them. So I suggest you get that understood tonight. A crush is one thing. But rubbing up on my husband and trying to leave your scent on him, is totally different. That's not something I'm gonna tolerate!"

"I'm ready to go now! I hate foul ass liars like you, Ajay!" Nickeia says, "You wasn't saying this when I saw you earlier!"

"Did you not hear what I just said?" Ebony asks Nickeia as she starts to get up off the couch. Ajay quickly goes to her and puts his arms around her. She's not done. She says, "You're not gonna talk to my man like that either. Do you hear me? Apologize or I'm gonna change the *fighting while pregnant rule, tonight.* Apologize to my husband!"

"Apologize Nickeia," Jarvis demands, "You were *wrong.*"

Nickeia is sulking. She doesn't want to apologize because she doesn't believe she's done anything wrong. She believed what Ajay said to her. But seeing how angry he's looking now that his wife is more upset. She decides to apologize. She doesn't want Ajay to be angry with her. She doesn't care if Ebony is or not. She says, "I'm sorry Ajay."

Ajay takes the time to explain to her *why* he said what he did.

"I said what I needed to say to get you to leave," Ajay tells her, "When I tried telling you the truth. You kept standing there pushing your point. I don't wanna have you or your virginity. Let's just get that clear now. I'm sure some guys would. But I'm not like anybody you know or will ever meet. I know what I have at home. Women don't come no better than Ebony. Now if I'd told you like that. You would've fucked up my meeting time and my ability to get there. So yes. I said I'd call you later so we could see what it was you were pushing. But when I made that call. It was to Jarvis. I was gonna talk to my wife first and then we was gonna call Jarvis and Gwen. *Together*. But she got mad as soon as she smelled your perfume on me. That talk couldn't happen until now. But when I made a call, it was to that residence. Not the number you gave me. It was for Jarvis to bring you here so you could see that the only woman I care for in that way, is my wife. And so you could come clean about what really happened. I'm in love with my wife, Nickeia. I'm not your typical male athlete. I come home to fuck. Do you understand me? That's how it is and that's how I want and need for it to stay. You're here to prove to my wife that I haven't cheated with you or anyone else. And I never will. I'm sorry if that hurts your feeling. But you tried to fuck up my home with that perfume trick. I don't owe you no sympathy. It's because of Jarvis that I tried to play you off without hurting your feelings. Ask some of them ho's around Cleveland State. I don't usually spare feelings at all. And if you don't take this as a warning and back off. I won't be sparing your feelings from now on."

"Take me home, Jarvis!" Nickeia screams as she burst into tears, "Now!"

She jumps up and runs through the house to the kitchen door and runs outside to Jarvis' car. Ajay looks at Jarvis with an expression that says he needs to handle her. His time there is done. Jarvis gets up and says goodnight to all of them. Before leaving, he gives a proper apology on Nickeia's behalf. Then Ebony has to say just 1 more thing.

"It may be because of you and Gwen's actions that she thinks it's okay for people to be unfaithful," Ebony says suddenly.

She doesn't give a damn if he didn't know. She wants some payback. Payback for him ever allowing Nickeia to get near her or her husband. Even in Cincinnati. For him and Gwen having secrets the other 1 doesn't know about. And for just being at the right place at the wrong time, for her best friend to collect a skeleton behind knowing her man was cheating. She's just not giving a damn how either of them feel. She wants them to leave her home and her life. No way is she going to allow her son or her daughter to pair up with kids from the likes of them. They aren't even open and honest with each other. How could they teach their children to be?

After Jarvis is gone and Ajay has closed the kitchen door, he comes back to the family room. Chill is still seated and waiting to do his part. But Ebony still isn't done.

"Why did you smell like sex, Anthony?" she asks.

Chill explains what they did at the photo store and Ajay's minimal involvement in it. All of it. After learning that Ajay had touched another woman and her genitalia. Ebony is right back to being pissed again.

Renee has driven around to bring Chill home, once his part is done. She's waiting on the driveway. Ebony is heated. She says goodnight to Chill and he leaves. Then she tells Ajay, she's still sleeping in the guest room. She leaves him standing in the family room and dares him to follow her.

"I *need* some time alone Anthony," she says, "*Please* respect that. Goodnight."

Ajay lasted less than an hour, on that salutation. He unlocks the door again to make another plea to Ebony.

"Anthony why can't you just respect what I asked you to do?" she asks.

"I can't sleep in this house without you next to me, baby," he says, "I'll do anything you ask me to do except stay away from you. You know that. I'm not gonna be able to do that. This house belongs to you. You don't ever have to sleep in no fuckin guest room. I'm not alright with that. Ebony I'm sorry for everything I did. But baby please, *please*, don't shut me off from you. I can't do it."

"Anthony, touching another woman is still cheating in my book," she says, "How would you feel if I touched another man's penis."

"I would kill his ass," he says without hesitation, "I hate what I did baby. I hate it *so* much. I'm so sorry I hurt you. But please know that I *can't* be without you. This is gonna haunt me forever. I have to tell my son about this, one day soon. Just knowing I have to tell him, is killing me. I don't wanna have to explain why we aren't sleeping in our room. I know you're mad at me. But please come to our bedroom and sleep. As hard as I know it's gonna be. I won't ask you to have sex with me. But please sleep in our room *with* me. Because I'm gonna sleep *wherever* you sleep."

She lays there staring at the ceiling. He's staring at her. Finally she gives in and gets up. She doesn't say 1 word. She just goes to the elevator with him hot on her heels. They go into the master bedroom and get into their bed.

"We're not gonna have sex Anthony," she says, "I *mean* that."

"I hear you," he says, "Thank you for coming to our room. I'll do whatever I have to do to make this up to you. And even though I know it's gonna be the hardest thing I've ever had to do. I'll give you the time you need to get through my mistake. I just wanna say thank you for sleeping in our room."

With that, they both lay in bed and try to go to sleep. Ebony has her back to him. She's not even comfortable because she's use to laying either in his arms or with her back up against him. He isn't trying to sleep as he lays there, looking at the back of her head. Still she attempts to fall asleep. That doesn't work. She finally turns to face him. She finds him looking at her with tears in his eyes. She wants to cry more but she doesn't want to feel as though she's letting him off the hook. She can hear her poppa's voice.

"But you still have to let him sweat. Even if he does come to you right away. That's so he'll remember. If he gets another chance. Not to hurt you again."

She can't help herself. This is her baby. The man she loves. He's crying silently from the pain and shame he feels because he's hurt her again.

Speaking softly, she says, "Don't cry Anthony. Okay? We're gonna make it, baby."

"Ebony I am *so* sorry I fucked up," he says, "I need for you to believe in me and trust me. And I don't even know how I can expect you to. Not when I did some dumb shit like that."

"I believe *in* you," she says, "I can see the pain in your eyes. I saw it from the time you unlocked that door. I'd forgotten how to even react to that feeling, Anthony. But I knew I wasn't gonna be okay without talking to you. It's what I've fought for all of these years. Getting you to talk to me."

"And I will," he says, "I hate what I did. Baby I didn't even wanna touch that trifling bitch. I was thinking more about how to make Lil Chill feel like I was participating without actually participating. He was looking forward to a crew caper with me. He's never been on one with me. And baby, he never will be. I knew I wasn't gonna fuck Farah. I knew it before we all got there. I just wanted him to see me there. I fucked up by even touching her. But I had on plastic gloves the whole time I was in the studio. I was more into taunting Marvin's racist ass. I just didn't think it through."

"I'm wondering how you ended up smelling like sex," Ebony says, "She must've had body odor or something."

"Baby, she fucked like seven or eight dudes," he says, "All of them wore condoms too. But I guess it was because it was all those different mixtures or something. I don't know. I just know mine wasn't one of them."

"Who all had her?" she asks.

"I'm just clearing me, okay?" he says, "You know I'm not gonna put nobody else out to make me look good or whatever. I only touched her because Kenny was asking me to share her with him. I knew that wasn't gonna happen. He wasn't even fuckin her, at the time. Two other dudes was. I only did it because we had video hooked up and Marvin was downstairs in the storage room, watching the relay. Ebony I'm not even suppose to be telling you any of this but I *love* you. You are more important to me than *any* crew rule, baby girl. I shouldn't have did any of it. And because I did touch her. I ended up doing the worse thing I could do. Hurt you and lose your trust. I've been working my ass off for years to try to build that trust up. And just like that. I fucked it up."

"Y'all got video ha?" she asks.

"Yea."

"So see, if I didn't believe you. I'd be demanding to see it," she says, "But I'm not and I don't wanna see it. I believe you. You've never lied to me. Neither has Chill. I'm good with the details I have about what actually happened. And I'm glad you didn't have sex with her."

"I am too," he says, "You don't know how glad I am that I didn't. I wouldn't have been able to come back here. I wouldn't come around you, back in the day, after we did that. I wouldn't even go to mama's house. I would stay at Chill's or down to Rich or June's. So I didn't have to face you. And a lot of it was before we was even dating. You didn't even like me and I still didn't wanna disrespect you by going to you after knowing I had been with another girl."

She smiles and says, "I've always liked you. You know that but I never liked that part about our crew. I know y'all use to do that. I use to eavesdrop on Tank and Jb. They use to be in their room giving Jesse the scoop, after y'all did what y'all call, *crew thangs*. That's what y'all call the females. Y'all use to do that a lot in the early eighties. Because they was always coming home telling Jesse to report to the room for a crew thangs update."

"Yea we did," he says, "It was a normal thing, back then. But since we got into legitimate business and wasn't really dealing with no drugs or guns. We had gotten away from having to make a nigga really feel us, like that. Plus we all got settled with our main girl. We was talking about getting married too. So the fathers kept us up on how we had to move from that. We got into being businessmen and that passed on to Bruce's crew."

"They still do it," she says, "I know they do."

"Yea but they're not married," he says, "Well Bruce and Archie

204

junior are now. And Steven or they're committed. They didn't participate tonight. They just wanted the chamber action and so did I. I can't even front. I've been wanting to kill Marvin since he was trying to ask you out."

"You notice how stingy you are with me?" she asks.

"Uh uh," he says looking into her eyes.

"I feel the exact same way about you, Anthony," she says, "I don't wanna share you either. I'm not going too."

"No baby," he says, "You won't have too. I never intended for you to share me. I was bugging when Nickeia came at me with that. I thought it was wingman again. On some; *let's see if I can get one up on the pilot*, type of shit. *Man*! When you said you knew about it. I was shocked."

"I'd just found it out when I was in my office today. But we had to go see Wheeler and that's what I was focused on today. I was gonna tell you as soon as you got home. But then the smell you had on you."

"I'm going to take a shower right now," he says as he jumps up.

"It was on your clothes," she says, "I don't smell it anymore."

"I'm still gonna take one," he says, "You wanna come with me."

She looks at him. He says, "I'm gonna honor your wishes baby. You know I'm ready to fuck you anytime and anywhere. But I respect you, to the utmost. I've grown up Ebony. For real. Every since we got our thing locked and I knew I didn't have to worry about some other man catching your eye. I cooled out on that, feeling like you're gonna fuck me whenever I say so. I know you're mine. I trust that, one hundred percent. That's the place I was trying to get to with you and before tonight, I was on my way."

"You didn't lose my trust," she says, "I was impressed by you going to get Chill and calling Jarvis. You've changed a lot. Because back in the day, you would just say I'm not gonna talk about that no more and that would be the end of it. That's where I've seen the most change in you."

"That's over, baby girl," he says, "I'm a man and a father too. I'm hurt by what I did. And I still have to tell my son about it and soon."

"Why would have to tell him?" she asks, "I don't get that part."

"It's a rule in the crew," he says, "All males have to learn what honesty is and we learn that from our fathers. My pops told me everything about his past. He never hid any of it. No matter how bad it was. He told me. Then he would tell me, he never wanted me to make the same mistakes he did and I didn't. Plus I knew I could trust him with anything I said to him and that he was gonna do right by my mother. Because he said he never wanted me to ever know he had done something to hurt her, more than once. I'll tell my son this before he even starts having girls. I want him to

205

know what's what. And I don't want him to make any of the same mistakes that I've made."

"Okay I get it," she says, "The men in this family are unique. I have to admit that. And I also agree. I want you to raise him to be as wise as you have *always* been. I don't wanna lose him for *any* reason. So I'm giving you my blessings and I will not interfere with you being upfront with him. But there will be absolutely *no more* crew *thangs* for you. Of *any* kind. Okay?"

"Okay baby," he says, "Thank you."

"Now let's go take this shower," she says, "But just the shower. As hard as I know it's going to be. I can't let you back in this quick."

She smiles. He finally smiles too and says, "Okay. I understand. I love you. I'm sorry I hurt you. I won't do it again. I promise you that baby."

"Okay. I love you too, Anthony."

"That's my blessing right there," he says as they go into the bathroom.

They take a long shower. They return to bed together where they still don't go to sleep. Though they don't have sex either, they just lay in bed and end up talking for the rest of the morning.

The next morning is Ellen and Dorothy's day to open the store. They're both in good spirits. Matt's kidnapping is still the top topic of their conversation. They open the store and get it running in preparation for Marvin's arrival. He would usually come in just before noon. At 9am it seems as like a regular day at the Insurance and Carpet store. Nothing seems abnormal until the mail comes. Ellen receives an Express envelope. The return address says it's from Marvin. She thinks it's strange he would mail her something rather than bring it in personally. But then, he's known to go to Pittsburgh on a whim and not show up at the store at all. Ellen opens the envelope and sees a DVD which reads:

"Play me like I've played you." It's in Marvin's handwriting.

"What the hell is this about?" she asks aloud as she opens it.

"There's not one customer in here," Dorothy says, "Let's put it in the D-V-D player in the backroom. See what's up wit his ass. He's probably on vacation. You know Thanksgiving's coming up."

"You're probably right," Ellen says as they head into the break room, pull the DVD case out, pop the disk in and begin to watch it.

"What the *hell*?!" Dorothy exclaims.

****

206

TIME TO FEEL-RELOADED-Time Will Reveal part 5

Matt escapes *"captivity"* and finds a police car on the beat. He tells the officers who he is and that he was kidnapped 3 days ago. The officers put him in the car and drive him to the precinct.

At the station, they have many questions for him. He answers each of them without putting any suspicions on any particular group. He tells the police he had $400 dollars on him and the kidnappers took that as soon as they got him inside of a building. But he isn't sure where the building is located. He tells them he'd been blindfolded with duck tape over the blindfold, the entire time. He saw no faces. He had only heard voices. He tells them the voices sounded Caucasian. Like, maybe Italian.

"They kept calling me a mullion," he says, "I only heard that in gangster pictures with Italian mobsters and stuff like that."
The officers ask him if they mentioned anyone in particular. Any names he recognized.

"They asked me about a lady I've gone on a few dinner dates with," he says as he plays it exactly as the crew had instructed him too.
The cops want to know more about the lady, so he tells them more.

"Her name is Farah Benson. She's a school teacher at Martin Luther King junior high school. She has me down for career day, each year. I'm head cosmetology professor at Cleveland State University. Farah comes to the salon I work out of, so she can get her hair done. She asked me, some years back when she first started teaching and coming to the salon. She asked if I'd be interested in speaking to her class on career day. I did it, that year. Every year since then, I knew she was interested in me. We became friends from there. They only asked me about her because of her fiancée, in my opinion. They really wanted to know about the guy she's engaged too. Marvin or Martin. Something or the other. I'm not positive of his name. They thought I knew him because they said they saw me out with Farah. But I told them I didn't know him. Every time I denied knowing him. They beat me up."
His jaw is swollen and his lips are busted. His eyes are swollen and black. He had gotten a royal ass whipping before they released him. The guys had roughed him up to make his story believable. The cops ask how he escaped.

"They was taking me somewhere to kill me. They said it was because, even though I didn't know the guy who owes them. They couldn't just let me live. Then yesterday they came in and I could hear them celebrating and cheering. One of them hit me across my eye, right here. It started bleeding again. The one that hit me, stood over me and said they found the guy they was looking for but they was still gonna kill me so I

TIME TO FEEL-RELOADED-Time Will Reveal part 5

wouldn't be able to rat them out. I'm worried for Farah. But I'm worried more about myself and my family. They said they was gonna kill my family. They said they was gonna get Farah too. I just feel like they got to her by now. That's what they said to me before we left today. They said they had her and her fiancée. And all three of us was gonna sleep with the fishes. I never heard anyone else being beaten up. I didn't hear anyone else who sounded like they was there against their will, like I was. I kept asking them not to kill me because I couldn't identify them. But they just beat on me some more, then drug me out to the car. The car had a new smell. I didn't know what kind it was but it had all of the beeps and dings like a new car. We got out in traffic this morning and they made a stop on Fitch road. I heard them say, "Stop on Fitch." Three of the guys got out and left one guy with me. I was still ducked taped and cuffed. I just decided if I was gonna die. I was going out fighting. So I made a move and started head butting the one guy. Then I beat him with my cuffed hands until he was weak and groggy. The tape on my ankles broke while I was kicking him in the backseat. That's when I made a break for it. I jumped from the car, still blindfolded and with my hands still cuffed. I was just running up the street, hands cuffed in front of me and yelling for help. I was trying to pull that duck tape from my face but it felt like it was tearing my skin."

"It did just a bit," the officer says, "That happens a lot after it's been on for awhile. We've got medics on the way to check you out."

"And it hurts too," Matt says as he plays it up. "Finally I got the tape off one of my eyes and I just ran as fast as I could. My legs was weak because I wasn't able to stand up the entire time. But I still ran the best I could. I didn't even look back because I didn't wanna know if they was coming or if the one guy was about to shoot me in the back. I just ran for my life for two blocks. I finally saw you on Bagley Road. I've never been so happy to see a police officer in my whole life."

The officers chuckle but they believe his story. After they're done with the questioning and taking his statements. Medics take him to the hospital to have his wounds checked. Genia and Kelly are there waiting when he arrives. They're overjoyed to see him. He plays the kidnap victim and lucky to be alive, role very well. The media soon shows up for the story that will be breaking news again. This time headlines will read:

'Matthew Johnson has escaped his abductors.'

Rudy calls the store for Ellen and Dorothy. She has just seen Matt on TV. She wants to be the first to tell Ellen.

"He escaped from whoever it was that had him and ran until he saw the police," Rudy says, "The police had to take the cuffs off that they put on him. They said those cuffs had been Cleveland Police issued too."

"What? Do you think the cops kidnapped him?" Ellen asks.

"I don't know girl. They're just saying they don't have a lot to go on. But they're looking to interview two other people in connection with it," Rudy says.

"Probably from fucking with that white bitch," Ellen says in a hateful tone. "They ain't shit but trouble. And always getting our black men killed behind fucking with they fake asses."

Dorothy agrees with Ellen. Ellen was already upset before Rudy called. The news of Matt has actually been good to hear. But right now, she's waiting to confront her boss man Marvin Huntley. It's 15 minutes before noon. He should be along soon. She has watched the disk. She watched Marvin in his condo, bragging about how she's *a psychotic nigger bitch.* He admits to buying the gun and sending it to her. He wanted her to kill Matt because he was fucking with his woman. He admitted to paying her bond too.

"So he was playing you, all along," Dorothy says, "He's Farah's ex! He was on one *serious* love hangover. That ho fuckin out of both *draws* legs. He wanted you to kill Matt and you was gonna go to prison."

"And he didn't give a fuck," Ellen says, "Wait until he comes in here. I should go get that damn gun and shoot his ass."

Just passed noon and Marvin hasn't shown up. But 2 Cleveland police cars with 2 officers each, do come by the store. They want to talk with Marvin too. Ellen tells them, he hasn't come in today. But he had sent her a DVD in the mail. She takes the police in the back to view the video. They inquire about how she knows Matt. She tells them they dated for years but had troubles recently when he started seeing Farah Benson. The cops recognize *that* name. There is an officer at MLK interviewing her now. They tell Ellen they will need to take the DVD with them for evidence.

At MLK, Farah is being interviewed in the teacher's lounge. She tells the officer, Marvin lives in Pittsburgh. The cop informs her that he has a local residence and a local business too. She says Marvin's family opened a business here and she was almost partner until she found out it was *his* family. She says she was sure he wasn't hands on. The officer tells her, he's sure that he was. She's shocked when she finds out Marvin had bought a place in Cleveland, was living here and running the business. She's happy she had gotten out of the investment. But now she wonders how well does

Chill know Marvin. Or if he knew him at all. After all, Ebony Jackson is the investment broker for the property and Marvin said they met online. She knows now that Marvin had lied to her when he said that.

"I had no idea he'd moved here. I ended my relationship with him four years ago. In ninety nine. I moved here and never let him know where I lived because he's abusive *and* he's the stalking type."

Also the officer mentions Matt and asks if Matt and Marvin had any connection.

She says, "No! Matt is my new friend here in Cleveland. If Marvin knows about him, then Marvin will try to do harm to him if he gets the opportunity."

The officer asks if she thinks Marvin could be behind Matt's kidnapping.

"Absolutely," she says, "If he knows he's *my* friend. *Yes*. Even though Matt and I are just professionals, who became good friends. Now he does my hair but Marvin wouldn't care. He doesn't like seeing the races in harmony. He would have tried to have someone harm him if he saw him around me. I've only seen Marvin here in Cleveland once. He came by my classroom. That was before the business opened up but he acted like he was only here, *opening* the business. He never said he lived here."

"How did he know where you worked," the officer asks.

"I told him I had a new job here and that I was moving here to take the job," she says, "I told him about this job on the same day I moved out of the apartment we shared in Pittsburgh. But I never told him *what* school."

The officer takes her statements then leaves. Farah hurries to get her items for home loaded into her car. She has a week to go before Thanksgiving. She's going to Pittsburgh to visit her family. But today she wants to see Matt. She'd heard the breaking news of his escape. After speaking with the officers, Farah believes Marvin was behind it. Because she *now* knows that he lives in Cleveland. And he most likely knew about her and Matt.

The officers seemed determined to find out what happened. They want to talk to Marvin Huntley immediately. Every lead from Matt to Ellen to Farah, leads back to Marvin. Just like Chill planned for it too.

The officers are still at the Insurance and Carpet store with Ellen and her friends.

"He's a person of interest right now," the officer tells Ellen, after viewing the entire DVD then bagging it again for evidence.

"I'm not interested in his ass no more," Ellen says, "I thought he was real. I should've known better than to fuck around with white folks. Y'all ain't nothing but the devil. And when you do see him. Tell him, *I* said,

210

he can kiss my black ass, for what he was trying to do to me. He even fired me on the video. So he can bring his *own* ass up here and close his damn store."

She's heated and for good reason. Her and Dorothy are preparing to leave but the officers asks them to stick around. They want to stake out the store in hopes of catching up with Marvin. For that reason and for a possible chance to curse him out. Ellen stays and tends to the store.

Farah shows up at CrewLand Mall for the word on Matt. Of course he doesn't come in to work today. But she does get the chance to speak with him by phone when he calls *Crew Cut's and Styles*. He lets the girls know he's okay and he's going to take a few days off to recuperate. Farah is waiting to speak with him, so Tonya passes her the phone. Matt isn't sure how he feels about Farah at this point. He tells her, he wants to talk to her in person and soon. Per his part of the plan, he does mention her ex trying to have him killed. She senses that he's holding back with her, so she volunteers the information which she'd received from the officer at MLK. She also tells him, she feels that his kidnapping was because of Marvin but she can't prove it.

"The police are looking for him as we speak," she says.

"He sounds like a maniac," Matt says.

"He is and he's dangerous when he's angry. He thinks his parents money can buy people. I wouldn't doubt if he paid someone to kidnap you."

"Money buys people," he says, "But you told me, you didn't wanna see me no more."

"That was then and this is now. That had nothing to do with him," she says.

"So how do you feel about it now?"

"We're cool. I consider you a really good friend with benefits," she says as they both laugh.

Then Tonya tells her, she needs to cut the call short because, "That's a business line."

Matt overhears Tonya and starts to close his conversation.

"Anyway I don't need no drama from him or you. You need to put him in his place," he says.

"I will if I see him. I'll have him arrested," she says, "I'll call you later. Okay?"

"Okay."

She hangs up with Matt and walks over to The Spot. She's looking for Chill.

Renee sees her first and she already knows the details of the *crew thang*.

"May I help you?" Renee asks with aggression in her tone.

"No thank you. I'm looking for-"

"What do you need, Farah?" Chill asks.

"Just the person I was looking for," Farah says, "Can we talk for a minute? I need to ask you about Marvin Huntley. Do you know him?"

"The white businessman from Pittsburgh?" Chill asks, "Ebony would know him best. I only met him briefly when he was trying to invest in the mall. He was asking about doing the same thing you was, when you first showed up here. Ebony helped him get set up. You remember, right? I had you onboard before you bailed."

"Because he was *stalking* me," she says, "He was my ex fiancée, Chill. I left Pitt to get *away* from him. He followed me here. I think he had something to do with Matt's kidnapping. I think I could be next."

"Sounds like a domestic problem to me," Chill says as he chuckles.

"I need protection from him. Can you help me?"

"Farah. Me and my wife are together," he says, "I can no longer have any dealings with you. That one night is just that. Please leave my establishment. We don't want your kind of trouble around here. We don't want some asshole running up in here shooting up the place. Or kidnapping *anymore* of our family members."

"So you're dumping me just like that? When my life is in danger?"

"I'm telling you, *you* can come to the club, the mall. What have you," Chill says, "But I'm not gonna see you. I'm not gonna lose my family and my home. Nor can I provide security for you. Do you understand?"

"You wasn't saying that, last night," she says in a semi whisper.
She tries to whisper so Renee can't hear her but Chill doesn't let her get away with it. He speaks loud enough for his wife to hear. He tells her again, they cannot be together.

"There's no way I'm gonna leave my wife for anyone. I'm not gonna fuck around with you. It was one night Farah. *One* night," he says, "I need you to recognize that you are a customer at businesses I own and run. That's all it will ever be to me."

"So *you're* dumping me?" she asks again.

"We was never together," he says, "We never fucked. You gave me head, screwed some of my boys and my son. Where in that do you find a relationship?"

"I think we can work it out and-"

"Good day Farah," Renee says, "Leave now please. Thank you."

TIME TO FEEL-RELOADED-Time Will Reveal part 5

Farah takes that as her cue to go. She heads to Parma Heights and home. She has to get up with her girls Alana and Darlene. She has been bragging about how good her night was since she made it home, last night. They had text messaged each other all day. She'd given them *many* details mixed with a *few* lies too. Alana and Darlene thinks she fucked Tank and Ajay. And they aren't happy about it *at all*. To keep the peace, Farah told them she would be hooking that rendezvous up again and they would be coming along the next time. They told her that until then, they was going to hold a grudge. And before Farah talked to Chill just now, she felt like that 3-way hook up was doable. Now she isn't so sure. She has to figure out what it was that made him want her, last night. So she can bring that again.

Alana asks about Matt. Farah tells them about the talk she had with him and the latest on Marvin too. And also that she believes Marvin was behind Matt's kidnapping.

"He would do something like that. With his stupid ass," Alana says, "He's a psycho ass nerd."

The ladies laugh. Farah doesn't want to tell them she had followed up with Chill today, only to be rejected. They would be pissed off with her if they knew she wasn't able to get them a hook up with Tank and Ajay. As if there is anyone else who could or a snowballs chance in hell, for either of them.

}*Jackson Heights*{

It's the Sunday before Thanksgiving and Marvin is still wanted for questioning. Today is the day for food preparations for the crew's big Thanksgiving dinner. The women have purchased the food for Thursday's big dinner to be held at Ajay and Ebony's estate. After church, the females head to Ebony's house for prep time. They have bottles of wine, grape juice for Ebony plus juice and soda's for the children.

"I love these subzero refrigerators, baby girl," Pearl says.

"I do too," Jo says, "We're suppose to get our kitchens remodeled for our anniversaries, this time around," Jo adds and the mothers laugh.

"Yes you *all* are," Rebbie says, "Brian, Ajay, Greg Jr, Jesse and Tank have already committed to it."

"And Eric too," Erica adds.

"Good and I'll drink to that. So pour me some wine," Rena says as they all laugh again.

All glasses are filled with the appropriate drink and they get busy with Thanksgiving prep, along with lots of discussion. It has been 5 nights and 6 days since Ebony told Ajay they would only *sleep* in their master bedroom

213

together. That scene hasn't changed much. The only change is Ajay has tried to rekindle their sex life and Ebony didn't give in. She hasn't talked to him about Tuesday night anymore. She found out exactly who did what to Farah, thanks to Renee. She can't even stomach the thought of it. However, in the past 6 days, her and the females in her crew have been talking a lot about their men, matrimony and crew rules. They're going to discuss it with the mothers and grandmothers today. One way or the other, Ebony is going to get some change. She needs the majority of the matriarchs and mothers to agree. Then put their foot down and demand that all of their men remain faithful. No matter the circumstance.

"I'm not gonna tolerate Anthony *sleeping* with another woman. *Touching* another woman. Letting them rub on him or none of that," Ebony says, "I don't care what the crew are doing. That's cheating, plain and simple and I'm not gonna stand for that."

"Well baby girl. Have you talked to him about it?" big mama asks.

"Yes I have," she says, "I've told him that's not gonna work."

"You'll have to put your foot down, baby girl," her mother-in-law says, "Jackson men are loyal *family* men. But they are diehards for their boys too. You'll need to get his undivided attention. Make him understand that *that* shit is not gonna be tolerated. I had that same talk with Allen."

"Did he listen?" Ebony asks.

"Hell yea, he listened," Jo says, "He wanted to live with me, didn't he? And he wasn't gonna be able to sleep under the same roof with me and live. If he ever fucked around with some tramp. I don't care how bad the person they was getting rid of, had it coming. It was about our marriage and him staying true to it."

"That's what I'm saying," Ebony agrees, "And I've been telling the ladies in my crew too. We stepped up our business game and we need to step up this fidelity game when it comes to our marriages too. We're all loyal to the crew. Us ladies are loyal to our husbands and boyfriends. But they get an excuse to be unfaithful and call it a crew thang."

"We need to put a stop to it," Renee says, "I don't like it either. But I wasn't born into the crew and I didn't wanna make waves-"

"You *are* crew. Tried and true," grandma Annabelle says, "From the day Kenneth *big Chill* introduced you."

"Same rights as everyone else," big mama adds.

"You sure are," Belinda says, "And all the girls in your crew, look to you for leadership. Just like we did with Deb and Jo."

"They sure did," Debbie says, "I dealt with a lot of infidelity from big Bradley. He was the boss, just like Chill. Every bitch with a split was after him. And when their men would come up owing our crew. I knew he was out sexing their girl and she wanted it."

"How did you get him to stop?" Nina asks.

"Gave him an ultimatum," Debbie says, "I was gonna leave and take Jr, Breanna and Bruce with me, if he didn't give me his word and stick to it. Mama Annabelle held my hand through all of it."

"I sure did. I had gone through it with Charles, in our early days of marriage," Annabelle says, "Fan dancers or strippers, as y'all call them. Women who had no husbands and wanted mine."

"We all had it happen to us at some point and time," big mama says, "But back then you didn't really make waves. You showed him in other ways that you deserved better. Our crew of ladies put up with a lot of it. Yes we did. But marriage was the only way to think about making a way out of nothing, for us. Divorce wasn't an option."

"Yes. So if we told them to straighten up. Either they did or they got slicker," Annabelle says with a snicker.

"Divorce is still not an option," Ebony says, "I'm married to Anthony for life. We're staying true to our upbringing and our crew. But loyalty to our vows and our marriage will take priority over some trick who disrespected one of the guys. They're gonna have to find another way to demoralize them besides sexing their females. That's gonna stop."

"So I take it there was a chamber meeting recently?" Brenda asks.

"Tuesday night," Brina tells her, "Kenny, Archie and Brandon was there. Archie swears he didn't do anything but I don't know for sure."

"Chill did and I know he did. So did Kenny," Renee says.

"Anthony smelled of it when he came in here," Ebony says, "Not so much of sex. But he smelled like a woman's perfume. I went off. Then I went to sleep in one of our guest rooms. *Child* he went and got Chill. Then called Jarvis to bring his sister-in-law over here so she could tell me how the perfume got on him. She admitted it and told it, just like he did. I told y'all about the crush she has on him. She was planning for him to deflower her. She sprayed perfume on him after he let her hug him. For y'all that don't know. After Anthony put her and Jarvis out of here. Him and Chill told me *his* part of the crew thang. He was massaging her clitoris while the others was having sex and getting oral sex from her. Then Renee verified what they'd told me, a few days ago. It was Farah Benson. The white girl that came back here with Alana and teaches at MLK."

"The one that's been having sex with all of the younger boys,"

Rena says, "The same way they use to do with Chill's crew and our crew too."

"And ours too," big mama says, "Older women have always come after guys in this crew. Me and Pearline use to be about to split Jackson and Percy into, over groupie girls and grown women too. Women that had sons their age. We wouldn't speak to them for three or four days. We would be on the road doing shows and not talking to them when we got off stage."

"I haven't had sex with Anthony since that morning before," Ebony says, "The twins are playing moderator and don't even know it."

"Get it settled and get it settled right now," Pearl demands, "Don't you put my babies in the middle of that mess. Fix it."

"I'm trying too," Ebony says.

"I know Jeremy did it," Nina says, "He went all the way but I've just put it out of my mind. It was enough finding out he'd been with Gwen before I ever got pregnant with Jerica."

"I tried to put it out of my mind too," Rebbie says, "But Brian swears he didn't and I know he did."

"I could smell a difference on Anthony," Ebony says, "I thought he'd had sex but he made it his business to make sure I knew what his night entailed. Still I told him, we wasn't gonna sleep in the same room. That part didn't work but I haven't given him any. We stayed up talking the whole night. Y'all I can tell he regrets his part in it."

"Eric didn't do it either," Erica says, "He told me he didn't. Him and Bruce just wanted the other action at the chamber. And he also told me that my brother didn't. No head or tail." They all giggle.

"Baby told me, he didn't mess with that girl," Kim says, "I wanted to believe him."

"He didn't," Erica says, "Eric told me. Neither of them did."

"What about Brandon?" Charlotte asks.

"He did. Archie did and we all know Kenny did," Chaundra says, "Those three went as far as Chill did, at least. And Ajay only played with her pearl tongue and rubbed on her back or whatever. Kenny even told me he asked Ajay to double team her with him. And Ajay said he wasn't wit it but he would help her get off."

"Brandon, Archie and Kenny aren't married," Ebony says, "The rest of them are. Except for Wes and Arthur. Something is gonna give and I mean that."

The ladies continue their deep discussion on the fidelity of their significant others while they prep Thanksgiving dinner items and sip cool drinks.

TIME TO FEEL-RELOADED-Time Will Reveal part 5

Ajay, June and the pro athletes are playing games on the road today. While the other crew men are at Stoney's watching the games on the big screens. Chill and his guys have caused an undercurrent of emotions with the crew women since the incident on Tuesday night. It's like a ticking time bomb, ready to explode. Al, John and the other fathers try to make light of it. But everyone's home is going to have tension in it after the women leave Jackson Heights. The men have their comfort foods of beers, hoagies and wings as preparation for whatever recollections their wives will want to discuss later.

As if any more explosives are needed. Farah, Alana and Darlene show up at Stoney's. This is definitely not the recipe for a smooth evening, to say the least. There's already enough tension between the genders in the crew. Ajay is on the road with his team. So are June, Bruce and Eric. Tank and Chill are at Stoney's. So is Wes, Jr and Arthur. Alana's face lights up as soon as she spots Tank. She feels a new sense of energy since knowing Farah has fucked the crew. But she still has no idea of why Farah was even let in or that she had fabricated part of her story.

"You got us back in, home girl," Alana says as they sit at a booth with a clear line of sight to Chill and Tank.

Alana wants to push up but she knows big Al is Nina's father. She isn't sure how he'll react to her approaching his son-in-law. However Farah doesn't feel she needs to hold back anything. She approaches Chill immediately.

"Hi baby. How are you today?" she asks.

"I'm not baby. Just call me Chill. I'm doing just fine."

"I agree. I still get chills thinking about the other night," she says.

John and Al start wiping the counters trying to appear busy. The other fathers laugh slightly. Chill pulls at his collar as if his shirt is choking him. He doesn't want to talk to Farah at all.

"Go on and have a seat, Farah," he says, "This is not cool."

"I'm trying to make it cool and dark too. In a little bit," she says, "I need that fix."

Chill doesn't waste time. He dials Renee's cell number immediately. They've had some discussion about Tuesday night in their home, this week. Renee is seething with anger, just knowing this Farah bitch orally fucked her man, while fucking her son at the same time. She knew it before Chill even admitted to it. She's been in the game dame near since day one, with Chill. She knows how things play out. She's angry with Farah, on every level. She fucked her family's men too. Renee wants to get even with Farah. Or at least beat her ass, just 1 good time. She'll get her chance today.

217

"Hello," Renee says.

"I'm at Stoney's. Old girl don't seem to understand that type of action from Tuesday night, ain't *happenin* again," Chill says.

"I'm on my way," Renee says as she heads to the door.

After her girls find out what's going on and where she's headed. They load up in cars and go too. They leave the mothers and grandmothers to finish food prep. Renee's crew of ladies come with her. She tries to get nearly 3-month pregnant Ebony to stay behind. That doesn't work. Ebony drives her Escalade with T-baby, Rebbie, Venitia, Erica and Kim. Nina brings Justine, Charlotte, Chaundra and Brina with her. Tonya, Ally, Pam and Ruthie ride with Renee. Michelle drives and Tameka, Courtney Freeman, Claudia and Shantel ride with her. They're going as witnesses mainly. The latter car load are the female crew's entourage or coworkers or both. They have loyalty to the crew and want to help out, however they can.

At Stoney's, Farah has no clue that Chill has called his wife. She continues to be obnoxious and overbearing while Chill bids his time. He wants Renee to see that he's staying cool and today, this is all on Farah.

Ten minutes later the females are parking in the lot. Even after seeing them show up. Farah doesn't sit down. She moves away from Chill's table and pretends to be browsing about the diner. Checking out the pictures on the wall and browsing but it's too late. Renee has the heads up plus she saw her standing over Chill when she first pulled up. She enters the diner with 1 thing on her mind.

"It's time for you and me to handle our damn business," she says as she approaches Farah swiftly.

Without another word, she punches her in the face. She continues punching as Farah stumbles backwards. John comes from behind the counter and grabs Renee. Farah had stumbled against 1 of the booths. She stands up and wipes her mouth to see if she's bleeding. She is. This angers her to the point that she lunges toward Renee. Ebony is closest to Farah so she grabs her and starts punching her repeatedly. You can see the anguish in her face, just as it was with Renee. She has a small score to settle too. Chill, Tank and Arthur rush over and pull Farah away from Ebony but Ebony keeps advancing. She keeps swinging, keeps punching Farah. Finally Al makes it to Ebony and grabs her. Her uncle Greg has to help him to hold her. That only makes room for T-baby and Rebbie to get to Farah. Nina turns and calls Alana. Tank comes to Nina's side instantly.

"Baby no," he tries.

"You need to move out of the way Jeremy," Nina seethes, "She's been had this ass whooping coming," Nina says, "Come on Alana. Don't stand over there like you don't think you got some ass whooping to take. Any time it's a fight and your dumb ass is present. You know I'm going in yo shit. So come the fuck on!"

"I work for your family," Alana tries, "I'm not gonna fight you and lose my job," she says as she moves toward the exit and behind the wall of fathers who are shielding the crew women from them.

"Your job has nothing to do with this ass whooping bitch!" Nina screams, "This has been holding for a *whole* decade."

The fathers manage to get Farah, Alana and Darlene out of the diner and to their car. They have security to lead them off the property because Shantel, Michelle and the rest of the entourage was about to jump them in the parking lot. Inside the diner, Al and John try to reason with Ebony.

"Baby girl. Please calm down," John says, "Sit down. You know *damn well* you're not gonna be fighting and you're pregnant. Who let you come up here?! I need to call Ajay right now."

"I'm calling Joanna!" Al says, "They must be so full of female discussion and wines out there. That their good judgment got drowned."

He's very angry. Ebony doesn't say anything. Everyone had tried to stop her from coming but they couldn't. She wasn't going to miss an opportunity to stomp a mud hole in *any* whore who had even come close to fucking her husband. Even if he was wrong for touching Farah. Ajay will know about this fight as soon as his game ends and 1 of the fathers can reach him by cell phone. She knows he won't approve of her fighting. But so what? She figures it like this. She didn't approve of him touching that bitch either but he did. So he'll just have to flex his toleration muscles when it comes her physical indiscretions too. She's over the anger side of his mistake now. At this point, she just misses her man and she looks forward to him returning home, in time for Thanksgiving and some make up love making sessions galore. But she knows their fathers are going to definitely discuss her actions here today. That side of Ajay hasn't changed and it won't. Not where her safety is concerned or the safety of his children. Ebony's actions today won't sit well with Ajay. Not at all.

TIME TO FEEL-RELOADED-Time Will Reveal part 5

CHAPTER   56

IT'S TIME FOR CHANGE

Never underestimate the power of a black man and his woman. It's Monday morning of Thanksgiving week and Marvin still hasn't surfaced. His parents had contacted the Cleveland police on Thursday, saying they usually talk with him daily. But the last time they'd spoken with him was Tuesday morning. He has been missing for 6 days now. Last seen leaving his condo alone, on Tuesday evening. The police inform his parents that he's wanted for questioning in a kidnapping case and he's also under protection order from Farah Benson, for harassment and stalking. The rental car he had was found Saturday, out by Fitch Rd in North Olmsted. The police also told them they found no signs of foul play, as far as the car was concerned. They assumed the same individuals involved with Matt, was involved in Marvin's disappearance too. Because there was a piece of duck tape found in the rental with Matt's DNA on it. Plus Matt had escaped and been rescued in the same area. Last Friday, the police officially listed Marvin as a missing person and reported his Porsche missing too. His father had contacted Jackson's Real Estate on Friday. This morning, they're in route to Cleveland. His father had contacted investor Jackson's Real Estate about taking over the Brook Park store. Ebony's firm is the investor that bought out Farah's interest, without Marvin or Farah's knowledge. Ebony had purchased a majority share of the store. Friday, she suggested to Mr. Huntley Sr that he square up with her, 1 way or the other. She told him he could put up his shares and she could secure them. Thus he wouldn't have any other interest in the store and she would takeover the day-to-day operations of business and own it outright. Or he could buy her out and own the entire share. He liked her 1st option better. He had no intentions of managing just 1 store in Cleveland. He told her, he could talk with her at another time about an expansion of his business because Cleveland wasn't *his* idea of expansion. Cleveland was his son's project. He'd also told Ebony that he was having the transfer paperwork drawn up and drafted to her. She should receive it within a week.

In the meantime, Ebony has Ellen to run the store each day, along with Dorothy. She has also hired Rudy and had them to train her. This way, they can keep the business open from 9am to 9pm. She'll look for a store manager in the week, following the Thanksgiving holiday. She keeps the contractor list which Marvin had started and the insurance reps agree to stay onboard as well. She will have a new manager there by the 1st week of

December. But today, she has more pressing business. Ajay is doing a video chat with her and the twins at noon. After making sure the store is in good hands and running smoothly. She heads to *Granny's house* to pick up the twins. She isn't going to her office until later. Her husband will be on live video satellite to catch up on how her and the twins have been doing since he's been on the road.

Most of the crew are up early, getting things done. Renee still isn't satisfied with the brief whooping of Farah's ass yesterday. She calls MLK for a conference with Farah Benson. Mr. Myers sets it up and moderates it, at Chill's request. Renee shows up for 930am as instructed. Farah walks up to the faculty building and they meet in the principal's office. Renee wants to make a few things clear to Farah.

"I asked for this meeting to get a few things out in the open," Renee starts, "Mister Myers is aware of your behavior, on and off campus. He also knows I got physical with you yesterday. But there's something you need to know and I'll let mister Myers tell you."

"What is it mister Myers?" Farah asks, acting clueless.
That's something she does often. Alana always said she's a brunette with blonde tendencies.

"Miss Benson I am fully aware of the behavior you've engaged in with students from this school. Both here at school and off campus too," he says, "More specifically, members of misses Payne's family. I had plans of firing you, years back. But misses Payne here, convinced me not too. She says the behavior wouldn't persist because she would handle it from her end. I didn't agree with that then. But without her testimony, the school has no case against you."

"And I wasn't gonna testify," Renee says, "I still don't care too. But I *will* tell you this. My husband and I are a strong couple. We compliment each others lives and we are loyal to each other. No matter what or who. We have gone from shit to sugar. Something you aren't familiar with at all. We've not only led our crew but we have become business owners and entrepreneurs *together*. That all started from the minds of a mighty black man and his woman. *Kenneth Chill Payne senior and myself.* Doing what we was raised to do. Stay loyal. Believe in each other and overcome *all* obstacles. The first generation of our family which moved to Cleveland, has spawned generation after generation of strong people. Kenneth and I are the head of our generation. We're bonded tighter than *any* blouse you'll ever wear. We're a force to be reckoned with. I need you to remember that and heed it. There's nothing we won't do to clear the other one of a problem. So Farah you need to stay away from my family, outside of business. Heed to that and you can keep your job."

"Is that it?" Farah asks obnoxiously.

"Did you understand me?" Renee asks for clarity.

"Sure."

"Then that's it."

Renee doesn't believe she's sincere. But she allows Myers to adjourn the meeting. Myers dismisses Farah and walks Renee to her car. They talk for another 20 minutes before Renee gets into her Benz and heads to The Chill Spot to do payroll.

In Jackson Heights Ebony is preparing a lunch for her and the twins as they wait for the video chat to start, 30 minutes from now. The sting of last weeks actions has lessened since she kicked off in Farah's ass yesterday. Actually she feels pretty damn good about it. But she knows Ajay will be upset that she had a fight while pregnant. She hasn't seen him in person since Wednesday morning and he won't be home for 3 more days. The Cleveland Cavaliers have been on a 4 game road trip and will return Thanksgiving morning. She misses her man and his sex too. Her body craves him so bad that she could've gotten herself off if she had tried too. But her husband doesn't like his pussy tampered with *at all* when it comes to her sexual fulfillment. They have a few more things to talk about, 1st and foremost. Things they won't dare discuss with the twins present. She feels that's the reason he's doing a video and asked for the kids to be present. Other than the fact that he misses them all. He doesn't want to go into their problems while he's away. He wants to listen, face to face. This video today will allow him to gauge whether her anger hasn't dissipated any. Or if she's missing him so much that she's ready to forgive him and move on. She's eager to see the video chat. But more so, she wants him to come home. She's ready to see him and talk to him. Then she wants him to fuck her like he really missed her. Missed her like she's missing him. She no longer has any of his shirts or their sheets with his smell on them. She had done all of the laundry on Saturday. Then relocated herself to having to sniff bottles of his cologne from his dresser, to get a whiff of him. She needs his scent on her body. The last loving she'd had was Tuesday morning before the chamber meeting. Being that she's already upset with him for cheating. She feels confident that he hasn't been fooling around since Tuesday either. So he has to be about ready to burst with sexual anticipation. His eyes will tell the story of his heart and soul. She'll know his pain with only 1 look at him.

222

TIME TO FEEL-RELOADED-Time Will Reveal part 5

From experience, she knows when he's hornier than a dog in heat. And she has an outlet for him if he could just get home.

A few minutes later and she's done preparing lunch. She goes to change her clothes. She wants to look sexy for their video chat. From her bedroom, she can hear the twins giggling. She gets instant butterflies. Daddy's video chat is on.

She can hear him as he asks the twins, *"Where's mommy?"*

"She's in y'all room, daddy," Lil Ajay says before he and Lannie both say, "Hi daddy!"

"Hey babies," he says, *"I miss y'all so much."*

Ebony rushes back to the family room where the twins are. She can't wait to see her husbands face. She spots him and Ajay smiles big as soon as he sees her come into view. She smiles at him too. The twins are so excited to see their daddy that they're hogging the chat.

"Daddy can you come home now?" Lannie asks.

"In three days I'll be home," he says, *"In time for Thanksgiving dinner. Okay? And I want my hug and kiss as soon as I walk in the door, baby girl."*

"Okay daddy," Lannie says as she giggles.

"Son have you been taking care of mommy and your sister?" he asks Lil Ajay but he's looking at Ebony.

"Yes sir, pops," Lil Ajay says, "And mommy told me to shovel snow, daddy. It was cold out there. But I handled it."

"So you're taking care of the house while I'm gone. Right?" he asks.

"Right. I do, pops," he says, "I'm the man. Just like you."

They all laugh.

"Mommy was sad, daddy," Lannie says suddenly.

"What's wrong with mommy, Lannie?" he asks, *"Why is she sad?"*

"Daddy I help mommy cook yesterday," Lannie says.

"Did that make her sad?" he asks with a chuckle.

"No daddy," Lannie says as she giggles, "We was cooking and mommy started to cry. I said what's the matter mommy. She said I just want daddy to come home. Daddy I told mommy it's gonna be alright. Daddy is coming home tomorrow."

"I'll be home Thursday, baby girl," he says quickly as he looks at Ebony again. *"That's in three more days."*

"Ahhh," Lannie says with a disappointing frown. She adds, "Daddy I want you to come home now. I'm sad too."

Ajay says, *"I don't want my girls to be sad. I'll be there Thursday, baby girl.*

Take care of mommy and your sister, Ant. Lannie don't you be sad and don't let mommy be sad either. Because if you're sad and mommy's sad. Then I'm gonna be sad too."

"I don't wanna be sad," Lil Ajay says, "Everybody's gonna be sad in this house."

"You don't want everybody to be sad, do you Lannie?" Ajay asks.

"I don't, daddy," Lannie says as she shakes her head.

"Okay," he says, *"Then I need for you to make mommy laugh everyday until I come home."*

"Okay," Lannie says with a giggle as she looks at Ebony.

"Okay," Lil Ajay says, "Pops, I'll tell mommy don't cry. Daddy coming back and he's gonna kiss you. Then you can laugh. He's gonna kiss you *these* many times," he says as he holds up 8 fingers and 2 thumbs. "Then you can laugh."

Ajay smiles as he looks at Ebony again. She's smiling as she looks at him. They both look back and forth at the twins.

"Were you sad, baby?" Ajay asks Ebony cautiously, while not knowing if she's ready to *really* speak to him.

"Yes. Yes," she says as she looks at his eyes, then she quickly looks away and blushes openly as her eyes become misty.

"I'll fix that if you allow me too," he says with baited breath.

"We can definitely talk about it," she says with a giggle.

"That's good enough for me," Ajay says and smiles big.

"See pops," Lil Ajay says, "She's laughing already and I didn't even do nothing yet."

"That's cause I'm the man," Ajay says and they all laugh.

Ajay's eyes tell the entire story. He's definitely sorry for his mistake. He wants eye contact. He wants to be closer to Ebony, *this* instant. She smiles shyly as their unspoken conversation seems to take over the giggling and fun chat that the twins are having with their daddy. Her insides are on fire as she watches him, watch her.

He misses me. And man does he ever. His eyes never lie.

It's 2 days before Thanksgiving. Farah, Alana and Darlene are preparing for a trip to Pittsburgh for the holiday. As Farah is packing her bags, she gets a call on her cell phone.

"Hello," she says.

"Hi Farah. This is Betty and Marvin senior. We need to know if you've heard from Marvin junior?" Mrs. Huntley asks.

TIME TO FEEL-RELOADED-Time Will Reveal part 5

"No I haven't," she says, "We aren't on speaking terms. We called things off between us, years ago."

"You did but he never did," Betty Huntley says with a smug tone to her voice. "Why was you so mean to my son?"

"I think you have that backwards, Betty," she says, "He was mean to me. He was always passing judgment on my friends."

"You was never good enough for Marvin," Betty says suddenly.

"Goodbye and don't call me again," Farah says, "You were always an asshole to me. And your son took after you because he talked down to me, the same way you are right now. That's why I left his ass."

Farah hangs up on Betty and immediately tells Alana and Darlene about the call.

****

It's the day before Thanksgiving and Ebony is at home with huge butterflies in her stomach. Pearl, Brenda, Jo and Lynn have a 4-way phone hook up when they decide to call her and discuss 2 very serious matters. She has taken the day off to get her home ready for all of the guest, her and Ajay will have tomorrow for Thanksgiving. She's preparing for her husband to come home as well. Actually, the latter is the real reason she has taken the day off. She wants to be able to give him her undivided attention tomorrow, when he does return. She's doing her cleaning and picking out what she'll be wearing. She's putting away the last of her cleaning supplies when the phone rings.

"Hello," she says.

"Hey Ebony. It's Lynn. I got mama, mama P and mama Brenda on the line too. We're calling about the golden wedding anniversary for big mama and poppa. But before I can get to that. I need to know. What do you want me to tell my brother on his next call?"

"On his *next* call?" she asks, "What do you mean?"

"He's been calling me every other day since he messed up," she says with a giggle, "And he's asking me what would I want John junior to do to make it up to me, if he messed up in *any* kind of way."

"Oh no," Ebony says as she smiles, "He shouldn't be doing that. He should not be worrying you about our problems. Jb wasn't involved in that mess."

"Because we live in Atlanta," Lynn says, "If he was anywhere near Cleveland that night. He would be in the dog house, right about now."

225

TIME TO FEEL-RELOADED-Time Will Reveal part 5

"You know Anthony is gonna call on his big sister for any and everything," Ebony says as she giggles, "He always does. I'm actually not surprised he called you. Now that I think about it. That's normal."

"He called me too," Jo says.

"Mama Jo?" she asks.

"Yes," Jo says.

"And me too," Pearl says.

"Mama he called you too?" she asks as she still giggles.

"He sure did," Pearl says, "He's called me twice."

"Oh Lord," Ebony says in disbelief, "I don't believe this. He's trying to get y'all to convince me to let him fool around?"

"No way. On the last call I told him I was calling you about the golden wedding anniversary and he went into that sad ass spill again," Jo says as she laughs. "He's like a lamb. He's called me about it, three times."

They all giggle.

"April the third will be fifty years since big mama and poppa got married," Ebony says, "Me and Anthony have a long way to go. But I can't believe he's calling all of y'all. Aunt Brenda did he call you too?"

"Not yet," she answers as she laughs. Then they all laugh before her mother has to say her peace about Ajay and what she thinks Ebony should do.

"I wanna know when are you going to forgive him?" Pearl asks suddenly.

The ladies know Ebony and Ajay are on speaking terms but they know that's not all there is to them and their healthy relationship.

"Ha? Mama where did that come from?" Ebony asks.

"From my mouth," Pearl says as she giggles.

"Ma I'm never gonna be okay with him cheating," she says, "You wouldn't tolerate that from daddy. Would you?"

Pearl is quiet.

"Well would you?" Ebony asks again.

"Ajay did some inappropriate touching," Pearl says, "That's true. But I put up with a lot worse, back in the early days."

"So have I," Jo adds.

"Me too," Brenda says, "And so did mama and every other woman in this crew."

"Well why did y'all put up with it?" Ebony asks.

Jo, Pearl and Brenda give her their rationalizations for accepting their husbands indiscretions, years ago.

226

TIME TO FEEL-RELOADED-Time Will Reveal part 5

"Ebony when we first got married," Jo says, "We did what we thought was the best thing for our families and our kids futures."

"We didn't like it at all," Brenda says, "But we couldn't be at every place, all the time."

"So we figured if we act like it was alright, if the whole crew of men participated," Pearl says, "Then they would be forthcoming about it when they *did* do crew shit. But we didn't start that. Mama and her crew had done the same."

"And that's the advice they gave us," Jo says and Brenda agrees.

"I'm not ever gonna agree with that," Ebony says, "He wants me to be faithful and I love being faithful. I'm proud of the fact that I nearly lost my life. *Twice*! To remain faithful to him. He's gonna give me the same respect. That's it. Point blank."

"Or what Ebony?" Pearl asks, "What if he doesn't?"

"He will," she answers.

"But if he doesn't?" Pearl asks.

"Then we can't be together," she says, "I love Anthony with all of my heart and soul. But I will not stay with him if he's gonna disrespect me like that."

"Sister he's wearing us out," Lynn says with laughter, "I told him he needs to find an apology that works. Then keep his hands to himself."

"Us who? I know he ain't ask Jb what he should do," Ebony says, "Cause he's gonna tell him to get all the pussy he can."

"He probably would," Lynn says, "But he's spoken with John junior more than one time. He probably did tell him that but he'd better not let me hear him say it. And yes, Ajay is wearing me, mama and Nina out. And mama Pearl too."

"Every day," Jo says, "Sounding like he's fifteen all over again." She starts to mimic him, *"Mama just call her and see if she's still mad,"* she says and she laughs and adds, "He's just pitiful with it."

"He's been trying to get me to call you too," Lynn says, "So I had to get it in. I know what it's about already. And yes, you *should* be mad. Whatever you do. Stick to it. Make him remember his vows and make sure he thinks about them next time. But like mama said. He's been quite pitiful. He called Nina last night, trying to get her to come over there and see where your head was at."

"Nina already knows what I have planned," Ebony says, "And even she's trying to get me to let him back in, all the way."

"Well tell me what you're gonna do," Pearl says, "Because if it
227

works. It may be something we can use and change the whole creed of this family."

"Matrimony *over* crew," Ebony says, in a matter of fact tone. "Basically that's what it is. He'll have to remember who he belongs to. Just like I do. Anthony has always moved the world for me. I believe he'll ask for this change to happen. Just so I'll know that he's never gonna hurt me again. I really do."

"Then you need to get at him with that, soon as he gets home," Jo says, "He'll be vulnerable and ready to make up. He'll agree to anything."

"He's gonna want sex and plenty of it," Brenda says, "Ask him for a million dollars for your auntie while you've got him at your mercy."
They all laugh at each others jokes. While Ebony feels like things aren't going to be as stressful as they're making it sound.

"I'm just gonna tell him what I need," she says, "He has always taking care of my needs. He never wants to see me stressing or crying. *Cheating* is surely gonna do that."

"Set a new crew precedence, Ebony!" Jo yells, "I know you can make some changes. Changes for all of us, Lannie and the rest of the daughters to come."

"If anybody can do it," Lynn says, "It's Ebony. Once she gets her hooks into Ajay. He'll give in. Then he can convince the men in our crew to agree to it too. And according to Renee, Tonya and Nina. That's gonna have to be *real* soon."

"Oh yes. Nina is fired up too," Pearl says, "But Tank's ass haven't called me."

"He called me," Jo says as she laughs, "He's pitiful too."

"I see what they're doing," Lynn says.

"I do too," Ebony agrees, "See that's the one thing about all of our families being so close. The men have been using that to their advantage. And they know we're gonna stay. So this is it. Tomorrow the ladies are gonna take a stand. Are y'all with me?"

"I'm with you," Lynn says, "And we're gonna get it done and done right, once and for all."

"I'll vote for that," Brenda says.

"Lynn what time does y'all flight arrive?" Ebony asks.

"We're leaving for the airport in an hour and we'll arrive before sundown."

"Tank and junior are picking y'all up," Jo says.

"We'll get the date set for the golden wedding while we're

cooking," Ebony says, "And we'll decide who's gonna do what, in the wedding party. But I think mama's crew should be the attendants and grandma Annabelle should be the matron."

"I like that," Pearl says, "I already had mama Annabelle written down as matron too."

"So we're gonna be bridesmaids," Jo says as she chuckles.

"Okay that's a good start," Brenda says, "We can finish the rest of the program once everybody is here in Cleveland."

"Better catch me, Bre and Jan before we go by *Crew Smokes and Drinks*," Lynn says as she laughs and they all laugh too.

"We'll get both of those issues ironed out tomorrow," Ebony says, "And if he wants to have his male party with his strippers. Then he'd best be ready to show me that I can trust him not to share my fingers, toes, penis or anything else."

"Oh my *God*," Pearl says, "I never thought I would be proud to hear that coming from my daughter's mouth. But I am."

"I've heard it from my daughters," Jo says, "The oldest two, that is. Erica's still in honeymoon bliss. But with Greg junior, she was pulling her hair out."

"She's happy now, all the time," Lynn says, "I like Eric. He's a big teddy bear and he loves to spoil her. Like Ajay is with Ebony. So Ebony and Erica are gonna get things turned around for all of us."

"Y'all let the foursome handle this," Ebony says, "Me, Nina, T-baby and Rebbie will get our men in line. Then they can influence the rest of their boys."

"Better hurry up," Pearl says, "Before my grandson gets out there. Because he has already picked it up."

"Let's not even go there, ma," Ebony says, "That's a whole other case and I'm probably gonna lose that battle."

"About Ajay junior having sex early?" Lynn asks.

"Yes," Ebony says.

"Ebony," Jo says, "That is a Jackson men thing."

"Brown men too," Pearl adds, "So he's got it on both sides. So does little John and Tank junior."

"We'll talk about it tomorrow," Ebony says, "Let's bring it all out while the entire crew are here."

"Okay," Brenda says, "Sounds like a plan."

They all agree. They soon hang up and Ebony gets back to the preparation for the following morning, before she wakes the twins.

TIME TO FEEL-RELOADED-Time Will Reveal part 5

Betty Huntley calls Farah back. Instead of communicating the worry she has over her son. She continues with the insults. For this call, Farah is in Pittsburgh at her parents place. She has finally finished unpacking. Today she has to help her mother with Thanksgiving dinner. Darlene and Alana are with their family, doing the same. They'll all hook back up to party, later tonight. For now, Farah has to deal with the woman who would've been her mother-in-law had she married Marvin Huntley.

"Hello *Farah*," Betty says, "We still haven't heard anything from Marvin junior. I know you should have *some* idea of where he is. He only moved to Cleveland to be with you because he loved you and you just tore his heart out."

"Marvin loved Marvin, Betty!" Farah shoots back, "He loved to control other peoples thoughts and ideas. As soon as he saw that he could no longer do that to me. He only talked with his hands. I wasn't gonna stay around and allow anyone to abuse me. Not in *any* form."

"He was not abusive," Betty says, "You are such a liar. If anything, you abused him with your promiscuity, bad manners and bad upbringing!"

"Go to hell, Betty! Which is most likely where Marvin will end up one of these days," Farah says, "So when he decides to call you. Tell him you'll meet him in hell. Then he won't have to worry about coming home."

"You're evil. Just evil and nowhere good enough for my only child," Betty continues her onslaught. "Marvin has pedigree-"

"Marvin has the same upbringing as me," she says, "We were educated at the same schools and college. And we belong to the same clubs! What *fuckin* pedigree? What manners? Calling people racial names is pedigree and manners? If so, I can do without it."

"He was only trying to help you understand that race mixing is a sin," Betty says.

"Oh my God! Bye woman!" Farah says as she laughs, "I guess Marvin never told you about that black cheerleader he was fuckin during our freshman year of college. Ha? Oh no! Mommy isn't ready to hear *any* of that. Ask him about Shanika Bradley! Ask him to let you watch the video he made of them! You should get a thrill out of it. Maybe big Marv won't need his *Viagra* that day! Get off my damn phone and stay off of it! I don't wanna hear anything else about Marvin and I don't wanna hear from you!" She slams her cell phone shut then turns it off. She doesn't want anymore calls from Betty Huntley. Especially not while she's helping her mother and aunts in the kitchen. There are a few things about her lifestyle that she would rather not have exposed to her family. But cursing is allowed.

Ebony was up at 4am. She has to get the twins and herself dressed before Ajay's shuttle arrives at 6a.m. It's pre-dawn Thanksgiving day when Ajay gets home. Ebony and the twins greet him at the door. He hugs his twins first. Lannie jumps up into his arms like she always does. He gives her a hug and a kiss. Lil Ajay gets a hug and a pound from his daddy. Then Ajay looks into Ebony's eyes. She's already looking into his. She can see the anticipation in his eyes and she's sure he can see the same in hers.

"I missed you, baby," he says suddenly.

His eyes are so lonely and sad. They're telling her that he's tormented himself, worrying about whether she would be ready to allow him to make up with her.

"I missed you too, Anthony. I missed you a lot," she says.

Without hesitation, he pulls her to him and hugs her tight. He holds onto her for more than 5 minutes while their twins cheer. She can hear their mothers arriving to start cooking for today's family dinner.

"I'm sorry I fucked up, baby," he whispers while still holding her, "I'm so sorry," he repeats before kissing her with fervor.

She can feel her insides melting. She's so hot and it's obvious he's hot for her too. She wants to take him their bedroom and fuck him like her body is telling her to do. But they're the host for today's Thanksgiving dinner and the mothers are already showing up to get things going.

"Looks like you two are ready to go to bed," big mama snickers as her, Annabelle, Jo, Debbie, Brenda and Pearl parade in through the kitchen entrance.

The twins had opened the door for them while Ajay and Ebony was still in the kitchen. Kissing each other like they were still in high school.

"Do y'all ever come up for air?" Jo asks as she laughs.

But she's happy to see them back to the romance.

"Only long enough to feed the twins and maybe themselves," Pearl says as they continue to laugh.

"Your husband is just coming home," Annabelle says, "Don't you worry about your mama and them teasing you, baby girl. You go on and take care of your marriage. We'll get the cooking going, just fine without you in here."

Ajay smiles at the women and they're smiling back at him. Ebony is holding his hand. Letting him know that she's okay with granny Annabelle's suggestion.

"The kitchen belongs to y'all until dinner time then," Ajay says, "We'll be-"

TIME TO FEEL-RELOADED-Time Will Reveal part 5

"-Out of the kitchen?" big mama says and laughs, "That's just fine. Y'all go on. We've got the kitchen, the twins and the twin dogs too."

"Yes we do. Dinner's at three," Jo adds as they rush them out.
They all want them to get back on the right track with their marriage. And soon. Ajay carries his wife to their master suite while the ladies laugh and shout many approvals.

Once they're inside the master bedroom, Ajay puts on his *Anthony Hamilton, Coming from where I come from* CD. As the track *Charlene* plays, he looks at Ebony with the saddest eyes. He's ready to talk or listen or answer questions. Whatever his wife demands. But she doesn't demand any of that. She knows he's sorry about his mistakes. She's seen it in his eyes. She heard it in his voice, the same night. The fact that he hadn't tried to force her to get over it, right then and come to bed for sex. Proved his maturity. Him taken the time to bring in others to prove his points, was major for her too. On that night, his actions toward her proved that he'd changed. In the past, Ajay had never accepted any type of break-up talk from her. Not where sex was concerned, no matter how angry she was. They would still have sex like nothing happened. He would just say,
"You can call us broke up or whatever you want. But I'm gonna get what's mine. No matter who, what or how. You're not gonna separate me from my pussy, baby girl."
He didn't even try that on Tuesday night. Nor the night before he left for his road trip. Today he tells her, he still felt that way that night. But because he'd made a mistake while married, is why he knew he had to let her have her say and her way. Plus respect whatever her say was. She knew by that statement that he'd grown up a lot. He wasn't worried about her being unfaithful. Back then he felt she might chose another guy to date and he wasn't willing to let another man have her. He also tells her, he hasn't worried about her thinking about another man for a *long* time.

"But I don't want it to seem like I take you for granted," he says, "Because that's not what Tuesday night was. It was crew shit. I didn't even consider the fact that I was breaking my vows by touching her. I really didn't and for that, I feel bad as *fuck*. Because I can still see your eyes and your expression from that night. That haunted me throughout this whole road trip. I never wanted to hurt you baby. I hate myself for that. I fucked up a perfect record and it didn't even dawn on me until I saw your eyes."

"I know you didn't," she says, "I know you wasn't focused during the trip either. I saw the games and your stats. You played average. That's acceptable for some but not for me. You was *way* too distracted."

"The coaching staff was telling me to send for you by Thursday night," he says, "They thought I was out of sync because you wasn't there. They didn't know it was because I knew I fucked up and you hadn't said you was okay yet."

"I'm okay," she says suddenly.

"Did you *have* to fight her?" he asks suddenly as he gets to the fight she had at Stoney's Bar and Grill.

"Yes I did," she says, surprised at how he brings it up. She adds, "I needed that."

"So now we've both put our baby in danger," he says.

She looks at him and shakes her head. He was incorrect. He had touched other females inappropriately. But she had a physical fight while carrying their baby. He had opened himself up to being harassed for the real act. That's true. But she had brought the dangers of being hit in the abdomen, same as T-baby did with her and Rich's 1st baby. Or she could've stumbled over something and fell. Thus injuring herself and their unborn baby.

"That was never my intentions," she says, "And I know you don't have plans of going any further with Nickeia or Farah."

"No I don't and if I would've taken a moment to think it through like I did after I saw you," he says, "We wouldn't even be having this conversation."

"I love you Anthony and I'm okay," she finally says, "I need for you to be okay. I need for you to be able to do your job. *All* of your jobs."

"Do you have some work for me?" he asks with yearning in his eyes.

"I sure do."

"I'm ready, willing and able to perform any job you've got for me to do, baby," he says.

"I need you to go to work on me," she says suddenly, "I'm so hot for you. I can't hold back your loving because I miss it. Just like you do. I can't even lie to you about that. I love our sex. Just as much as you do."

He gives her a sexy smile while he's pulling her to him.

"I'll never cheat in *any* way again," he says, "That's my word. I wish I wouldn't have done that much. And no more fighting, okay?"

"Okay Anthony."

She shows him she understands and agrees. She gives him a sweet kiss with plenty of tongue. She wants to taste him but she knows he won't allow her to suck his dick while she's pregnant. But he's certainly going to taste her though. And does he ever!

TIME TO FEEL-RELOADED-Time Will Reveal part 5

After her 1st orgasm, she's back in the groove. This is her man and though he'd make a mistake while participating in his male meeting. He has and still is, showing remorse. She can feel that in the way he's holding her today. He makes love to her with extra passion. With tears in his eyes, he kisses her and sucks all over her body. He's happy to finally be able to touch, tease and tantalize her again. This is what makes his house, a home. She's just as much his home as the huge estate that he'd put in *her* name. She's his sanctuary and he's so glad to be *home*.

After 3 passionate sessions, they refresh themselves with juice and Gatorade from their mini fridge. Then they talk about what changes *she* needs him to make when it comes to crew thangs.

By the time dinner is served, Ebony and Ajay have fucked, talked and decided on some suggestions for their family and crew. During dessert, Ajay opens the floor.

"Tonight we need to do something a little different," he says, "I need the men *and women* to attend the party in my basement."

Ebony smiles as she looks around at the men. They're mean mugging her.

"Don't give my wife mean looks, brothers and fathers and grandfathers," Ajay orders, "She didn't know anything about this part. She's just hearing it, same as y'all are. But I need y'all to walk with me on this one."

They all agree as they adjourn to the basement after dessert. On the way downstairs, Renee and Tonya pull Ebony to the side.

"What did you do, girl?" Tonya asks.

"How did you get Ajay to change the tradition?" Renee asks.

"I don't know," Ebony says, "I just missed him a lot. I just told him and I showed him that. This isn't about something I said or did. This is from him. *He* wants to make some changes in our traditions. He *wants* this because he truly loves me and our daughter too. He doesn't want to break my heart again and he don't want Lannie to *ever* be hurt like that."

Then Renee says, "He told Chill he wants them to take the whole *fucking someone's girl thing* out of the equation, for the next time when they go to the chamber."

"He told Brad that too. And that he didn't want none of them to do that again," Tonya adds, "Even the guys who aren't married. What did you *do*, baby girl."

"He's knows what real love and loyalty is," Ebony says, "He had time to think about it. I haven't said anymore *to* him about Tuesday night. This came from him. *Trust*. With me, he's learned what it's like to be the *absolute* best for your partner and he knew that wasn't his best. He wants

234

me to have his best and that's a beautiful thing. I know our love is strong enough to get that accomplished. I knew that when I was a girl. But then, I just didn't know when or how long it would take before it came. I knew in my heart that it *would* come though. Now is as good of a time as any."

The motion is put forth by Ajay. Tank seconds him and then, 1 by 1, all of the males in the family from papa down to Brandon, agree never to employ that act again.

Matrimony will trump crew loyalty from now on. The ladies are happy to hear this one. After this change is agreed upon. Many of the ladies start to open up about the hurt they'd suffered because of that crew chamber ritual. They also agree that they'd done something right, in the teaching of Ebony. For she had learned what real love is about and because she had grasped it, in it's purest form and was able to convey that to her husband. He stepped up and demanded the men never do that again.

Out of Ajay's love for Ebony, he committed to suggesting the change for all of the males. They all agreed. And just like that, change had come to the Cleveland Crew. The Atlanta crew are home for Thanksgiving too. Lynn, Jan, Bre and Brittany are happy with the change as well. Being away from home is hard enough. But the crew men in Atlanta had still been practicing the *crew way*. This change couldn't have come at a better time for Jan and Brittany. With the music business Rob and Reaper are in. That infidelity thing was becoming a huge obstacle in both of their relationships. Yolanda and Carolyn are happy to hear it too because David and Ron had fallen right in with that practice. Shortly after becoming family with the crew.

"Good Riddance," Bre says and all the ladies 2nd her.
Thanksgiving 2003 is wonderful. Ebony and Ajay add this night into their wedding diary. It's a very significant 1 for them and for their entire family.

TIME TO FEEL-RELOADED-Time Will Reveal part 5

CHAPTER 57

WHAT THE CHICAGO WIND BLEW IN

It's a week before Christmas and the crew have gotten *plenty* of shopping done already and still have more to do. The December party is set. Nina and Ebony will turn 28 this year. Kenny will be 20 while Ruthie had her 22nd birthday at UC. Ruthie has transferred colleges and is now attending in Cincinnati, along with Pam. That's since Greg and Jesse graduated and left Baton Rouge. Jesse is on the Cincinnati *Bengals* team now. Which works out perfect for both of them. Jesse wanted her to be familiar with the city because they'll live there until his contract expires or he gets traded.

The crew are having a huge celebration for December birthdays, holidays, anniversaries and all. The Atlanta and Houston crew's are coming home to attend. Kenny and the college crew are coming home as well.

Tonight at the club, Farah strikes again. She goes after Kenny, who's in the adult club helping out. She asks him about coming to her home after the club closes. He tells her, *"NO."* Less the 20 minutes later, she corners him and Chill, next to 1 of the back bars on the 1st floor. She propositions them both. This time they both ignore her and go on with their work, as though she isn't even talking. Chill is 1 person who doesn't repeat himself. He'd told her weeks ago, he wasn't interested in fucking with her ever again. After seeing that neither of them are going to give her any play. Farah heads up to the *Juice Bar* on the 2nd floor to watch dancers. While she sips a few drinks, she notices Matt come in and sit in a booth in the back. She already knows she can use him. Slowly but surely, she makes her way over to him.

She says, "Hello stranger. You're looking good. I haven't seen you since your kidnapping ordeal."

"Why *thank* you," Matt says, "I feel good. And I haven't seen you either."

She sits down with him and orders a bottle for the table. They share the bottle and plenty of suggestive conversation. By the end of the night, he's ready to go home with her. Farah leaves with Alana. Matt trails them to Parma Heights.

"Matt must be whipped by that bitch?" Jr asks Chill.

"He can have it. I wish them luck," is Chill's response.

On the Friday before Christmas, Marvin's body is discovered. It makes it onto Cleveland news, though his body is found near Pennsylvania.

TIME TO FEEL-RELOADED-Time Will Reveal part 5

His body was discovered just off the coast of Erie Pennsylvania, near Presque Isle Bay where his family docks several boats. His Porsche 944 was parked in the parking area with the other boat owners. The car had been discovered a week ago. Police had staked out the dock, hoping to catch Marvin coming in. A check of the Porsche's trip speedometer revealed that the car had been driven 187 miles. The exact mileage for a trip from his Cleveland Condo to Erie's Presque Isle. Early speculations are that he'd driven here to meet someone, went out on the lake in their boat and was killed while sailing. Then dumped in the lake and his body floated back to shore.

Shortly before noon, Mr. Huntley Sr contacts Ebony at her office. He tells her to go ahead with the liquidation of the store. He says his son's body has been found. She makes him an offer for the store and he accepts it. She transfers the funds to his bank before the close of business. Then she calls in her final 3 manager choices. Amongst the 3 applicants is Mario Scott, the witness from the Angel Taylor murder trial. He had completed his degree in Business Management and needs a job. She needs a manager whom she's familiar with. He was the best choice. She calls him in for his final interview just before 5pm. Today Venitia is working in Ebony's office. Her and Mario's eyes meet and Ebony notices the obvious sparks, right away.

By 6:30pm Ebony, Venitia and Mario are at the Brook Park store. She introduces Mario to his assistant manager Ellen Barnes. Ellen and her friends had done a great job keeping the store going after Marvin's disappearance. Ebony is impressed and so is Venitia and Mario. They decide to allow Ellen to keep her assistant managerial position. They give her a 20% raise plus change the store name from Huntley's Insurance and Textiles to *CrewLand Insurance and Carpeting,* by New Year's 2004. Ebony is glad to have the business set up and running well before the end of the year. Venitia expresses interest in making it her permanent job which brings a huge smile to Mario's face. This is the crew's 29th business in total. Venitia and Mario are happy for the opportunity to be under the Crew Enterprise umbrella.

The December party is another great 1 for the crew. There's much talk about the body of Marvin being found in Erie. Farah uses his death as a way to gather sympathy. The crew play along for a week or so. But by New Year's Eve, they're over it and ready for her to stop playing it up. Because for the crew, they give less than a damn about her or Marvin.

"I never saw you with him," Courtney Freeman says, "I would never have known you all even *knew* each other. Are you the reason he was snooping around here?"

"For real," Wayne adds, "All he did around here was spy and snoop. What was he involved in? That's what I wanna know. And are you involved in it too? Because if you are. You could be the next one to get it."

"Yea I know," Farah says, "He was following me and I didn't even know he was *here*. I left him because he was abusive to me. I don't know what all he was involved in. But I wasn't apart of it. He was a mean spirited and a racist person."

"Looks like somebody got tired of that," Courtney says, as she goes back to her duties.

Before long, Matt's at the club to meet Farah. He's her counselor, now that she's lost a loved one. He's consoling her on the regular *these days*. Or better yet, she's using him again. Ellen and Matt are still friends, believe or not. He has hooked up with her a few times since his fake kidnapping too. He'd seen the video of Marvin's plan to set her up. He found it interesting that Marvin was trying to use her to kill him. She'd showed him the video but she didn't let him see the part where Marvin admitted to sending her a gun. She didn't volunteer *that* part of the information either.

}*Chicago Family*{

Eric's siblings had come to Cleveland to visit with him and Erica for the Christmas holidays. Leilenne, Alan and Kimmie are staying in Jackson Heights with their big brother and new sister-in-law until Chicago school's resume in January. The Jackson twins have playmates for the entire holiday and they love to have company. Erica has brought Alan and Kimmie over to play with the twins each day since they've been here. They had even spent a night or 2, back and forth. Erica is at Ebony and Ajay's today. She's helping out with the twins while Ebony cooks her and Ajay's 6th year anniversary dinner. Lil Ajay and Lannie love playing with Alan Anthony and Kimmie. They'd played together a lot at the reception and during the 2 days following it until the McNair's returned to Chicago. Alan and Kimmie wanted to stay but Eric told them they could come back and visit another time. Before leaving, Alan and Kimmie had begged Eric to let them come back and play with the twins. Eric promised them they could come back and stay for Christmas break. He kept his word. He'd also told his parents, he would be Santa Claus this year, for his siblings and for them too. Eric's parents spent their days with Jo, Al and their crew.

TIME TO FEEL-RELOADED-Time Will Reveal part 5

Eric's 17 year old sister Leilenne hung out with the other twins from the crew, Brandon and Brina. They're 17 now as well. She hung out with 18 year old Archie Jr and 19 year old Charlotte also. They had her working in The Spot II by her 2nd night in town. She was already loving the crew and their club. Alan and Kimmie had played with Lannie and Lil Ajay every day. They'd become so close that Kimmie was begging her mother to let Lannie and Lil Ajay come home with them.

Today as they play, Lil Ajay still keeps a close eye on Alan Anthony. Same as he'd done during the wedding week.

"I know you got me and my daddy *same* name," Lil Ajay tells Alan. "And you got my papa name too. But yours is spelled different. That still don't mean you can like my sister though. Didn't I tell you one time that she can't have no boyfriend? My pops said that. He's the man. Okay? You feel me?"

"I can like her if I want too," Alan says, "She smiled at me and she's pretty. I like her, just like Kimmie likes you. And she's my Lil sister."

"I done told you. You can't like my sister," Lil Ajay repeats, "If you do. I'm gonna beat you up."

"No you're not," Alan says.

Erica and Ebony can hear the boys arguing in the playroom. They don't say anything. They just listen and laugh. The 4 kids are having quite an interesting conversation.

"But Ajay didn't you say you wanna be Kimmie's boyfriend?" Lannie asks.

"Yep I *am* her boyfriend," he says, "That don't mean nothing. You can't do what I do. You know what daddy said."

"That's not fair," Alan says, "She can be my girlfriend if she wants too." Then he turns to Lannie and asks her, "Atlantis do you wanna be my girlfriend?"

"I can't," Lannie says, "You heard what my brother said. I don't wanna get in trouble. I never make my daddy mad."

Ebony and Erica are about to burst as they go into the playroom to check on the kids.

"How's everyone doing in here?" Ebony asks.

"Good!" the kids yell and, "Fine!"

"Okay then. I need some help in the kitchen," Ebony says, "Ladies would you like to help me out?"

"Yes!" Lannie and Kimmie scream as they follow Ebony and Erica into the kitchen.

239

Lil Ajay and Alan stay in the playroom for another 5 minutes. Then they head to the kitchen.

"Oh the boys wanna cook *too*?" Erica asks with a smile.

"I don't," Lil Ajay says.

"Me either," Alan agrees.

"Then why are y'all in the kitchen?" Ebony asks as she smiles.

"My girlfriend is in here," Lil Ajay says.

"And mine too," Alan tries.

"No yours *not*," Lil Ajay says sternly but as calm as his father would say it. He adds, "You'd better not say it again."

He's getting upset. Ebony and Lannie know it, even if the others don't.

Ebony says, "Ant don't be rude to him. He's only saying what *you're* saying. You can't say you're his sister's boyfriend and then tell him he can't say it about *your* sister. That's not the way you negotiate with family."

Her and Erica try to hide their grins. Lil Ajay isn't having it. He's dead set against Alan even saying he's a boyfriend to his twin sister.

"I am Kimmie's boyfriend but he's not Lannie's," he says, "Watch this." He turns to Kimmie and asks, "Am I your boyfriend or not?"

"Yes," Kimmie says with a smile.

"No," Lannie says, "My brother can't have no girlfriend and I can't have no boyfriend. So we're all friends. Now let's just help my mommy cook and stop all this fussing. Ajay's already gonna tell my daddy."

"You got that right," Lil Ajay agrees.

Everybody thinks that's funny. All except Lil Ajay. He doesn't laugh.

Ebony has everything prepped and ready for a romantic dinner later. The twins are staying at Erica's tonight but that'll most likely change after Ajay finds out the revelation. Or at least it's going to change for Lannie.

Ajay makes it home by noon. He spends the first 4 hours with his twins plus Kimmie and Alan. The 5 of them play with the new Christmas toys or just doing whatever the twins wanted him to do with them. After the twins are satisfied that they've had daddy time. They go home with Erica, Alan and Kimmie so Ajay and Ebony can have alone time.

Once the twins are gone, Ajay and Ebony start off with a Jacuzzi bath. They have plenty of their normal activity while in the tub. Then they get dressed in their finest attire and she serves him dinner. They sit at their formal dining room table to feast on the great meal she'd cooked for them. They enjoy each others company over some great conversation.

"This smells *so* good," he says of the 6th anniversary meal she'd spent all morning preparing and cooking, as he inquires about how they'd spent their time without him.

"Thanks baby," she says, "I figured you wanted something *spicy* tonight."

She'd made seafood gumbo and Empire salad for appetizers. Ajay had tried gumbo on 1 of their trips to New Orleans, back when June and Rich was playing college bowl games. He loved it then and had asked Ebony to learn how to make it. Kilo had his aunt to email her the recipe. She got it right on the 1st try, with big mama coaching by phone.

"This shit is good, baby girl," he says with a smile, "I'm a blessed man. I got a woman who's smart beautiful, fine sexy, got some good ass pussy and can cook too."

She giggles and says, "Thank you sexy man. You're sexy yourself."

He gives her another seductive smile with eyes to match. He's always ready. She tells him she has to feed him a full meal before they can get back to their sex marathon. He agrees to be patient as she fries up the entrée while he tries to assist her. Then they have their golden brown Catfish fillets with jumbo Cajun sautéed shrimp and hot links Jambalaya on the side.

"This kind of food will keep us warm without even turning on the heat or lighting one these fireplaces, we got up in this estate," he says as he flashes her another seductive smile and adds, "But I already know I got something in this house that's way spicier than this food."

"Yes. You know that already," she answers and giggles.

"Yes indeed," he says, "We're about to set two thousand and four off with a five alarm blaze." They both laugh hard.

"How is my little baby doing," he says, "The one that's still cooking?" he chuckles which makes her laugh even harder.

She's still giggling as she says, "She's doing fine. You said this is a girl. I guess that means we'll be having another baby ha?"

"You still want two boys?" he asks, smiling at her.

"Yes," she says, "We're that special couple of *this* generation. So I know we can break your blood line legacy too. If nobody else can. We can."

"Already," he agrees.

They dig into their dinner and keep the conversation going. He wants to know how his twins are treating their Chicago family.

"Oh boy," she says and smiles, "*Little you* acts just like you. He says Kimmie is his girlfriend."

"Okay. That's my son," he says with a huge smile and adds, "He's gonna be on the girls. I know she likes him. She said that the first day she

241

was here for the wedding. And her pops told her to get in the will."

They laugh hard. Then she gives him a look of uncertainty before telling him the rest of the story. He knows there's more.

He asks, "What is it?"

"Well Alan Anthony," she says as she giggles because she knows he's going to interrupt her and he does.

"I know he don't think he's gonna go at my baby girl?"

"Yes," she says with a sigh.

"No," Ajay says, "What did Ant say?"

"The same thing you just said," she tells him.

"Damn right," he says, "Ant knows what the rules are. Alan can come back in thirty years and ask me then."

"Anthony that's crazy," she says, "But I don't want either of them picking mates. They're not even five years old yet."

"Ant's ready to fuck by now," he says with confidence.

"*No way*," she snaps back.

"Not with Kimmie though," he says, "She's to young for him, right now. But she might be his wife."

"*Anthony*."

"I'm serious," he says, "I see how he looks at her. He just wants to keep an eye on her, at this point. He likes to watch her. If he didn't like her. He would've already touched her."

"Oh no," she says and they laugh.

Then he says, "Let's get done with dinner so I can go around there and get my daughter. I'm not about to let Alan think up a plan for her, right now. She's not spending the night. *Period*."

"Are you serious?" Ebony asks.

"As a heart attack," he says and starts to inhale his food.

She laughs and says, "You are a bit much to take. Do you know that?"

"Yea. I'm pretty hard nosed. I know," he says, "Let's eat while the food's hot. We're gonna pick up Lannie when we're done. I mean that."

Sure enough, when they finish eating and Ebony has loaded the dishwasher. They drive her Escalade around to Erica and Eric's house to bring Lannie home. Ajay even brings Kimmie back to spend the night with her.

}*The Spot II*{

Leilenne is having the time of her life with Archie Jr and the crew. Shortly after the new year rings in, Brina has to head home. Brenda is there to pick her up. Brandon is able to stay because he's a crew male. That part of the double standard *didn't* change. Charlotte and Archie Jr are still there, so Leilenne has someone to kick it with. Ally is there as extra holiday work crew, along with Steven, Holly and Jamal. Leilenne is having a blast. She's already sweet on Archie Jr. He's feeling her too. He tries not to let the crew girls see him. He's going to visit *DePaul University* this spring, just to get his visits in. But he's already assured Ajay that he's going to sign with Cincinnati. Leilenne has promised to show him a great time in Chicago, when he gets there.

}*Ajay and Ebony's house*{

Ajay and Ebony have just finished a heated session of lovemaking. Ajay is holding her close to him but he can tell there's still something on her mind.

"What's up baby?" he asks.

She sighs and says, "I can't believe you made Lannie come home."

"I don't know why you can't," he says, "You know me."

"She's four years old Anthony," Ebony tries, "And she's not gonna do anything she thinks will make you mad. She said it herself."

"And I believe her," he says, "I trust her to do what I tell her to do. I don't trust Alan. He's a young me, just like Ant. That's why I brought Kimmie with us too."

"Okay. It was because of the boys and what they might try to do?" she asks, for clarity.

"Exactly," he says, "What they was *gonna* do. Not *try* to do. I know my son and even if Alan wasn't thinking it. He was gonna mimic what Ant did, just to stay even with him. And no. You, Lynn and Nina wasn't no *one* up for me, Jb and Tank. Y'all are the ones *for* us. Y'all crew. We was born to be together."

"Like you said. *We* are the *ones* for *y'all*," she adds with a smile.

Then she giggles but she knows he's probably right about their son. After all, Ajay was that way very early in his life. And so far, their son has mirrored his father's childhood in every aspect. Right down to the fighting.

****

It's 2 weeks after Valentines Day. Jan and Rob have come to Cleveland for an appointment with Ebony. This time she has to prepare land for Jan's pediatric office. Jan will graduate from Georgia Tech school of Pediatrics and Medicine this May with a doctorate. She'll become *Dr. Janice Marie Logan-Jenkins MD*. She'll do her first 2 years of residency at Grady Hospital in Atlanta. Then apply for dual residency in Cleveland. She'll get her start in labor and delivery at East General. The same hospital Pearl has just retired from.

The month of February also finds *CrewLand Trucking* growing more clients. Just as Pearl and John had guaranteed, the trucking company is profitable enough to maintain it's own office. Ebony sets up the construction for the next strip mall. This will be the 3rd strip for the crew. Dr. Janice Logan-Jenkins office and CrewLand Trucking will be the first 2 to open. Kimberly Logan-Wilson and Chaundra Coleman, the future Mrs. Kenneth Payne Jr, will both have their future law offices in this strip. The law office will carry the name; *The Wheeler Firm*. Trina Yvette Sloan-Wheeler will have her office there too. For now she still works out of Ebony's office when she's in the Cleveland area. Kim and Chaundra are both going to work with Attorney George Wheeler and his wife Trina Yvette. Wheeler has been wanting to put his Law office right there on the business property of his most important clients. Kim is getting a degree in Family law while Chaundra is studying to become a corporate attorney.

But with CrewLand Trucking's increase in clientele, John had to hire and train more drivers. He already has 4 employees. This week he hires Joe and Woody. He'll train them to drive rigs. They'll start out doing local deliveries with him. After they rack up 24 months of driving local delivery. They'll be able to apply for over-the-road driving. By January 2005, John and Pearl will have their own office at CrewLand mall, in the split entrance style. Which John will share with his brother Greg Sr and Sam Sr, as soon as their ready to open up their side. John also hires Andre and Pac Man to load and unload for the CrewLand businesses.

"Self contained man," John says to the 4 of them, "We make money for our neighborhood and spend it right *here* in our communities. We're trying to hire right here within our own people. Ex-offenders have a hard time getting legal work as it is. But not with this crew because we're gonna give you a chance to make something of your life. Something legal and something that will help you to build a future with benefits."

"I always knew that knowing this crew was gonna be a benefit," Woody says.

"No joke," Joe says, "I can't even find the words to say how much I appreciate every lick I've hit, just from knowing big Chill and the crew."

TIME TO FEEL-RELOADED-Time Will Reveal part 5

Andre, Joe, Pac Man and Woody appreciate the opportunity to do legal work, for a change.

Nina and Tank celebrate 8 years of marriage on the same day Archie Jr and his dad, Big Arch fly to Chicago to visit *DePaul University*. DePaul had recruited Archie extremely hard. Eric had begged him to consider DePaul or Northwestern. Archie Jr had promised him he would visit at least 1 of them. Him and his father arrive in Chicago to find not only DePaul's recruiting team staff members waiting to receive them at *O'Hare International*. But Eric Sr and Jillian McNair, along with Leilenne, Alan and Kimmie are there also. The McNair's have made plans to host big Arch and Archie Jr once the official visit is complete, on Saturday morning. They want to show them a great time before they leave the city. Eric and Erica flew in with them to visit with his family for a few days before they jet off to Barbados, the home of *Rihanna*. Friday night is the start of their official honeymoon.

By Saturday, the DePaul visit is done. Big Arch and Archie Jr go stay with the McNair's until Monday. When they'll head back to Cleveland. MLK will be on Spring Break when they return home. Archie Jr enjoyed his visit with DePaul but he's going to sign with Cincinnati. He has already given his word to Ajay and no one else.

Saturday the McNair's take them out to *really* see the city. They visit the *Sears Tower* and the *Museum Campus, Navy Pier and Crown fountain in Millennium park* before shopping at *Chicago's Magnificent Mile*.

By late evening, they've finished with the *shoreline tour* which had given them a beautiful and full view of the city from Lake Michigan. Eric Sr takes them to see *Soldier Field* where the *Chicago Bears* play. *The United Center*, home to the *Chicago Bulls* and *The Cubs* home; *Wrigley Field,* before they have an elegant dinner at *Gibson's Steakhouse.* The McNair's tell them they should come to Chicago for *4th of July* and go with them to *Grant Park* for *Taste Of Chicago.* It's the largest food festival in the world which runs from the last week of June through 4th of July week. Archie Jr enjoys his time in Chicago. He has thanked the McNair's several times for their hospitality. By Saturday night, Leilenne is his hostess. She's taking him to a party for 1 of her Southside friends birthday. *Finally*! Some youth excursion, he thinks to himself as they dress and leave in Leilenne's 2004 Mercedes-Benz C-Class which Eric Jr had bought for her 17th birthday.

"I'm gonna show you how we party in Chi-Town," Leilenne laughs.

"Okay. Let's do this," Archie Jr says.

TIME TO FEEL-RELOADED-Time Will Reveal part 5

They have a ball at the party. Archie receives a lot of female attention but Leilenne isn't going to allow *any* other girl to get closer to him then she is.

"He's with me," she tells her fellow Chicago friend girls, "He's my man as long as he's in Chi town."
Archie smiles. He's cool with that. Leilenne is already sexually active. She had broken up with her 2nd boyfriend, 2 weeks before she attended Eric Jr's wedding. By now, all of her relationship wounds are healed and she's ready to move on. She has her sights set on Archie Wilson Jr. After the party, she drives Archie Jr back to the shoreline.

"We're gonna check out the shoreline, *my* way," she says, "All twenty nine miles of it."

"We've got a shoreline too," he says as he smiles, "We took you to the shoreway. Gordon park. You remember that, right?"

"Yes," she says, "I love Cleveland and your family is *so* cool. Your crew has got it going on, Archie and I wanna be down."

"Oh yea?" he asks, "Down how?"

"With you," she says suddenly, "You know that too. Don't try to tell me you didn't know I was feeling you."

"I felt that when you was in C-town. But you held back on me," Archie Jr says, "You never said anything."

"Because your girlfriend was there," she says as she laughs, "So are y'all still together?"

"I am a single man," he says, "I'm not married. I'm not engaged. So you could've said whatever was on your mind. That's the only way to find out what's *really* going on."
Archie Jr doesn't want to answer that question honestly. He's still with Brina but he wants to fuck Leilenne. He senses that she wants to fuck him too. Otherwise why would she have driven him out to what looks like *Inspiration point*. She has parked at the southern most end of *Navy Pier*. First they go for a walk along the Pier and ride the Ferris Wheel. Archie finally kisses her. He'd wanted to do that from the 1st time he saw her, back in October. He's trying to figure out how he can have a relationship with Leilenne while having 1 with Brina, at the same time. That's going to be tough. Leilenne tells him she wants to hook up with him. She has a girlfriend that attends college at DePaul, who has a spot off of *Sheffield avenue*. This is where Leilenne takes Archie Jr so they can hook up. They go by there and he meets her friend Iona. Him and Leilenne have sex, several times before going back to the McNair's home to go to sleep. Their entire date lasted 7 hours. They arrive back in *Burbank*, shortly after 5am.

246

TIME TO FEEL-RELOADED-Time Will Reveal part 5

In Cleveland, Brina has been trying to reach Archie Jr on his cell phone all night. She has called and sent text messages, over and over. Neither was answered. All of her calls had gone directly to his voicemail.

"He's got his phone off," Brina says to Charlotte, "He's had it off since like ten o'clock. I talk to him at nine thirty and they was just finishing dinner."

She's spending the night at Charlotte's house after leaving The Spot II.

"I hate when they do that," Charlotte says, "Your brother does the same thing to me when he's *fuckin* around."

"That's what Archie's doing too," Brina says, "I'll bet you, he done met some lil freak while he's over there. And acting like he's a single man too."

She has no idea of how right she is. Only she doesn't realize she's already met the girl whom her boyfriend is in Chicago fucking around with. And that the same girl is considered family. Brina will have plenty to question Archie Jr about when he returns to Cleveland tomorrow. Her and Charlotte try to go to sleep. Mama Jackie will be in to wake them up for Sunday school, in 2 hours.

Eric Jr and Erica return from Barbados on Tuesday, the first official day of spring.

"Stop at *Best Buy* on the way," Erica says as they head to Jackson Heights from Cleveland Hopkins international airport.

"We've got to get that new *Usher*. Ha baby?" Eric Jr laughs.

"Yes indeed," Erica laughs.

Usher Raymond drops his highly anticipated CD; *Confessions* the 4th Tuesday in March, as his relationship with *Chili* from *TLC* gains more popularity and attention. Folks already speculate that this CD is personal. They contemplate whether his singles, *Confessions Pt 2, U Don't Have To Call* and *Let It Burn* are aimed toward her. And if they're an admission of his infidelity which many figure caused the end of their relationship. But the club banger, *Yeah* which features *Lil Jon* keeps folks dancing and jamming long enough to forget the drama going on with the couple.

The end of spring break week party at The Spot II which carries the title; *The Confessional,* turns out to be just that for Archie Jr. Leilenne's spring break is starting the following Monday. Her, Alan and Kimmie are back in Cleveland to visit Eric Jr, for a week. Leilenne brings 3 friends with her. Iona, who's apartment Archie Jr and Leilenne hooked up in. Charity, who'd just had her 18th birthday party in Chicago and Felecia

247

came too. All 3 girls look forward to meeting all of Archie Jr's crew. They'd heard so much about the crew from Archie Jr while he was in Chicago last week. Plus Leilenne has talked about the crew a lot since her oldest brother had become a member of it.

"Where the boys at?" Charity asks as they pile into The Spot II.

"Girl my crew owns all of this you see around here," Brina says, "We own this club, the whole mall and more. And the boys are always up in here, in full effect."

"That's off the chain," Iona says, "I wanna meet some Cleveland boys. Let's see what they working with."

"Amen to that," Charity cosigns her.

Leilenne doesn't have a comment. She isn't interested in meeting anybody new. Her and Archie Jr have plans to hook up at his sister's house while she's here staying at Eric's. Brina and Charlotte play hostess to Leilenne and her 3 girls, this week. They introduce them to their whole crew without any knowledge of Leilenne and Archie Jr's involvement.

But by Tuesday, the news of Archie Jr staying out at Rebbie's house on Sunday night and Leilenne sneaking over from Eric's to spend the night, gets out. Brina is in class when she hears a teammate of Archie and Brandon's speaking on it. She's livid as she ask her teacher for a pass to go to the restroom. She goes directly to the gymnasium and confronts Archie Jr. He's embarrassed but acts unaffected by what Brina is saying. Brina is about to get sent to detention for causing a disturbance during the boys basketball team's, time in the gym. But instead, the girls coach comes to get her and escorts her to his office for a talk. Archie Jr takes that as his time to break away. He leaves the gym before Brina is done talking with her coach. She does catch up to him later at CrewLand mall. He's at The Spot II, working his normal shift.

"Archie is it true that you're fucking Leilenne?" she asks.

"Brina baby, don't come in here with this madness," he tries, "I'm fucking you and you know that."

"Did you hook up with her, Sunday night? Don't lie, Archie."

"No."

"That's what I've been hearing all week. I also heard that you and her have been taking ecstasy too and that started in Chicago."

"Brina, I'm a ball player. What drugs have you seen me take?"

"I know you smoke weed but her friends have been popping those X tabs all week. So I know they do it. Did you do it *with* them?"

"No. I don't do drugs," he lies.

248

TIME TO FEEL-RELOADED-Time Will Reveal part 5

Brina knows some of her crew take ecstasy pills, from time to time. She has even tried it herself. But Archie is particular about his body. He hasn't *ever* been willing to try *X* around her. However, he likes when she takes it because as he says, her sex is more intense. He has never taken any with her, to her knowledge. He dodges all of her questions about Leilenne and manages to get her to calm down. That won't last long because outside in the parking lot, Erica has just pulled up for her shift at The Spot II. She's brought Leilenne, Iona, Charity and Felecia with her. They're going to earn extra cash by working at the club this week. Leilenne runs in and goes right up to Archie Jr. She gives him a giant hug and a kiss on the cheek. She's smiling from ear to ear. Brina takes this opportunity to ask her the same line of questioning.

"Did you fuck Archie? Yes or no?"

"Wait. Why are you asking me that? Archie is single, right?"

"He's my boyfriend. Tell her, Archie."

Archie doesn't say anything. He walks away to avoid the conversation. He gets on the elevator and goes up to the 3rd floor to Tank's office. While Brina and Leilenne continue the conversation without him.

"I asked him if y'all were still together when he was in Chicago," Leilenne says, "And his exact words was, *'I am a single man. I'm not married. I'm not engaged. So you can say whatever's on your mind. That's the only way to find out what's really going on.'* After that, I said what was on my mind. Then we started talking about him and I getting closer."

"Did you fuck him or not?"

"I don't really see where that's any of your business, Brina. Like that's personal and y'all aren't together," Leilenne says.

"We are together, Leilenne," she says, "We've been together since I was thirteen."

"He's never said that to me. And besides, he just walked away when you asked him to tell me that. I don't think he's with you anymore."

Brina doesn't say anything else to Leilenne. She's hurt by Archie Jr walking away. So she leaves Leilenne, Iona, Charity and Felecia on the 1st floor and goes to find Archie Jr.

She finds him on the 3rd floor. He's still in Tank's office having what looks to be a *very* intense talk with Tank. Brina barges in and starts going off on Archie, right in front of Tank. Immediately Tank tries to calm the situation with his younger crew.

"Hey Brina. What's the problem?" Tank asks.

"He's been messing around on me with Leilenne."

"Did *she* say he did?" Tank asks.

"She said it's her personal business and since we're not together. Then I shouldn't be asking her that," Brina says.

"You shouldn't be, Brina," Archie Jr tries, "If you know we're together. Then why do you let that bullshit get to you? I'm just saying."

"Because I want to know the *truth*, Archie. You're always fucking with some tramp and you expect me to just believe *whatever* you tell me," she says, "But I'm not stupid. I know you did."

"Then why did you ask me?" Archie Jr asks impatiently.

"Hold on Lil Arch," Tank insist, "Chill out. Don't talk to her in that tone."

Brina starts to cry. She's torn up by this rumor. She wants Archie to tell the truth. The real truth and what *she* knows is the truth. But he's acting very nonchalant about the whole thing. Tank is reminded of Ajay and Ebony, as he watches Archie Jr and Brina go at it. Archie Jr has ways like Ajay and he idolizes him. Brina is subdued like Ebony had been when it came to street shit and player ways. She believes in happily ever after and first loves being true to their 1 and only. Archie Jr loves Brina. He wants to be with her forever. But he isn't willing to fuck, *only* her. Tank knows this isn't going to go away with ease. It never had when him and Ajay was in school and doing similar things. Their ladies can give Brina books and books worth of proof that Archie is indeed doing shit the crew men before him use to do. Tank doesn't want this to get to Nina and her girls. For it will *surely* rehash a lot of bad memories. And perhaps bring back a lot of the discussions they'd had during the Thanksgiving holiday when him and none of his male crew was getting *any* loving. Or worse. It could bring the whole issue about Gwen, Nickeia and Jarvis back into play. He doesn't want any of that.

"Arch junior and Brina, I need for both of y'all to calm down and go to work," Tank finally says, "This is the type of thing that happens when males are still growing up. He can love you and still mess up. Because he's not perfect and he's a boy. That's what boys do."

"I thought that was suppose to stop after Ajay and all of y'all messed up, last year," Brina says.

"It *has* for us, Brina. But we're married," Tank says, "Archie junior is not married. He needs to get all of that out before he marries you. You don't want him to save it up. Then have an affair on you, when you get married. Do you?"

"I don't want him to do it now either."

"I'm not," Archie Jr says, showing he'd rather lie his way through this. "Let's go to work baby. Because if this shit is gonna be the talk of the day. Then I'm gonna head home."

"No. Both of you are gonna work and I'm going down there and let everybody know. This conversation will not be had up in here," Tank says, "You two need to talk later. But for now, it's time to get both of y'all asses to work."

They all laugh briefly before going back to their stations. Archie Jr is going to DJ. He hits the booth on the 3rd floor where Brina is in charge of keeping the VIP tables and area clean. She listens to the song selections Archie is playing. He plays *Confessions Part II* and *Let It Burn,* every 20 minutes. Brina feels as though he's talking directly to her. Eventually, she approaches the DJ booth.

"Why are you playing the same songs? Are they for me?" she asks.

"If you want them to be. They can be," Archie Jr answers, "I'm not gonna have that discussion. You heard what Tank said."

"You need to get out some *Alicia Keyes*," she suggests, "*A Woman's Worth!* That's what you should be playing."

She storms away from him as she feels tears forming in her eyes. She takes a bathroom break. Leilenne and her girls have been told to stay on the 1st floor and work concessions with Charlotte, Destiny and Jada. Brandon goes upstairs to check on Archie Jr. He knows it has to be rough up there working next to his twin sister.

Tank has called Rebbie and June. He wants them to come down and talk to their siblings. Tank feels like they may be able to deal with them more effectively. But when June hears the story, he becomes angry at Archie Jr. Rebbie insists he calm down and keep in mind, he operated along these same lines with her, when they were teens.

"And even some *since* teen hood," Rebbie says with conviction.

She doesn't bother to offer any revelations about her kissing session with Jarvis. Tank wants to call Ajay but he has a game in Dallas tonight. His team will head to Milwaukee on Friday before returning to Cleveland to play Golden State, this Saturday. Tank is looking forward to the weekend *and* Ajay being back. Leilenne and her girls are returning home this weekend too. He sees that as taking the fuel away from the flames. At this point, he's just glad Leilenne lives in another state. That might be an aid to Archie Jr. By not having her here in Cleveland.

Tonight June isn't backing down. He lets Archie Jr know, in many colorful words, that he isn't going to be okay with him messing over his baby sister. He also makes his teammate Eric Jr aware of what his sister has been up too. Eric Jr puts Leilenne on a strict routine for the remainder of her trip. He also threatens to tell their parents, if she gets involved in any more unflattering discussions during her visit. Needless to say, he won't let her visit again if he hears anything else along the lines of her sneaking out or having sex. She tells him, she understands. But by the time Ajay returns home on Saturday morning. Things have grown to a fever pitch. Not only had Archie Jr fucked Leilenne again but Brandon had fucked Felecia. Kenny was home visiting and he fucked Iona and Charity too. Chaundra, Charlotte and Brina are ready to fight by the time Ebony and Erica are preparing them for their ride to the airport. Neither of the 4th generation of crew girls want to accompany them *to* the airport. Ebony and Erica will be picking up Ajay during their trip to Cleveland Hopkins Airport.

"Some things in our crew, never change," Erica says as they drive.

"Being dogs in heat isn't just a crew thing," Ebony says, "However, our crew seems to get more than their fair share."

Her twins have enjoyed having Alan and Kimmie here for the week. She can't say the same for her younger sisters, in the crew. They're about ready for war. She's *too* familiar with what her 1st cousin Brina is feeling. She almost hates to think about those days as a teenager when she'd caught Ajay fucking around. Or just found out that he had been. She's going to talk with Brina as soon as possible. She wants her to know, she isn't alone. And that Archie Jr sees Ajay as his role model. He's mimicking what he'd seen and heard about the men in the crew doing, for years.

Ajay arrives home and jumps into the past weeks discussions with both feet. June is rambling on about Archie Jr. Ajay reminds him of their own indiscretions. Again without mentioning Rebbie's.

"June do you remember Farah?" Ajay asks, "What about Diana? Or Deloris? I know you hit her. Right out there in the security house. Do you remember them? Or are you just overlooking your own fuck ups?"

June is quiet for a moment. He finally says yes, he does remember them.

"I hate to admit it but Archie and them, they're doing the same shit we did," Ajay says to him, "Brandon fucked one of them girls too. Why you not in *his* face?" June says nothing as Ajay continues. "I know why you're not. It's for the same reason I'm not. *We've* done the same shit. It's okay with us as long as our sons do it or our brothers do it. But not our sisters or our daughters. And nobody better not fuck over our sisters. Unless they're crew," he continues, "June man I was out there with you, Rich, Tank and Jb. Fucking ho's. Knowing all the time *my own* sisters was being fucked over. And Rebbie was being fucked over too. So how can I tell Archie junior that he can't get as much pussy as he wants? When I did. So did you. He's still a single man."

"Leilenne is family, Ajay," June tries, "Crew don't fuck with two females from crew. Archie Jr needs to not go there. She's Eric's sister and Erica's sister-in-law. If this shit gets out of hand. It'll have lasting effects."
He's trying to get Ajay to see his side. No crew member has ever messed around with more than 1 female from the crew. But this is a new day and time. Bruce's crew has always been *even more* reckless than Chill's crew. They've been more flashy and more outspoken than Chill's crew was too. Neither Chill's crew nor the crews before them, saw fit to change that in the beginning. Greg Jr from Bruce's crew, lost Erica due to abuse, infidelity or some other form of disrespect. Which seems likely to be Archie Jr's fate with Brina. No one had told them about the repercussions and made it resonate. Rich Jr and Greg Jr had been violent with their mates. They weren't made to pay a *huge* price for it either. The crew should've known something else just as severe, would come next and it has. Ajay feels like that's their fault too.

"Then we should've been better role models," Ajay says, "We did the same shit. That's why I said what I said at Thanksgiving dinner. I'm making a change in myself, for my daughters sake. *You know*? I don't want her to be hurt like I hurt her mother. My wife and my love Ebony. She's your first cousin June. You was right out there with me while I was fucking over your cousin. You didn't have a sister old enough to get fucked over, when you was doing it. But I did. It's no different than when you and me did it. Lynn and Nina got fucked over. So did Ebony, Rebbie and T-baby. We can't be hypocrites man. We can't take that *holier than thou* approach with this next crew. They're not gonna go for it. They're crew too. They was raised under the same ceiling as us."

"I know you're right, Ajay," June says, "I'm her big brother though. She expects me to look out for her."

"And you will. But you can't be ready to fight crew for doing the same shit you enjoyed doing yourself," Ajay says.
Then they have a talk with Archie Jr, Brandon and Kenny. They let them know they have to be more discreet. And for Archie Jr, he has to decide between Brina and Leilenne. He can't have both. Archie Jr was trying to bring a totally new equation to the crew standards of fucking around. But the crew aren't going to allow that. No one can fuck around with 2 females from the crew family. That is *never* getting a pass.

CHAPTER 58

NEW BREED OF FEMALE

In May, Archie Jr graduates from MLK and signs with Cincinnati the same week. Him and Brina are still a couple. Jan receives her Doctorate of Medicine this month from Georgia Tech. Pamela Jackson and Ruthie Williams both graduate from the University of Cincinnati and T-baby starts online studies with Cleveland State University. She wants her Masters in Accounting. The talk that stirs throughout the crew is about 3 things.

Angelise Taylor's lawyer managed to get her a parole hearing asking for time served on good behavior. Ajay and Ebony met with the parole board in opposition. George Wheeler had set it up.

The 2nd bit of news came out of Chicago. Leilenne is pregnant and says Archie Joseph Wilson Jr is the father. Her parents the McNair's, expect him to do the honorable thing and marry their daughter.

"Just like I said a few weeks ago, Ajay," June says, "If this shit gets out of hand. It's gonna have lasting effects. It's all the way out of hand now. They want him to marry her."

June is feeling his baby sister's pain. Her only love has a kid on the way and a family and crew who believes he has to do the right thing. He'll have to face his responsibilities. Brina doesn't know where that'll leave her. She's devastated.

The 3rd and last thing is huge too. On the last day of May, Ajay and Ebony adds to their family. Ebony gives birth to another little girl while Ajay and the twins are in the delivery room with her. Lil Ajay detest it because either he doesn't understand it or he doesn't want to see it. Lannie is afraid for her mother and her sister. She feel they've been injured after seeing the blood. That brings many laughs. Ajay manages to keep his twins calm and relaxed during the birthing process. He feels like a veteran.

"I was in here when you two were born," he tells them. "That's when I was nervous because I didn't know what to expect. But now I do and I'm just excited and ready to hold her and watch her grow up."

"We didn't have all that stuff on us," Lil Ajay tries.

"Oh yes you did," Jo says with a smile.

"Especially you Lil Ajay because you came out first," Pearl adds, "You was taking charge from day one and protecting Lannie."

"We didn't even know if she was a girl or a boy until the day she came," Ajay tells his son, "Because you was in front of her the whole time while y'all were in mommy's stomach. You were shielding her, from the beginning. Protecting your twin sister from the eyes of the world."

"He was *hiding* me," Lannie says and laughs, "Blocking my *shine*." They all laugh including Ebony. She's worn out and ready to rest but she's also enjoying the delivery room chatter of her family. Her twins are always the stars. They have everyone else in stitches from their unforced humor. Today, they become a big sister and a big brother. They're both really proud and that's evident through their eyes. This is *their* baby.

AALIYAH IMANI JACKSON aka LEA
BORN: MAY 31, 2004
TIME:10:12AM
WEIGHT: 6LBS 12 OZS
HEIGHT:18 INCHES

"We have some May babies now," Nina shouts as she comes in to check on Ebony and to see the baby.

"This is *my* baby, auntie Nina," Lannie says, "Me, Jerica and Orian are gonna keep this baby with us."

"You, Jerica and Orian are gonna have plenty of babysitting to do too," Nina says and laughs as she kisses her niece.
Then turning to Ebony, she asks, "How are you feeling kid?"

"Like I just gave birth," Ebony says and they laugh.
Now the crew has 6 birthdays in May. Kim, Pam, Lil Jb, Orian, Lil Tank and now Aaliyah aka Lea. Ajay is thrilled to see his 2nd daughter born and he can't take his eyes off of her.

"I told you it was a girl," he says to Ebony.

"Yes you did, Anthony and you were right," she says and smiles.
She's ready for some sleep. Lannie wants to be the 1st one to feed her new little sister but Ajay explains to her that Ebony has to try breastfeeding her and only she can do that.

"If that don't work," he says, "Then we can try to give her a bottle. That's the same way we started with you and your brother."
Lil Ajay wants to make it clear that he's still the only boy, as he sticks his chest out.

"I might be taking after papa Al," Ajay says to his son, "You might be the only boy, like me. But who knows? Mommy said she wants to keep trying until we have another son. So you can have a little brother."

"I *do* want a brother, pops," he says, "So me and my brother can
255

take care of our sisters by ourselves and take over the world."

"Oh daddy *will* be there to help, son," Ajay says, "*Believe* that."

"If I don't get another brother. I am gonna be *you*, pops," Lil Ajay says as he laughs.

"You're already my junior and my only son," Ajay says.

"Mama you can't have no more sons?" Lil Ajay ask Ebony.

"We can't control that part Ant," Ebony says and smiles, "But right now. I'm not thinking of having anymore of anything. Not right after having a baby."

Everyone laughs. Lil Ajay doesn't laugh because he's still waiting to get the answer he wants.

"Mommy that means I will be the only boy like my daddy?"

"Yes Ant. For now, you can," she answers.

"We'll see about that son," Ajay interjects.

He wants 5 children. Him and Ebony have been discussing it since she was in 8th grade. He's not going to pressure her about how many kids she wants to carry. She has already said she's going to have 2 sons. But he still teases.

"Don't be slick, baby girl," he giggles and says, "You told me I can't stop until I give you two boys. You must really need some rest?"

"I think we all do," she says, "Especially if y'all feel like talking about having more kids, after the one I just delivered today. I'll volunteer one of y'all to get up here and have the next one."

There are no takers on that, as she figured. Lannie is holding Aaliyah with Pearl's help. Lil Ajay is observing and not sure if he wants to handle her yet. He's just watching.

"Can my baby sister break or something, pops," Lil Ajay asks.

Ajay says, "You have to be real careful with her."

"I won't break her, pops," he says, "I won't let nobody else break her either."

Ajay likes his son's response. Tenischa is still in there with them too. She's been around Ebony and Ajay a lot. So she's very familiar with them by now. She can tell Ajay took major pride in Lil Ajay's statement. She smiles at Ebony as Ajay tells the staff to prepare his wife for her private room.

"She needs her rest," he says, "It's enough family here to handle the baby."

The staff take Ebony to her room immediately. Ajay and the twins stay at her side and at the hospital, all night.

Welcome to the world………………………..Aaliyah Imani Jackson!

TIME TO FEEL-RELOADED-Time Will Reveal part 5

Its a few days into the month of June. Ajay takes his family home from the hospital where he and Ebony receives more good news. Angel was denied parole. Her new attorney was no match for Wheeler and Associates. Which is a good cause for *more* celebration. It was *their* testimony which persuaded the board to deny Angel's request. They're glad she's not going to be free to walk after only 8 years. Ajay, Ebony and the twins welcome Aaliyah to her home and her new room. They're already calling her Lea, for short. Ajay doesn't fail to mention to Ebony that he would have 4 kids now, if he had never fucked with Angel.

But the news about Leilenne being pregnant for his protégé, troubles him. He knows Archie Jr has to be feeling the pressures of responsibility. He's glad he never got caught up like this back in his premarital days. He feels for Archie Jr. The crew was taught to do the right thing. The *responsible* thing. Leilenne is 10 weeks into her pregnancy. She had just graduated high school and had plans to attend DePaul. But now she's going to Cincinnati where Archie Jr will be playing basketball. Both of their parents had insisted they go to the same school. So after a much improved basketball season, Ajay finds himself pre-occupied with his protégé's situation. The *Cav's* had more than doubled their win totals over last season since the addition of *Lebron James*. He'd made Rookie Of The Year. An honor Ajay enjoyed after his 1st season with the *Miami Heat*. Cleveland finished 5th in their division this year. Still Ajay is tormented over what his uncle Archie and Aunt Rena are insisting Archie Jr do about his pending fatherhood. He has already pitched an idea to both sets of parents, as well as to Archie Jr and Leilenne. He'd like to help them with the financial part of it. So Archie Jr can go to college, finish and get drafted. And so far, everyone is open to the offer. No one is forcing them to get married. However the suggestion is being thrown out there more and more by Eric Sr and Eric Jr. Leilenne doesn't even want to get married. Her father and her big brother are upset with her for not wanting too.

In mid July, Ebony has her 6 weeks examination with Weston. She's fine and healthy. Her and Ajay hadn't made it passed 4 weeks, this time either. He was ready for her to resume her normal activities by the 3rd week and so was she. Lea's 6 week check up is normal. She's up-to-date on all of her immunizations and so are the twins. While there, Ajay and Ebony ask Tenischa to be Aaliyah's Godmother. She cries and happily accepts. They'll set a date for it and get it done before the end of this 2004 year.

With that done, the Jackson family are all set for their vacation to *Disneyworld*. The trip includes more than just Ajay's family of five.

257

TIME TO FEEL-RELOADED-Time Will Reveal part 5

Pearl, John, Jo and Al are going. Big mama, Ashanti, Jarvis Jr, Poppa and Papa are going. Mrs. Ida Graves is going too. It's a trip for 15 with all of the amenities, expenses and 1st class treatment.

Ajay turns 30 the week before they fly to Orlando. The twins celebrate their 5th birthday with *Mickey and Minnie Mouse* at Disneyworld. They have the time of their lives.

On July 27th Ebony, Ajay, their kids, God kids, parents and grandparents are tuned in to the Democratic National Convention. They get a chance to see first hand, the Senator Eric Jr has been talking about since becoming apart of their family.

Barack Hussein Obama gives the keynote speech for the *DNC* this year and he rocks the house. In his speech, he says some things that really hit home with the crew, such as; *'There's not a liberal America or a Conservative America. But there is the United States of America.'* He emphasizes the importance of unity and makes veiled jabs at the Bush administration and the news media's perceived oversimplification and diversionary use of wedge issues. He says, *"We worship an awesome God in the blue states. And we don't like federal agents poking around in our libraries in the red states. We coach little league in the blue states. And yes, we've got some gay friends in the red states. There are patriots who oppose the war in Iraq. And there are patriots who support the war in Iraq. We are one people. All of us pledging allegiance to the Stars and Stripes. All of us defending the United States of America."*

"At the end of the day. I'd say it's time for Barack Obama to speak for the United States of America," Ajay says and the rest agree with him wholeheartedly.

In August, Kilo takes Justine to his family reunion in New Orleans. She meets all of his family including his son and the friends he'd grown up with. She thoroughly enjoys her trip and thinks the food is the best she's ever tasted. Kilo proposes to her while they're there and he invites his family to come to Cleveland to visit them.

Justine comes back to Cleveland raving about the time she had in New Orleans. She's the most fond of Kilo's grandmother.

"She didn't play around," Justine says, "She kept it real and told it just how it is. And she can cook better than a chef."

In late August, the crew pick up copies of *Straight Outta Cashville*, the solo CD from *Young Buck*. It's very raw, just as they had expected.

"He kept with the whole *Straight Outta Compton* name and feel on this joint," Jr says.

TIME TO FEEL-RELOADED-Time Will Reveal part 5

Him and Wayne are setting up the music for both clubs. *Buck* had bangers on his CD just as *Lloyd Banks* had on his, *Hunger For More*. Favorites from Young Buck are, *Let me In, Bonafide Hustler, Prices on My Head* and *Black Gloves*. But *Shorty Wanna Ride, Walk With Me* and *Stomp* keeps the dance floors packed.

"Young Buck did a damn good job with this solo project," Chill says, "My gee kept it all the way gutter."

"Definitely street shit," Tank agrees.

****

Brad III turns 13 on the 1st of September. He's being initiated to the crew, along with his 1st cousin Chastity Jacquel or CJ as she's known, at their coming out party at The Spot II. Him and CJ are very excited and so are the crew. They are the 2nd and 3rd of the Chill crew children who are becoming a legitimate part of the crew. Stoney's only child will finally be crew. Jr has looked forward to his sons initiation since his birth in 1991. He loves the fact that his son is getting initiated. Brad III will be the leader of the 5th generation of the crew.

School starts after Labor day and Brad III is in the 7th grade this year. Ashanti turned 5 last October and is about to turn six. Her, Lil Ajay and Lannie, who turned 5 while at Disneyworld, starts Kindergarten at Beachwood Elementary. Ebony cries all morning as she realizes she has to leave her twins in the care of someone other than crew, for the first time in their lives. She's familiar with their teacher. Mrs. Tasha Gates, who had done student teaching at MLK when Jesse was there, is the twins kindergarten teacher. Ashanti is in Miss Jeffries class, right across the hall. Mrs. Gates is very familiar with the crew. Coincidentally, she is the teacher who had been hired the year after the foursome graduated to replace Debra Wittman. Debra Wittman was the "Farah Benson" of Chill's crew school days. The foursome had nearly come to blows with her at her apartment, 1 spring break after finding Ajay there and Wittman undressed. Jo, Pearl and the other mothers had saw to getting her fired. Much like Renee and Tonya are contemplating doing with Farah Benson.

"I had their uncle Jesse, Aunt Erica, Aunt Pam and all of the crew who attended after ninety four," Mrs. Gates says, "I know it's hard to leave them mama. I've done this over and over. Just *this* morning."

Ebony can't speak, so Ajay takes the opportunity to say his peace.

"My twins are well behaved but very mature and intelligent," he

259

says, "They're gonna want to help out a lot. That's how we raised them."

"Well I can surely use the help," Mrs. Gates says.

She selects Lil Ajay and Lannie as her assistants for the 1st week of school. After getting their assistant assignments, Lannie is ready for her parents to leave. She wants to get on with her 1st day of school. She takes Ebony and Ajay by the hand and leads them to the door.

"Bye mommy. Bye daddy," she says and smiles as she puckers her lips to them for a kiss.

Lil Ajay isn't as enthused. He isn't crying but he doesn't seem particularly happy about staying in *this* place. He takes his desk and moves it next to Mrs. Gates desk. He does the same with his sister's desk. Then he sits down and folds his arms. Lannie takes her seat next to him and folds her arms, like her twin brother had just done. 1 by 1, all of the little kindergarteners sit in their desk and fold their arms just like the twins had done.

"They're going to be okay," Mrs. Gates says, "They've already brought the class to order for me."

She says goodbye to Ebony and Ajay and gets on with the business of her 1st day of teaching kindergarten.

MLK starts the fall semester 2004. Farah is happy to be allowed back. She's still under a microscope. Not only by Principal Myers but by the investigators of Marvin's death too. That murder case hasn't been closed yet. Brina and Brandon are seniors and the last of Chill and Bruce's crews. Brina has had a very tough summer after finding out Leilenne is claiming to be pregnant for her 1 and only love, Archie Jr. Even worse, Leilenne is down in Cincinnati living in the big house with Archie Jr while she's stuck in Cleveland finishing high school. Before the drama with Leilenne started, Brina looked forward to her senior year. For 4 years she has planned a future with Archie Wilson Jr. Now those dreams are looking bleak. Leilenne, who Brina thought of as a sister less than a year ago, has other plans for Archie Jr's future. Brina is hoping for another Mya and Greg Jr situation when it comes to Leilenne's baby. Because she knows Leilenne wasn't a virgin when she started seeing Archie Jr, like she was. Leilenne had other boyfriends before, during and after Archie Jr. Where Brina has not. Brina knows Leilenne had been seeing 1 of her guys in Chicago at the same time she was seeing Archie Jr. She hopes that guy had fathered the unborn child Leilenne is carrying. Brina was raised to believe a young lady gives herself to only 1 young man and she is to stay loyal and faithful to *him*. She's done her part. Still her love is in need of a rescue. Her and Archie Jr have always said they were going to be just like Ebony and

TIME TO FEEL-RELOADED-Time Will Reveal part 5

Ajay. Brina is still seeing Archie Jr and he's still proclaiming his love to and for her. At the same time, he's now accepting the responsibility for Leilenne's baby. Only not when he's talking to Brina James. To Brina, he denies the baby is his. *Time Will Reveal.*

Kerry lost the presidential election to Bush, much to the chagrin of the crew. Dirty politics won out again. That's something the Cleveland crew will never understand. Why would the American people elect someone simply because they talked more bullshit and trash than their opponent? George Bush's campaign had destroyed his republican rival John McCain. They did the same to John Kerry, using the swift boat ads. Karl Rove's playbook was implemented unrelentingly. All in all, there's a bright light for the crew and the Democratic party. That beacon had shone brightly at this years DNC. So immediately with the McNair's and other politically active citizens in and around their city of Chicago. The crew in Cleveland help to launch a presidential campaign for *Barack Hussein Obama.* They started recruitment for volunteers who wanted to see some *real* change come to America. Their memberships in alliances like the *NAACP* and the *ACLU* helped to get the word out. They joined the campaign *Barack for America* in late November 2004. Before it was a twinkle in America's eyes.

At the Vibe Awards taping in Santa Monica, the crew's favorite living thug, *Young Buck* and his *GUnit* crew got into a brawl. Some guy later told to be Jimmy James Johnson, had initiated an assault on *Dr Dre* and got his ass filet by *Young Buck* and a dinner fork. *Young Buck* hid out for days until terms of his surrender was negotiated. Then he turned himself in. The 4th generation of crew ate it up.

"Young Buck *forked* that fool up," Brandon says as they all roar with laughter.

"They putting the whole charge on him," Archie Jr says, "What about the rest of GUnit? Them niggaz was in the shit too."

"They letting Buck take the fall," Brandon says, "Watch."

"Yea you probably right," Archie Jr says, "The east coast dudes gonna let a dirty south dude take the fall. I'll bet you you're right."

"Buck needs to leave them niggaz, man," Steven adds, "He's not like them."

"I said that too," Jamal says, "He's living his real life and doing what he would normally do. No matter where he is."

"They living *Hollywood* while he's living *Hollyhood*," Steven says.

"Young Buck is still my nigga," Jamal says, "Dude is humble for real. New York rappers never come off as humble."

"They don't," Archie Jr agrees, "They just claim shit all the time. Like the whole art of Hip Hop. It started in the South Bronx. But damn it's everywhere now."

"With a lot of different styles," Steven adds.

After failing to get Angel Taylor paroled, her attorney goes to the police in Cleveland and asks for a missing persons report to be filed on James "Bulldog" Taylor. He visits the prosecutor and all but insinuates the crew had to have done away with him. Only because they must've learned that he was related to his client. The police inform him they've had a missing persons case on James Taylor on file for years. But they've had no response on it. The prosecutor tells him without any evidence to support his claim. They can't go after anyone just because he *thinks* they may have done away with him.

Meanwhile Julie Von Reese has moved to Atlanta and reconnected with Lynn. On paper, she isn't working for Crew Enterprises. Not until the dusk settles behind James Taylor. But she is making money with them. Only it's under the table for now. She has been contacted by Cleveland police and brought into Atlanta police stations for questioning several times, over the past few years. But she's not considered a suspect. Just 1 of his many girlfriends. She hasn't even been called a person of interest. Though through Lynn and the crew, she was able to off the bulldog without any suspicion whatsoever. When she went in for questioning, she was as cool as a cucumber. Just as she had been when she competed in the 1500 run and relays. She never sweats. She gave the police the same story she'd given to Angel on her last visit to the Ohio State penitentiary.

"James left me without even as much as a text message," she had said, "I called his phone for weeks. He didn't bother to answer nor did he respond to the many voicemails I'd left him. He dropped me without even telling me. I'm so glad I wasn't dumb enough to fall for his lies about wanting to be with me. I feel he only used me to stalk Ebony and her family. I told him I knew Lynn Jackson since sixth grade. I feel like that's the only reason he stayed in touch with me. Once we went out to their club and he got familiar with the scene. He never even called me again."

That's her story and she's sticking to it. She has phone records to support her claims. She knows he isn't coming back but until they find his body and try to figure out how he ingested arsenic. She's going to continue her life as

TIME TO FEEL-RELOADED-Time Will Reveal part 5

she has been. As a solid friend to Lynn since grade school. As an honorable woman who believes in justice and a fair one for everyone plus her newest title; *undercover* crew. She's smart. She's going to let the police think they led her to find Lynn again. Afterwards, she won't have to be undercover. She'll be crew, tried and true.

****

Thanksgiving is a blur for the crew as they go full steam ahead with getting petitions signed, emails and websites together with others. Others who support their suggestions to Senator Obama that he should run for President of the United States. But he declines the initial suggestions.

Young Buck had turned himself in after a few days and bonded out. He seems to be in a good space and his legal team are some of the best according to George Wheeler and Trina Yvette Sloan-Wheeler.
"He should be okay," Trina Yvette tells the crew.
"The worst he'll get is probation," Wheeler says, "But his business will probably suffer."
"Then we'll have to schedule him to perform at our venues," Chill says and with Jb on a long distance call, they put Young Buck on the calendar for all 3 spots.

****

Archie Jr and Leilenne are already having trouble getting along down in Cincinnati. Every chance he gets, Archie Jr is visiting Brina. They spend almost as much time together as they had before he went to college. He comes to every 1 of her games he can get to without messing up his own schedule. 8 month pregnant Leilenne has had her share of mess ups too. She's been caught several times with other guys in the house, down at UC. 2 of her ex's came to visit while Archie Jr was on the road with the team during preseason or when he's in Cleveland. Leilenne is a free spirit. She's the independent type which is what Archie Jr liked about her from day 1. But Archie Jr hasn't been a saint either. He's had Brina come down and stay with him at the downtown Clarion Hotel nearly every weekend. Ajay had suggested it and rented the suite for them. He wants them to make it. He told him it was the same hotel him and Ebony stayed in when they'd gone down there for his 17th birthday. But Brina isn't the only girl Archie

263

TIME TO FEEL-RELOADED-Time Will Reveal part 5

Jr has seen since him and Leilenne have been living together either. Brina is just the only 1 *he* says has his heart. Archie Jr and Leilenne are making a career out of fucking over each other. They have the weirdest relationship. They love to fuck each other. But as soon as the other 1 isn't around. They see and fuck someone else.

By now, June, Rebbie and Eric Jr have let go of any hard feelings they may have had. All 3 of them see how volatile these 2 are and how stupid and careless they act with their lives. They decide to butt out of it and let the chips fall wherever they may. Leilenne had gone home for Thanksgiving after taking her finals early. She's officially on maternity leave.

In early December, the crew get some good news from Atlanta. Bre and Ced are expecting their 1st child together. The baby is due August 21, 2005. Though CJ calls him daddy, this will be Cedric's 1st biological child. Him and Bre have already talked about it with CJ. She's eager to have a sister or brother. Her and her 1st cousin Brad III have turned 13 and become crew. Jr and Tonya have a 3 year old son named Donavan. But for Bre and Cedric, there will be nearly 14 years between CJ and the new baby.

More baby news for December comes from Chicago. On December 12th Leilenne gives birth to a baby girl she names Ashley Josetta, after Archie Joseph. A paternity test is pending before Archie Jr will agree to sign the birth certificate and give Ashley his last name.

Nina and Ebony turn 29 years old this Christmas season. Kenny turns 21. Him, Chaundra, Ally and Steven have a huge *Turning 21 party* at The Chill Spot.

Ebony and Ajay celebrate 7 years of marriage on New Year's eve 2004. They add a huge copper fountain to their landscape as their 7-year traditional gift to each other. It's also noted that had Ajay's maternal grandparents still alive this would've been their 52nd wedding anniversary. Big mama and Poppa had just celebrated their Golden Wedding anniversary, this past April. They received brand new diamond and golden wedding bands from their crew family.

Robert Leon Jenkins Jr turned 5 years old in Cleveland on New Years day, 2005. He has his party at *Big Mama's house*. This is a 1st for him, since he lives in Atlanta. The crew do it up extra special for him. His mother Jan is here to apply for her residency at East General. She wants to start it in another year. Her and Rob are going to commute once her East General residency starts.

TIME TO FEEL-RELOADED-Time Will Reveal part 5

The office for *CrewLand Trucking* has been completed in the 3rd strip of the mall. Pearl and John move out of Ebony's office officially by Tank's 30th birthday. Jan's pediatric office is nearly complete and will be ready long before she'll need to take up occupancy, next Winter.

Finally Pittsburgh police have ruled Marvin Huntley's death a homicide. But they still don't have any solid leads as to what happened to him. The case hasn't advanced in a year. He's filed into the cold case file and his murder case is closed. Farah is happy to finally have them out of her business and her face. Her, Matt and Ellen had been questioned so many times, each of them have lost count. Farah and Matt have gotten closer since Marvin's death. Matt knows who killed Marvin but he isn't about to tell anyone. The police see him as a lucky bastard who had escaped the horrible hand that Marvin was eventually dealt. They feel like Matt was kidnapped because he knew Farah. And whomever killed Marvin had been watching Farah to get a lead on how to find him. They still feel like Marvin was killed because of his dealings with some criminal underworld. That is partially right but they don't know which underworld. The good part about it is, the crew aren't even on their radar. They had followed the Italian American lead into the ground. It went absolutely nowhere, just as the crew had planned for it too.

As the MLK girls and boys finish the state tournament, the crew get some more baby news. Brandon and the boys team are runner ups in the state. Brina and the girls had won 1st place while Brina was 3 months pregnant. The majority of the crew didn't even have a clue that she was pregnant. This is a shock to everyone except Brina and Archie Jr. He'd confided in Ajay during December when Ashley Josetta was born and swore him to secrecy. Since then, Ajay has told Ebony. Both of them tried to get Brina to tell aunt Brenda and uncle Brian Sr that they had conceived. She'd refused too. She thought they would make her abort it and she didn't want to do that. Once finding out about the pregnancy, Brenda and Rena take Brina to see Dr. Weston. Brina is indeed pregnant. Her and Archie have a due date of July 27, 2005.

"Brina are you okay?" Ebony asks her.
Brina and Archie Jr are visiting at the house with her and Ajay.
"Yes I am cousin. I wanted this baby. We was both trying to make this baby," she admits and Archie Jr agrees with her.
"I didn't wanna lose her and I thought I would after Leilenne," he

says, "But she stuck in there with me. I'm not ever gonna do anything like that to her again."

Then he does something that shocks Ebony and Ajay. He proposes to Brina, right then and there, in their family room.

"We're gonna get married in two weeks," Archie Jr says.

"We don't need a big wedding. We just wanna get married and go on with our lives together," Brina says as she glows.

The 2 of them look really happy right now. Ajay and Ebony vow their support for them as they all leave to go share the news with the crew.

Two weeks later, Archie Jr and Brina get married. It's big news because of Archie Jr's celebrity status. Though it was short notice, *Crew Gear and Alterations* pulls it off. Rena, Belinda and Sandy put together a nice wedding for them. It's small and elegant. But most of all, it has what the 2 of them wanted. Each other. Their wedding is the 2nd day of March 2005. Ebony and Ajay send them to Jamaica for a week during spring break. Leilenne acts as if the wedding isn't a big deal. She still expects to have Archie Jr at her leisure. But she'll learn that isn't going to be the case.

In late March, Kim, Chaundra and George Wheeler say goodbye to their hero. *Johnnie L. Cochran Jr* dies. He was an African American lawyer best known for his leadership in the legal defense of *O. J. Simpson*. Back when OJ was charged with the murder of his former wife Nicole Brown Simpson and her friend Ron Goldman. He had also represented *Puff Daddy* during his trial on gun and bribery charges. *Michael Jackson.* Actor *Todd Bridges*. Football legend *Jim Brown.* Plus rappers *Tupac Shakur* and *Snoop Dogg*. Cochran also represented *Reginald Denny,* the truck driver who was beaten by a mob during the 1992 riots in Los Angeles. After police were acquitted for the beating of Rodney King on videotape. In the crews opinion, Johnnie Cochran was the best lawyer in the world, if he could get a black man off after he was accused of killing 2 white people.

At the end of March, Rena and Brenda find out they're going to be grandmothers, twice this year. Not only is Brina and Archie Jr having a baby but so are Rebbie and June. They're expecting again and due in early October. Still nothing has come out about Rebbie and Jarvis' kissing session from 1993 and Ajay still suspects that Jarvis is still in the picture.

On Easter Sunday, Farah attends 1st Baptist Church of Cleveland with Matt. The word gets back to Ellen before dusk. She looks for Matt but she isn't able to locate him. At least not while she's still angry. After church, Matt and Farah went to Pittsburgh to have dinner with her parents. Farah introduces Matt to her parents as a college professor who's trying to get her placement at CSU. Matt has still played back and forth between Farah and Ellen. Only Ellen thinks her and Matt are exclusive. Matt told her, he was no longer willing to mess with Farah after he'd been kidnapped and damn near killed because of his relationship with her. He'd only said that to sleep with Ellen. And once again, he's caught in a lie.

Ajay's Cavaliers go through not only a coaching change but an ownership change too. *Dan Gilbert* of *Rock Financial* buys the team. *Coach Paul Silas* had been fired mid-season and replaced by *Brendan Malone* for the last 18 games. *Gund* Arena was renamed *Quicken Loans* or *The Q arena*. Ajay's contract was renegotiated for what will be his 4th season with the home team and 9th season in the NBA. The Cavaliers fell just 1 game short of making the playoffs. They finished 4th in their division.

"We're over five hundred, man," Ajay says to Chill as he smiles, "That feels better."

"We're getting a ring real soon, brother," Chill boasts, "I can see it coming together."

"So do I," Ajay says.

"You're staying around until then?" Chill asks.

"I can't retire without a championship," Ajay says, "I'm going into my ninth year. I got about seven good years left."

"We'll get it," Chill says, "I'm sure of it."

Kenny has bypassed the NFL draft this spring to the dismay of many of his fans and hopefuls. He elects to stay in college. He'll be a senior for the 2005-2006 season. He promises Renee he'll get his degree. Even though he's going to go to the draft next April.

"I'll get my degree from Ohio State, mama," he says, "I promise."

"That's all that matters to me, son," Renee says.

Graduation 2005 is still huge for the crew. The 1st crew twins Brandon and Brina James graduate, both with full athletic scholarships to UC. 6-month pregnant Brina didn't have to forfeit her scholarship and the Alumni are stepping up again for the crew. Ruthie, Archie Jr and Leilenne still have the house. The twins will join them this fall. Brina figures it'll be an awkward situation but Archie Jr tells her, him and Leilenne are no longer sleeping together. Not since she'd left on maternity leave. He has been faithful to Brina and he plans to continue to be. Now that she's his wife. Ajay had insisted on that.

Charlotte will be going to Cincinnati too. She has waited for her boyfriend Brandon to finish high school so they can attend college together.

Archie Jr and Leilenne are the parents of 5-month old Ashley Josetta Wilson, as the paternity test finally proves. They aren't much else, not to each other. The luster had truly faded for them once the baby came and reality set in. Leilenne no longer wants to be exclusive with Archie Jr. She had decided that before knowing he was marrying Brina and he wasn't willing to just fuck around with her. After getting to college and seeing all that she saw. Leilenne told her parents, Archie Jr wasn't the man she wanted to marry. Brina wasn't mad to hear that, at all. She still loved Archie Jr and always will. She's happy they never stopped seeing each other during the Leilenne saga. Archie Jr had long told her they would share a bedroom at the Cincinnati house. He solidified that when he married her in March.

Chaundra Coleman finishes at Ohio State and gets her pre-Law degree but she's going to stay there and enter law school. Kenny is happy about that because he has about 2 years to go before he qualifies for graduation.

This May, Ally and Steven, the 2 crew members who had become parents at 15 years of age, get their degrees from CSU. Their parents Archie Sr, Rena, Sandy and Greg Sr are very proud of them. Their 6 year old daughter Ashanti, who starts 1st grade this fall is there to see them. She has a great time with her God siblings Lil Ajay and Lannie. Although Lil Ajay acts more like their babysitter, these days. Ebony has noticed a change in her sons behavior. She's not quite sure what it is but she's going to discuss it with Ajay, later tonight. For now she reminds Lil Ajay that he isn't the boss of the girls and he has to play nice and not selfishly. The 3 kids will start 1st grade at Beachwood Elementary this fall.

TIME TO FEEL-RELOADED-Time Will Reveal part 5

CHAPTER   59

COME HELL OR HIGH WATER *OR BOTH*

There's 1 week left in the month of May. John III has turned 8 years old. He's in 2nd grade and still being home schooled in Smyrna. Orian turned 8 yesterday. She had her party at *Granny's House*.

Ajay and Ebony's youngest daughter Aaliyah is at home with her daddy today. It's 1 week before her 1st birthday. Ajay has been keeping her since his season ended. He keeps the camcorder set up, all day everyday. He doesn't want to miss *1* thing Lea does. He had Ebony doing this with the twins when he was still playing in Miami. They continue to record them now too. Today Lea suddenly starts crawling faster. She's trying to follow her daddy from room to room. But that just isn't working out well enough for her. Ajay picks her up and brings her into the kitchen with him, so he can feed her while he grabs lunch for himself too. He sits her down on the floor next to the island counter while he preps their food. He goes to the sub zero's to get her milk and a fresh bottle. As he heads to the sink to pour it. He can see her moving in his peripheral vision. He looks toward her and makes eye contact to let her know it's okay to come to him. He gets a pleasant surprise. She's coming to him. Only she isn't crawling. She had pulled up on 1 of the legs of a barstool and is now walking to meet her daddy at the sink. She's smacking her lips together to let him know she's hungry. Apparently he isn't getting her lunch, fast enough.

"*Hey!*" he says in excitement and almost frightens her off of her feet. "Look at daddy's baby! You're walking! My baby girl is walking!"
He makes sure the camera is getting this new accomplishment. He grabs the camera from the tripod and zooms in on her. He keeps moving away from her and filming. To his delight and hers too, she continually walks back and forth over the kitchen floor.
"Come on daddy's baby *girl*. Come on, Lea. Walk to daddy."
She knows she's doing something *big*. He can tell by her expression. She giggles and high steps her way to him, over and over while patting her hands along with him.
"We got it on tape too. We have to show mommy, your big sister and big brother what you learned today while they wasn't home."
He's so proud of his baby girl. He's proud of himself for being here to witness it. He'd missed both Lil Ajay and Lannie's first steps while on the road with his team. He had to see it on video. Lannie started walking before she was 8 months old. Then Lil Ajay started at 10 months while Ajay was in

Miami, packing up for the off season. He was determined he wouldn't miss Lea's first steps. She hasn't made a year old yet but she's the slowest to start walking out of their 3 children. Ajay has waited for this day for the past 3 months.

"Daddy didn't miss his baby start walking this time," he says with excitement as he giggles and adds, "Daddy see you, Lea. I *see* you."
She clowns and laughs with him. She has had a ball with her daddy everyday since the season ended. He's been keeping her at home with him, instead of taking her to *Big Mama's House*. He wants to keep her for the 2 months he isn't training and before the summer league kicks off at his recreation center. He calls Ebony at her office and gives her the news. She can hear Lea giggling in the background. She's so busy walking that she doesn't even want to take the phone from her daddy like she usually does. Ajay promises to have the tape cued up for when she gets home.

"Okay," Ebony says, "I'm picking up the twins and getting dinner from Crew's house. Big mama made those buttered mashed potatoes that Lea loves. She's got some chopped steak, just for her. She cooked dinner for us today."

"What did she make?"

"Peas with snaps and okra, Chopped Steak with gravy, Rice and mashed potatoes, yams, buttermilk rolls and peach cobbler."

"Big mama's gonna make us fat around here," Ajay says and laughs, "But we can stand it."

"I know that's right," Ebony says, "She's *always* coming through for us."

"She knows you work a stressful job. She's just being big mama," he says, "A woman who loves to cook and can cook *anything* your heart desires."
They laugh and talk for several minutes. After accepting that Lea is to busy walking to come hear her voice over the phone. Ebony soon hangs up.

It's 2 days before Lea's 1st birthday and there's a buzz around the CrewLand mall. The type of aura that usually surrounds the crew when something memorable is about to happen. They have all seen Lea walk, by now. It is the Sunday of Memorial Day weekend. Nina and Ebony have planned a huge party for Lil Tank, who has turned 3 and for Lea, who'll be 1 on the last day of May. The 2 them and their families have just left church and dropped by Big Mama's House to do a final check on preparations. Everything is ready to go.

TIME TO FEEL-RELOADED-Time Will Reveal part 5

As they're leaving the property, they see Matt and Farah turn in. They speak to each other, then Matt and Farah proceed to Crew's house to eat. Nina and Ebony head to Jackson Heights to get the children dressed for their party.

At Crew's house, Farah and Matt are having the special. A wonderful Sunday dinner of Sirloin Roast, red potatoes with carrots, cabbage, yams and cornbread. Today's special is a recipe from grandma Annabelle that she use to cook when the foursome would spend the night at her house. Sirloin roast is her granddaughter Rebbie's favorite. Farah and Matt have gotten closer since Marvin is officially out of the picture. Matt is really beginning to *genuinely* like her.

"I just remember you telling me, you wasn't really feeling me. And that you really wanted to get with Chill," Matt says, "That really threw me for a loop. That's why I wasn't going after you after my kidnapping. Because I figured it was just another part of some elaborate game you was playing."

Farah smiles. She doesn't respond right away. Partly because what Matt is saying is true. She still desires Chill more than she does him. But who else can she get to share time and meals with, in sight of Chill and his crew? Other than Matt? No other male is going to do that.

"I just didn't have my priorities straight then," she lies, "I had to sit down and evaluate things after I found out Marvin was dead. He really wasn't the right guy for me either. I'd made the mistake of getting engaged to him and look who he turned out to be. I didn't wanna make that mistake again," she says, "So I was just being careful with you."

"I need to do the same with you," Matt says, "I mean. I'm taking a risk just *being* with you," he smiles and goes on. "I have other women who like me. But they get angry and don't talk to me because I spend time with you. So if you're not serious. I don't wanna waste time."

"I'm not seeing anybody else," she says, "Which is more than I can say for you."

"I'm not either," he lies, "I have other women who *like* me. But I'm weighing my options."

They share a laugh as he looks at his watch. He's suppose to meet Ellen at 5pm. They have a date to go see the movie, *Crash* starring *Ludacris*, *Larenz Tate* and *Don Cheadle*. He's heard that the movie is about racism from every perspective. He doesn't feel comfortable seeing a movie like that with Farah. He finishes up his dinner with her and tells her, he has to go. He calls for the check so he can leave and get on to Ellen.

"I'll call you tonight and see what you're up too," he says, "If you're not busy. Maybe I'll come by. Tomorrow is a holiday. Neither of us have to work, so maybe we can sleep in."

"That sounds great," Farah says with a smile.

Matt leaves a tip for Corey, who is their server today. Then he and Farah leave. She goes to Parma Heights while Matt hops in his Durango and drives straight to Euclid Avenue to pick up Ellen.

Farah makes it home to find Darlene and Alana waiting to talk to her. Darlene doesn't have an expression on her face but Alana does. It's obvious to Farah, she's upset.

"What's up?" Farah asks.

"You tell me," Alana says.

"I don't know what you mean," Farah says.

Darlene takes the liberty of explaining *why* her and her niece are upset. She says, "Farah you've been giving us the run around for over a year now."

"How so?"

"Remember all of this new found love you said you was getting from the crew?" Alana breaks in, "For the longest time, you've been telling us to give you more time to work the shit out."

"For all of us to hook up and get shit jumped off again," Darlene adds, "But all we see is you getting your swerve on and us being kicked farther to the curb."

"Chill is playing it off, you guys," Farah tries, "His wife is on the prowl like crazy. Nina and Ebony got a party planned for Tank and Ajay's kids today. I know he can't get them away today. All he's been telling me is that he'll let me know when it's cool and that I'll have to let him handle it. That's what I've been doing. I'm just dating Matt for the same reasons as before. Y'all know he's just a diversion. Somebody to go to the mall with and let Chill see that I have other options. He said he don't like to share and y'all was there when his wife and Ajay's wife jumped me. So you know they know about our encounter. You two was the ones who told me how those females get when they know you've fucked their men."

"Yea, well me and Darlene are gonna press the gas a little bit on our own," Alana says, "*Shit*. I could've got my own shit *crackin* by now."

Darlene agrees. She's seen Ajay at his recreation center a few times. She had invented an excuse to go by there and speak with her son Jamal. The 1st instance, she spoke to Ajay and he spoke back. The 2nd time, she made light conversation. He was cordial but she couldn't read him well enough to know if he was interested in her or perturbed by her. But a smart 1 who

who knows Ajay would guess the latter because he was raised *well*. Darlene is only encouraged by the fact he hadn't snapped at the sight of her. But he hadn't either time. So of course, she plans to press the issue.

Ebony and Nina have all 5 of their children ready and at the party by 5:30pm. Rebbie and Ally bring Orian and Ashanti. T-baby brings Rich III, Richaunda and Jada. Destiny is almost 12 years old but she still wants to come hang out with her best friends, Jerica and Jada. Renee and Tonya bring her and soon-to-be 4 year old Donovan. Ajay and Tank come by to celebrate with their babies.

"Lea's cutting her own cake," Ajay announces.

"Daddy, she's gonna mess it up," Lannie warns him.

"So did you," he says and laughs. "You saw the pictures and video."

Lannie and Lil Ajay laugh hard. They pull out their birthday books and video's often and share laughs at their own expense.

"We wrecked our cakes when we was one," Lil Ajay says.

All in all, they have a great time at the party for Lil Tank and Lea. They get many matching outfits, toys and games. Ajay is known to give all the crew kids *Certificates of Deposits* on their 3rd birthdays. Lil Tank receives his today as another birthday gift.

"My nephew has got to be balling in another ten years," Ajay says as he smiles.

Lil Tank seems to know that the gift is money. Just like his father, he's a blood hound for cash and he's frugal too. He gives the gift to Nina.

"Take it mama," he says, "That's money?"

"Yes it is, man," Nina answers her son with a chuckle, "Your uncle Ajay got that cake. Stay tight with him."

They laugh as the party comes to a close just after 7:30pm. The clubs are opening for *Memorial Day*. All other crew businesses are closed tomorrow except the clubs, *Crew Smokes and Drinks* and Ajay's sports center. *Stoney's Bar and Grill* is doing the cooking for the crew family and more. The family celebration will take place in Jackson Heights. But all of the crew have to donate 2 hours each at Stoney's, to help feed the homeless and the senior citizens whom Crew's House caters to *daily*. Ebony and Nina head home with the children. Ajay and Tank stay at CrewLand with Chill, Arthur and the guys to run the clubs and party some too. Erica and Eric are there to party along with the rest of the crew. Nina and Ebony are keeping the Jackson Heights kids while Rebbie, T-baby and the rest of the crew hook up at The Spot and The Spot II for a huge Memorial weekend celebration.

TIME TO FEEL-RELOADED-Time Will Reveal part 5

Matt and Ellen's movie ends around 9pm. They stop in at *Crew Smokes and Drinks* to get a bottle of liquor. Ellen is planning to spend the night with Matt but he has other plans. He drives to her house, enjoys a few drinks with her, then they have sex. Instead of him spending the night. He tells her a lie, in order to make a *quick* getaway.

"I promised Kelly she could use my Durango," he says, "She wants to meet Greg junior at the club. I'm gonna go home and get some sleep."

"Ah why not have her drop you back off *here*?" Ellen asks.

"Because I don't want her driving out here by herself," he says, "And you know I don't like being parked out here a long time. Somebody already tried to break in my shit, once before."

"Then we should go to *your* house," Ellen suggests.

"We can but another time," Matt tells her, "I'm just tired tonight, Ellen. I've been up since five this morning."

"I don't like this," she says, "It seems like you're always in a hurry when *we're* together."

"I tell you what," he says, "I'll see if I can get her mama's car. She won't let Kelly drive it. But maybe I can borrow it since Kelly will have mine. Then I'll come back and pick you up."

"That'll *work*," Ellen says and smiles.

"I'll call you," Matt says as he prepares to leave.

He has lied, yet again. It's true he's going to get Kelly and bring her to the CrewLand mall to meet Greg Jr at the Spot. But she isn't keeping his 2005 Durango. He's meeting Farah at the club too. He leaves Ellen none the wiser and pulls away, headed to Genia's house to pick up his daughter. He isn't aware that Ellen and her girls had their CrewLand Mall privileges restored after showing exemplary improvement in their behavior since working at the Brook Park store. Venitia and Mario are meeting them for a workplace *get* together. Ellen gets a call from Rudy around 11:00pm, begging her to come to the club with her and Dorothy. Ellen accepts.

At the club, Matt and Farah have a cozy table on the 1st floor, in the back. Alana and Darlene are floating the club and being bold tonight. They try flirting with Tank and Ajay but get no response. Still they keep trying. Darlene approaches Ajay while he's at the 1st floor bar, in the back. She walks right up to him and starts a conversation.

"Ajay can I ask you a question?" she asks.

"Sure. What is it?"

"Is it true that you fucked Farah?"

He doesn't respond. He wants to ask her how would that be her *fucking* business, if he had. Though he hasn't. But he knows he can piss her off worse by answering positively and acting pleased about it. So he does.

"Hell yea I did," he lies, "I fucked the shit out *o* that ho. Why? Is she bragging? Did she say I fucked her *good*?"

"She rubbed it in, pretty good over the past year and some. *Yes*," Darlene says, "It pissed me *the fuck* off though."

"Why is that?"

"Because you haven't even looked my way. So I figured it was because you were happily and *faithfully* married," she says, "If you was gonna fuck over your wife. I think I deserve that honor. Don't you?"

"Darlene it's been a decade and a half since we fucked around," he says, "What are you talking about?"

"Even after fifteen years, Ajay," she says, "I still have desires for nobody but you. You was a man *then*. In *every* way that counts. A woman doesn't forget that."

"What the *fuck*? You was like twenty two and I was twelve," he reminds her, "I was a foolish boy. I'm a wise man now."

"I'm Forty and you're thirty now," she says, "Older, wiser and no doubt *better*. I would give anything to feel you and taste you again."
He lets her know it isn't going to happen.

"I don't fuck over my wife, Darlene," he says suddenly, "That shit with Farah was a crew gangbang. Believe or not. It's what she wanted, so that's what they obliged her with. For the good of the crew. That shit was a one time thing and just so you are clear on it. I did *not* fuck Farah. She wanted me too but I didn't fuck her. Me nor Chill did. Neither one of us wants too and we never will."

"She doesn't believe that's how it's gonna be Ajay," Darlene says.

"She don't have to and neither do you," he says, "Or maybe she just wants you to believe it. But I know I'm not gonna fuck *her*, you or no other woman *but* Ebony. I'm done with all of that old school shit. Crew bang or not. I'm happily married and I love fuckin my wife. Do you understand that? As a matter of fact. I can't wait to see what she's got for me when I get home. You have a good night."
With that, he walks away and leaves her standing alone. It's something about Darlene that turns him off *royally*, these days. She hasn't excited him since he was 13 and that was only because she was 10 years older than him, with her own place and a car that he could drive before he had a license.

After walking away, he joins Tank who's by the front bar. Tank had just gotten some things off of his chest with Alana and pushed her off.

She'd come to him with the same type of conversation Ajay had just foiled with Darlene.

"There is no fucking way I would let that bitch slob on me again," Tank says to Ajay and laughs, "Farah got her ho's going crazy. Telling them she got some dick from the crew."

"She ain't been keeping it real with them though," Ajay says, "If she was. She would've told them, Chill nor I fucked her. And that Chill told her we never plan too. Nor can she have anymore crew dick. *Period*."

No shit, Cuz," Tanks says.

Ajay says, "Even if I had fucked Farah. I still wouldn't fuck Darlene. I was dry heaving just having that washed up bitch in my face."

They laugh as they leave the 1st floor and go back up the elevator to VIP.

Shortly after Ajay and Tank leave the ground floor, Ellen and her girls stroll in and go straight to the bar.

"Hennessy and coke please," Ellen says to the bartender, "And give my girls whatever they want. We don't have to work tomorrow. Our store is closed and the Brook Park crew are *all* here."

"I know that's right," Venitia says as she joins them at the bar to say hello.

Mario is with her and they are both full of smiles.

"Let's make this a great night," Mario says, "We're turning that store into a legitimate crew money maker."

The ladies laugh in agreement. Mario and Venitia head up to VIP. Ellen, Dorothy nor Rudy can go up there. They have the privilege of coming to the clubs and businesses, so they're not going to try to push it any further. They get their drinks and explore the club.

It isn't long before Ellen spots Matt at the table with Farah. She goes directly to him and questions him about the lie he'd told her earlier. He's embarrassed and caught off guard. He keeps saying Ellen isn't suppose to be in the club.

"Our banned status has been revoked," Rudy tells him.

Matt gets up and goes to the cash cage to question Tonya, who tells him the 3 women are no longer banned.

"Ebony cleared them 6 months ago," Tonya says, "So now it's up to you to let her know what's up with *you* two. You know we don't turn down no money for the businesses. Nor do we allow our personal lives to affect our businesses, Matt. You need to be straight up with both of them. Do it soon before they bring anymore drama to CrewLand."

Matt heads back to his table. He feels trapped all of a sudden. He text Kelly and tells her, they need to leave. Within minutes, her and Greg Jr come down from VIP to the 1st floor. They meet Matt and Farah at their table where Ellen insist on questioning him. He doesn't want to answer her anymore. He tells Farah they need to leave. Farah doesn't want to leave but Matt insists. So she gets up and follows him, Kelly and Greg Jr out of the club. Ellen and her girls follow them outside too.

Alana and Darlene see them following Farah. They go outside as well. Before Farah can get into the Durango, Ellen grabs her. They start to fight until security intervenes and separates them. Farah manages to get on into Matt's SUV. Matt, Kelly and Greg Jr get in and Matt starts his engine. They pull away while Ellen cries and explains to Bronson why she's upset, this time. Bronson and McDaniel are familiar with Ellen and Matt's relationship by now. They know Matt is playing both sides. They don't charge Ellen nor Farah with anything. They just tell Ellen, she has to leave the property and the crew will let her know *if* and when, she can return.

Ellen leaves but she isn't satisfied with not being able to beat Farah into the ground. Her and her girls get in the car and head to Matt's house. Ellen is going to finish what was started in the club parking lot.

When they arrive at Matt's place, he isn't home. Ellen drives out to Parma Heights. On the way into Farah's Subdivision, she see Matt's Durango leaving out. Rudy can see the driver and it isn't Matt.

"That's his daughter driving with that football player from the crew," Rudy says, "The one that plays with Detroit."

"That's Greg junior," Dorothy adds, "He's our big bosses first cousin, y'all. Don't mess with them. He'll get us fired."

"Let's go home Ellen," Rudy says, "Matt ain't worth you getting in trouble. No more. You see how he is. Find you another man and pay his ass back like *that*."

"Find a man like we did," Dorothy says, "They're meeting us at the house. So we *really* need to get there."
Ellen isn't use to backing off and she isn't going to give Matt up that easily. She's the best girl for him. Whether him or his daughter or anyone else, realizes it or not. Kelly didn't notice Ellen because she isn't familiar with Rudy's car. Ellen's *hooptie* is at her home on Euclid avenue. Ellen leaves Parma Heights and heads home. But she isn't done. Not by a long shot.

Kelly and Greg Jr drive to Jackson Heights. They're spending the night at T-baby's. Greg Jr has broken ground for his home in Jackson Heights already. But T-baby is always staying at Wesley's home since they'd gotten engaged on her last birthday. Greg Jr has decided to rent the home which T-baby and Rich had originally lived in. He's still going to build his own home. But for now, he's renting from his older sister. T-baby and Wes are getting married in less than 2 months, on July 25th which is Lil Ajay and Lannie's 6th birthday. It's also 1 day after T-baby turns 29 and 1 day before Wes turns 30. Wesley's birthday is 2 days after T-baby's. He was born in 1975 and lacks just 2 days, being a whole year older than her.

Greg Jr and Kelly arrive at T-baby's house where he continues to try and calm her down. Kelly is still upset about Ellen's actions in The Spot parking lot.

"Come on in baby," Greg Jr says, "It's always a wild ass night whenever we kick it with your dad."

"I know," she says, "He needs to chill out, for *real*. Him and all of these crazy ladies. Mama still loves him but they've been separated *damn* near all of my life, since I was four. They separated twenty years ago."
She calls Matt and lets him know she's safe inside of Jackson Heights. He tells her Ellen has still been calling his phone and leaving threats because she knows he's at Farah's home and she'd seen Kelly leaving in his truck.

"So stay where you are until I call you," Matt warns, "I'll have you to come get me before the sun comes up. Keep your phone on. Okay?"

"Okay daddy. I will," Kelly says, "I'm really worried about this Ellen woman."

"I'm not," he says, "Don't worry. I love you."

"I love you too," she says and they hang up.

Ajay arrives home just after 3am. Ebony is in bed but she isn't asleep. Something has prevented her from sleeping. She has an eerie feeling and when she gets these types of feelings. She can *never* sleep. Not until she figures out just what the dangers are. With her husband home now, she's relieved that the eerie feeling wasn't about some possible harm coming to him. But she still feels like something is going to happen and very soon. She can't shake the feeling that somehow, her crew is going to suffer a lose. Her gut tells her that. And her gut never fails her. Ajay joins her in bed.

"I love it when you wait up for me," he says and smiles.

"I know and I love to wait for you to come in too," she says, "But I couldn't sleep tonight anyway. I have one of those feelings, baby."

"Oh my God. Not one of those premonition type feelings. Ha?" Ajay asks, "I'm home now. My kids are safe and asleep in their beds. So are *all* of our crew. You can relax your mind baby. We all made it home safe. I've got something that'll help relieve your mind for a good night sleep."

She lays back in his arms and tries to clear her mind. But he can sense that she's having a hard time doing so. She's still uptight.

"Can I give you a massage, baby?" he asks.

She smiles and whispers, "Sure."

"Lay on your stomach," he says, "While you *still* can." He laughs.

"Oh Lord. Do you know something I don't?" she asks with a smile.

"No I don't know anything for sure," he says while smiling, "I'm just saying, while you still can."

"Our baby will be one tomorrow, Anthony," she says, "Are you telling me Lea won't be the baby for long? Tenischa just became her Godmother, two weeks ago. Lea loves being the baby too. So you'd better slow your role. You don't want that fireball to get angry with you."

They laugh and he says, "I'm not gonna hold back baby. You know how potent your man is."

They laugh for a few minutes after that comment. Ebony has been feeling some sickness in the mornings. She has already made plans to visit Dr. Weston's office before Ajay starts preseason training.

"I sure *do* know how potent you are," she smiles, "You're always *so* in tune with your biological clock. Uh huh. That's why we have to go see doctor Weston this week."

They share another short laugh. Then he remembers Darlene's actions at the club.

"Baby, Darlene was pushing up on me *hard* tonight," he says.

"Oh she was?"

"Hell fuck yea," he says with a disgusted look on his face. "She got on my nerves too. Talking all that *back in the day* shit. Alana was after Tank extra hard too. They saw that you and Nina wasn't out there. So that's it baby. From now on. You have to go to the club when I go. To keep these groupies in check." They laugh.

"But do you think that's really it? That we *wasn't* there?"

"That and Farah told her about the crew thang," he says.

"Uh huh. So she's probably been telling them it's gonna go down again," Ebony says, "They've got her trying to hook it up so they can be down too."

"Maybe so," he says, "At first I was gonna just let her think I fucked Farah and wanted her. So she could step off of me for good. But I told her the truth. I told her that her and the rest of them can forget about that shit. Because it's ain't happening. *Ever* again."

"You told her that?"

"Not exactly," he says, "What I told her was. *I don't fuck over my wife. That shit with Farah was a crew gangbang. Believe it or not. That's what she wanted so we obliged her. For the good of the crew. That shit was a one time thing. And Chill nor I fucked her.* But baby, you know that bang was all about getting rid of Marvin, *right*? I couldn't tell her *that* part."

"Yes I know. What did she say after that?"

"She said Farah didn't believe it was over, just like that. So I told her *Farah don't have too. I know I'm done with all of that. Crew bang or not. I'm happily married and I love fucking my wife. I can't wait to see what she's got for me when I get home*," he says and smiles, "Then I told her to have a good night and I left her where she stood. Then I went to relieve Tank of that ho bag named Alana."

Ebony laughs and says, "I'm proud of you, Anthony. I believe you. One hundred percent."

"That's what I live for, Ebony," he says, "That and an NBA championship." They laugh.

"Well this is what I have for you," she says.

She's already naked. She starts kissing him aggressively. She rolls over on top of him. She has her hair wrapped in a scarf to keep her do fresh for the Memorial day events, later today. He starts to remove it as he always does.

"I need to get into this hair," he moans.

"I can't keep a good hair style when you're home, baby," she says.

"Consider yourself *blessed*," he says, "I can pay for another style."

"You already did when you opened up the salon," she giggles, "And then put a station in our bathroom."

"Then come here and give me my money's worth," he says with a chuckle.

"You know I'm wit it, daddy."

Anytime she has her hair up. He always wants it down. And he *always* gets his way.

"Baby quit playing with me and let me get into this hair," he says as he pulls the scarf completely off.

"Daddy, no!" she shrieks and puts her hand on her head trying to hold her hair in place.

"Don't tell me no, baby girl," he says, "You know I love to play in your hair. Especially when we fuck."

"We make love, baby," she corrects him, "Our sex life has always been about love."

Still she tries to make a case for keeping her hair style fresh for the holiday

280

Festivities but he isn't going to back off. She concedes to her man and leaves the scarf off. She knows he'll make it worth her while. And he'll get Nina to touch it up for her today, if she desires. She lets him have his way because his freedom to do what he pleases during sex. Is for *her* benefit. The way he runs his fingers through her hair while they make love. Is 1 of the things that makes their sex *so* passionate. Even when he grabs handfuls of it as leverage to push himself deeper inside of her. She loves the way it hurts, *so* good. She knows she'll never wear weave.

"I can get it fixed again, right?" he asks, "Don't I take good care of this?"

"Like I said," she purrs, "You already did that when you built me my own salons."

"I'll make Nina come over here at the crack of dawn. Or open up crew cuts *today* to fix my baby's hair, if I need too," he says as they both laugh and move in closer to each other. "Like I said earlier. I love to fuck my wife."

He grabs a hand full of her hair and puts his tongue in her mouth. She sucks it like the pro he has taught her to be. He moves in for the kill. Tasting every inch of her body. She returns the favor.

"This is what I love about *not* being pregnant," she says as she takes his dick to the back of her throat. "I get to taste *my* man."

"Taste me then, baby. Devour me," he whispers, "I love this mouth you got, baby. You turned me out up in the Pocono's mountains. I couldn't believe how good my baby was on the first time. I love it and I love you. Only I'm not so sure you're not pregnant though. But we'll go with it tonight until I see different." He pulls her up on her pillow and says,

"I need to feel this sweet pussy, right now though."

He enters her and with that, the majority of the talking concludes. The rest of this early morning is filled with heated exchanges and sweaty fuck sessions. They haven't lost any of their lust for each other in their 15 years as a sexual couple. Nor any of the love for one another after being a couple for almost 18 years. Ajay loves Ebony and she loves him back. Their love is as solid as ever. The sex gets better with every session. These 2 have the staying power they were raised to believe in. They affirm their real love, all morning.

Meanwhile out on Euclid Avenue, Ellen Barnes is still not a happy camper. Rudy and Dorothy had gone into their rooms a half hour ago, with the men they'd met at The Spot. Each of them are in their bedroom doing what grown folks do after a night of alcohol, weed and flirtatious dancing. They're getting and giving lube jobs with their 1 night stands. Ellen isn't going to let the sun rise with her feeling as neglected as she feels right now. After several more attempts to reach Matt by phone, she gives up. She grabs Rudy's keys and drives back to Parma Heights.

She arrives, gets out and knocks on Farah's door. Darlene gets up and looks through the peep hole. She sees that it's Ellen so she doesn't open the door. She goes to Farah's bedroom door and yells through it. She lets her and Matt know Ellen is outside. Matt gets up and goes to the door. In so many words, he tells Ellen to go home and he'll call her later. But she isn't accepting that. The many drinks she'd had at The Spot plus the ones she'd had at home, are telling her *she* doesn't have to accept no for an answer. Matt had sex with her less the 12 hours ago. He told her he wanted to spend the night with her but his daughter needed his vehicle. She now knows that was a lie. Just another 1 of his famous lies to give her false security. She isn't going to be made a fool of *this* time. Matt has closed the door and is now, talking to her through a window with the blind pulled back. He's refusing to reopen the door. She leaves and heads back to Euclid Ave. It's nearly 5am when she gets home.

The house is quiet and she assumes Dorothy, Rudy and their men have fucked each other to sleep. She isn't in the mood for sleep. She wants revenge and she's going to have it *today*. She goes into her room and grabs the box which houses her brand new 9mm. The gun sent to her by her *now* deceased asshole boss Marvin, who had been trying to set her up. He wanted her to get angry just like she is right now. Angry enough to kill Matt. She takes the 9mm out of the box and puts it in her bag, along with the extra clip. She goes back outside, gets back into Rudy's car and starts the engine. She starts to cry as she puts it in gear and starts her drive. She thinks about Marvin as she heads back to Parma Heights. She's in a drunken stupor and livid with anger by now.

"He tried to play me for a fool, for that bitch. Now Matt's doing the same shit,…. *FOR THAT BITCH! I HATE CRACKERS! I HATE LIARS! I HATE TO LOSE!*" she screams to herself.

Before long, she's reentering Parma Heights. She drives back to the front of Farah's house, parks and sits there.

While she was gone, Matt had called Kelly and told her, he was ready to leave. Kelly and Greg Jr arrive, just after Ellen. They pull into the driveway, get out and start toward the door. That's when Ellen gets out of Rudy's car and heads toward the front porch where Kelly and Greg Jr are ringing the doorbell. They hadn't noticed her this time either because neither of them know Rudy's car.

"*It's me daddy,*" Kelly says, calling for Matt through the door.

Matt comes to the door. Before he opens it, he can hear Ellen screaming obscenities to his daughter. He opens the door to protect Kelly because now, her and Ellen are in a heated exchange.

"Ellen leave here now!" Matt screams, "I said I'll call you later! Leave me and my daughter the hell alone!"

"That's not what you said last night. You lying son of a bitch!" Ellen screams back.

"I am not married to you!" Matt yells back, "I'm a single man, Ellen! You need to get wit that. Or fuck the whole thing!"

"Oh! Fuck the *whole* thing! If I don't wanna be fucked over for a white bitch?! Is that it?!" Ellen screams.

"Yea that's it!" Matt yells, "If that's how you see it. Then yes!"

"Can't you see he don't wanna be bothered with you?" Kelly tries.

Farah is inside. She's peeking through the same window Matt had talked to Ellen from earlier. She doesn't say anything. She just watches and smiles. It makes her feel good to know Ellen is put out because Matt wants to spend time with her. She grins as she watches. That is, until it takes a turn for the worse.

Ellen gets tired of arguing with Kelly while Matt plays her off. She draws that gift from Marvin from her bag. She points it at Kelly. Kelly is still arguing with her but isn't looking in her direction. Matt and Greg Jr notice Ellen pointing the gun at Kelly. Greg Jr darts toward Ellen while Matt jumps in front of Kelly. Ellen fires the gun, hitting Matt in his center mass. She'd learned that at the range. Matt falls to his knees. Ellen fires again, striking Kelly twice. She turns and shoots Greg Jr in the arm and shoulder. Only because his pro football speed affords him rapid spurt ability. He'd been able to get halfway into the door frame of the still open door. But after being shot, he falls backwards and lands not far from where Matt and Kelly are now laying. Ellen spots Farah looking terrified in that window now. She's frozen in her tracks. Darlene had run out of her room and towards the door, after hearing the shots. Instinctively she throws her weight against the open door which slams shut. She locks it.

"Get down girl!" she yells at Farah as she pulls her from the window in the nick of time.

Ellen fires more shots through the window. Darlene and Farah seek cover. Ellen's rage leads her to continue firing into the house until the weapon is empty. All while she's screaming for Farah to bring her *ass* outside.

"Don't hide *now* bitch!" Ellen screams, "Bring your bad ass on out here! Let's see how funny you think it is *now*! I got a nice pile of these *muthafuckahz* out here! Your ho ass is next!"

Alana, who'd been asleep in her room with her trick of the night. Is awakened by all the commotion. She appears at her bedroom door. Peeking around it to see her aunt and her friend crouched behind an over turned bookshelf.

"Call nine one, one!" Darlene yells to Alana.

Alana slams her bedroom door and in a nervous flutter, she locates her cell phone. She manages to dial 911. Her date is on the floor next to bed wondering what the hell is going on. He dials 911 from his cell phone too. A neighbor has done so as well.

Meanwhile Ellen has run back to the car to reload her gun. Greg Jr is hit but he's not fatal. He tries to move Kelly and Matt to the door. At the same time, he is trying to get the ladies inside to open the door and help him move Matt and Kelly before Ellen can reload and return. Alana's date opens the door. He has a gun in his hand. He helps Greg Jr pull Kelly and Matt inside of the house and closes the door back. They hustle to slide the bookshelf, Darlene and Farah was behind, in front of the shot out window. Greg Jr can hear the police sirens in the distance. He becomes weak. Ellen hears the sirens too. She takes this opportunity to break camp. She jumps in, starts up the car and speeds away. The police arrive in droves as Ellen speeds out of the subdivision on the opposite end, in haste.

There are 2 ambulances arriving by the time the police get up onto Farah's front porch. They see the blood and the blood trail which leads back into the house. They draw their weapons, not knowing what the situation is, they've been called out too. 2 of Farah's neighbors run out of their homes screaming to the police that the shooter had just left. They describe the car Ellen drove while telling them the residents of the house had drug the victims indoors when the shooter went back to her car. The police knock and identify themselves. Darlene opens the door. The police quickly access the situation. Farah is screaming for them to attend to Matt and Kelly. They're both lying motionless on her living room floor. The police motion to the paramedics to come in, right away. They do. When they get inside, they quickly determine both Matt and Kelly are fatally wounded. Neither of them have a pulse. They're pronounced dead at the scene. Greg Jr is treated on the scene first. Then he's taken across town to East General as he'd requested. The police notify Sandy and Greg Sr of his injuries and

284

where they can find him. Then they contact Matt's wife and Kelly's mother, Genia Johnson. Less than a half hour later, Ellen is arrested and held without bond. Rudy's car is impounded.

The word of Matt and Kelly's deaths spread quickly throughout the crew and the Cleveland area. Greg Jr had a superficial wound to his arm. His shoulder wound is a bit more serious but not life threatening. Because of his muscular mass, the bullet had been lodged under his shoulder blade. Dr. Stansfield will remove it and release him. T-baby and Wes are there within an hour of getting the news. Before long, the rest of crew are there to check on him. Greg Jr tells them what happened and Ellen had done it. He's very emotional about losing Kelly. The crew contact Genia and tell her that Jr, Tonya, Tank and Nina are on their way to where she is, in the hospital, to be of assistance.

"Ebony said something was gonna happen," Ajay says after arriving and getting the story. "And I'll be damned if it didn't."
Genia has to claim the bodies of Matt and Kelly. She's a wreck. Renee and Tonya help her contact family members and whatever else she needs them to do. The crew still have obligations for this Memorial day.

They help Genia handle things for her deceased husband and daughter while feeding senior citizens and homeless of their community. They do manage to have their Memorial Day celebration in Jackson Heights. It's bitter sweet for all of them. Namely Greg Jr, who has started to feel like he has bad luck with women and relationships. As he gathers with the crew in Jackson Heights, he can't help but look inward.

"I lost Erica because I was an immature jerk," he says, "Now Kelly's gone because of some psychotic woman who wanted her daddy, bad enough to kill them both. Maybe I'm just suppose to be single."
His crew tries to lift his spirits but aren't able too. They're having a hard time believing 2 of their business associates are dead and 1 of their business associates is the killer.

"I can't *believe* Ellen could kill somebody," Venitia says and Mario agrees with her. "She was a good worker and she kept the store on point."

"She sure did," Mario agrees, "And I had just hired Matt as my permanent barber. He knew hair like no one I'd ever met."

"Matt was next to me *all* day before I walked down the aisle to marry Anthony," Ebony says as she looks through 1 of her wedding photo albums. "And now he's dead. The world has gone crazy locally and nationwide. We've got a president and vice president who lies to us. The

TIME TO FEEL-RELOADED-Time Will Reveal part 5

CIA creating alliances that don't exist. Just to support war for money. Babies being raped. Children killing children. Children killing parents. Parents and children dying together. Friends killing friends. Lovers and friends, killing lovers and friends. The *real* axis of evil is a hell of a lot closer than Korea."

"I know that's right," Rebbie agrees, "George Bush needs to look inward for that one. We've got all the worst type of crime and criminals in the world. Right here in America."

"Torture. Espionage. Illegal wiretapping. Treason. Plus lies and murder," Nina says, "Sounds like a movie of the week."

"Oh but it's real life though," T-baby adds.

They do their best to savage their Memorial day holiday. The children certainly have a great time. Ajay had brought out another cake for Aaliyah and Tank Jr. He started them another birthday party. The crew maintain and make it through another tragedy. For they know there is truly more good times coming for their family. They just have to be patient and work hard for it.

Matt and Kelly are laid to rest the following Monday. The entire crew attend their service. Coincidently, Ellen is arraigned the same day. She will be held without bond until her upcoming court date. She had asked Dorothy and Rudy to contact George Wheeler's firm. They did but his wife Trina Yvette had given them an emphatic, "No. Thank you."

Before they could even finish saying her entire name.

"We here at the Wheeler firm. Represent the crew family," she told them, "And the three victims *were* crew family. This firm will not provide any type of counseling for anyone who has wronged the crew family. That's final."

****

In June, Sandy, Rena and Belinda start the preparations for T-baby and Wes's wedding. It'll be a small ceremony and a large reception at Allen Saul's Recreation center. Rich III and Jada are going to be the best man and maid of honor while Richaunda and Ashanti will be the flower girls. Tank Jr will be the ring bearer. Ebony, Nina and Rebbie will be the bridesmaids and their husbands will be groomsmen. Renee and Wesley's mother, siblings and their family's will be attending as well. Lannie, Jerica and Orian are the miniature brides-in-waiting with no grooms.

TIME TO FEEL-RELOADED-Time Will Reveal part 5

Darlene's oldest son Rodney Casey, now 27 years old, is released from prison on Renee, Chill, Tonya and Brad Jr's 14th wedding anniversary. It's been 7 years for Jarvis and Gwen. Rodney had talked to Jamal about asking Ajay for a job at the center. Ajay had set up an interview for him with Ally and Steven. He's hired today. The last day of June. He'll start within the week. Rodney is more radical than Jamal. He's more loyal to their mother Darlene than Jamal is. Darlene is already planning to pick him for any information she can get about Ajay. Like what days he'll be at the center.

Luther Vandross had never fully recovered from the stroke he'd had in 2003. On the 1st day of July 2005, he passes away in New Jersey. The entire 2nd generation of crew attend his funeral services in New York City, on the 8th of July. They return home the following day.

It's Saturday morning. 9 days into July and 2 days before Ajay turns 31 years old. He's had a sneaky suspicion about his wife and kids, for the past week or so. They've been sneaking off and not telling him where they're going. He tried to play it cool but being the hard nose that he is. He has to know what they're up too. Ebony isn't telling him anything. So he decides to ask his kids.

"Lannie come here," he says as he still sits at the breakfast nook.

His oldest daughter has finished her breakfast and heads to the playroom to watch *Nickelodeon* with Orian, Ashanti, Richaunda and Kimmie who had all slept over.

"Yes daddy? Did you call me?" Lannie asks as she skips back.

"Yes I did. You love your daddy, right?"

"Yes sir," she says as she looks at him with her big brown eyes. "I love you, *this* much."

She spreads her arms out as far as she can stretch them and bucks her eyes. Kimmie mimics her as all the girls laugh. Ebony is doing the breakfast dishes. She observes her husband trying to pry his surprise out of their oldest daughter.

"If you love daddy. Then you wouldn't want me to be sad, right?" Ajay asks Lannie.

"No sir, daddy," Lannie says, "I don't want you to be sad. Why are you sad?"

"Because I don't know where you, your brother, your sister and your mama keep going off too and leaving me by myself," he says as he makes sad lips.

TIME TO FEEL-RELOADED-Time Will Reveal part 5

"We're not gonna leave you *anymore* daddy," Lannie says, "Okay? So now you won't be sad. I'm gonna play now daddy."
She kisses him on the cheek and smiles. She knows how she is to answer her daddy's inquiries about his surprise. Ebony had sent Lil Ajay to spend the night at Erica's with Alan, to keep him from telling while her and Lannie keep a close eye on Lea. She isn't able to converse as well as Lannie did, at her age. But Ebony knows as slick as Anthony is, he may find a way to get it out of her. His birthday surprise is something Ebony had planned to do since Lea was born. Update the family photo on his office desk and in his team players album. Her and the 3 kids have had 2 pictures done. 1 is a portrait and 1 is a painting. Both were done at Que Psi Phi Studios. Arthur had an artist, he and Jr knows from their fraternity, to come into his store and do the painting. Ajay is going to be photographed with his family today. But he won't be allowed to see the surprise portraits until Monday. He will be added to the painted 1 and they'll hang it in the 1st floor family room over the mantelpiece.

Tonight his crew are celebrating his birthday at The Spot. They tease him with the naming of the party. They're calling it *"The over the hill bash and flashback jam."* Arthur has videos lined up that go as far back as the late 70's. Which he'll show tonight on the screens throughout the club. It will include pictures of Ajay, from birth until now. But before all of that. Ebony and the kids have another surprise for him. He wasn't able to get Lannie to reveal anything. Finally Ebony sends Lannie, Orian, Ashanti, Richaunda, Kimmie and Lea on into the playroom. She smiles at Ajay.

"Daddy are you trying to milk our oldest girl for information?" she asks, still with that smile he loves.

"Yes. Of course I am. You won't tell me," he says.
He's never a happy camper whenever there's a secret he isn't up on.

"Because it's a surprise for your birthday, Anthony," she says, "Be a sport, for a change."
He looks frustrated as he says, "Uh huh. Whatever."

"I've been trying to surprise you for more than fifteen years. I've never been able too," she says, "This time I am going too."

"And I've been telling you for fifteen years. That I don't like surprises too."

"Well hopefully I can pull this one off successfully," she says.
He gives her a stare with a doubtful look. He isn't done yet. He still has to question Lea and his Jr. Ebony is determined he won't find out.

Erica arrives to drop off Lil Ajay and pick up the other girls just as
288

Ebony is finishing her kitchen chores. Ajay asks her if she's in on the secret birthday plot. But Ebony intervenes quickly.

"We're taking you out to lunch today," she says, "And we're all wearing matching gear."

She smiles and summons her 3 kids to follow her, as she heads upstairs to lay out their outfits for the family portrait. Erica takes Ashanti, Orian and Richaunda to her house, along with her and Kimmie.

Ebony and the kids take Ajay to have the family portrait done at Arthur's studio. Then they go to Crew's house for lunch. After lunch, they go to the Mercedes Benz dealership. As part of his birthday gift, they had upgraded him to a *2006 Mercedes Benz SL Class Roadster Coupe* with platinum 22 inch wheels, navigation, Bluetooth capability with XM Satellite radio. This car isn't even available to be bought for another 3 months. But Ajay is a preferred customer. He loves his new car. Before driving from the showroom, he immediately calls his youngest sister Pam, down in Natty. He tells her, he's going to sell her his 2002 coupe.

"So now you'll have my first Benz and you'll be living on my cul-de-sac, so I can see it," he says, "Sam Jr has already gotten the keys to the house that use to be Jarvis and Gwen's. Archie Jr and Brina are gonna be next door to y'all."

"Oh big brother! Thank you," she says, "I wanted that car, *bad*."

"Actually you wanted your own," he says and chuckles, "But it's still just like new. So there you go."

She'd always wanted that car. She's excited to know she'll get it when she comes home for T-baby and Wes' wedding in 2 weeks. Ajay said he's selling it to her. But she knows he's going to let her have it. She's his baby sister. He has always given her *everything* she wanted as long as she makes him proud.

It's a week after Ajay's 31st birthday and 1 week before the twins turn six. Ebony and Ajay wake up in their normal way with a hot session of sex before their feet hit the floor.

"Baby you're back to being horny as fuck, all the time," Ajay says as he's trying to catch up to his breath.

"I am ha?" she says, "It's a good thing we're going to see doctor Weston today."

"I already know the results, baby," he says, "You've got that *hot just like an oven*, pussy again."

"Yes and I'm gaining weight too," she says.

"Oh I didn't notice," he says.

She giggles and says sarcastically, *"Really*? So you don't see Henny and Penny has put on another two pounds?"

"Nah I thought they was just happy to see me," he says and they both laugh all the way into their master bathroom.

They get dressed and then dress Lea while the twins get themselves dressed. When everyone comes down for breakfast, Ebony is pleasantly surprised as she says, "We're all dressed alike."

"We're a tight family, ma," Lil Ajay says, "We go like that."

They all laugh as they have breakfast, then hurry off to the medical complex to confirm that there will be another addition to their family.

Tenischa is all smiles as she hugs her Goddaughter Lea and the twins too. She says, "Y'all just couldn't let my Goddaughter be the baby for awhile. Could you?"

"That's Ebony, Tenischa," Ajay says as they all laugh, "She's so demanding. I'm like a puppy when she gives me those bedroom eyes."

"Yea I know, right?" Tenischa says, "Well I'm looking forward to my babysitting days. If the twins will volunteer to come too."

"Lannie can help you," Lil Ajay says, sounding just like his father would at his age. "I got to get my bread up. I work at my daddy's gym. I work at the detail shop too. When it's not cold."

They all laugh hard as they head back to the examination room. Doctor Weston meets them in the hallway and they all walk in together.

"Okay I know this drill," Ebony says, "I got my cup. I'll be right back."

"Why she taking a cup to the toilet," Lil Ajay asks and everybody laughs.

"That's how she finds out if she's having a baby," Tenischa says.

"Ha?" Lil Ajay asks and Lannie takes notice. "In a cup?"

Lannie asks, "How does that tell her if she's having a baby?"

Tenischa and Dr. Weston look at Ajay. He's smiling as he takes the liberty of answering his twins and Lea, who's trying to repeat what her big sister has just asked.

"She has to pee in the cup," Ajay says, "Then the doctor here, will stick one of these strips in the cup. If it changes colors. That means mommy has a baby in her stomach."

"Ugh!" Lil Ajay says with a disgusted look on his face.

"Is that nasty, daddy?" Lannie asks.

"Nat-tee, daddy?" Lea mimics.

"No girls. It's not nasty," he says, "That's the way y'all got here. The only way me and mama can have you guys. Is for the baby to grow in her stomach."

"And you got to kiss mama a lot of times. So the baby can get in there too," Lil Ajay adds.

They all laugh. Even Lil Ajay. He knows a bit more about how babies are made, then he shares. He knows his daddy doesn't want him to expound on his knowledge in front of his sisters. He smiles as his daddy gives him a pound.

Ebony returns with the cup and takes her position up on the table. Ajay positions the kids away from the table, so Ebony can be examined without them having front row seats. Tenischa does the stick test with the cup. She smiles as she turns to Ajay and the kids. She reveals the stick to them.

"It changed colors!" Lannie yells.

"Tang colors!" Lea repeats.

"Me and mama having another baby," Ajay says proudly.

"My daddy is the *man*," Lil Ajay says proudly as he chuckles.

He knows where babies come from and he's alright with it. Because according to his daddy's explanation to him. That's what happens when a man and woman loves each other unconditionally. He loves knowing that his daddy loves his mama. That makes him more proud. They have a due date of February 13, 2006.

"That's about the time Lil Kenny, Jesse and Cupid will be getting married too," Ajay says, "It's hard to believe Chaundra, Roo and my baby sister Pam are old enough to be getting married, baby."

"It sure is," Ebony says, "We're on child number four in six years. They're slow compared to our biological clocks. Anthony, Lea didn't even make a year old before we made this baby," Ebony says and smiles.

"I'm just glad she made a year old before another baby *came*," Tenischa says and they all crack up laughing.

****

T-baby and Wes get married on Lil Ajay and Lannie's 6th birthday. They're going to honeymoon in Hawaii. During the week that follows, the Raymond case takes a serious turn toward Jr, The Omega's and the crew.

Wheeler contacts the family to let them know they will all need to make statements. They've had their story in order for a long time now. They're ready. The Ann Arbor prosecutor seems particularly interested in Jr and the Omega's. He feels definite that they know exactly what happened to Raymond White. He seems more determined than ever to convict someone. Ebony has constant butterflies for the 2 weeks that follow the giving of statements. The nervousness she feels, just by having the name Raymond White in conversation again. Coupled with the morning sickness from the new pregnancy, leaves her more than willing to comply to Ajay's demands that she stay home, in bed and off of her feet as much as possible.

As August 2005 rolls in, the Raymond case is once again hanging over the crew's head. Ebony is having anxiety attacks each time she allows herself to remember him. She only wants to enjoy her children, her husband and take care of herself and the baby she's carrying. She doesn't want to have any thoughts about Raymond White. Nor does she want this case to be on the front burner. But it is. It most *definitely* is. And it's taking everything Ajay has to keep her calm.

Ron and Carolyn fly into Cleveland the 2nd week of August 2005. They've come for Arthur and Michelle's wedding which is on the 13th plus they have some news that Wheeler will be very interested in too. Wheeler meets with them on the 9th and they give him something which once it's introduced to the Ann Arbor prosecutors, it will bring closure to the Raymond White ordeal for good, for the crew. There are 4 guys from Ron's crew who have confessed to killing Raymond White. The 4 of them are already in the system for murders and they are already sitting on death row. They started out at Huntsville. Then went to the Ellis unit while there, they was apart of the escapees in 1999 and was then sent to the Polunsky unit to await their executions. They remain there today, exhausting appeals and confessing to other unsolved murders. Some they did. Some they just claim to have done.

1 of the 4 guys is Tony *"Big Tony"* Robinson, the first cousin of 1 of Raymond White's rape victims by the name of Ayesha Robinson. Her rape happened before Ray attacked Ebony but she never reported it because she was too afraid. Sonya, Shuntay and Tina had threatened to kill her mother. When her rape happened, her father was serving in Kuwait. Ayesha was a 13 year old, straight A student who was an only child of Tony's brother Sergeant Travis Robinson and his wife Bonnie. They lived in the same 5th ward community which Ron and Carolyn did, before they bought big mama and Poppa's property. The same neighborhood Raymond White was bussed from to play basketball at Smiley high school. Ayesha is no longer alive.

TIME TO FEEL-RELOADED-Time Will Reveal part 5

She committed suicide the same year and day, Granny Pearline died. She still never told anyone. But she did leave a secret box which her best friend found and gave to Big Tony. In that secret box was all the details of what *Sweet Ray and his Rats* had done to her. She had newspaper clippings about her attack with Ray and the Rats photo's taped to them. She'd also left a long letter describing how she'd met Ray, everything he'd said to her, as well as a detail letter about the date he was taking her on. The date night that she became 1 of over 30 of his rape victims. When big Tony viewed the contents of that box. It solidified what he'd thought all along. His brother Travis came to believe it was Raymond White after Tony told him about Raymond's past occurrences and what his reputation was around town. Big Tony had already told Ron he felt like Raymond had done it. And when Raymond attacked Ebony, they believed it all the more. It became big Tony's mission to see Raymond White dead before Ayesha's suicide was even attempted. But then his discovery of who'd raped her after she was comatose, made big Tony and his squad go full steam ahead in finding out Ray's whereabouts so he could meet his maker. When they learned Ray had gone to Ann Arbor University. Ron told big Tony the Cleveland crew was closer to the college and could get to him without a travel plan. He also told him, Ajay wanted that honor. Ron assured big Tony that Raymond was going to die, a horrible and very painful death. Still wanting some closure of the murderous kind, big Tony was given the task of taking out Raymond's coach and the family members who'd helped to keep his rapist profile out of the news. Big Tony and his 3 killers did that and then some. They also got to Sonya, Shuntay and Tina. They made them dope fiends, so they could die a hundred times before they did them in. Unfortunately, they got arrested on charges that stuck and they hadn't been able to get to the killing of the 3 rats. But that's going to be done too. Ron assured big Tony of that. Big Tony and his 3 killers pledged to take the rap for Sweet Ray's murder, if the crew did them that solid.

Ron came to Cleveland for the specific reason of letting Wheeler know he had a confession waiting for him at the Polunsky unit in Texas. Being that big Tony and the 3 killers are never going to see the light of day again. They relieved some of their comrades, the crew, who are still under suspicion of crimes committed before 1994. That's when they'd gone in the system for good. Ron has kept their families fed since their convictions. Now him and the crew are going to continue doing that. Plus see to the murders of the 3 rats too. These lifers from Ron's crew was convicted in Texas of 7 counts of capital murder, for killing a family of 7, in the Dallas area.

293

TIME TO FEEL-RELOADED-Time Will Reveal part 5

Then they confessed to more murders throughout the United States. They were labeled as *The Interstate Bandits* because they had confessed to killing over 30 people from Texas to Michigan to California to Florida. They had gotten word to Ron when Ray's body was discovered and made the national headlines. They reminded him that they would take that ride for whomever did it, if they were loyal to him and would keep their family's fed after their executions. Plus avenge the rape and subsequent suicide of Ayesha Robinson. After getting the offer, Ron made certain they had the details they needed to give a proper confession. They took the rap for Ray, Ray's family, the coach and the coach's family. These were 4 of the same guys who had helped to beat Ray's ass, back in 1991 when he was messing with Ebony in the school hallway before the assault. Since they had history with Ray, they knew the story would go over better. Though he knew these guys was straight killers, Ray still didn't learn from that ass whooping. Because he assaulted Ebony, less than a month later. The attack on Ayesha had happened nearly a year prior to the day that he attacked Ebony. Too date, Ron already employs more than half of the families of the 4 killers.

Immediately after the meeting with Ron, attorney Wheeler takes the information and contacts Ann Arbor with the names of these 4 killers. The prosecution follows up by getting their confessions on tape. There is already testimony from 1996 which places them in the Ann Arbor area during the Thanksgiving holiday of 1991. The police know that was the same time frame according to the lab results, that Ray would have likely been killed. As a matter of fact, bus ticket receipts proved they'd traveled to the Michigan area several times during the months from September through November of 1991. To make the case even firmer, the guys had recently chatted it up with other inmates and said they had made those trips trying to catch him off guard but they didn't see him until Thanksgiving weekend. This for Wheeler, was an open and shut case and enough reason for releasing his client's of any other scrutiny.

By the close of the week, the Ann Arbor prosecution removes Jr and the Omega's names from the case, *once and for all*. By Arthur and Michelle's wedding day, Jr and his frats are free from any more implications in the disappearance and subsequent murder of Raymond White. Chill and Ron are at Ebony and Ajay's side when Arthur makes the announcement at his reception.

"It's finally over, baby girl," Chill whispers to Ebony, "There will be no more talk about investigating who took that asshole from the world."

"I told you in ninety one," Ron says "I would *not* allow him to hurt

294

you or your life. It took longer than I wanted it too. But I never stopped thinking of a way to clear *all* of my family."

"You're always on time brother," Ajay tells Ron, "I've got mad love for you, Fam. *Mad* love."

"Me too," Ebony adds, "You was always there for me, April and Yolanda. I always felt safe with you and Carolyn on my team. I'm just glad it's over."

The next day after church, Chill and Al dig up the tapes from Al's backyard. They meet with the other fathers from the 2nd generation, at CrewLand mall. John starts up the largest BBQ pit at Stoney's Bar & Grill. 1 by 1, they burn their video taped confessions to Raymond White's murder which they had recorded, back in 1996. It's finally over and the crew are all safe from any further prosecution dealing with Raymond White.

The crew sent Arthur and Michelle on a 7-day trip to the Bahamas for their honeymoon. Kilo had suggested they fly instead of taking a cruise because it's storm season. Michelle had ladies from the crew as bridesmaids and their husbands was Arthur's groomsmen. Michelle having the crew ladies on her team isn't something that was even likely, back when the crews troubles with Raymond White began. That has all been resolved now and Michelle is official crew. The ladies of *Crew Gear* had pulled off another breathtaking wedding. Though Michelle had once been good friends with Alana, Darlene, Tameka and Angel. She's loyal to the crew nowadays. So is Tameka, who's the only 1 she still considers a friend from her school days. Tameka was her maid of honor. She still works at Crew's House of Soul food. She's now a manager for the restaurant's evening employee's. She's been employed with the crew for nearly 9 years.

****

The prosecutors in Cleveland have called on the crew to give statements about their knowledge of Matt and Ellen's relationship. They're building their witness list against Ellen Barnes. Through Wheeler, each of the crew give their statements. They miss Matt and Kelly terribly. They only wish Matt hadn't carried on the relationship with Ellen, based on lies. They gave that as their reason for lifting Ellen's ban from their business property.

"It wasn't fair to ban her and not Farah and Matt too," Tonya says in the crew meeting. "Matt worked on the property part time. But he did bring full time drama. Still I miss having him around because he did keep all of us laughing and he could do anything with *any* grade of hair."

"I just know he was a special part of me and Anthony's wedding day," Ebony says, "But I didn't know what kind of player he was."

"I didn't either or I would've objected to him hanging around you all day, on our wedding day," Ajay says, "Even when he came to our games. He sat by you. Was he trying to get at you, at any point?"

"No," Rebbie says with a giggle, "No way. He *knew* better."

"He never said anything out of the way to me," Ebony says, "He knew not too. Jr had hipped him to how my man gets down."
They laugh.

"I feel so bad for Greg junior though," T-baby says, "He really cared for Kelly."
The crew have a brief meeting before going to T-baby's game in Detroit, on Tuesday night.

Back in Cleveland, mama Brenda is up all night with Brina and Archie Jr. Brina isn't feeling good at all. She's way past her due date. Big Mama is there with them. She tells Brina she's going to have the baby within the next 24 hours. Brittany J is home from Atlanta to be there for the birth of her new nephew. Archie Jr's big brother Shannon "Da Reaper" had come home with her. The crew don't get to see them a lot because of their music careers. But they're going to stay in Cleveland for a few days and catch up on all the latest happenings with their crew.

"We're gonna perform at the clubs before we leave," Brittany J tells Brina.

"Good. It's been a minute since y'all did that," Brina says.
She's in a lot of pain. By 4am Archie Jr takes her to East General where Dr. Weston and nurse Tenischa are waiting for them.

It's the 17th day of August. Brina gives birth to a son whom she names after his father and her husband. Grandpa Joshua tells them their son is born on the 36th year anniversary of the worst Hurricane he'd ever lived through. *Hurricane Camille.*

"She was a real monster," he says, "Tore the Mississippi gulf coast, clean up."

"We should've named my lil dude, Hurricane," Archie Jr laughs, "Cause he's gonna do some damage to the league."

"Naming him Archie is just fine then," Rena adds with a smile, "He'll do damage enough as Archie."
They all laugh. Brina had to have a C-section. She's still in recovery while

TIME TO FEEL-RELOADED-Time Will Reveal part 5

the crew view and admire their new male addition to their huge family.

NAME: Archie Joseph Wilson III
BORN: August 17, 2005
TIME:7AM
WEIGHT:6lbs 2 ounces
LENGTH:23 inches

"Being a father is the best feeling in the world," Archie Jr says as he holds his son. "I feel love for both of my kids. I just love Brina. I wasn't in love with Leilenne. She's cool though. But I sometimes wish I wouldn't have messed with her."

"Son it's too late to say that," Archie Sr says, "My granddaughter can *never* know that."

"That's right," Rena says, "Never make her feel like she's not the most precious gift in the world."

"Oh I know," Archie Jr says, "I love her to death. I just hate I hurt Brina by messing around with her friend then making a baby too. That tore her up for a long time."

"Well you made good on it, grandson," Grandpa Charles says, "I'm proud of you."

Welcome to the world.........................Archie Joseph Wilson III

Kilo has been feeling antsy this whole week. He's from the south. He knows the dangers of the hurricane season. He's been watching the weather channel since June when the season started. His family resides in New Orleans. It's 23 days into August and some of the crew are packing for Atlanta. Kilo has plans of making the trip. But today he changes his mind. Justine can't understand why he doesn't want to go to Atlanta with the crew. She's disappointed because she's been anticipating the trip.

Today Kilo learns of and begins tracking *Tropical Depression 12* which has formed over the Bahamas. This is the very reason he warned Arthur and Michelle against going to the Bahamas during hurricane season and definitely, not by cruise.

"I have a bad feeling about this season," Kilo says to Justine, "The *IN-OH* hasn't had a storm in years. I have a feeling my family is gonna need me to help them evacuate."

"Oh okay. Then what should we do?" Justine asks.

"I need to call them and see who's coming," he says, "Because I know most of them are gonna need finances too."

He calls his family to see if they have a game plan. Just like he figured. None of them are planning to flee the city.

"Y'all gonna trust them levees?" he asks his mother.

"Yea we don't have a way to get all of us out of here. And no where for all of us to stay," his mother says.

"Come stay with me and Justine until hurricane season ends," he says suddenly.

"KeJuan, you say that *every* season," Mrs. Thomas laughs, "Your daddy's gonna board us up and stock the pantry. We'll be alright."

"I don't feel good about y'all staying there," Kilo says.

"I've been in my house for forty years," his mother says, "No storm is gonna run me off."

That's final. She isn't going to entertain anymore talk about running away from the weather.

"Nu Aulins has always *been* below sea level and we always survived," she says, "God will take care of us. Don't you worry none. You hear me?"

He tells her, he won't worry. Though he knows he will. He worries plenty but his mother isn't going to change her mind. Not even after it hits Florida, 2 days later with the name *Katrina* at a Category 1.

He calls back and tries hard to convince his mother to travel but to no avail. However his sister Patricia Thomas takes him up on his offer. She's a senior at Dillard University. She tells him her dorm is going to close if the storm tracks west. It appears that it's going too. She tells him to reserve a ticket for her because she's coming. He tells her to pack enough gear for a week and go to the airport. She goes to *Louis Armstrong* airport where a ticket is waiting for her on Southwest Airlines, round trip to Cleveland.

Kilo, Justine, Courtney and Wayne take the crew to the airport for their flight to Atlanta. They'll pick up Patricia, in the process. Her flight arrives just in time for her to meet the crew before they depart. Ebony isn't feeling particularly well today. Ajay is very concerned about her and the baby she's carrying too.

"Baby are you sure you wanna make this trip?" Ajay asks.

"I wanna go, baby," she says, "I'm just pregnant, Anthony. I'll be okay. I'm gaining a lot of weight with this baby. Like I did with the twins."

298

"I think it's more than one again," he says and smiles.

"You're probably right," she says and smiles too. Then she says, "You seem to know this whole pregnancy thing better than I do. It's a shame you can't carry the baby too."

They laugh hard as they take their 1st class seats and prepare for their flight departure.

It's August 25th when the crew fly to Atlanta. Bre and Ced's baby is coming soon. Ebony, Ajay, Nina, Tank, T-baby and Wes make the trip with Bre's parents, Deb and Brad Sr. Rebbie is too far along in her pregnancy and June is into his preseason schedule. They can't leave. Ced's parents fly in from New York. Bre isn't in active labor yet but she's been experiencing pressure in her lower back. She knows the onset of labor isn't far away. He mother Deb and her mother-in-law Sedina make her as comfortable as possible.

"I've been through this before," Bre says, "But it was over thirteen years ago and I did not miss that part of it."

They all laugh but Bre doesn't. She's very uncomfortable at this point.

2 days later, August 27th and Bre still hasn't gone into active labor. They all watch the weather because the same hurricane they heard about 4 days ago is still a hurricane. Katrina had hit Florida 2 days ago as a category 1 and weakened while on land. Then it went back into the Gulf of Mexico and regained intensity. It's up to a Category 3, by the morning.

By evening, 9 hours later, Katrina is a category 5. The most intense category a hurricane can be, according to the *Saffir-Simpson* scale.

"I think Kilo needs to make his family leave there," Lynn says.

"If he could've they'd be in Cleveland already," Jb says.

Him and Lynn are hosting Ebony, Ajay, Nina and Tank at their house. They're all glued to the TV while they keep in touch with T-baby and Wes, who are staying at Jan and Rob's. Bre and Ced hosts their parents. CJ is happy to have so much company.

Kim flies down on Sunday and brings Brad III with her. That makes CJ's day, even more to have her closest cousin visit her in Atlanta. They had been inducted into the crew together, last year at The Spot II. No one in the crew will turn 13 in 2005. But the crew are going to officially induct Shantel Jacobson, Venitia Walker and Mario Scott. The crew in Atlanta stay fixed on the weather channel while they're discussing the new inductees.

"Man those highways are packed in Mississippi and Louisiana," Kim says.

TIME TO FEEL-RELOADED-Time Will Reveal part 5

She's staying at her sister Jan's home while in Atlanta. She has been in touch with Bruce. Him, June and Eric are preparing for a preseason game.

"People are trying to get to safety," Bruce says, "Two of our teammates had to bring their families to stay with them. They lived in Biloxi."

"That's in Mississippi," Kim says, "Grandpa Joshua told me all about that place. He said it's time for another bad storm to come there."

"They're saying New Orleans," Bruce says, "It can be either one."

"Or both," Kim adds.

Bruce and Kim soon hang up after he told her to be sure and call him back when his sister gives birth. She promised him, she would.

By 4am, Bre and Ced are in Labor and delivery in Atlanta. While Kilo, Justine and Patricia are on pins and needles in Cleveland. Katrina is still a category 5 and roaring through the Gulf of Mexico. The cone of the storm covers land from the Florida panhandle into western Louisiana. Nobody knows her destination. Citizens all along the gulf coast brace for the worse. Bre gives birth to a son at 7:10. While at same time, Katrina is making her 2nd landfall at Buras-Triumph Louisiana as a category 3 with winds of 125 miles per hour. Katrina moves over southeast Louisiana, then heads back over the water at the Breton Sound. Katrina makes her 3rd landfall in Pearlington Mississippi. Still at a strong category 3. The crew in Cleveland and Atlanta watch as the storm pounds the 2 states, well into the afternoon. Dumping water and hard winds for hours.

By late evening, Kilo is beside himself. He's unable to get a call into his family in New Orleans. He can only watch the news broadcast and pray. He watches as the news starts to show the damages along the coast of Mississippi. All through the night, he continues to try and reach his family. But before the dawn of the next morning, all hell breaks lose in New Orleans. He's watching footage of his hometown while Patricia cries and prays. Justine feels so helpless, just watching. She's never experienced anything like this. Then suddenly, the levees which surround New Orleans start to breach. Like a domino affect, 1 by 1 they fail. And by the sunrise, 80% of New Orleans, 1 of the largest and most popular cities in the world, is underwater. News crews who had flocked to the coast in anticipation of the hurricane, are now stranded in unfamiliar circumstances. While whole towns in Mississippi are wiped out. Citizens in New Orleans are perched on their roofs, hanging off of balcony's and out of windows signaling for help. Still others seek refuge in their attics from the still rising water. The water continues to rise. Katrina is still a hurricane as she moves inland and does

300

damage in Northern Mississippi. Katrina has traveled more than 150 miles inland and is still at hurricane status. It isn't downgraded to a tropical storm until it reaches Clarksville Tennessee and she has left *major* destruction in her path.

Bre slept until the late evening while her visitors watched the weather and stay in touch with Kilo for updates on his family. They watch in horror as coverage shows citizens still stranded. Lil CJ never takes her eyes off her new baby brother. At the same time, she watches as children who are smaller than her, sit on adults shoulders and wade through waist deep filthy water, at night. But Lil Ced is bundled up warm, on her lap.

NAME: Cedric Leroy Hamilton, Jr
BORN: August 29, 2005
TIME:7:10am EST
WEIGHT: 5lbs 13 ounces
LENGTH:19 inches

Even 2 days later, Katrina's fury can be tracked into the Great Lakes and beyond.

"We got three boys and CJ is still the only girl," Deb says to Brad Sr about their grandchildren.

"CJ ain't mad about that. Are you, CJ?" Brad Sr asks.

CJ laughs and says, "Sometimes I wish I had a girl cousin to play with around here because it's only boys, down here. Lil Jb, Lil Rob and now Lil Ced."

"You'll just have to show these boys who's the boss," Sedina says.

They all laugh as they escort Bre in a wheelchair, down the elevator. Her and baby Ced are going home today.

"Man, Katrina damn near went to Cleveland," Ced says.

They gather around a TV in Grady hospital's lobby. Brad Sr and George go get the vehicles while Bre catches up on the tragedy that is Katrina.

"Why the hell are those people still sitting on the roof? The storm was two days ago?" she asks in a very irritated tone.

"Girl you know Bush don't give a damn if they bake up there and die," A black male nurse says as he waits with them.

"I hate to admit that it's the truth, when someone says that," Sedina offers, "I felt the same way after the September eleventh attack."

"I don't hate too," Deb says, "I love to admit it. I was raised to say it. If that was white folks stranded out there. There'd a hundred helicopters

buzzing overhead. And for every fifty people, there'd be a rescue person down there on those rooftops with them."
The wrath of Katrina isn't nearly over for the people on the Gulf Coast.

Welcome to the world.................Cedric Leroy Hamilton, Jr

Kilo is losing his mind. He's been watching the newscast and trying to get any type of transportation he can that will take him to New Orleans. No one is flying nor driving into the storm region because there are no inlets. Katrina tore up highways, interstates, forest, lakes, whole neighborhoods, towns and cities. The entire Gulf Coast is in shambles. It's already been recorded as being the 6th strongest hurricane of all time.

"All circuits are still busy, baby," Justine says to Kilo somberly.
He's been trying to call his family since Monday. It's Wednesday morning and he hasn't heard a peep from anyone in New Orleans. He's more terrified than ever because the news has reported that there have been many deaths, from drowning and shootings. They report looting, pillaging and lawlessness is at an all time high. Kilo and Patricia worry for their loved ones as they watch news coverage, 24 hours a day.

"I talked to Sharon at three this morning, low," Patricia says to Kilo, "She said they was evacuating to the convention center. Now I'm hearing that women and little girls are being raped in there."
Patricia is still in tears. She prays her family will be spared. But seeing all the faces of the people in front of the Superdome and convention center filled with despair. They know their family hasn't faired *any* better.

By Friday September 2nd, Ebony and the crew in Atlanta have signed up as volunteers to be aid to the Katrina victims. Ajay isn't going to allow Ebony to move 1 muscle. Lynn, Jan nor Brina can house a family because the crew are staying with them. But they give money donations and help out at shelters, Red Cross and FEMA sites.

In Cleveland, CrewLand Enterprises is ready to move supplies southward for the victims of Katrina. They started gathering aid the day before the storm.

"George Bush was on vacation at his ranch in Texas when Katrina hit," Patricia says.

"Shit. On his way back to DC, he flew over the bitch and looked

down," Kilo says, "He didn't even land. I know he don't give a fuck."
His frustration is evident to all the crew in Cleveland. While the crew in Atlanta are volunteering all week, the crew at CrewLand mall have been gathering and loading more supplies. John is sending 9 of his 18 wheelers, loaded with supplies which had been donated by the crew and their business partners. Mr. Parkwood joins him and they expand it to 18 trucks. Andre, Joe, Woody and Pac Man are 4 of the 36 drivers who will drive the trucks down south and unload them. Kilo makes Patricia stay behind with Justine but he packs a bag and crowds into 1 of the rigs. He's headed to the Gulf Coast by Friday morning. Still he's had no contact with any of his relatives.

Nina and the crew notice there are many evacuees already in Atlanta hotels. More are coming in everyday. Still, 5 days since the storm and black people in Louisiana are still on roofs or still packed into the unsafe and unsanitary conditions at the Superdome and convention center. They have no food, water, sanitary products, running water or bath facilities. They have nothing. To make matters worse. Some news media has started to refer to the citizens of New Orleans as refugees. Still nothing gets moving until today. Friday the 2nd day of September.
5 FUCKING DAYS LATER!
"They're not no *damn* refugees!" T-baby screams as Nina cries. They're helping folks get registered for FEMA and watching coverage on TV's placed throughout the community center.

Many entertainers, comedians, sports stars and politicians slam Bush and response team for lack of effort. Chertoff and Homeland Security haven't done a damn thing either. But still, Bush compliments Michael Brown saying, "Brownie, you're doing a heck of a job."

At an *NBC* benefit concert for Katrina relief, *Kanye West* has had enough. It's been *5 FUCKING DAYS*! His frustration comes out as he's presenting an award while standing next to *Mike Myers*. He creates a lot of controversy and movement with his comment. He makes a serious plea for his people, to the dismay of some. The crew agree with Kanye's statement.
"I hate the way they portray us in the media. You see a black family. It says, 'They're looting.' You see a white family. It says, 'They're looking for food.' And you know it's been five days [waiting for federal help] because most of the people are black. And even for me to complain about it. I would be a hypocrite because I've tried to turn away from the teacher-the TV. Because it's too hard to watch. I've even been shopping before even giving a donation. So

TIME TO FEEL-RELOADED-Time Will Reveal part 5

now I'm calling my business manager, right now to see what is the biggest amount I can give. And just to imagine if I was down there and those are my people down there. So anybody out there that wants to do anything that we can. Help with the way America is set up to help the poor. The black people. The less well-off. As slow as possible. I mean the Red Cross is doing everything they can. We already realize a lot of people that can help, are at war right now. Fighting another way and they've given them permission to go down there and shoot us!"

Next to him, Mike Myers attempts to carry on with the script but when Kanye gets to speak again, he says,
"George Bush doesn't care about black people."

That video clip is played for days afterwards. Causing many Americans to come out and speak on the side of Kanye West.
    "I see why Kanye said what he did," Ebony says, "And I agree with him. This government don't give a damn about my people."
She's very emotional because it is 5 days later and they still haven't gotten the people out.
        The first breakdown which may have caused the disastrous lack of efforts could've been when President George W. Bush declared it a state of emergency in select regions of Mississippi, Louisiana and Alabama on Saturday the 27th, 2 days before Katrina made landfall. But what he hadn't done was to include the Louisiana coastal parishes. Even after learning that the NHC had extended the cone and expressed concern that the levees wouldn't hold Katrina. Bush still didn't expand the state of emergency. On the 28th he even called Governor Blanco [Louisiana] and suggested she issue a mandatory evacuation. Later FEMA director Michael Brown would blame Blanco for not including the coastline of her state in her request for a state of emergency to be issued. But Blanco shows proof via her letter that she *had* included them and the government just didn't adhere to her letter. And even though Bush gave Brown a compliment. He and Chertoff called him back to Washington DC in 8 days. Three days after that Brown resigned from his position as FEMA director. No assistance had been given to the majority of the storm victims in 120 hours or 5 days. Still the relief efforts wouldn't have been successful if it wasn't for *Lieutenant General Russell L. Honore.* Even after they moved citizens, things weren't smooth. They took 5000 people to Reliant Astrodome in Houston but there was only 2000 cots available.

304

TIME TO FEEL-RELOADED-TIME WILL REVEAL 5   Black Coffee

TIME TO FEEL-RELOADED-Time Will Reveal part 5

By Saturday, all of the people have finally been evacuated from the city but many families are broken up. They're spread all across the nation, not knowing where their other family members are.

"That evacuation procedure was worse than the slave trade," big mama says, "They have small children who are separated from their parents. Husbands from wives. Families are split up all over the United States."

"They're even putting folks on a cruise ship now," Grandma Annabelle adds.

"This is the saddest thing I've seen in a long time," Mrs. Ida Mae Green says, "This was more than a hurricane. This was hell and high water."

TIME TO FEEL-RELOADED-Time Will Reveal part 5

CHAPTER 60

THE REAL AXIS OF EVIL

By Saturday Kilo finally talks with his mother. She's been evacuated to Utah while his father was bussed to Houston. 1 of his aunts and a cousin are in Tennessee. 4 other family members who are in Ohio, contacts Patricia. The crew are going to Toledo and bringing them to Cleveland. After finally reaching his mother by phone, Kilo learns that some of his relatives perished and each of them had died after surviving Katrina. His uncle drowned in his attic and floated out into the streets where his bloated body remained on the following Monday, for Kilo to see.

Now on a boat with rescuers, he tours his Lower 9th ward and historic neighborhood. It's still underwater, a week later. His grandmother died at the superdome. 1 of his cousins was killed by Jefferson Parish deputies while trying to cross the bridge to escape rising flood waters. He was amongst the people Kanye had referred to on Friday. Kilo is devastated. Still he has to keep going. There are so many things that still have to be done with no obvious way to get started.

In Atlanta the crew give housing to many of Kilo's family, just as they're doing in Cleveland. On Labor Day many victims flood the Atlanta area. They're 90% black. It's sad how black citizens have been treated. Chertoff claims the Katrina scenario doesn't exist. But CNN releases an article today which proves engineers had long been told that the levees wouldn't be able to handle more than a category 3 hurricane. And a category 4 would turn the city which is already below sea level, into a swamp. And that's exactly what happened.

For an entire month, Hurricane Katrina dominates the news. Many of the Cash Money artist lost their homes. Juvenile speaks out numerous times, about the lack of effort. Also about the monies raised by the entertainment industry and others which never made it to the victims. Over 1800 people from 7 states died from Katrina. More than 1700 are still missing. Katrina is recorded as the costliest natural tragedy of all time.

Less than a month later, on September 24, Louisiana is hit on the Texas side by Hurricane Rita. Rita causes damage as far inland as Hammond and Baton Rouge. By now, all of Kilo's family that he could locate, are in Cleveland. The crew have given them free rent at the condo's for 6 months. But things are getting heated amongst Kilo's relatives and the crew. Some of the younger family members, along with other evacuees in the Cleveland area are becoming apart of a new wave of crime.

"They're *so* ungrateful for the help we're giving them," says a very pregnant Rebbie, "I don't trust having them working in my dance school. They don't even show up for work, first of all. And when they do, they don't do *any* work."

Kilo has made it back to Cleveland. He starts the actions to get them into FEMA travel trailers and apartments. Those who have income, have to get an apartment and pay their own rent. Those who don't have income and are causing trouble. Kilo makes them leave the crew property immediately. In a heated pitch, he yells, "Here it is! My Ohio family is doing all of this shit for y'all! And still you muthafuckahz is acting like clowns! Fuck it! Get your own shit! But you're getting the fuck out of my pockets!"

They spend the end of September moving those who was yet to do anything to help themselves. Which was only a select few. They're heading south to Houston and Atlanta. Some are even going back to New Orleans. Kilo doesn't care where they go, as long as they leave the crew property by Rich III 10th birthday. The last day of September. Kilo has had enough.

The 1st day of October is Ashanti's 7th birthday and the 3rd year anniversary of Rich Jr's death. Alicia Mallory Wilson or Ally as she's known and Steven Davon Brown get married in a small romantic ceremony at their workplace, Allen Saul Recreation Center. Ashanti and their parents are their wedding party. Ajay and Ebony's gift to them is a trip to the Pocono's mountains for the honeymoon excursion *they'd* enjoyed in 1997. They keep their Goddaughter Ashanti while the newlyweds are away. Ebony doesn't have much energy due to her pregnancy. But she's a trooper. Ajay is into preseason practice. Big mama is staying with them. She plans to stay until the new baby or babies come.

In the wake of Katrina and the crew being so close to the destruction via Kilo, their children became quite inquisitive about *how* disasters happen. America has had her share of tragedy's. Both by humans and by nature, during the foursome's lifetime. Katrina had brought forth a lot of questions from their children.

It's 2 days into October. The foursome and their children sit at Rebbie's house while she deals with the early stages of labor. June has a bye week and is finishing up the decorations on the room for the twins, they're expecting. While the foursome are on their lanai trying to name disasters and big news making events which happened during their lifetime. They have their kids out there too. Their informing them about the disasters which had happened and sparked national attention.

"Mount Saint Helens erupted in nineteen eighty," Nina starts, "That's the first one I can remember watching on the news."

"The F five tornado in Niles Ohio in nineteen eighty five," Ebony says, "Also there were no F five tornado's during the year me, Tank and Nina was born. None in nineteen seventy five."

"How did you know that mommy?" Lannie asks.

"I did a report on tornados when I was in the sixth grade," she says, "I won an award from the Ohio Scholastics board. Your mommy is smart."

Lannie likes that a lot. Her and all the kids smile and look at Ebony with adoring eyes while the foursome continue to recount history.

"Oh how about the OJ Simpson trial and acquittal in nineteen ninety five?" Rebbie asks, "I did a report on that my freshman year at Natty. I got picked to represent the University in the college bowl."

The adoring eyes continue as T-baby speaks on an incident of school violence which sparked talk and soon action for the betterment of school security. She mentions, "The Columbine school massacre in April nineteen ninety nine."

"Oh yes and almost a year to the day of that one. The *Murrah building* bombing in two thousand," Nina chimes in.

"By American terrorists Timothy McVeigh and Terry Nichols," Ebony adds.

"Yes but has America called them terrorist? Or profiled those who look like them?" T-baby asks sarcastically.

"Of course not," They all answer as the children giggle.

"They killed babies and all, just like nine eleven," Rebbie says, "Which I saw up close and personal."

"You did mommy?" Orian asks.

"Yes sweetheart," Rebbie says, "Mommy was there for a dance audition when the planes hit."

The kids eyes get *very* large after hearing she was there *when* the 2 planes *struck* the 2 towers. Jerica remembers when it happened and being told she would've gone next, had the terror strike not happened and destroyed the facility.

"Uncle Ced's brother and sister-in-law got killed in the buildings," Jerica says, "Y'all know Valene and big Aaliyah from New York? Their mommy and daddy died in those towers."

"You talking about CJ's cousins?" Ashanti asks.

"Yes they're from New York," Jerica clarifies.

308

"She's got my little sister's name," Lannie says.

"She's older than Lea," Rich III says, "But my cousin Lea is the bomb."

They all laugh.

"What about the Beltway sniper attacks for three weeks of October of two thousand and two?" T-baby asks, "While I was in a coma. We had black serial killers out there killing people."

"That bugged me out," Erica adds, "All of my friends in Oklahoma who was from the DC, Baltimore and the Virginia area was freaking out."

"Us too," Rebbie says, "Then the Sumatran Tsunami, last year."

"That was crazy," Ebony says, "That's why I can never go with Bush and be against foreigners. Just because they *aren't* Americans."

"That Bush white house and his administration are the *real* axis of evil," Nina says, "And we're gonna make sure our children know the truth. *Always*. Our first generation wants us to keep the knowledge flowing."

They end with more discussion about hurricanes Katrina and Rita before wrapping up today's talk. The crew will continue to volunteer their services in Louisiana and Mississippi for the next 3 years. Only breaking for pregnancies and delivering babies. Hurricane relief will remain their focus until it's time for them to start their day-to-day campaigning for the new Democratic Nominee, Barack Obama by late 2007.

Though she tires very easily these days. Ebony picks up her children, her goddaughter Ashanti plus Orian from aftercare today. Rebbie had called her at noon, at her home office. She told her, she was in active labor. Rena and Brenda are at the house with her in Jackson Heights, trying to reach June. He's on the practice field preparing for their next game against the *Chicago Bears*.

"I got Orian. I'm on my way home," Ebony says to mama Rena via cell phone, "She can have dinner with us. I got Shaunny too. Ally can be at Rebbie's, to help y'all out."

"Okay baby girl. Thank you so much," Rena says, "But don't you overdo it. I don't want Ajay to go off on us for letting you baby sit all these *extra* kids."

"He's gonna do that regardless," Ebony says as she giggles, "He don't want me to lift a finger. But big mama is here with me too."

"I appreciate you for always helping out. Since you're working out of your home now," Rena says, "And tell Ajay I said that."

"Oh don't even mention it, auntie," Ebony says while still laughing.

TIME TO FEEL-RELOADED-Time Will Reveal part 5

"You know Ree Ree is my sister and so does he. We're always here for each other. Besides, Lannie and Lea was looking forward to having *both* girls at the house for as long as they can stay."

Rena thanks her again. Then she tells her, they'll be headed to the hospital within the hour.

"She's still gonna try the V back, ha?" Ebony asks, referring to the term used when expected mothers who previously had a cesarean section, elect to try a vaginal birth.

"Yes she doesn't want to have a C section if she doesn't have too."

"Tell her I'll be there after Anthony gets home," she says, "I'm gonna ask him to bring me, so I can check on her and see the babies. Big mama is here to stay with the kids and Erica's coming by later."

"Okay Ebony but you be careful," Rena says, "You're carrying twins, for the second time. And just like the last time. You need your rest."

"I stay off my feet all day until it's time to go get the kids," Ebony says, "Anthony finally said it was okay for me to pick them up. As long as security is available to drive me. I had to promise to come straight home and sit down."

"Well *good*," Rena says, "I know my nephew is gonna take care of *his*."

They laugh before hanging up.

Rebbie and June have twin boys coming. It seems they'll be here tonight. Rebbie had a c-section with Orian but Dr. Weston told her she's in perfect shape and healthy enough to try to deliver the twins vaginally. And if she sees any complications, she'd take her to surgery immediately. Both Rebbie and June agree, they prefer to try natural child birth.

Brenda is able to reach June before they leave for East General. She tells him, he has time to shower. But then meet them at the hospital as soon as he can get there.

"Well alright!" he screams, "I'm about to have me some twin boys running around my house!"

His teammates are shouting their congratulations to him. Brenda can hear them clowning around in the background.

Before hanging up and running to the showers, June says, "Tell my baby I'll be there on time and please take it easy. Don't take any chances with the birth. If she needs to have surgery. Please let the doctor do it."

Brenda tells him she'll pass the message along. She can tell he's nervous as he rushes her to get off the phone so he can shower and leave. They hang up.

310

TIME TO FEEL-RELOADED-Time Will Reveal part 5

He isn't in panic mode yet. But his mother could hear the anxiousness in his voice. He's always wanted a son. Sometime this evening, he'll have 2 of them.

Tank and Wes agree to help big mama keep the children while Ajay drives Ebony, Nina and T-baby to visit Rebbie. They make it just in time to see her wheeled into surgery. She wasn't able to deliver the twins.

NAME: Brian James III----------------------Brent James
BORN: October 6, 2005
TIME; 5:10pm---5:14pm
WEIGHT: 5lbs---4lbs 4ounces
LENGTH: 16inches-18inches

Brittany J and Reaper show up to view the twins, just after June opens up the celebratory cigars.

"Our siblings are showing us up, baby," Reaper says to Brittany.

"I know *right*? First Brina and Archie Jr," she says, "Now its big June and Ree Ree *again*."

"We'll get us one in there pretty soon," he says.

"Get that marriage in there first. Okay?" Rena says as she smiles.

"We're engaged already," Reaper tells his mother, "We got engaged right before we flew home this morning."

Brittany smiles brightly. With that announcement, the crew have something else to celebrate at the clubs tonight. Chill and Tank was already throwing a party Sunday after the Browns game, to celebrate the birth of the James' twins. Now Shannon Da Reaper Wilson and Brittany James are getting married next Valentine's day. That won't be all. There's still more good news coming for the crew to celebrate and more wounds to heal as well.

Welcome to the world.............Brian James III and Brent James.

Before the crew can leave the hospital, T-baby turns weak and becomes ill. This puts everyone on alert because of the head trauma she'd suffered several years back plus the gunshot to her chest. The crew have taken special notice of T-baby's health since those 2 traumatic occurrences. She doesn't have the strength to walk. Ajay and Nina hold her up. Suddenly she faints in the corridor. The staff takes her to emergency and Wes is called. He and Renee rush to her side. The staff run neurological test. All of her results are positive. Dr. Weston is still in the hospital, being that

TIME TO FEEL-RELOADED-TIME WILL REVEAL 5   Black Coffee

Rebbie hadn't long given birth. Sandy calls for her to come down and give T-baby a pregnancy test.

"Gladys these symptoms are familiar to me," Sandy says as Dr. Gladys Weston comes into the room with T-baby. "I just wanna satisfy my mother's intuition."

"Have you had dreams of fish again?" Weston asks with a smile.

"Big trout's and blue gills too," Sandy says as she giggles.

"Hmm Salt *and* freshwater fish?" Weston says, continuing the humor. "Then let me give you a diagnosis to go along with your motherly wit. You're going to be a grandmother again."

Everyone around T-baby's bed starts to cheer and applaud. T-baby's diagnosis is 1 her, Wes and everyone else can live with. She's pregnant. Her and Wes are expecting their 1st child together.

"I tell you what," Weston says with a laugh, "This crew has put all of my children and family through college. We've done round two with Nina, Ebony and Rebbie. Now we're going round two for you, T-baby."

"I know and Ebony will complete round three before this baby comes," T-baby says with a giggle.

"The foursome do *everything* together," Nina adds with a laugh.

"No matter what the path is to do it, ha," T-baby says.

"We still manage to do it similar and together," Ebony says.

T-baby and Wes are ecstatic. They've been trying to conceive since her basketball season ended. They find out they've been successful. They have a due date of June 20, 2006.

"I'm gonna get this baby into the world just before I turn thirty," T-baby says as she giggles.

"That biological clock is *ticking*, home girl," Nina says as they all laugh, "Lil Rich is ten years old."

"And Jada is turning twelve, next month," T-baby adds.

"Woo, she gets crewed up next year," Ebony offers.

"She sure does," Nina says, "Her and Destiny together."

"The two *Lil Renee's* will be crew this time next year," Ebony says.

"And we'll have five or six kids by then," Ajay adds with a chuckle as Ebony's eyes stretch.

"With a new *Stewart* addition to the crew too," T-baby says.

"That's so true," Ebony says before turning to Ajay and asking, "You said *we'll* have five or six kids by this time next year? Do you know something I don't know?"

"Baby there's lots of movement going on in your belly, for you to

be *only* five months," Ajay says, "A *whole* lot of movement and it's constant movement in here."
He's standing behind her as she leans back and rests her head on his chest. He has his arms around her mid-section with both hands on her protruding belly.

"That's true but Ant and Lannie moved around a lot too and it was just the two of them," Ebony tries as she can't help but smile.

"Ajay thinks he got more than two babies coming?" Nina asks as she smiles and shakes her head.

Then Dr. Weston says, "Her weight gain is a little bit higher than it was with the twins, at this stage. Ajay if you're right. I'm hiring you to work in *my* practice."
They have a good laugh as they all head back up to Rebbie's room to give her and June the good news on T-baby and Wes.

"No matter what path we take to get there," Rebbie says with a smile, "The foursome is still doing our thing *together*."

"We just said that too," T-baby says as they all laugh.
Before long everybody heads home. Leaving June at the hospital with his wife and new twins. Orian leaves with her grandmothers, Rena and Brenda. They'll get her off to school in the morning.

On Sunday June, Eric, Bruce and the Browns beat the Chicago Bears 20-10 and pull their record even at 2-2. June is still reeling with excitement over the birth of his twin sons. In today's game, he has 4 solo tackles and 2 sacks which is even more reason for him and Rebbie to celebrate.

At Ajay's, he and Ebony have gone to bed. She tires very easily these days. He wants to make sure their kids are in bed early and her also. After they're relaxed and cuddling together. They talk about the pregnancy which has them both so excited and him, a little worried.

"Baby are you sure you're doing okay?" he asks.

"Yes I'm just pregnant, Anthony," she says with a smile, "It's apart of it. *Remember*?"

"Yea I remember. That's why I always stress about you getting your rest too," he says.

"You do a great job of it too baby," she says, "And I'm doing what you want me to do. So wrap me up as tight as you can. Because I know this belly is getting big, faster than the last two."
They laugh. She's backed up to him in their bed. He wraps his arms around
313

her, fairly easy and begins to plant sweet kisses on the back of her neck.

He says, "You're not as big as you *think* you are, baby. But you *are* bigger at five months than you was with the twins. *And* with Lea. Shit, at seven months your stomach was still flat with Lea." They laugh again.

She says, "I didn't get big with Lea at all. I guess because she was a single."

"She's a *new* breed of female," he says and smiles.

"You really think I'm having more than two babies this time?"

"I really do," he says, "I've *been* saying it. It's a lot of movement going on in here. It has been for over a month. I don't remember that with either of the last two pregnancies. Even with the twins, you was over four months before you felt them moving."

"You're right," she says, "And I felt movement with this pregnancy, the week of the twins birthday. While we was preparing for T-baby's wedding. I was *barely* three months."

"Right," he says, "So I'm glad we're seeing Weston in the morning. Because I need to know what's up before the season starts."

"She's doing an ultrasound," she says, "Are we bringing the kids again?"

"Why not," he says, "They survived the first one." They laugh and he adds, "I think Ant understands that it's not nasty now. I've been talking to him. He's getting into his big brother role. He's looking forward to it."

"He loves that *second* in charge status too," Ebony says.

"That's just cosmetic," Ajay says and chuckles, "He's third in charge because *I'm* second." They laugh hard.

Ebony says, "I notice the puffiness in my face, more too."

"I see it in your hands more," he says, "Are your rings tight?"

"Kind of but-"

He says, "No butts, baby. I don't want you to be uncomfortable *anywhere*."

"But these are my wedding rings," she says, "I took off the promise ring, last month. But my wedding rings are *not* coming off. I can't get em off anyway."

"If they're too tight. Then we'll get them cut off," he says.

"*No way*," she says as she tries to turn and face him.

He helps her to turn around so they can look *eye-to-eye*.

"Ebony I bought the rings," he says, "I paid nearly a hundred grand for that set in ninety six. It's worth almost a million dollars now. If they're too tight and cutting off blood to your fingers. They're coming off. I'll get em resized and redone for when you can wear them. Our circle is in tact. Not having them on for the sake of your health, won't do anything to

314

change who they belong too and that you belong to me. I know that. I need the person wearing my rings to be here, alive and healthy while you're wearing them. That's my priority. Do you understand?"
She looks into his eyes but she doesn't say anything. He wants an answer.
"Do you understand me?"

"I *love* my rings," she says, "They mean a lot to me."

"You mean more to me then the rings do," he says, "Your health is what's important here. You have to be well in order for these babies to be well. Having to remove them for awhile or to resize them. Won't change shit about what we have or who we are. Do you understand me baby?"

"Yes I do," she says.

"And are you gonna tell me if they're uncomfortable?"

"Yes."

"Are they?" he asks.

"Not yet," she says, "But they might be as I gain more weight."

"Let me know when and we'll have them taken off," he says, "And how they go back on will depend on you. We can make them bigger, for now. Then shrink them after the babies come. Or we can have them mended back to the same size and you can put them back on after the babies come. That's up to you."

"Okay," she says, "We'll resize them so I can wear them while I'm pregnant."

"Cool," he says, "I'll add some more diamonds to them like I do every year. Just tell me when....., no. Actually we're gonna do it before I have to go on the road. I can make sure they do them *exactly* like they are now with no flaws in the bands. Is that cool?"

"That's cool," she says and smiles, "Thank you Anthony."

"You're welcome baby," he says, "Now let me see how wet I can get this *pregnant* pussy of mine, tonight."
She giggles as he slides his finger into her tight but soft vagina. The sensation is great. She purrs as he sticks his tongue in her mouth and starts to kiss her *very* aggressively. She's more than ready for some loving from her man. That's her 2nd favorite part of being pregnant. Because the extra hormones keep her horny all the time. There's no need for more discussion. It's *daddy* time.

The next day Ajay and Ebony visit the doctor. Tenischa is her usual vibrant and clairvoyant self. She'd already predicted they'd have another set of twins, this time. But she's only partially right. Ajay had the correct prediction. Ebony is pregnant with triplets. Ajay was dead on. She's having 3 babies this time. They can already see that 2 of them are girls.

"And no we don't wanna know what the third one is," Ajay says.

"We guessed that much," Tenischa says as they all laugh.

Lil Ajay, Lannie and Aaliyah are thrilled to know they'll have 3 more siblings in a few months. Lil Ajay's only demand now is that they all be girls.

"I want a brother but I want him to come by himself," he says, "I already came with a sister. He gotta do it bigger than me."

They all laugh which makes him crack up laughing too. Ebony and Ajay make note to say, if the 3rd baby *is* a boy. That would be bigger. Lil Ajay doesn't agree with that either. Fact is, if they have another son at anytime, they'll be the 1st couple in the history of Ajay's paternal legacy to bore a 2nd son. Richard Williams Sr had already changed the maternal side.

"That *will* be bigger," Lil Ajay says and chuckles.

"Well if it's not a boy. Then I guess we won't-" Ajay starts to say, as Ebony cuts him off and says, "Well I guess we'll be trying again."

Ajay smiles. He likes that answer. He gives her a sweet kiss and smiles big.

He says, "Whatever you say baby. I know I'm second in charge."

They laugh it up as Ajay, Ebony and their kids prepare to leave the office.

When they get in the parking lot, they realize they aren't the only couple with an appointment to see Dr. Weston. Michelle and Arthur are here for a visit too. They speak and talk for a few minutes before leaving. Arthur and Michelle head on up to Weston's office.

When they go back to the exam room, they find out they're expecting a baby too. They're due sooner then T-baby and Wes. Their due date is May 10, 2006. But even before their new baby comes. Arthur has a quadruple wedding to video and photograph in early 2006. The crew just keeps doing it *bigger*.

Reaper and Brittany are going to share the alter with 3 other couples from their generation. Lil Chill better known as Kenny, will marry Chaundra Coleman, the oldest of Stoney's 2 younger sisters. Ebony's baby brother Jesse is marrying Ruthie, who is the deceased Rich Jr's, *only* sister. The 4th couple is Ajay's baby sister Pam. She's marrying her longtime boyfriend Sam Logan Jr, who the crew has always called Cupid. He's Jan and Kim's *only* brother. The tradition in the crew of best friends children marrying each other is still very much alive. At tonight's celebration, the James' twins, the expecting mommies and the newly engaged are all the toast of the evening.

"This crew don't stop!" Reaper says during the engagement party.

316

"We're doing this shit *now*," Jesse says, "Our family's the *shit*."

"Ain't nothing to it but to do it," Kenny adds.

"Do it crew style, at that," Sam Jr says.

"I wouldn't have wanted *any* other family," Eric adds.

"You got the best family possible right here, man," Bruce tells him.

"To the C-town crew! What it do?" Steven says as he toast to the newly engaged couples of his crew.

Tonight the rest of crew join them. They all celebrate getting engaged, in front of an audience at the club.

"Our crew is gonna break Lynn, Jan and Bre's record," Pam says, "All the wedding records before us."

"Yes we are," Ally says, "They had three couples in theirs."

"Renee, Chill, Jr and Tonya had a double wedding," Ruthie says, "Rich Jr and big June had a double wedding with T-baby and Rebbie."

"But we're setting it off," Chaundra says, "Our crew has to top the crews before us. That's the rule. So we're just gonna go ahead and start it off by breaking that *most couples to get married at one time,* record."

"That's how it's always been," Brittany says, "Seventh Heaven are getting it in."

"That's right home girl," Erica adds, "Kim, Brit, Me, Roo, Pam, Chaundra and Ally are all *growwed* up as *The Rugrats* say it."

"Yes indeed," Kim says, "The crew is doing it bigger and better, each time."

They laugh as they enjoy their huge engagement party which is given at both clubs. Crew Gear has already started preparing the dresses. The crew have always shared a nickname for their individual age groups.

For Renee and Tonya. They're the *dynamic duo*. Lynn, Jan and Bre are *3 the hard way*. Nina, Ebony, T-baby and Rebbie are *The Awesome Foursome*. Now the *7th Heaven* of Kim, Brittany, Erica, Ruthie, Pamela, Chaundra and Ally are having their moment to shine. Their guys share the same names. Except in Chill's crew, its slightly different. Chill and Jr are the *dynamic duo*. But Stoney, Rob and Jb wasn't 3 the hard way. Stoney and Rob are known as *2 of kind*. The foursomes guys didn't share the name they carried. Jb has always been grouped with Ajay, Tank, June and Rich. Their nickname is *The Horsemen*. Eric hadn't been in that group of 7 guys when they grew up. Neither was Cedric but they was given the spots with their prospective groups when they'd gotten engaged to Bre and Erica. Only Wes was added when he'd gotten engaged to T-baby. Greg Jr grew up in that 7 and he inducted Eric, himself to show that he held no bias toward

317

Him and that he had no hard feelings. He knew he'd messed up. Being crew, he was raised to accept his faults like a man and move on. He had done so. But he feels a little out of place tonight. All of his age group are in happy marriages or relationships. He just can't seem to find and hold onto *Miss Right*. He has a condo at Crew condominiums. His huge home in Jackson heights is complete too. Everyone refers to both of his spots as bachelor pads. Ajay and Chill encourages him to enjoy his bachelor hood while he still can. He's the only male of age in the crew, who isn't married, engaged or in a long term relationship. He doesn't see it as a plus. Greg Jr wants the companionship the rest of his crew has. His father Greg Sr would always tell him, "It will come when the time is right. Live your life to the fullest, son."

For now he does just that. For he has no other choice. His 1st love Erica will celebrate her 2 year anniversary tomorrow. His last love Kelly was violently killed less than 5 months ago. But there is a *Miss Right* for Greg Jr. She will be unveiled soon. She's nearly apart of the crew already. When her and Greg Jr do meet and become engaged. The 7th Heaven title will change to *The Elevated 8*. A nickname big mama always used for the foursome and their guys. All that's left for Greg Jr is the meeting and her induction. But they haven't even been introduced yet.

Ellen has been incarcerated since the double murder of Matt and his daughter and Greg's girl Kelly. The judge has denied her bail up until this point. But after her good behavior, attorney Wheeler though he isn't representing her, was able to help her court appointed attorney convince the judge to give her a bond until her trial. Which Wheeler *was* going to delay for the maximum time allotted. Her bond is set at $500K the following week. The crew aren't going to secure her bond. They'd only convinced Wheeler to help her to get one. Rudy and Dorothy have stayed by her side and so has her new bosses, Mario Scott and Venitia Walker. She was a great employee. They're also saving her job until her trial comes and the verdict is announced. The crew don't want them to abandon her. They have even invited all of the employees of Crew Insurance and Carpeting to celebrate Thanksgiving with them in Jackson Heights, next month. Greg Jr is going to host. His mother Sandy and the ladies will do the hostess honors for him since he's single. Also being a *Detroit Lion*, he'll have a game before dinner on Thanksgiving day. They'll have dinner after his game ends and they arrive back. He will host the basement party which has already been labeled as coed, thanks to Ajay's movement this time last year.

Ajay's on the road in Indiana for Thanksgiving, where they suffer their 6th lose of the season in an early game. He'll get back in time for dinner with his family.

Kilo and Justine have a home in Jackson Heights. They're on Wilson's Way with Bruce and Jr.

Mya Dean and Corey Grey attend Thanksgiving dinner. They're no longer a couple but they're still friends. Corey shows up with his new love partner Bobby White. They met at CSU and started dating when Corey was still living with Tameka and Mya. They needed a bigger place, once Bobby moved in. The 4 of them rented Stoney's old 4 bedroom house on Union Avenue. 1 for Tameka, 1 for Mya, 1 which Corey and Bobby shares and 1 for when Mya has her son, once a month. The crew have become a lot less homophobic since Corey came into the picture in 1999. They love him and extend the same crew honors and expectations upon him, as they do everyone else. He has enjoyed the last 6-plus years with his extended family. They're happy to have him too.

Another couple gets together while sharing Thanksgiving dinner with the crew. Greg Jr is seated with Patricia Thomas, Kilo's sister who's still staying in Cleveland since hurricane Katrina. Her and Greg Jr hit it off instantly and are inseparable all night. Mya and Greg Jr speak but don't say much more for the rest of the night. Their tension from their school and college years have eased off a bit. They're able to be civil and keep it moving. Greg Jr lets Mya know he isn't interested in starting another relationship with her and he's willing to let the past stay there.

He says, "I don't hold any grudges toward you. I wish you the best."

"That's cool with me," Mya says, "And thank you for that."

They're all going to the clubs after the party in Greg Jr's basement ends. But before they can leave, they get a call from Jan and Rob down in Atlanta. The have several bits of good news to share.

They're moving back to Cleveland and building a home in Jackson heights. Jan's pediatric care office will be opening November 2007 at CrewLand mall. Also they're expecting another baby in July and Jan wants to be home with Dr. Weston for *this* birth.

"We've got a lot of baby's coming and a lot of folks getting married in two thousand and six," Ajay offers.

"Me and Justine are gonna get in that baby line, after awhile," Kilo says with a smile.

"Is she pregnant?" Ajay asks.

"No not yet," he says, "We still got my family living with us and it cuts down on our ability to get as freaky as we want too. But we've been talking about it and planning it. With all these babies coming. I know she's gonna be back in my ear."

"You gotta get in her ear too," Ajay says, "That's how you get the babies to come. Get in her ear and a couple of other places too. A couple of times a day. You know *I know* how to make babies, man. Listen to me."

Him and Kilo laugh hard. Kilo wants more kids. He always has. It took him years to realize him and Justine are a good fit. Chill introduced them in the nineties, shortly after she moved to Cleveland with her uncle Jason Carr. Jason is Stoney's stepfather and husband to mama Jackie. He liked Kilo for his niece, from day 1 because Kilo is motivated and wants a great future just like his crew. But he's never had a female in his life that he trusted enough to marry and settle down with. He found that in Justine. They were married during the golden anniversary ceremony for big mama and poppa, on April 3, 2004. They are already crew with a share in crew businesses.

"We're set up pretty good," Kilo says to Ajay, "We can go down that road now."

His sister Patricia has gotten her transcripts transferred to CSU. She's planning to make Cleveland her home. She's a full time student and has worked at CrewLand Mall for the last 2 months. She floats from store to club to restaurant to office. Wherever she's needed. She makes great money too. However, tonight's Thanksgiving dinner is her 1st time meeting Greg Jr. She likes what she sees, so far. She ask Kilo to hook her up. He promises her he will but he tells her, he has to do it *the crew way*. It has to be done right. Patricia agrees to be patient.

****

The Cleveland sports fans are overdue for a championship of some sort. The city of Cleveland hasn't won a title since 1964. Years before the active crew was even born. The crew are hoping with their family as apart of the teams, they can get 1 in the near future. The Browns season isn't going the direction they wanted it too. They aren't expected to make the playoffs. They have a 4-11 record by Thanksgiving weekend but the Cavaliers are 15-7 by the end of November. With new head Coach Mike Brown, they're planning for the best season in their history. Ajay and the crew have high playoff hopes too. While they enjoy the high of a winning record and the players and coach to get them that elusive title. Something has to come up to spoil the fun. The 1 thing the crew hadn't counted on is the news they get from Wheeler, the 1st week of December.

Attorney George Wheeler calls Ebony at home. He reminds her that Angelise Taylor is up for parole for 2007.

"I know that's over a year away but they've begun the process," he tells her, "Looking at her prison record and time served."

"She got twelve years," Ebony says, "She needs to do all of them." Wheeler guarantees her, she won't be out before 2007. However, she will most likely be freed in 2007 with prolonged probation.

"She'll have another eight to ten years of probation," he says, "That's the best we can do. She will have served her time by then."

Ebony tells him she understands and she won't lobby for her to receive more time. She adds, "But she needs to stay away from me and my family. Especially if she hasn't gotten over my husband."

"Understood," Wheeler says, "I'll secure a restraining order. If she violates that, I'll have something in place to send her back to prison."

"Or crew will put her in the ground where she belongs," Ebony says, "That's the only way to get rid of vile trash like that, for good."

Wheeler agrees. They hang up. Ebony calls Ajay, who's on the road. She tells him. He wants Angel to remain in prison for the rest of her natural life. He knows that's not going to happen. He's angry. He knows his only son Lil Ajay will never be okay with letting Angel live out her full life. *Period*!

Alana, Darlene and Farah get the news too. Alana is excited Farah kept Angel's lawyer paid. But Darlene isn't looking forward to her release.

"That bitch can't come around me if she's still making plays for Ajay," Darlene says, "He might've *said* he ain't gonna fuck over his wife. But even if he tells her *dumbass* that. She'll try something else stupid. Hell I might get back in if I kill her ass."

"Auntie you'll never get over that dick, will you?" Alana asks.

"Hell no. Obviously she hasn't either," Darlene says, "I know she still calls here and wants you to give her the play by play on him since you work for them. I'm glad you wised up and stopped hooking her up on three way with the club. But I don't want her out. I know Ajay. He'll kill that bitch and mess up his whole life."

Darlene is still angry about Alana's friendship with Angel. As if *that's* what's stopping Ajay from fucking with her. Alana agrees Angel hasn't let go of her obsession with Ajay. Even after being behind bars for the last 10½ years. She knows Angel will be right back out here trying to get his attention.

Alana says, "She said she'd never give up on that dick and she didn't."

"Thing is," Farah adds, "If he don't wanna be bothered with her.

Then she's gonna be a problem. And a huge problem for us too, if she's a nuisance. We've got enough problems from the crew already."

"For real, Alana," Darlene agrees, "If she's around you and do some dumb shit. Then all of our asses are out. She may fuck up things for my sons *and* you, with y'all jobs."

"Shit. She better not fuck up my money," Alana says, "I got my degree now and my money. I can send Olivia money for nice things. I'm not gonna let her fuck *none* of that up for me. *Trust!*"

Jamal's girl Holly is there at the house with her and Jamal's kids. She doesn't join in on the conversation the 3 of them are having. What she does do is she goes into Darlene's room to call Jamal at the *Rec* center. She tells him about the conversation his mother and her friends are having.

"Nobody's gonna fuck up my situation with Ajay and this crew," Jamal says clearly.

Holly can hear it in his voice. He's going to tell Ajay as soon as he gets back from his road trip. That's exactly why Holly called him. She wants him to tell Ajay. They soon hang up.

Jamal goes into Ally's office and ask her to set up a meeting with Ajay, for him. He wants it at Ajay's earliest convenience.

"Is everything okay?" Ally asks.

"*Oh* yea it's cool," Jamal says, "Just wanna let him know about some drama my mama and the *suspects* was discussing. It's no biggie."

Ally laughs and says, "Some things just don't change, do they?"

"Hell no," he says, laughing as he heads back to his duties.

Ajay arrives home the next afternoon. After checking on his wife and kids, then stopping to speak to his crew at the CrewLand mall. He goes on to his Rec center. He and Jamal have their talk, 1st thing. Ajay thanks Jamal for the loyalty and heads up. After his work is done. He picks up Lea from *Big Mama's house daycare* and heads home. He's going to be sure and tell Ebony about his conversation with Jamal, as soon as they get some alone time.

After the twins get home from school, do their homework and spend quality time with their daddy. They all have dinner. After getting their 3 kids to bed, Ajay and Ebony can finally settle down in their own bed and talk. He gets right to the discussion he'd had with Darlene's youngest son at his Rec center today. Ebony isn't a bit surprised to hear that she's still plotting on getting with her man. She can also tell that Ajay is over it. And it makes him angry nowadays to even hear her name.

"Darlene is delusional too," Ajay tells her, "She's talking about *fuckin* Angel up. Like *she's* got a chance in hell of getting with me. Stupid."

"She sure is," Ebony says as she giggles, "She's upset like whatever Angel says or does affects *her*."

"I know *right*?" he asks as he chuckles. Then he says, "I hope they wipe each other out and save me and my son some time."

"Anthony I don't want you to do anything that'll disrupt our happy home life," Ebony tells him, "We need you here with us."

"I won't baby," he says, "As long as neither one of them cross me."

"Do you promise *not* to do anything rash?" she asks.

"No."

"Anthony?"

"I don't, baby," he says, planting a kiss on her forehead to keep her calm. "All I can say is. As long as they stay out of my way and don't come near my kids, you or my family with no bullshit. Then I won't go looking for them. But *be clear*. I'm not gonna let nobody fuck with my happy home and my ability to have peace in it. I learned that from that incident with Nickeia. Then the Farah thing that followed. I'm focused baby. I can promise you that. I got my mind on what keeps me living and getting from day to day. And that's you and my babies."

She gives him a kiss. She knows he isn't going to change his mind on that. Nor is he going to promise her, he won't get rid of Angel, Darlene or anyone else he views as a problem to who and what is important to him.

"I mean we make enough money now to have it done," he says and chuckles. "We've got killers on the payroll now. Shit's gonna run smooth or else."

"I'm glad I'm a person whom you view as important and very necessary," she says with a smile. "I'm reminded of something big mama says to me all the time."

He gives her a sweet kiss, then asks, "And what's that?"

"She said you are the type of person who only cares about a very few things. And those things, you're willing to move the world to protect."

"She's right, like always," he says, "Big mama knows me. She was always and still is a person I can tell anything. And she always has the answer. She could always say something to paint a clearer picture for whatever it was I went to her with."

"That's the truth," Ebony says, "She's always been that person who can weigh the situation out and make anything make sense."

"She's a wise woman," Ajay says, "And I got her namesake. That's who I always knew you would listen too. Even before mama Pearl. I knew what I was getting when I set my eyes on you, baby girl. Don't even think I don't realize the quality of woman I have. Big mama is correct. I'll do whatever is necessary to make sure you're happy. That was my plan and the job I wanted from day one. It's never changed. No matter what irresponsible things I did while I was growing into the man that I am. You was always the person I wanted to love me and wanna be with me. That's what saved my life. I believe that with all my heart. Once I started having real feelings for you. I did what I had to do to make sure you felt the same way about me. That's what saved me from ruining my life, by putting street shit first. Knowing I had a girl who was gonna be a woman of quality with that kind of wisdom, gave me a lot of confidence. You are the best thing that happened in my life, Ebony. Still to this day," he says, "If I hadn't started to want you and realize what it took to have you. I would've fucked up all of this. But look at us now. It was only you who could give me something to live for. Something that was more important than my ego. And that something is my babies. Thank you, baby. I love you."

"I love you too," she says as they smile at each other.

"So are the rings more comfortable now?" he asks.

"Yes," she says, "I can move them around on my fingers."

"Do they still look the same as they did when you first got em?" he asks with a smile.

"Well no," she says, "They have even *more* diamonds now."

They both laugh and he says, "I had to fill in that other inch they added."

"You're wonderful baby," she says, "Like I said. I'm so glad and proud to be the object of your affection."

"Well that's good because my affections are rising," he says with a chuckle.

"Then come here," she says as she pulls him to her.

It's time for a night of passion like *only* they have. They have gotten to the good part of love and life. Nothing is going to come between this love they have. As long as it's a priority for Anthony *"Ajay"* Jackson, Sr. Ebony loves their bedtime talks. Their bedroom is where they are definitely the most comfortable and open with each other. That started years ago, when he made it his sexual *priority* to please her. Along with that pleasure, her comfort and security was key also. She knows love is such a beautiful thing when it's nourished *and* cherished.

The next day the foursome plan to do some Christmas shopping.

324

TIME TO FEEL-RELOADED-Time Will Reveal part 5

Ebony gets a call from Gwen. It's been awhile since she's called. Actually she's only called twice since the night Jarvis brought Nickeia to their house to explain her actions in the CrewLand parking lot. Jarvis is at practice and so is Ajay.

"How are you doing Gwen?" Ebony asks.

"I'm alright," she says, "But I really miss having *all* the family to be around."

"We never said you couldn't come around us Gwen," she says, "We didn't get to add you to the crew. But that doesn't mean you was banished for our existence."

Suddenly Gwen says, "Jarvis still doesn't know about Tank. But somehow, he thinks it's his fault we didn't get voted in. But I know it's my fault because of the one night stand I had with Tank, in college."

Ebony knows why Jarvis believes it's his fault. But she doesn't offer up *that* info. She makes small talk with Gwen until her girls show up. Nina and Rebbie have taken half days at work so they can shop with the very pregnant Ebony. And T-baby, who hasn't even begun to show yet. She's only a few months along and due in June of next year. But Ebony doesn't look like she's going to make it through the week. Most predicted she would've had the triplet's by now. Her due date is mid-February. That's still 2 months away.

"I would love it if these babies come on my birthday," Ebony says to her girls as they head to the malls.

"We're due for another Christmas baby," Rebbie says.

"Me and Ebony will be thirty years old in less than two weeks," Nina says.

"Y'all getting old," T-baby says and they all laugh.

They she says, "But remember when we use to think thirty was old?"

"Yep," Rebbie says, "When our parents was in their thirties, we did. Now that it's us. I see that thirty ain't old."

"Thirty is when you start to figure it all out," Ebony says, "Because my life *and* my relationship are on point. I remember when I wasn't so sure if this day would ever come when I felt secure with me and Anthony's relationship."

"We *all* remember that," Rebbie says, "We all had those same hang ups and growing pains."

"I still think about Richard," T-baby says suddenly.

"We all do," Nina says, "No matter how he left us. We'll never be without the memories of the good ole days."

"I agree," Rebbie says.

Ebony changes the subject. She hasn't forgotten that letter Keno brought to her office. It's obvious Wes has kept his word and never told T-baby about it because she's never mentioned it.

"Lil Kenny will turn twenty two, this year," Ebony says, "That's a long time without a Christmas baby. April had a Christmas birthday too. I miss her, so much."

"We all miss her too," Nina adds, "Yolanda called me last night. We talked about April. She said she's calling the twins tonight."

"I hope she's coming to visit soon," T-baby says.

"She is," Nina says, "She said she's planning to come after Ebony have the triplet's. She said April's cousin Black from Gulfport, still wants to visit. They're gonna come together."

"Oh she is *so* cool," Ebony says, "I met her when the crew first came to Houston. She had April's back, big time. Just like Renee has *always* had ours."

"I can't wait to meet her," Rebbie says.

Nina and T-baby agree. Then Ebony goes somewhere they don't expect.

"I remember when we didn't *ever* keep secrets from each other," she says, "That changed when we got married and older."

"Somewhat yes," T-baby says, "But I don't have any secrets that y'all don't know about."

"Neither do I," Nina says.

"Rebbie does though," Ebony says as she looks at Rebbie.

She says, "Sis when are you gonna tell us about your kissing session with Jarvis? I know Tank voted against them being in the crew. I'm sure you was the second *negative* vote against them. Right?"

Nina and T-baby look shocked, as Nina screams, "What!?!"

"No shit," T-baby adds.

Rebbie sighs deep and looks at her girls. She decides to come clean.

She says, "It was one night in late nineteen ninety three. Ebony, you was at Ajay's apartment. I asked to use your car to go to mama Jo's. I told Nina and Tee I was going to my mom's to sleep and I was gonna come back the next morning. I went to Natty because I knew Brian was cheating."

"We know you didn't come to mama's," Nina says, "I thought you stayed with Ebony."

"And I thought she stayed with y'all," Ebony says.

"What went down?" T-baby asks.

"I'd called Brian a lot before I came up with the idea of driving up

326

there," Rebbie says, "At first he wasn't answering his phone. So I knew I had to go find him. Once I was on the road and called, he finally answered. We talked for over an hour. I talked to him from the time I got on the highway until I was almost in Columbus. But after I stopped to use the bathroom and called back. He didn't answer again. He didn't know I was on my way there. He just thought I was calling him from my room at mama's. I kept calling him. Eventually he turned his phone off. When I made it to Cincinnati, I knew how to get to the house, so I headed that way. On the way there, I passed him walking. He walked to a car and got in. It was a female in the car. I pulled off and turned around. Then I followed them to a hotel. As he was getting out, I called his phone. It was still off. He went in that hotel and stayed in there for hours."

"Oh God," T-baby says.

Rebbie continues, "I was sitting in that parking lot feeling like my life was over. I finally got out and went to the reception desk. Y'all know our guys was *the shit* in their sports. So the clerk knew him. She wouldn't tell me the room number but she did tell me he wasn't checked in under his own name. And get this. He had fucked around with the clerk too."

"Damn," Nina says.

Rebbie says, "She said they was under Diana Keyes name. That's the same woman he cheated with at Ajay's bachelor party. And the one Ebony saw him with when she saw Rich with Regina. I knew he was cheating. I never brought it up because I didn't want what Jarvis and I did, to come out."

"What did y'all do Ree?" T-baby asks.

"Jarvis saw me when I was going back to the car," she says, "That's how I know the crew guys *knew* Brian was cheating on me. Jarvis knew exactly where to find him. I knew they knew it. I wasn't gonna go to the house so they could feed me a lie. I was crying and screaming. Jarvis pulled up, got out and ran over to me. He opened the drivers door and put his arm around me. He comforted me and asked if I needed to talk. I said yes. It was freezing. I went and sat in the car with him. He listened to me. Something Brian never does unless I'm angry. I was in that car for two hours. I was attracted to him since I first saw him. Like whenever we went to visit or tour the campus, he always got my attention. He gave me his too. That night he told me he was attracted to me at first sight too."

"Wow," Nina says.

Rebbie says, "I reached over, pulled his face to mine. He kissed me. Y'all I liked it. I *loved* it. It was *so* genuine. I could tell he'd wanted too, for awhile. Just like I did. We kissed a lot. He sucked on my neck and my breast…"

"Woo Ree!" Ebony adds.

"He ate me out that morning too," she finally admits.

"*Downtown*?" T-baby asks.

"*Lord* yes," Rebbie answers, "And it was the bomb. It didn't even feel wrong and it still doesn't."

"Still doesn't?" Nina asks, "What does *that* mean?"

"We did it more than one time," she admits, "At Natty we didn't hook up. The next time was after they was living in Jackson Heights."

"*Rebbie*!?!" Ebony screams.

"We've never had sex *with* penetration," Rebbie says, "But we've done everything else."

"You've done him too?" T-baby asks.

"Yes," Rebbie admits, "After I found out Brian was cheating with that bitch again. I wanted too. Hell I was hurt. I really think I'm the reason Jarvis wanted to come to Cleveland. Whenever I see him or think about him. I put it on Brian, big time. I wanted him here but I couldn't vote for them to be crew because I knew that would be too close for comfort. Plus I didn't want Gwen in the picture."

"So Rebbie. You're having an affair?" Nina asks.

"No," Rebbie answers, "The last time was the day after they moved out of Jackson Heights. We met at the Fillmore. He still calls me and we talk. He got a condo and he said he got it for us. So we can still see each other whenever I need him. He said all I have to do is say the word and he'll divorce Gwen to be with me. I knew he was taking Nickeia to Ebony's house and set the record straight about how she tried to come on to Ajay. We was on his cell phone when Ajay called. Ajay couldn't wait for him to click over, so he called their house phone. Gwen answered and told Jarvis it was Ajay. Jarvis was in their master bathroom on the phone with me. I was in my dance room, playing with my pussy and working up a sweat. I don't feel bad. Brian fucked Farah on that crew *thang* night. So it's whatever."

"Tank did too. I told y'all about his one night with Gwen, down in Natty," Nina says.

"Yes but that shit was *only* one time," Rebbie asserts quickly.

"Oh I know," Nina says with a look of certainty on her face.

"I can't say I'm not gonna see him again," Rebbie says, "A part of me wants to know what his fucking skills are like."

"Oh my Lord," Ebony says, "You're gonna make me go in labor."

"Not at the mall," T-baby says, "*No!*"

They all laugh. Ebony finds it strange that she isn't mad at Rebbie. She

TIME TO FEEL-RELOADED-Time Will Reveal part 5

knew about the 1 time. But she had no idea it had continued.

She says, "Rebbie I don't even know what to say. I can't even be mad at you because I know my cousin cheated on you for years. I even saw him cheating and he kept it going. I'm just gonna support you regardless. Are you in love with him?"

Rebbie says, "I get hot every time I see him. I think that's just lust. He tells me no woman has ever made him feel like he feels when he's near me. I just don't know if I'll ever be able to trust him. When I first learned Brian had cheated on me. It really changed my ability to trust. I don't know."

Then she changes the subject and says, "Y'all let's get this shopping done before Ajay calls us and goes off about Ebony being out this long."

"He knows *I* ain't in no make out session," Ebony says and laughs.

"No but he's probably ready to start one," Nina adds.

"Y'all remember what I told y'all he said, back in the day when the rats from Houston came to visit?" Ebony asks.

"Oh about killing you, if you cheat?" T-baby asks.

"Yes," Ebony says, "His exact words was, *'If you ever let another muthafucka touch mine, in any way. Ebony I'll kill you. Do you hear me? Do you understand me? I'll kill your ass, I swear to God. I'll kill you and then fuck your dead ass body before I get rid of you. You got that?'* That's what he said. And he was griping my pussy *so* tight. Then he said, *'This is mine. Always have been. Always gone be. You understand that?'* Honey he was holding me against Chill and Renee's wall with my pussy in one hand and my chin in the other one."

"And he would too," Nina says, "You best know that."

"I think she knows it," T-baby says, "She remembers what he said *word for word*. She got it."

"I'll say she got it," Rebbie adds, "And that was nineteen ninety."

"Damn right," Ebony says, "Fifteen years later and I still shiver when I recall it."

"It *worked*," T-baby says, "I ain't even mad, cousin. Let's get this shopping done before he calls one of our phones and give us a threat that we can't shake until we're forty five."

They all laugh as they head into store number 8, enjoying some lighter conversation. Ebony's sure the Rebbie and Jarvis situation is far from over.

****

Ebony celebrates her 30th birthday with Nina on the 22nd of

329

TIME TO FEEL-RELOADED-Time Will Reveal part 5

December. Ajay and Jarvis are on the road for a game against the Chicago Bulls. The foursome are still reeling over the admission from Rebbie, a week ago. Ebony has told Ajay. His response was, "It just makes me love you more, every time I hear some shit like this about our crew, baby girl. I'm so glad we don't have none of that type stuff going on in our relationship. I don't even wanna waste time talking about it no more. They will all have to figure out how to get to where we are."

"I agree," she'd said, "We'll just keep doing what we do. Focusing on our *own* marriage."

Tonight's party is another great one. Ebony is seated in VIP at The Chill Spot. Ajay will be home before morning. The Cavaliers have a home game tomorrow against Indiana. Ebony plans to go and bring their 3 kids but Ajay hasn't given the final word on that yet. He doesn't think she'll be able to attend. He feels like she'd be much too uncomfortable. Still she says if she's not in labor, she wants to go. He calls after their win against Chicago, before he boards his flight home.

"Happy birthday, baby," he says with a chuckle.

"Almost," she says.

"It's your birthday everyday," he says, "The big three oh and you're still looking sixteen."

"I feel sixty though," she says.

"How *are* you feeling?" he asks.

"Pregnant," she says and laughs.

"No signs of labor yet?" he asks.

"Big mama says it's gonna be any day now because the babies have dropped," she says with excitement in her voice.

"Well don't let em drop before daddy gets back," he says.

They laugh. They have to hang up so his flight can depart. She gets with security so they'll know she's ready to leave. She wants to be home and in bed when they go to the airport to meet him.

"We'll get you ready to go, misses Jackson," Joiner says, "I'll have Davidson pull the vehicle around."

"Thank you," she says.

She lets her crew know she's leaving. Her girls go down with her and wait until she gets into the car. John and Al leave Woody and Pac Man in charge at Stoney's and follows security to take her to Jackson Heights. Then they'll go to Shaker Heights and bring the kids home before meeting Ajay at the airport.

TIME TO FEEL-RELOADED-Time Will Reveal part 5

It's Christmas eve morning. The Cavaliers beat Indiana, last night. The twins and Lea went to the game with all the men. While the crew ladies ran the clubs, the restaurant and opened up Stoney's Bar & Grill. Just until the men returned. Ebony stayed home with big mama by her side. Big mama, poppa and papa are staying in their guest house until she delivers the triplets and recovers. After all, Ajay wasn't going to be okay with her being home alone with less than 2 months to go before she's due.

Big mama makes breakfast at Ajay's house. With the weight of the triplets, Ebony has swelling in her hands and feet lately. She's in the master bedroom wrapping gifts. 1 of their Christmas CD's plays on the mansion's acoustic house stereo system which has wall speakers installed in *every* room. Ajay is in the garage apartment putting together toys for their twins and Aaliyah aka Lea. He has practice this evening for their home game against Chicago, the day after Christmas. Big mama calls everyone inside to come eat. Ajay comes in and helps Ebony to the breakfast nook. Big mama watches her as she glides slowing to the table.

"You ain't got much longer to go, baby girl," she says, "Those babies look like their sitting on your lap."

They all share a laugh as Ajay pulls out her chair and helps her to sit down.

"It's smelling *good* in here," he says to big mama as Ebony, poppa, papa and the kids agree.

"Thank you Ajay," big mama says, "I'm cooking some of the sweets for Christmas too. I figured I'd get an early start. Annabelle and the ladies will be coming by to help me get some of the foods going before you leave for practice. It's Christmas eve and we always try to get the sweets done a day early."

"That works for me," Ajay says with a smile. He adds "I insisted we do Christmas dinner here. Because I don't want Ebony to have to leave this house unless she's headed to the hospital."

They laugh and he adds, "Doctor Weston and her family are invited. So if she goes into labor. Her doctor will already be in the house."

"Thank you daddy," Ebony says with a smile, "I like that a lot."

"Plus one of the perks of being the host is. I get to pinch off of all the foods before anybody else gets here," Ajay says and they all laugh. Before he asks, "So do you think we'll have three more mouths to feed before our marriage is eight years old?"

"I sure do," big mama says, "She's gonna have those babies soon."

"Well alright!" Lannie chimes in, "Lea, you'll get to see the new babies being born."

"Yea. We saw you being born," Lil Ajay says, "It was gross too."

"*Gwhoss*," Aaliyah says, mimicking her big brother and everybody laughs.

"I'm ready for them to come on out," Ebony says, "I've survived another pregnancy without stretch marks. I don't wanna get *any* bigger."

"I'll take you however you come to me, baby," Ajay says with a smile, "I know where to look."

Everybody laughs and digs in. After they're done with breakfast, big mama takes the children to the guest house. She's going to read Christmas books with them. Ajay helps Ebony back to their bedroom to finish her gift wrapping while he goes back out to the garage apartment to do some more toy assembly. Poppa and papa come out to help. They're having great conversation while testing out the new toys.

In the master bedroom, Ebony has grown tired of wrapping gifts. Now she wants to wrap up with her husband. She's feeling horny. Ajay isn't done in the garage apartment but she's going to get his attention, so he'll come back in and lay down with her. She calls his cell phone.

"Hello baby," he says with a smile.

"I'm done with all this gift wrapping for now," she says as she giggles. "I'm lonely. The kids are at the guest house."

"I've got help out here today," he says, "Our grandfathers can do this *for* me, if you need them too. Even if they won't. I'm saying they will. I'm on my way," he says.

While poppa and papa are teasing him and chuckling, he makes his way to the house.

When he makes it to the master bedroom, Ebony is completely nude. The way he demands she be *whenever* she's in bed. Their Christmas CD is still playing. *Have Yourself A Merry Little Christmas*, the song *The O'Jays* performed on the night he proposed to her, is playing. He walks up to their bed with a seductive smile on his face. He loves what he sees.

"My favorite chocolate," he says.

"I thought you'd wanna feed your sweet tooth," she says, "I've got mistletoe too."

She's in the center of the bed with mistletoe draped over the head and footboards. She's leaning back on bed pillows with her legs spread apart, wearing nothing but a large bag of *Turtles* between her legs.

"Uh, uh, uh," he says, "You always know what I need. Don't you?"

He smiles while he slides out of his clothes and gets up on the bed with her.

"I know Turtles are your favorite candy," she says and smiles.

"Second favorite," he says.

He gives her a sweet kiss as he moves the bag of candy to the edge of the bed. He puts his face between her legs and gives her pussy a kiss too. He starts to lick her and suck on her clitoris like a man starved for her taste.

"Mmmm," she moans.

"This is my favorite candy," he says, "My pussy moved them damn Turtles right on up out of the number one spot on our honeymoon."

"It feels so *good* daddy," she oozes, "I'm in the mood like you wouldn't *believe*."

"I'd believe it," he says from her southern end. "Hell, I live for it."

He pulls her down toward him so that she lays flat out on the bed. He goes to work on her pussy.

"I need to take this stress off of my babies," he says, "Help you relax. So they can come on out here and meet daddy."

"Mmmm yes!" she screams.

"You're so fuckin hot baby," he whispers, "I love these pregnant hormones. They keep my pussy hot like a summers day in fuckin Miami, in *July*."

He talks to her while he eats her pussy. She loves it. Within minutes, she's screaming his name.

"Oh Anthoneeeeeeeeee! Oh baby yes! Yes! Ssss Oooooooooooooo!"

"Sing that shit baby," he orders, coming up on his knees while rolling her over on her side at the same time. Then moving up behind her, he says, "I need to feel how wet this *sweet-as-sugar* pussy can get today."

"Oh daddy," she whispers, "I feel *so* good."

"You know that's what I'm here for, right?" he whispers in her ear and penetrates her.

His dick slides all the way into her moist pussy with ease. She purrs.

"My pussy's gonna handle all of daddy," he says, "It's ready for *all* of me."

He's into it instantly. She's moaning and pushing her ass back to him. He loves it.

"Oh shit yea!" he says loudly. "Oh this muthafucka is ready, Ebony. Bring it here. Bring my pussy to me baby!"

"It's all yours daddy!" she screams as she reaches back and pulls him into her.

They're enjoying each other thoroughly. He's experienced with pregnancy sex, enough now. He knows he can't hurt his unborn. He's going for broke.

333

TIME TO FEEL-RELOADED-Time Will Reveal part 5

"Is daddy doing you *good* baby?" he whispers in her ear, sending her farther into ecstasy. She's *cumin* and he's on the verge of getting his too. "Uh! This shit is so *good*," he says as he throws his head back.
He's pulling her to him and sweating profusely. He sucks and bites on the back of her neck and her shoulders while his dick beats into her pussy overtime. She knows he's about to make it rain.

"Come here daddy," she purrs and he lets it go.
It's massive. He bites his bottom lip and squeezes his eyes closed tightly, as he yells, "Ooooooooooooo *shiiiiiiitttt*! Oh damn baby! This shit *soooo* good Ebony! Mmmm! I love it baby. Ah *damn*! I love you!"
She pushes against him until he's drained himself. Leaving it all in her. They're both gasping for air as they grind to a slow stir. He wraps her up in his arms. With 1 arm under her shoulder and the other arm around his triplets. He's planting sweet kisses on the back of her neck and on both of her shoulders. With not much breath available, he manages to say,
"You always feel *so* good Ebony. I'll never get over this addiction. I don't even want no rehab."
She giggles and says, "I don't want you to get rehab either. I'm addicted to the way you hold me Anthony. I have been for *forever*. Every time you make love to me. It just gets better and better."

"That's what I'm living for Ebony," he says, "Just know that."

"I know and I'm so proud to be loved by you," she says as she turns to face him. She says, "I often wonder if there's a love *anywhere* in this world as solid as ours."

"Nah," he says, "It can't be. We'd know about em and they'd have to know us too."
They smile and kiss each other repeatedly. Then take a much needed nap.

Poppa and papa are taking the twins with them to the Cleveland Browns game at 1pm against the Steelers. 17-month old Lea is staying home. She isn't quite old enough to sit out in the frigid temperatures at the stadium. The ladies have shown up to start the cooking for tomorrow's Christmas dinner. Nina, T-baby and Rebbie stop by on their way to the game. Rebbie is taking Orian. But her and June's 2½ month old twin boys Brian III and Brent are staying at Ajay's with mama Rena. Mama Brenda is going to the game with Rebbie, Nina and T-baby. Rich III, Jerica and Lil Tank are going, along with the men in the crew. It's Christmas Eve and the crew have done all the shopping they plan to do. Eric's family are in from Chicago to go to the game. Eric's siblings are here with Leilenne and Archie

334

TIME TO FEEL-RELOADED-Time Will Reveal part 5

Jr's 1 year old daughter Ashley Josetta. She's staying at Ajay's with Rena as well. Brina and Archie bring Archie III by before heading to Browns Stadium.

"Y'all enjoy the game and be careful, okay," mama Rena says, "All us grandmothers are gonna watch the small children *and* cook."

"Is Ebony and Ajay in the bed?" Nina asks with a smile.

"Where *else?*" T-baby asks and everyone laughs.

They soon leave for the stadium. The women get to their cooking and babysitting duties while they have the game coverage on the TV's.

}Browns Stadium{

As they take their seats, Rebbie glances over her shoulder to see Jarvis and his son heading down the steps. They take the 2 seats behind her. Those are the ones *she'd* left at Will Call for him. Nina and T-baby look at her, then at each other and smile while shaking their heads. They know Rebbie had *everything* to do with the seating arrangements.

The crew stay at the stadium for the entire game which the Browns lose miserably, 44-0. It's after 5pm. They're preparing to leave the stadium. As they file out, T-baby and Nina are ribbing Rebbie. Jarvis had sat in the seats directly behind her and right next to her father Archie Sr, by design. Chill and Renee sat on the other side of Jarvis Jr. Gwen didn't come. Nina and T-baby were the only ones in the crew at the game, who knows about the affair. Tank only knows about the 1 night in Natty. But his guilt about fucking Gwen the same night, still makes him feel uneasy around Jarvis. He knows Jarvis still wants to be apart of his crew.

Rebbie, Nina and T-baby are about to head to Ebony's house to help with the food prep. But before she can leaves the stadium, Jarvis calls her cell phone.

"Hello?" she answers.

"What's up?" he asks, "I wanted to talk to you before you leave. Where you heading too now?"

"Jackson Heights," she says, "The ladies have cooking and gift wrapping to do."

"Are you okay?" he asks, "Is everything okay?"

"I am now," she says, "I wanted to hear your voice." She giggles.

"Oh wow," Jarvis says, "Me and my junior are coming to dinner. My big brother invited us, since he knows Gwen and Nickeia are gone to Indiana for Christmas. Ajay wanted us to come."

335

"I'll see you there then," she says.

"I was hoping I could see you before tomorrow," he says.
She's blushing and can't hide it. Nina and T-baby are looking at her with half smiles. When she hangs up, Nina says,
"June is gonna bust a cap in his ass if y'all don't chill out."

"He wants it to continue," T-baby says, "And Rebbie does too."
Rebbie doesn't comment. She just walks with them to her Navigator which had been upgraded to a 2006, after her twin sons were born. All the ladies in the crew had their vehicles upgraded to 2006 models, this year. Ebony's 2006 Escalade is her Christmas present this year but she doesn't know it yet. Nina and T-baby continue poking fun at Rebbie as they strap on their seatbelts.

"Get yo butt in this car and lets go," Nina barks as she laughs.
They continue laughing as Rebbie pulls away, heading to Ajay and Ebony's house.

****

Alana gets a call from Angel today while her, Darlene and Farah are doing some last minute Christmas shopping.

"Hey girl," Alana says, "How are you?"

"Ready to get out of here," Angel says, "They're moving me to Cleveland's jail for my last year. So they can see if I'm rehabilitated."

"Oh wow!" Alana yells, "When do you move?"

"They don't tell us *that* part," Angel says, "But my lawyer told me I would be moving within the month. That's all I know."

"Well that's good news," Alana says, "You'll be *back* in the city."

"And maybe you can come visit me for a change," Angel says with a little urgency in her voice. "I haven't had a visit since my cousin's old girl moved to Atlanta."

"For sure," Alana says, not really trying to sound thrilled.
Darlene is giving her an evil look while Farah is grinning from ear to ear.
Farah says, "The new year is gonna be interesting."

"For who," Darlene says doubtfully.
They head into another store while Alana stands out in the mall to finish her conversation with Angel.

"So what's up with Ajay and have they had those babies?" Angel asks, "The news said they're having *triplets*. That bitch got her game *on*."

"Now you know that shit would be on the news if they had," Alana
336

says, "I haven't heard anything. But she was at her party the other night, as big as a house. Ajay was playing in Chicago that night."

"Now you know I watched the game," Angel says, "His fine ass *killed* it too."

"He's on his game, for sho," Alana says, "So girl. I know you called with some juice to tell me. What's up?"

"I got the new number for the club," she says, "I hope you and Farah will hook me up over the holidays."
Alana thinks about that option, then she says, "I'll see what I can do Ay. You know my aunt can't know anything about this."

"She'd better not be thinking *she's* gonna fuck with my man," Angel says, "She's forty one *fuckin* years old. It's time for her to fall back. I'm gonna be the one he cheats with when I get home."

"Oh damn!" Alana says.
Darlene comes back out of the store to get Alana. Angel's 15 minute call is about to expire. Alana says bye to her quickly and joins Darlene. They walk back into the store and to meet Farah.

"I hope that little murderous bitch don't have plans of getting near Ajay when she gets out," Darlene says, "I know my position is higher than hers. After the bullshit *she* did."

"Oh Lord," Alana say as she giggles, "That big dick muthafucka got y'all going at each other."

"You ain't seen nothing yet," Darlene says, "Wait until she gets out. I'm gonna knock a hole in her, if she comes around me with her fatal attraction ass."
Alana lets that go up into the air. She doesn't even want to hear talk or have any knowledge about what their plans are for each other or Ajay.

****

It's 7pm and time for Ajay to get to *Quicken Loans* for his 8 o'clock practice. Jarvis is picking him up while the crew ladies are buzzing around the mansion, setting the cakes and pies on the dinner hutch for tomorrow's dinner.

In the master bedroom, Ebony wakes up feeling very heavy. She needs to go to the bathroom. As she struggles to get up, Ajay wakes up.

"What you need baby?" he asks.

"I got to go to the bathroom," she whispers, "I feel like I can do a number two. For *real*."

337

TIME TO FEEL-RELOADED-Time Will Reveal part 5

He chuckles and asks, "You've been looking forward to that?"

"Yes *indeed* I have," she says as she giggles slightly. "Constipation is the one thing I *don't* like about being pregnant. I'll never be regular in *that* department again."

He gets up and helps her to her feet, then walks her to the bathroom.

"Big mama was right," he says, "Your stomach is sitting a lot lower than it was last week."

"I hope that means they're coming," she says, "My back is killing me. No matter how I lay in bed or sit or whatever. It still hurts. I'm gonna soak in the tub after I use the bathroom. Let those jets massage my back. That's the only thing that seems to help it. Other than when you do it."

"Okay," he says, "I'll start you a bath and bring you some water and something to put on, for when you're done. Then I can see if the grandfathers left anything that still needs to be put together, for when I get back from practice."

"I hope you didn't overdo it on toys, Anthony," she says.

"Of course I did," he says and chuckles.

She makes it to the toilet and he helps her to sit down. Then he exits and goes to get her a bottled water and a maternity dress to put on when she's done. He comes back with her supplies and starts her bath.

Suddenly, he hears her scream out!

"Oh my God! It's feels like the head is coming out!" she screams.

When she sat down on the toilet. She'd started the birthing process. 1 of the babies feels to her like it's about to crown. She has her hand under her vagina like she's trying to hold it in. Ajay rushes to her.

"Hang on," he says, "Let me get you back to the bed."

With his adrenaline alone, he lifts all 270 pounds of her and hurries her to their bed. Her water isn't even broken but she has started to have some *mild* contractions. Ajay doesn't panic. He grabs his phone and calls Dr. Weston, who answers on the 1st ring.

"Are we ready?" Weston asks.

"She thinks one of the babies is about to come out doc," he says, "We're not gonna have time to talk long because I might be delivering my *own* kids, if we do."

"You know the drill," Weston says, "I'm already here and I'll be here. I've signaled the ambulance and they'll have a police escort, so they won't be impeded on the drive in. Come on as soon as they get there."

They hang up and Ajay runs into his kitchen to inform the ladies that Ebony is in labor.

338

TIME TO FEEL-RELOADED-Time Will Reveal part 5

"Let's go!" he yells, "Ebony's about to have babies back here!"
Pearl, Jo and big mama rush to the master bedroom, followed by Nina and T-baby. Rebbie is in the parlor talking to Jarvis while he waits to give Ajay a ride to practice.

Ebony's laying on the bed. Besides the grimace on her face, she doesn't seem to be in labor at all.

"Are you in any pain?" Pearl asks, rushing to the side of the bed.

"Surprisingly no. I just feel like I have to pooh-pooh."
She cracks up laughing. Ajay isn't ready to laugh. He wants her to be at the hospital. He can hear the sirens from the ambulance and police cars. He's going to meet them on the driveway. He gives Ebony a kiss before telling the ladies, "Help her get dressed. These sirens are for her."
He tells Jarvis to head on to practice because he isn't going to make it.

"And Rebbie," he says, "Go check on your girl."
He has no patience for her and Jarvis, this evening. He lets that be known by his expression. Rebbie hurries to the master bedroom. She's not trying to piss Ajay off. That would be *way* to risky.

Within minutes, the paramedics are entering the house through the front foyer. Ajay leads them to the master bedroom, as he yells,
"Call daddy and tell him to bring the kids to the hospital."

"I'm talking to him now," Jo says, "Him and John are getting them ready to leave the spot two. They had all the older kids out there so we could get toys hid and all."

"Well we're about to have some more kids," Ajay says as he helps the paramedics get Ebony on the stretcher."

"This is the first time I've ever gotten on one of these and wasn't in *any* pain," she says, still laughing.
Ajay just looks at her. He can't believe how calm she is. But she's helping him to stay relaxed too.

"You're laughing Ebony?" he asks.

"I'm a pro now Anthony," she says, "I'm just waiting to see if this is the last time I'll be pregnant or not."

"Not," Pearl and Jo say simultaneously and they all laugh.

"She said she wanted another boy," Ajay says, "So if there's a boy in there. She might lock it up on me."

"Not," big mama says as she chuckles, "Y'all got a few more baby making years in you."

"They're going for number six in three tries," Jo says, "That's how you get it over with Ebony. Y'all got six kids out of three pregnancies.

That's a record in itself for Ant's bloodline. And if y'all get another boy. That's a change in the legacy."

"That would be a changing of the guard too. And big Ajay is gonna set some rules then," Ajay says, "See, cause my baby ain't going for no crew thangs. I'm living for my baby. My junior loves that already. So I'm good. Ask him. He'll tell you. I'm the *man*."

They all laugh as Ajay tries to shield his nervousness. Even the paramedics laugh as they roll Ebony out and put her in the back of the ambulance. Jacobson is off today but he calls Ajay as soon as he gets the news. He says he's coming to the hospital. Ajay gets into the back of the EMS unit with Ebony while Pearl, Jo and big mama get into Pearl's van to follow them. With 2 police cars in front of the ambulance and 1 behind Pearl. They speed to East General with 2 security vehicles trailing the convoy.

"I retired from this place," Pearl says as she drives, "And I *still* see it as much as I did when I worked there."

"Oh but these are the best trips here," Jo says, "I don't mind rushing to the hospital to see another baby come. I knew these two was gonna have a huge family."

"So did I," big mama says, "So did I."

They rush through lights and arrive at East General with Ebony still feeling like all she has to do is number *two*.

"Bring her on back," Tenischa says, "We got the room ready to go. With three little beds for the new Jackson babies."

She's all smiles as she asks, "Is my goddaughter going to make it here?"

"They're on the way," Ajay tells her.

"You seem a little out of sorts, daddy-to-be," Tenischa says, "Has she been mean to you already?"

"Not at all," he says, "She's still laughing. I just hope it's not a false alarm."

"Hardly," big mama says, "Those babies are coming. It may take a half a day. But their coming before she goes home."

"Her birthday is in *four* hours," Jo says, "She just might be sharing her Christmas birthday with my triplet grandbabies."

By 9:30pm Ebony and Ajay are set up in their private birthing room. Ebony is still having only mild contractions and her water still hasn't broken.

"I'm going to give you time to do this the natural way because I know you would love to have Christmas babies," Dr. Weston says to Ebony.

While Tenischa checks her cervix, Weston adds, "I'll wait as long as I can. But if there's no water by midnight. We'll go ahead and break it. That should make the contractions pick on up."

"She's at 6 centimeters," Tenischa tells Weston.

"She's progressing with no real pain, daddy," Weston says to Ajay.

"She's a professional now," he says as he laughs, "That's what she said earlier."

"This is the third round," Weston says, "I'm just here for the technical support."

They all laugh as Weston leaves the birthing room to go check her patients charts and prep for Ebony's delivery.

At 11pm Ebony's water breaks and her contractions become more intense. Tenischa checks her again and reports that she's at 10 centimeters.

"You're ready to push, Ebony," she says, "Are you ready?"

"I am. But apart of me was hoping they'd have my birthday," she says as she looks at Ajay. Then she says, "But if I do well and the babies are all good. Do you think doctor Weston will let us go home so we can do Christmas with our kids?"

"I'll go ask her," Tenischa says, "She's going to want you to have it set up to monitor you and the babies."

"Y'all coming for Christmas dinner right?" Ajay asks.

"We sure are," Tenischa says.

"If she says yes, right now. We can go on and get that set up going," Ajay says, "So it'll be ready as soon as the babies come and we can move her from here as soon as possible."

"I really do wanna be at home when my children wake up for their Santa Claus surprise," Ebony says, "They're sleepy now."

She looks over at the twins and Lea. Lannie and Lea are already asleep in John and Al's laps. While Lil Ajay has his daddy's frown on because he's so tired. He can barely hold his eyes open.

"I'll be right back," Tenischa says and leaves to go see what Weston says about letting them leave after the birth.

Only a few minutes later, Weston returns with Tenischa and says she'll sign off on it. *Only* because Dr. Susan Mahoney agreed to be out there for 48 hours or until she feels it's okay to stop monitoring the babies.

"Great," Ajay says, "Let's get this show on the road."

Ebony is set up in the stirrups. John and Al wake Lannie and Lea up and bring them closer so they can witness the births of their new siblings.

TIME TO FEEL-RELOADED-Time Will Reveal part 5

Ajay and Ebony have already decided on 3 names. They have 3 girl names and 1 boy name, just in case. By 11:30pm Ebony has started the pushing process. Weston is in position but the babies are slow to move into the crowning position. She has Ajay to turn Ebony on her side for more leverage. This seems to work.

By 11:45 the 1st head pops out. Weston clears the nostrils and works the shoulders through. Then pulls the 1st baby out.

"It's a girl!" she says as she passes her to her staff.

"That's Ariel Shantell," Ebony says.

Lea is transfixed on the new baby. She looks like she's seen a ghost. Lannie grabs her hand and says, "That's our little sister. See the baby?"

"Baby," Lea says as she finally blinks.

Weston starts to work Ebony's abdomen for the 2nd baby. It takes a few more minutes but finally the head pops out.

"They were snug in there," Weston says, "But with the first one out. That made it a bit easier to get baby two."

She clears the nostrils and pulls gently and the shoulders come out easy.

"It's another girl!" Weston says and passes baby 2 to her staff.

"That's Arianne Nicole," Ebony says as her girls Rebbie and T-baby smile.

They're there to witness the births and to see their middle namesakes come into the world.

"Now Ebony has a daughter with all three of our middle names," Nina says.

"Go Ebony go!" Rebbie yells, "Y'all got a foursome already."

"What if it's another girl?" T-baby asks, "Who's middle name will she have?"

"It's a surprise," Ajay says, "Let's just see if we can get number three out here first."

Nina, T-baby and Rebbie smile. They have a feeling what name the 3rd baby will have if it's a girl. The thing is, the clock strikes midnight before the last baby is delivered.

"Well this last baby held out for Christmas," Pearl says as her, Jo and big mama smile.

"That's a gem," Ajay says, "We have triplets and one has a different birthday. That's *got* to be some kind of record. What y'all think?"

"It's definitely the first time I've ever known babies to share the same womb and have different birthdays," big mama says, "I knew y'all was gonna be some trendsetters. My, my, my! I knew it was golden!"

TIME TO FEEL-RELOADED-Time Will Reveal part 5

They all laugh. Dr. Weston has been in position the entire time. She's massaging Ebony's belly. Pushing down and in a forward motion. She's trying to inch the 3rd baby on down the birth canal. It's proving to be a challenge though.

"Let's sit her all the way up and try to rest her chin between her knees," Weston says.

"You wanna fold her up?" Ajay asks as he chuckles.

"Pretty much. Yes," Weston says, "Number three baby is very stubborn."

"It's a boy that's taking after his daddy," Al says as they all laugh. Ebony sits as far forward as she can. She pushes as hard as she can. Baby 3 doesn't seem to be coming down as rapid as the first two.

"It's been fifteen minutes since Arianne came out," Ajay says, "This is crazy. How's a baby gonna *refuse* to be born?"

"He's been listening to his bossy daddy," Jo says as they laugh again.

"It's probably because I haven't had a hard time, this time," Ebony says, "So now the last baby wants to put up a fuss about meeting me." They're full of laughs as Weston is finally able to get baby 3 into the birth canal.

"Good," Ajay says, "Save Christmas son. Save Christmas for your siblings."

"Ha?" Lil Ajay asks, thinking his daddy is talking to him.

"I'm talking about the one that's still in there, son," Ajay tells him.

"That's another girl baby, pops," Lil Ajay says with very little excitement.

"Oh yea?" Ajay asks him.

"Yea pops," Lil Ajay says, "I'll be the only boy until my new brother comes *first*. Or by his self. Boys have to be born first. Like me." They all laugh as Weston announces that she can see the head. She smiles as she looks at Ebony.

"What?" Ebony asks, in mid push.

"There's a lot of hair," Weston says as the head pops out.

"Our male babies come with a lot of hair too," Nina offers. Her and Ebony's girls are hopeful that Ajay might get his 2nd son this early Christmas morning. Everybody in the room has surrounded the bed. Jo is holding Ariel and Pearl is holding Arianne, as they all watch to see what sex baby 3 is going to be. Weston tugs and gets the shoulders out.

"Ready to know what it is?" Weston asks, just to tease them.

343

"Come on now," Ajay says as he chuckles.
Weston pulls the baby out and everybody laughs.
"It's a girl!" Weston yells.
Ebony looks at Ajay and smiles. He gives her a kiss and wipes the sweat from her face.
"It was simply meant for us to give her life again," he says as him and Ebony continue to smile at each other.
As Weston passes the 3rd girl to her staff to be cleaned and weighed. Ebony announces her name.
"That's April Leshay," she says, "And how much of a blessing it is, that she has me and April's birthday too. It's perfect."
"She got my Godmother's name," Lannie says.
"Alright!" Nina, Rebbie and T-baby yell.
They had no idea Ebony had even thought of naming the bonus baby after their deceased best friend April, who died in 2000.
"She's back," Ajay says as he kisses Ebony, over and over.
"You did so good this time, baby. You didn't even go off on me. Not *once*."
"I wasn't ever really in any pain," she says, "I had three babies in thirty minutes. And I didn't have *one* contraction that was off the chart."
"You're a professional," Ajay says and they all laugh hard.
Then Pearl and Jo take over and tell them they need to get Ebony and the babies prepped to head to Jackson Heights.
"We've got to get these children in bed so Santa Claus can come to their house," Jo says.
"Santa's going to sleep," Ajay says with a chuckle.
He's only kidding. He can't wait to get his kids home and in bed, so he can go to the garage apartment and pull out the $20K worth of Christmas goodies he has for them. He has gifts for all 6 kids plus he has to get Jacobson to drive Ebony's new Escalade from big Al's garage in Shaker Heights.

Ariel Shantell Jackson, Arianne Nicole Jackson, April Leshay Jackson
Born: 12/24/05, 12/24/05, 12/25/05
Time: 11:52pm...11:57pm...12:20am
Weight: 4lbs 6ounces, 4lbs 3ounces, 4lbs 1ounce
Length: 20inches, 18inches, 16inches

Welcome to the world Ariel, Arianne and April Jackson!
THE END OF PART FIVE!
344

TIME TO FEEL-RELOADED-Time Will Reveal part 5

Get the Time Will Reveal short story series by Black Coffee
#1 MORE THAN 4 ADMIRERS-RELOADED
#2 MR. WRONG AND THE RATS-RELOADED
#3 THE CREW'S PRIORITY [TBA]

BE SURE AND PICK UP THE FULL SERIES!
The Time Will Reveal, the series
Time To Learn-RELOADED part 1
Time To Grow-RELOADED part 2
Time To Love-RELOADED part 3
Time To Know-RELOADED part 4
Time To Feel-RELOADED part 5
The Making of AJAY- Every Man- RELOADED, A Time Will Reveal novel
Time To Show-RELOADED part 6
Ajay and Ebony-Time Will Reveal part 7-Time To Give [TBA]
Ajay and Ebony-Time Will Reveal part 8-Time To Live [TBA]

All works by Black Coffee at: www.truesrelatepublishing. com
www.blackdollone.com

Like the fan page on Facebook:
Author Black Coffee & True's Relate Publishing, LLC
Or the group: The Time Will Reveal-RELOADED series Crew Nation #Crew4Life
Twitter: *AuthorBlkCoffee*
Instagram: *AuthorBlkCoffee*
Facebook & Tumblr: *Lovely T. Brown*
LinkedIn: *Lovely T. Brown*

WHAT'S NEXT?
http://blackcoffee.homestead.com/WHATSNEXTFROMBLACKCOFFEE.html

TIME TO FEEL-RELOADED-Time Will Reveal part 5

On online sites, be sure to
LIKE the titles and ADD YOUR REVIEW FOR ALL TITLES

If you'd like to be added to the author's website, on the readers page;
http://www.blackdollone.com/Reveiws-and-Covers.html
please contact us through either of the options below:

New Series by Author Black Coffee: The Organization
All By My Lonely-part one [1/1/2014]
Still By My Lonely-part two [11/2014]

Thank you for your support and I look forward to chatting with you soon. -
Author Black Coffee, True's Relate publishing

www.ingramcontent.com/pod-product-compliance
Lightning Source LLC
Chambersburg PA
CBHW061321170626
46817CB00001B/262